Praise for *Still Life*

"[A] cunningly crafted fifth novel featuring Det. Chief Insp. Karen Pirie . . . McDermid expertly balances the book's multiple mysteries, giving none short shrift. Vividly sketched characters, a colorful narrative, and myriad twists keep the pages turning . . . McDermid continues her reign as queen of the police procedural." —*Publishers Weekly*

"We read crime fiction for enjoyment, comfort and reassurance. McDermid provides all this. She is a writer with a clear sense of right and wrong. In tune with contemporary life, she remains also a moralist. *Still Life* shows that she is still at the height of her powers; it is deeply enjoyable, one of her best." —*Scotsman*

"McDermid is at the top of her game and readers will be highly rewarded for taking this new journey at her side." —*Crime Reads*

STILL LIFE

By Val McDermid

A Place of Execution
Killing the Shadows
The Grave Tattoo
Trick of the Dark
The Vanishing Point
Resistance

TONY HILL/CAROL JORDAN NOVELS

The Mermaids Singing
The Wire in the Blood
The Last Temptation
The Torment of Others
Beneath the Bleeding
Fever of the Bone
The Retribution
Cross and Burn
Splinter the Silence
Insidious Intent
How the Dead Speak

KAREN PIRIE NOVELS

The Distant Echo
A Darker Domain
The Skeleton Road
Out of Bounds
Broken Ground

LINDSAY GORDON NOVELS

Report for Murder
Common Murder
Final Edition
Union Jack
Booked for Murder
Hostage to Murder

KATE BRANNIGAN NOVELS

Dead Beat
Kick Back
Crack Down
Clean Break
Blue Genes
Star Struck

SHORT STORY COLLECTIONS

The Writing on the Wall
Stranded
Christmas is Murder (ebook only)
Gunpowder Plots (ebook only)

NON-FICTION

A Suitable Job for a Woman
Forensics
My Scotland

Val McDermid

STILL LIFE

Grove Press
New York

Quote from *Artful* by Ali Smith reproduced with the author's kind permission.

First published in Great Britain in 2020 by Little, Brown

Printed in the United States of America
Published simultaneously in Canada

First Grove Atlantic hardcover edition: October 2020
First Grove Atlantic paperback edition: October 2021

Library of Congress Cataloging-in-Publication data is available for this title.

ISBN 978-0-8021-5745-4
eISBN 978-0-8021-5746-1

Grove Press
an imprint of Grove Atlantic
154 West 14th Street
New York, NY 10011

Distributed by Publishers Group West

groveatlantic.com

21 22 23 24   10 9 8 7 6 5 4 3 2 1

To friends and colleagues in New Zealand, including – but not exclusively – the Raith Rovers FC Kiwi Supporters Club, all the Lesleys/ Leslies and their sidekicks, and the baristas at the Dispensary. We miss you and I'll be baaack.

Art is always an exchange, like love, whose
giving and taking can be a complex and
wounding matter, according to Michelangelo.

Ali Smith, *Artful*

Prologue

Saturday, 15 February 2020

Billy Watson cast off from the quay without the faintest flicker of a premonition. He nosed the 23-foot creel boat out into the east harbour's main channel with casual familiarity. The morning was no different from countless others: bitterly cold, a sharp northerly wind slicing through flesh and making his cheekbones ache. But at least it was fair, and the eggshell-blue February sky held no promise of rain to come. On the far shore, the outlines of Berwick Law and the Bass Rock were crisp as a painting. The chill waters of the Firth of Forth parted before the scarlet bows of the *Bonnie Pearl*, a thin line of white foam marking her passage.

Billy reached for his thermos mug of coffee and took a short nip; it was still too hot for a full swallow. He always liked to give it a wee blast in the microwave after he'd added the milk to make sure it stayed piping hot for as long as possible. A man needed all the help he could get to stay warm on a winter morning in the Forth estuary.

His cousin Jackie opened the wheelhouse door a crack and squeezed in, trying not to let the heat out. 'Braw day for it,' he said. It was one of Jackie's limited and predictable

1

conversational gambits. 'Bit rough the day,' was another. 'Gey wet,' his invariable response to rain.

'Aye,' Billy said, giving the engine some throttle. They left the shelter of the harbour for the choppier waters beyond the zig-zag pier that stretched into the sea and protected the harbour walls from the tideline surges that swept along the coast. A touch on the wheel and their course shifted till they were heading east, the Isle of May breasting the horizon like a humpback whale. As they drew level with the old windmill and the hollows and hillocks of the former salt pans, Billy slipped the engine into neutral and in a practised manoeuvre brought the *Bonnie Pearl* alongside the first marker buoy.

Jackie's son Andy swaggered into view, his rolling gait compensating for the low swell. With the ease of experience, he reached over the side with a boat hook to snag the buoy that marked the end of the fleet of D-shaped creels containing the day's first catch. Just like every other morning, he led the rope to the creel hauler and started the winch.

Even from the wheelhouse, Billy could see there was a problem. The rope was taut but no creel had emerged from the water. Andy was struggling, leaning over the gunwale, trying to manoeuvre the boathook. 'Better give the boy a hand,' Billy said to Jackie, who sighed and made his way down to the deck. The two men wrestled with the rope. Something seemed to be tangled in it, something that was a drag on the winch. Billy could see Jackie swearing eloquently, his words whipped away by the wind.

A rogue wave caught the bow and swung the boat through ninety degrees. Enough to make the men's job easier. They staggered back a couple of feet, giving Billy a clear view of what was in the water.

STILL LIFE

For a moment, it made no sense. Billy's brain translated the strange sight into a battered white creel marker buoy with slash marks. Then he recalibrated. No buoy ever came with a neck and shoulders.

Their first catch of the day was a drowned man.

1

Sunday, 16 February 2020

Detective Sergeant Daisy Mortimer wasn't easily put off her food. But for once, she stared at the bacon and egg roll she'd made for breakfast with a distinctly jaundiced air. In that crucial moment between sliding the egg on to the crispy bacon and squirting it with tomato ketchup, her boss had rung. 'Morning, Daisy,' DCI Charlie Todd had greeted her cheerily. She could hear his two kids bickering in the background.

'Morning, sir.' Daisy matched his cheer with perkiness. She liked her job and she liked Charlie Todd, after all.

'A lobster boat out of St Monans pulled a body out of the Forth early on. Unexplained death, so we need to attend the PM. Meet me at the mortuary in Kirkcaldy at ten o'clock. Sorry to mess up your Sunday.' He chuckled. 'At least you'll have time for a second cup of tea.'

Daisy ended the call and stared at her phone, a hollow ache in her stomach. Her first post-mortem. Did the boss actually know that? Did he assume she'd stood at the side of an autopsy table often enough to take it in her stride? It was less than six months since her transfer to the Fife-based crime squad and they'd not had a murder in all that time. There had been one suspicious death, but she'd been on a long weekend and, by the time she got back, it had been filed away as an accident.

Before that, she'd been in a general CID office in Falkirk. There had been plenty of crime but nothing that had ended on a pathologist's slab. She prodded her roll with a neatly manicured finger, her lip curling in distaste. The thought of what she might be confronted with – the smells, the sounds, the sights – had killed all appetite. Given how squeamish she was about visits to the dentist, she anticipated she'd be one of the ones everybody took the mince out of, throwing up in the sink or, even worse, dropping to the floor in a dead faint.

In a different case, she could have weaselled out of it by volunteering to supervise the crime scene. But with a corpse fished out of the sea there was no crime scene to be preserved. There was no way out of this. She was going to have to face it some time. It might as well be today.

She stared out of the kitchen window of her rented flat. It looked across a busy dual carriageway to fields and woodland beyond. It had been the only aspect of the former council flat that had appealed to her, apart from the fact that she could afford it. Even so, most mornings, she looked out into the slowly brightening sky and felt good about her life. Not today, she didn't.

Daisy binned her roll and headed for the poky bedroom, deliberately refusing to think about what lay ahead. She shrugged out of her dressing gown and put on what she thought of as her uniform – straight-leg black jeans with enough Lycra to make a chase possible, a close-fitting fine merino layer in dark grey and a deep plum sweater that made her actual shape a subject of speculation in the squad room. A skim of make-up, mascara to emphasise the bright blue of her eyes, then she tucked her thick curly hair into a scrunchy and she was ready to roll.

She was first to arrive. Professor Jenny Carmichael was checking her instrument tray before she began. Daisy introduced herself to the pathologist, who was swathed in full surgical greens, her fine silver hair reduced to narrow triangles in front of her ears. The professor raked her with a hawkish glance and said, 'First time?' Daisy nodded. 'Thought so. Away and stand over there against the wall, far as you can get from the sharp end. That way you can suss out whether you're a fainter or not without getting in the way.'

Daisy did as she was told and Professor Carmichael busied herself with preparations Daisy didn't want to think about. The pathologist looked up when Charlie walked in and gave the barest nod of acknowledgement. 'White male, in decent physical shape for his age,' she said.

'I've told you before, flattery'll get you nowhere.' That was Charlie all over, Daisy thought. Always a quip, whether it was the right moment or not.

Carmichael snorted. 'You're the one doing the flattering.'

'And what sort of age would today's customer be?' Charlie peered across at the pale white body, bloated by its immersion in the sea.

'Forty-nine,' she replied with a quick sidelong glance.

Daisy thought she could see a twinkle and noticed Charlie decide to rise to it. 'You're not usually so precise.'

'We don't usually find a passport and a driver's licence in the back pocket of our victims' jeans.' That seemed odd to Daisy till she remembered the body had turned up in the East Neuk of Fife, a popular tourist destination. Nobody wanted to leave their ID lying around in an Airbnb.

'Victim?' Charlie picked up on the key word.

The pathologist tutted and took a sideways step so she could turn the corpse's head. 'A sufficient insult to the back of his skull to prove fatal. And an absence of sufficient water in his lungs for him to have drowned. He'll have been close to death when he went into the water.'

'He couldn't have fallen and hit his head on the way in? There's plenty of rocks along that part of the Fife coast.'

'The injury's too regular for that. If you pressed me, I'd incline towards a baseball bat or a steel pipe.'

'So, homicide.'

The professor gave a sharp sigh. 'You know it's not my job to make that judgement.'

'I wasn't asking, Jenny.' He softened his words with a bashful smile, then turned to DS Mortimer. 'The passport?'

She spotted the evidence bags on the side counter and picked up the two relevant ones. 'It's a French passport. Issued just over two years ago to a Paul Allard. Like the prof said, he's forty-nine. His driving licence was issued in Paris at the same time—'

'What? Exactly the same time?'

'Same date. That's weird, isn't it? I mean, nobody has a passport and a driving licence issued on the same date, do they?'

'Is there an address on the driving licence?'

She shook her head. 'Nope. Only where it was issued, his name and date of birth.'

'Well, that's your first job, Daisy. Talk to somebody at the French consulate. Tell them we need to know all they can tell us about Paul Allard. What about next of kin? Who to contact in the case of an emergency?' Charlie turned back to Professor Carmichael as he spoke.

'Nothing. He left that part blank.'

'So it's down to you, Prof. Fingerprints? DNA?'

She looked up. 'We should be able to get prints, he's not been in the water more than twenty-four hours, I'd say. I need to talk to someone with more expertise in this area, though. DNA is no problem.'

'Really?'

A swift eye-roll. 'Charlie, it's been nearly twenty years since we managed to extract DNA from a corpse that had been submerged in the Holy Loch for thirty-five years. Trust me, you'll have a DNA result in a couple of days. Though whether that'll help you, I don't know. Can you still get the French to run things through their databases for you?'

Charlie groaned. 'Nobody wants to do us any favours after Brexit.'

'Maybe we'll get a hit on our database,' Daisy said brightly. 'I mean, people who end up murdered are usually a bit dodgy, sir.'

'We should be so lucky,' Charlie said gloomily. 'Have you got anything else for me, Jenny?'

'He's got a tattoo on his left shoulder blade. We photographed it; I'll ping it across to you. It's like a torch with seven flames and a ring below it.'

'No handy inscription, I suppose?'

'That would be too easy.'

He turned back to Daisy. 'There you go, Daisy. A proper mystery. We don't often get one of them, do we?'

The professor raised her eyebrows. 'Surely the only interesting question is whether you can solve it?'

2

Lazy Sunday mornings in bed with coffee and the Sunday papers on her tablet were a relatively recent experience for Detective Chief Inspector Karen Pirie. In the past, she'd have been up early, out for a walk, planning the week ahead, working out her strategies. But she'd been seeing Hamish Mackenzie for the best part of six months now and he'd persuaded her that it wasn't a sin to take time off from her job running Police Scotland's Historic Cases Unit. 'You don't get paid overtime,' he'd reminded her. 'It's not good for you to work all the hours in the week. And if you genuinely care that much about your job, you'd recognise that you perform better with refreshed mind and body.'

Karen didn't relish being told what to do by anyone, but in showing concern for how she could best do her job, Hamish had hit the right note. He hit the right note in so many ways. He was the first man she'd even contemplated any kind of relationship with since her lover Phil had been killed in the line of duty, the fate dreaded by anyone who loves a police officer. Somehow, Hamish had eased his way past her defences and here she was on a Sunday morning, in his bed, in his flat.

And why not? He was smart and funny, easy on the eye, kind and thoughtful. She looked forward to spending time with him. She enjoyed his company, whether they were out having fun or staying in doing nothing much. She liked those of his friends that she'd met. She loved his croft in Wester Ross. But she had reservations about waking up in this lavish New Town flat with its secret roof terrace. Like a lot of things about Hamish, it all felt a bit too much.

If she was honest, the sex was more exciting, more adventurous than it had been with Phil. But afterwards, she never felt completed the way she had with Phil. She'd never had a moment's doubt about the love between them. But with Hamish ... Karen hadn't been able to say, 'I love you.' She'd sensed it on the tip of his tongue, hoped he wouldn't give in to temptation.

Karen realised Hamish had said something she'd missed completely. 'What?'

He was frowning at his screen. 'I said, I think I can get us a table tonight at that place in Newport we've been wanting to try. They do rooms as well, I could see if we can stay over?'

'Not tonight,' Karen said in a tone whose finality she hoped he'd recognise.

'Why not? If we take both cars, you can shoot off in the morning in plenty of time to get to work. And I can head north from there.' From Monday morning to Wednesday night, Hamish worked on his croft in Wester Ross. The rest of the time he spent in Edinburgh, where he ran a small chain of coffee shops.

'Not tonight. I have to be a place first thing in the morning.'

'OK. How about we go for dinner and drive back afterwards?'

11

She wished he wouldn't push it. 'I need to be by myself this evening, Hamish.'

A hurt look sprang into his eyes. 'Have I done something to upset you?'

'It's nothing to do with you.' She hoped that would do it, but no. He had to persist.

'Then what is it? I don't want us to keep secrets from each other.'

Karen pushed herself more upright on the feather pillows. She didn't want to discuss this in a slouch. 'Tomorrow morning, the man who killed Phil is being released from prison. I want to be there.'

'What are you planning?' Anxiety vibrated from Hamish as if he were a freshly struck tuning fork.

'Nothing. I want to see where he's living, that's all.' Now she'd said more than she intended. 'And I don't want company.'

'Do you think that's a good idea?'

Before she could respond, Karen's work mobile rang. Automatically, she reached for it on the bedside table. 'DCI Pirie, Historic Cases Unit,' she said.

'Good morning, DCI Pirie. This is Sergeant Pollock from Barrack Street in Perth. We've got a walk-in this morning that I think is more up your street than mine. Any chance you could come up and help us reach a decision?'

Karen felt a familiar prickle of interest and turned away from Hamish. 'Could you give me a wee bit more to go on?'

'Well, it's like this.' He spoke slowly, keen to make sure he got his points across. 'A member of the public came in and made a report at the bar. Her sister died in an RTA a few weeks ago and she's just getting round to sorting out the deceased's house. There was a camper van in the garage that the woman says definitely didn't belong to her sister. She took a look inside and there's skeletonised human remains in the back of the van. Now, the fact that they're skeletonised says cold case to me and my boss. So we thought we'd cut to the chase and get you involved from the start.'

'Are you telling me you've not already got a team on site?'

A pause. 'We're a bit stretched today, to be honest. We've got a royal visit, not to mention an armed robbery at a club last night.'

Karen sighed. 'And a skeleton isn't time-sensitive, right?'

'Well, it's not going anywhere, is it?'

In spite of her irritation at the lack of urgency, Karen was eager to be involved from the start. She never lost sight of the lives devastated by the cases she found herself investigating. But that didn't mean she didn't get a buzz at the thought of a new case to unravel, a mystery to explain, an aching gap in some strangers' lives to fill with answers. 'We'll meet you at the house,' she said. 'Ping the address to my colleague.' She ended the call and was about to make another when Hamish put a hand on her arm.

'You're not going to work?'

'It's a new case that looks like a cold case. I need to attend the scene.'

Hamish sighed and fell back on his pillows. 'I can't compete with the dead.'

She turned and kissed him. 'It's not a competition, it's an obligation.' And then she was out of bed, self-conscious in her nakedness. 'I'll have a shower then I'll be out of your way.'

In the bathroom, she called her bagman, Detective Constable Jason Murray. 'Morning, Jason. Sorry to screw up your Sunday but we've got a new case. Meet me at the office in twenty minutes.'

'OK, we going anywhere interesting?'

'Perth.'

'Suspicious death?'

'Correct. We don't get many of those in the petty bourgeois capital of Scotland.'

3

North Woodlands Crescent was a short drive from one of the big roundabouts that interrupted the dual carriageways sweeping round Perth, carrying traffic to more urgent destinations in all four points of the compass. Substantial whitewashed bungalows sat on their individual plots behind sturdy evergreen hedges trimmed to uniform heights. It had the air of a street determined that nothing should disturb its equilibrium. Nobody here would be having to call the police about rowdy teenagers doing drugs, or domestic disputes that spilled out beyond trim front doors, or joyriding car thieves doing wheelies on the litter-free streets.

'This is the kind of place people get totally outraged about a murder on their doorstep,' Jason remarked, pulling into the kerb behind a marked patrol car. 'Like it's a personal insult.'

'We don't know that it's a murder yet,' Karen said.

'Fair enough, boss. But tucking a body away in the garage isn't how most people react to natural causes.'

He was, she thought, definitely becoming both more insightful and more confident. Karen allowed herself a moment's pride. Supporting Jason to be the best he could be was a cause Phil had recruited her to. Slowly but surely, the Mint was getting there. She grinned. 'I don't know. It is Perth, after all. Could be death to your social standing to admit to having a body in the boot.'

A uniformed sergeant emerged from the patrol car and raised a hand in greeting. He waited for them to approach then said, 'DCI Pirie? I'm Sergeant Pollock. We spoke on the phone.'

'Still no detectives on the scene? Or CSI?' Obviously they did things differently in Perth.

'I spoke to my inspector, he thought we should wait to see what you thought. It's not like there's going to be a hot pursuit or anything.'

'It might have been an idea to get a forensics team out. It doesn't matter whose case it ends up as, we're going to need a full sweep of the scene.' Karen spoke mildly but Pollock caught her grim expression.

'Do you want to do that first, then? Before you take a look?'

'Call them. While we're waiting for them to get here, DC Murray and I will get suited up and assess the scene. And then we'll want to talk to the woman who made the discovery. Is she down at the station?'

Pollock shook his head. 'We let her go home. She was pretty shaken up, you know? I thought she'd be better in her own house, rather than here or sitting in an interview room for who knows how long.'

It wasn't what Karen would have done, but she was getting the message that Barrack Street definitely wasn't on the same page as the Historic Cases Unit. She hoped their response to live cases was more by the book. 'What's the name of the householder?'

'Susan Leitch. She's the one who was killed in the RTA. The woman who made the discovery was her sister, Stella. Also Leitch. Neither of them's got any previous, not even a speeder.'

Ten minutes later, clad in rustling Tyvek and blue plastic shoe covers, Karen and Jason made their way through the front door and down the bland carpet of the hallway into a tidy kitchen. Karen clocked the assortment of oils and spices by the hob, the stoneware jar of utensils and a row of cookbooks with dinged corners and cracked spines. It looked like a place where cooking actually happened. In the far wall, a solid door opened on to a double garage. Their eyes were drawn to the half-uncovered VW classic camper van, but Karen forced herself to take a look around the rest of the space. First impressions were often a reliable indicator when things were out of kilter.

A rack for two bikes was fixed to one wall but only one bike hung there, a sturdy mountain bike with fat tyres and a mount for an electric motor. On the floor below it, the motor was plugged into a charger. Next to the bike rack was a board that held an array of tools that Karen assumed were the sort of thing you needed if you were going to take care of your own bike, rather than wheel it round to the local bike shop every time your brakes squeaked.

'You know anything about bikes, Jason?' she asked, without much hope.

'Only the kind with engines, boss.'

On the opposite wall there was a workbench with an assortment of tools for minor DIY and maintenance – screwdrivers, adjustable wrenches, a couple of hammers and a hacksaw. Neatly stacked next to them, half a dozen paint tins, clearly partly used. By the looks of things, Susan Leitch was a well-organised woman. None of the signs of chaotic behaviour that often characterised domestic crime scenes. If that was what this was.

Karen crossed to the camper van, noting that the one tyre she could see was flat and looked as if it had been like that for a long time, to judge by the distressed state of the rubber. She opened the driver's door with as little contact as possible. Stella Leitch had doubtless destroyed any fingermarks there might have been, but it never hurt to follow forensic protocols. Karen stuck her head in and sniffed. There was a faint smell of musty decay, but not the overwhelming stench produced by a rotting corpse. She noticed the passenger window was open an inch or two, which, coupled with the passage of time, would account for that absence. Keys in the ignition still.

She peered over the seat but couldn't see much of the main cabin. 'I'll have to go in,' she said, preparing to clamber on to the driver's seat.

'There's a side door that lets you in, boss,' Jason pointed out. 'Maybe it's unlocked too?'

Karen backed out. 'We should wait for the CSI team. But the sister's already disturbed the cover.' She considered for a moment. 'Get your phone out and take pics all round the van, so we've got a record of how it was mostly left before the sister shifted it. And don't forget the number plate.'

'There isn't one,' Jason said. 'At least, not on the front.'

'That's interesting,' Karen said, moving to the rear of the vehicle and carefully lifting the tarpaulin. 'Same on the back. Somebody was thinking this through. OK, on you go, get the rest of the pics done.'

She stepped back and waited. A score of clicks later, she gingerly moved the tarpaulin away from the side door and tried the handle. It opened easily, sliding back on well-oiled runners.

On the floor of the van lay a disarticulated collection of bones, the skull with its corona of shed dark hair towards the front end, the scatter of tarsals and phalanges pointing towards the rear. Maggot pupae cases, like macabre Coco Pops, were scattered everywhere around and among the bones, evidence of why the body was stripped clean of flesh. It looked as if the victim had fallen or been placed on their side. What was clear from the first glance was that 'victim' was the right word. Across the back of the skull was the jagged crack of an obvious depressed fracture. Someone or something had hit this person very hard indeed.

The incongruity of the human remains was made more poignant by the tidiness of the rest of the van. Everything was stowed in its proper place; books on a shelf, clothes in slatted plastic boxes in an alcove, artist's paints and brushes in a custom-made caddy. A few watercolours of lochs and mountains were tacked on the front of a cupboard. To Karen's untrained eye, they looked like the kind of generic painting stocked by every Highland craft shop she'd ever been in.

She withdrew her head from the van. 'We definitely need CSI. And River.'

Back at the car, stripped of her protective suit, Karen made the call. Fortunately, Dr River Wilde was in her university office in Dundee rather than the lab or the lecture theatre. Karen briefed her on their discovery. 'Can you free yourself up for a wee trip to Perth?' she asked.

'Sure, these bones aren't going anywhere. I'll be with you within the hour.'

Reassured that the remains in the VW were in the best

hands, Karen brought Pollock up to speed. 'You'll probably want to get some PCs up here to guard the scene, keep the nosy neighbours at arm's length.'

'Not to mention the bloody citizen journalists,' Pollock grumbled.

'And ask the techs whether they can find the VIN. Somebody's removed the number plates, but they might not have known to erase the identification number. Even if they tried, the lab has ways of revealing it. Once the CSIs have done, Dr Wilde will want the remains uplifted to her mortuary in Dundee,' Karen continued. 'She'll liaise with your officers on that. We're off now to talk to the sister. Thanks for bringing us in so early. That way, nothing gets lost in the cracks of a handover.'

'Aye, well, it's not often we get something that's so obviously a cold case from the get-go. Let me know if there's anything you need back-up on.'

As they headed for Stella Leitch's address, Jason said, 'This is a funny one. Why would you keep a body in your garage?'

'River always says that murder's easy. It's getting rid of the body that's hard. It looks like Susan Leitch hadn't figured out what to do with the second part of the deal.'

'I get that, boss. But this is just bones now. Could you not smash them up with a hammer and take a wee bag at a time down to the beach and chuck them in the sea?'

'It'd be worth a try, I suppose. But you'd have to be pretty cold-blooded to do that. Especially if the person you'd killed was somebody close to you. Even serious gangsters employ people to do their body disposal for them. They call them "the cleaners".'

'You're kidding, right?'

Karen shook her head. 'Wish I was, Jason. It's apparently

considered a skilled operation. There was a case a few years ago, down in England, where bits of a body kept turning up all over the countryside. I think by the end there were body parts discovered in five or six different force areas. They eventually did nail the guy responsible, but the full story didn't come out in court. Apparently the organised crime gang responsible for the murder had fallen out with their regular cleaner because they thought he was charging too much. So one of the eejits in their gang thought, "How hard can it be?" and took on the job for a fraction of the fee. And it turned out he was rubbish at it. Rubbish to the tune of fourteen years inside.'

'You're not serious? How d'you know that?'

'Because it was one of River's cases. When they went to the pub afterwards to celebrate the guilty verdict, one of the serious crime squad guys told her the back story.'

Jason shook his head. 'How do you get a job like that?'

'I don't think they recruit at careers fairs,' Karen said drily. 'I'm guessing Susan Leitch discovered that getting rid of the body in your VW wasn't as easy as she thought.'

4

Monday, 17 February 2020

It was barely half past six in the morning, but already the
traffic heading into Edinburgh on the A71 artery was scle-
rotic. Detective Chief Inspector Karen Pirie was glad to be
travelling in the opposite direction, moving steadily if not
swiftly. She'd worked her way across the waking city to the
background murmur of a playlist as familiar as the streets
themselves. Music had never been that big a deal for her, but
when she'd lived with Phil, he'd gently eased her into his
preferences. Now, when she was off duty and didn't have to
keep one ear on the radio, she always returned to the playlist he'd imported to her phone. Elbow, Snow Patrol, Franz
Ferdinand. The lyrics had made little impression over the
years, but she liked to hum along to the tunes.

Out of habit, she flicked glances to either side as she
drove, alert to anything out of place. The houses on her
left looked substantial, but that was an illusion. In reality,
they were blocks of four flats, two up and two down, built
when social housing was a public good taken for granted.
They'd been sold off years before, the clue to their private
status being the different colours and styles of front doors.

Karen didn't begrudge their occupiers the chance to own their own homes; what she minded was the politicians' failure to replace what they'd sold off. She hoped they saw the city's growing homeless population as a reproach, but mostly doubted it.

At a break in the row of houses, she turned left into a narrow roadway lined with thick hedges, their winter foliage copper brown. Straight ahead, a modern frontage, all bulletproof glass flanked by solid pillars and cement blocks designed to look like dressed sandstone. A casual observer might have taken it for the offices of a minor insurance company except that where the logo should have been, bold black letters read 'HMP EDINBURGH'. A second look, and the high concrete wall stretching far into the darkness would have hammered home what the acronym stood for – Her Majesty's Prison.

Karen swung left into the car park. She was early enough that the slot she'd previously identified as perfect for her needs was still empty. She was driving her personal car this morning. Nobody would take her five-year-old Nissan Juke for a police car, not even an undercover one. Phil had always taken the piss out of her for her choice of wheels. 'The Nissan Joke,' he'd dubbed it. But this morning, it was the perfect camouflage.

As the minutes ticked past, a trickle of cars turned into a stream. Some were clearly prison staff, driving round to their designated parking zone. Others stopped near Karen, there for the same reason if not the same purpose. Some of the drivers and passengers stepped out into the cold morning, drifting towards the prison buildings, clouds of warm breath mingling with steam from vapes and smoke from sparked-up cigarettes.

They obviously hadn't done this before, she thought. Seven o'clock might be the official time for prisoner release, but that didn't mean the ones they were waiting for would walk out of the doors on the stroke of the hour. There was paperwork to be done. Medications to be issued. Property to be checked. The welcoming committees would be lucky to see their loved ones by half past seven. By eight, there would be a ragged procession – mostly men, a few women – re-emerging into the world, clutching their black bin-liners and trying not to look as disorientated as they felt.

Karen didn't mind the wait. She'd been preparing for this moment for years, turning over what it might demand of her. If revenge was a dish best served cold, then the timing was spot on. An extra half hour or more was neither here nor there.

So focused was she on the prison frontage that the opening of her passenger door physically startled her. She whirled round in her seat, fight or flight pumping through her reptile brain. Heart pounding, she registered who was climbing into her car and felt her muscles relax. 'What the fuck, Jimmy? You trying to give me a heart attack?'

'Did you not see me walking up to your car? I wasn't hiding, Karen.' DCI Jimmy Hutton, head of Police Scotland's Murder Prevention Unit, settled himself into the passenger seat like a man who was readying himself for a long journey. He pulled off black leather gloves and unbuttoned his dark navy overcoat.

'What are you doing here?' she demanded, scowling eyebrows drawn down, attention back on the prison.

'Taking care of you,' he said mildly.

'What's that supposed to mean?'

'I reckoned you might be here this morning. I thought I'd

swing by and make sure you had somebody in your corner. In case you were tempted.'

'Tempted to do what?'

'Something you'd regret.'

Karen scoffed. 'I'm not a hormonal teenager, Jimmy. I'm not going to flip my lid and run across the car park like a banshee with a machete. All I want is to see Merrick Shand for myself. To see what three and a half years in the jail has done to him.'

'Really? That's all?'

She shrugged. 'And maybe check out whoever's here for him. And where they take him. I'm not planning on doing anything, Jimmy. But I need to keep tabs on him. I need to know where he's living, what he's doing. I don't care whether he sees me doing it, either. In fact, I'd quite like that.'

'That's a big risk to take. All he's got to do is report you to Professional Standards for harassment.' Jimmy shifted in his seat and gave her the hard stare.

'I won't give him grounds. Nothing stalkery, you understand. Just the odd unsettling glimpse out the corner of his eye. Enough to fuck with his head but not enough to put my job on the line.' She chanced a look at Jimmy. She hadn't seen a look that sceptical since she'd told her granny it hadn't been her who'd eaten all the butter tablet, in spite of throwing up like a sick dog.

'Is that why you brought your back-up? So's you wouldn't get spotted tailing Shand away from the jail?'

Puzzled, Karen cast a quick sideways glance at Jimmy to check whether he was at the wind-up for some unfathomable reason. But she'd never seen him look more serious. No, not serious. Pissed off. 'What are you talking about? I wouldn't drag the Mint into this.' For all sorts of reasons, Detective Constable Jason Murray was the last person Karen would have brought along that morning.

'Come on, Karen, don't come the innocent with me. I'm not talking about Jason. I'm talking about Captain Coffee.'

'What?' Karen couldn't have faked such outraged astonishment.

'The row behind you, four cars to the left. Did you not see him parking up in his big fuck-off Range Rover?'

Wildly, she looked around, instantly spotting what should never have got past her in the first place. 'I'll fucking kill him,' she raged, throwing open her car door so hard it bounced back on its hinges and caught her hip as she jumped out. But Karen on the warpath wasn't going to be hindered by anything as mundane as pain. She stormed towards the Range Rover, determined to deal with the one person who had no right to be there.

5

Daisy glared at her computer screen, turning in a fine performance of a woman lost in concentration. At least, she hoped it was a fine performance. The reality was that, although she'd got in early the morning after the post-mortem, she could make no significant progress until she heard back from the French consulate staffer she'd been sweet-talking the afternoon before. Their first conversation had been brief. Daisy was convinced she could actually hear the Gallic shrug when she passed on Paul Allard's details.

So she'd been surprised when he phoned back inside the hour, sounding like a different person. 'Sergeant Mortimer,' he began with a flourish. 'I have some very interesting information for you.'

'Glad to hear it. Thanks for calling back.'

'No, not at all. What I have found out is that Paul Allard is a jazzman. He plays saxophone in a quintet. Comme des Étrangers. Not my sort of thing, but I hear they're pretty good. He lives on the Left Bank. Do you know Paris?'

'No, sorry to say I've never been.'

'No matter, it will still be there when you decide to go. Monsieur Allard lives – lived, I should say, in one of the little streets that leads to the Odéon, in the Sixth Arrondissement.

It's a nice area but, looking at his address, I think it's probably a small apartment in the roof.'

'Well, that's a start. Can you get your local police to go
and knock his door, see if there's anybody else living there?
Or even get a search warrant, to see if there's anything in
his apartment to give us a clue as to what he was doing in
the East Neuk of Fife?'

He made an indeterminate noise in the back of his throat.
'You would need a warrant from your courts, I think.'

A stifled sigh. 'OK, maybe you could ping across the
address and I'll see what I can get moving at this end.'
Who knew what hoops she'd have to jump through for that
these days?

'Of course, but not so fast. There is something much more
interesting. There is no record of Paul Allard before that
passport and that driving licence were issued to him. It's
like he never existed.'

'What?'

'I know. I thought maybe he was in a witness protection
programme or something like that. I talked to my colleague
about this and she said, no, no. If he was in witness protection, he would have a proper paper trail. We would not be
able to access it, but we would know of its existence.'

Daisy had sat up straight in her chair, a buzz of excitement in her head. 'That's right. A legend.'

'Ah, we have the same word. And then my colleague, she
said he could have changed his name. That would explain
the dead end.'

'And did he?'

'I don't know yet. I have sent an urgent request to the
Ministry of the Interior, but I will be honest with you, I
have no idea how long it will take to come back. But when

someone changes his name officially in France, he has to place a notice in the *Journal Officiel de la République Française.* I will check out whether it is searchable online. Maybe that will be a shortcut.'

'That's brilliant. I'll see what I can do at this end. Thanks so much. I really appreciate your help. And don't forget to ping that address over to me!'

Which had all been very exciting. DCI Todd had been much more sanguine about it, barely acknowledging what she'd learned. 'Let's wait and see what Inspector Clouseau comes back with before we get overexcited,' he'd said, turning away to shout at one of the detective constables. 'Have you made any progress with the coastguard and where the body might have gone in the water?'

Todd had sent them home shortly after six. He wasn't the kind of boss who believed in working all the hours in the day for the sake of looking busy. When Daisy had started working for him, he'd taken her to an improbably cosy café on an industrial estate on the outskirts of Kirkcaldy and laid out his philosophy over home-baked cherry scones and Earl Grey tea. 'There's no overtime in CID. When we've got lines of inquiry to pursue, we work the hours we have to. But cases get stalled. You're waiting for an address or another key piece of information before you can take the next step. So you might as well be waiting at home. Half the time, you can't get access to records out of office hours. So you might as well be watching a box set on your own settee. That way, when you do have to work thirty-six hours out of forty-eight, you're not already knackered. Pull your weight when it's needed and you'll get no complaints from me. But God help you if I catch you skiving when you're needed.'

It couldn't have been clearer. But still Daisy struggled to turn in late and go home early. So she was first in next morning. She unwrapped the roll and sausage she'd picked up from the roadside snack van and ate as she checked through the files again, making notes as she went. When her phone rang with the ID of the French consulate, she carved a tear in her notepad with her pencil point in shocked excitement. 'DS Mortimer,' she almost shouted.

'Good morning, Sergeant. My name is Guillaume Verancourt. I believe you spoke to my colleague from the French consulate yesterday?' He sounded more Edinburger than Parisian.

'That's right. And you—'

'He passed your inquiry on to me. I'm associated with the Ministry of the Interior.'

Was that code for him being a spy? Or just a bureaucrat? Daisy was starting to feel she might be out of her depth. 'And have you anything for me?'

'I have some information, yes. But before I do so, I need to make clear to you that the responsibility for investigating the death of a French citizen rests on the shoulders of the French authorities. We are very willing to cooperate with Police Scotland, but we must be assured that you are equally prepared to cooperate with us. To share information. Are you in a position to give that assurance?'

Daisy thought quickly. She knew she should pass this up the line, but she was pretty sure nobody was going to refuse the French request. Not if it meant dead-ending the investigation before it had even begun. 'The dead man may have been a French citizen, Monsieur Verancourt, but he was killed here in Scotland. It's in everyone's interests to work together on this.'

'So you will send me what reports you have? And you will continue to do this?'

Daisy took a deep breath. She was determined to make her mark with this case, but she didn't want that mark to be a blot on her record. On the other hand, she needed to make progress. 'I'll be honest. We don't have much to go on, but we will share what we have. And will you pass on what you have?'

'I will email what I have discovered to you, but I think it might be helpful to run through it verbally first. In case there is anything that isn't clear. And of course the details from us will be in French.'

'That's very kind of you.' Plenty of time later to reveal her competence in French if necessary. 'So, what have you found out?'

'So, you already know Paul Allard did not exist officially until two years ago. The reason for that is that he changed his name.'

'Can you tell me what he was called before?'

'Well, this is where it becomes complicated. Almost ten years ago, a man joined the French Foreign Legion calling himself Paul Allard. That was not his real name, but the Legion allows recruits to self-declare their name when they join. Conventionally, the surname should have the same initial letter as their actual name, but that's the only link to their past.'

'You're kidding, right? This is like something out of an adventure comic. You're saying they really get to join the Foreign Legion to forget?'

Verancourt cleared his throat. 'It is a tradition. There is nothing comic about it, believe me. There will have been nothing humorous about Paul Allard's military service.

31

And like everyone who signs up, he will have had to provide proof of his original identity so we could check that
he was not a convicted criminal or the subject of a warrant
for a serious crime. If applicants are clean, they can choose
the name they serve under. That is the only name on their
records. Under those terms, the man called Paul Allard
signed up. He was a competent musician so he was assigned
to the regimental band, which is part of the 1st Foreign
Regiment. He attained the rank which corresponds to cor-
poral in your army.'

'All that's very interesting. But obviously he wasn't
in the Legion any more. He was living in a flat in Paris,
playing jazz.'

'Correct. He left the Legion after seven years. Because
of his service he was entitled to claim French citizenship.
There is a drawback to that for a man who wants to stay
invisible. To claim citizenship, he must revert to his original
identity. So Caporal Paul Allard had to resume his former
name and status as a UK citizen.' He paused, clearly savouring the dramatic moment.

'And that was?'

'James Auld.' He spelled out the surname. 'This is a
Scottish name, I think?'

'It is,' Daisy said, scribbling on a fresh page. 'Very much
so. But if that's the case, how come he had the passport and
driving licence in his Foreign Legion name?'

'He applied almost immediately for a legal name change
back to Paul Allard.'

'And he got it? Just like that?'

Verancourt chuckled. 'No, Sergeant Mortimer. Not "just
like that". To change your name in France is not as simple as
it is in the UK. There are strict conditions. But he met one of

those conditions quite easily. Because he made his living as a musician and his reputation had been established as Paul Allard, he could argue that he needed to be officially known as Paul Allard to avoid confusion in terms of payment and tax liability. And so, two years ago, he became officially a French citizen called Paul Allard.'

Nothing like a bureaucracy for dotting the i's and crossing the t's. 'But the date of birth is the same? James Auld would have had the same date of birth as Paul Allard?'

'Undoubtedly. We only sanction a change of name. As I said, I'll email the details over to you, but I think this is the only really important detail for your purposes.'

'It's too early to say that,' Daisy said slowly. 'The man's been murdered. It may be that the motive for that lies in his military service.'

Verancourt made an indeterminate noise. 'You may struggle to uncover much information about that. The Legion is not noted for its willingness to be open about its operations.'

'Great,' Daisy sighed.

'And you will send me your reports? The autopsy and whatever else you have?'

'I will. Thanks for your help. I might have to come back to you again, though? We may want access to his apartment, for example?'

'For that you will have to deal with the local police in Paris and the *juge d'instruction*. But I may be able to assist with that. Goodbye for now, Sergeant Mortimer.'

As the line went dead, Charlie Todd walked into the room. Daisy stood up and caught his eye. 'The dead man, boss? He ran away to join the French Foreign Legion.'

6

Later that morning and Karen was still fuming as she marched along Duke Street, an implacable woman on a mission. On entering Aleppo, the Syrian café where she'd arranged to meet a friend, she was so wrapped up in her fury that she barely managed to nod hello to Amena, not too busy with her front-of-house duties to beam a welcome at Karen.

Karen made straight for the woman sitting at the furthest table from the door. She'd known Giorsal Kennedy since schooldays, but in spite of a fifteen-year gap when Giorsal had been working down south, her reunion with the senior social worker over a recent case had formed a closer bond than they'd ever had as teenagers. Karen sat down heavily and sighed.

'I take it things didn't go according to plan,' Giorsal said, her keynote mildness instilled by years of social work.

'You could say that.' Karen half-turned to try to catch a waiter's eye, but she was too late. Amena was already headed for the table carrying a small cup of the intense cardamom coffee Karen had learned to love.

'Royalty here, you,' Giorsal said as Amena left them in peace.

'It's embarrassing. I still don't get to pay for my coffee.'

'But you always chuck money in the charity box. I've seen you. Besides, they owe you. If it wasn't for you—'

'They'd have found somebody else to help them.' Karen shifted in her seat, awkward at being reminded of the help she'd given the Syrian refugee group to find premises and get their business off the ground. 'But never mind that. I'm absolutely raging, Gus.'

'What's happened? You told me you were only going to keep an eye on Merrick Shand. Track him to where he's staying. That's all. You promised, Karen.'

'And that's all I was going to do. Until bloody Hamish stuck his oar in.' She took a sip of coffee, feeling the need of its strength.

'Hamish? What's this got to do with Hamish?'

'Absolutely bloody nothing, that's what. Stupid me, I know you're supposed to share things when you're ... I don't know, getting into a relationship with somebody. I didn't think that gave him the right to stick his nose into my business.'

Giorsal frowned. 'You're going to have to give me a bit more to work with here, Karen.'

Another sip. 'I told him I couldn't stay with him last night because Merrick Shand was getting out this morning and I'd have to be up at the crack of sparrowfart to make sure I could get on his tail.'

'He knows who Merrick Shand is?'

Karen gave a weary sigh. 'He knows Shand is the animal who used his car to deliberately crush the life out of Phil. Yes.'

'So, what? Hamish tried to stop you?'

'No, he's not that daft. Though that would have been

understandable. I think he secretly thinks I should put the past behind me and move on. But all he said was, "Do you think that's a good idea?" and I said, probably not but it was something I had to do. And we left it at that.'

'I'm guessing that wasn't the end of it?'

'Correct. Fast forward to this morning. I'm sitting in the car park, eyes glued on the door, waiting for Merrick Shand to creep out from under his stone. And I just about jump out my skin when Jimmy Hutton opens the passenger door and breenges into the car.'

'Presumably there to stop you doing anything you'd regret?'

'Exactly.' She rolled her eyes. 'Gus, you've known me a long time. Do you have me pegged as the sort of person who loses the plot and runs amok at the slightest provocation?'

Giorsal couldn't suppress a chuckle in the face of Karen's indignation. 'No,' she managed. 'No, you're more the "creeping up from behind when they least expect it" kind.'

'So why is it all these men who should know me better think I need a minder?'

'I suspect Jimmy was there for his own sake too, Karen. He loved Phil like a son. And it was his operation that went south and ended up with Phil being killed. He's got all that guilt to carry too.'

Karen considered. 'Aye, you're right. I'm not being fair to Jimmy. But Hamish? That's a different story. So, Jimmy gets in the car, like I said, and casually mentions he's spotted Hamish parked in the row behind me. He assumes I've asked him there as back-up, to help me tail Shand when he leaves. I mean, really? Me? Why would anybody that knows me think I'd need back-up on a piece of piss like that? And if I did, that I'd choose a civilian whose only experience of tailing anybody comes from playing *L.A. Noire*?' She paused for breath and another sip.

'What did he do?'

'He did nothing. He saw me coming for him and had the sense to get out the car before I had to drag him out. I gave him a bollocking that must have stripped the wax out his ears and stood there till he got in the car and drove off.' Karen's sigh came from the depths of her lungs. 'And while this was all going on, Merrick Shand walked out and got picked up.'

'Oh no! Tell me Jimmy followed him?'

Karen shook her head. 'That's not what he came for. He did at least get the car reg, so I can follow up on that. But Hamish? How can I trust him after this?' Her brows drew together in a stubborn frown.

'Are you not being a wee bit harsh? Sounds to me like Hamish thought he was doing the right thing, covering your back because he cares about you.' Giorsal shrugged. 'It's not a hanging offence.'

Karen fiddled with her cup, not meeting her friend's eye. 'It's one more thing that makes me wonder . . . '

'Wonder what? Karen, Phil would probably have done exactly the same thing.'

'Don't compare him to Phil. He's nothing like Phil. Phil and me, we were like two sides of the same coin. It's not like that with Hamish.'

'Maybe not. But Hamish is one of the good guys. He's solvent, he's single, he's sexy and from what I've seen he's quite clearly smitten. What more do you want?'

Karen sighed. 'He's not . . . straightforward. You remember

when I first met him on his croft, on that case up in Wester Ross? He played the handsome Highland crofter to a T, kilt and big boots and sheep on the hill and everything, and it was several days before he let on that he's actually got the coffee shops here in Edinburgh to pay the bills.'

'I thought that was funny, Karen.'

'So did I. But now I'm not so sure. I think Hamish has always got one eye on the impression he's making on his audience. Like for my birthday.'

Giorsal laughed. 'You're complaining about your birthday? He whisked you off for a surprise long weekend in Venice, Karen. In a hotel even I'd heard of!'

'He'd already asked me what I fancied doing and I said I'd like to spend the weekend up on the croft.' Karen's jaw had settled into stubbornness. 'It's not what I want, it's what he thinks I should want. Nothing's ever simple with Hamish, it's all razzle-dazzle. Even his bloody porridge.'

'His porridge?' Giorsal looked bemused.

'How do you have your porridge?' Karen demanded.

'Oats, skimmed milk, a teaspoon of honey. Why?'

'Hamish has oats, buckwheat flakes, a mix of ground flax seeds, brazil nuts and CoQ10, a pinch of chai spices, a spoonful of almond butter, a handful of blueberries and a mix of lactose-free oat milk and coconut water. How in the name of God can you have porridge where oats are the minority ingredient?'

Now Giorsal was giggling like a teenager. 'I can't believe you're judging him on his porridge.'

'It's symptomatic, Gus. It's a class thing. Our backgrounds are so different. His parents are academics, he spent his teens in California where money was never an object, he's got a degree and he's a successful entrepreneur. Me? I was born in a council house in Methil, I left school at sixteen to become a polis. I think we're just too different.'

There was a long silence. Then Giorsal put her hand over Karen's. 'I hear you,' she said. 'But how does the porridge taste?'

7

The proposed extension of the tram line to the heart of Leith provoked daily gridlock in the north of the city. Even the buses struggled to keep to anything like a timetable. Karen had given up on any form of transport more sophisticated than her own two feet for getting to work. As she marched up Leith Walk from Aleppo to the office, she couldn't avoid thinking about the two hundred medieval skeletons that were being exhumed and relocated to satisfy the needs of Edinburgh commuters. How long, she wondered, before some idiot tried to hide a more recent body among the historic remains? If there was one certainty she'd earned from policing, there was no limit to the stupidity of criminals.

She was still smarting from what had happened outside the prison. She hoped Hamish would have the good sense to take her at her word when she'd told him not to make contact with her till she was good and ready to talk to him. He'd looked hurt and baffled. It worried her that he seemed to miss the crucial point that when Karen wanted help, she asked for it. That she didn't appreciate anybody second-guessing her when she didn't. Really, had he assimilated so little about her?

During the last case they'd worked together, she'd

confided in her closest friend and ally, forensic anthropologist River Wilde. River had met her eyes with a steady gaze and said, 'Phil was the love of your life. You'll never feel like that again. But that doesn't mean you have to give up on love. It's not second-best. It's different.'

Karen wanted to believe that. She hadn't quite managed it yet. And that morning's row had thrown everything out of kilter. But in spite of that, she knew she didn't want to let him go. She turned into Gayfield Square and cut across the park to the police station. Time to put Hamish back in his box and concentrate on work.

The office was still empty but Karen barely had time to log on to her email account before Jason arrived, out of breath and clutching two cups of coffee. Karen had schooled him well. Whenever he departed the office, he stuffed their reusable vacuum coffee cups in his backpack so he could refill them on his way into work every morning. It wasn't taking advantage of him, Karen reasoned. She was always easier to work with when caffeinated.

'Thanks, Jason.' Karen took the proffered cup and handed Jason a post-it note. 'Can you run this car index number for me?'

Jason gave her a sideways look. 'What case is it attached to?'

A scatter of cases where cops had done favours to friends by checking the database for car details had provoked a recent memo from the Assistant Chief Constable (Crime) reminding them that all database searches had to be legitimately attached to cases. Which was why Karen had passed the task on to Jason in the first place. 'Just tidying up a loose end on the Joey Sutherland case,' she said with a note of finality.

He frowned but said nothing. Even Jason knew better than to push against a brick wall. 'OK, boss.' He turned to his screen.

'Later,' she said hastily. 'We've got somebody to go and see.'

Stella Leitch's home had little in common with her sister's bungalow. It sat in splendid isolation at the end of a steep single-track road that climbed up from the busy dual carriageway between Perth and Dundee. It must originally have been a single-storey cottage for a gamekeeper or a shepherd, Karen reckoned. But only its bare bones remained, dwarfed by a two-storey glass extension built out like the prow of a ship to provide stunning views across the Tay estuary to Fife. From the outside, they could see that the lower level was laid out as a living space, with sofas and a dining area off to one side. The upper level appeared to be an artist's studio, with three easels facing in different directions. 'I wonder how she got planning permission for that?' Jason muttered, gazing up at it. 'My dad just about had a nervous breakdown trying to get his conservatory past the building inspectors.'

'It'll be architecturally significant, Jason. If you're going to dream, dream big.' Karen walked up to the front door, past a bright red Mini Cooper S convertible that looked like it had been abandoned rather than parked. Before she could ring the bell, the door opened. 'I'm Stella,' the woman on the doorstep said. 'I'm guessing you're the police?'

Karen identified herself and Jason. 'Can we come in?'

'Sure, I've been expecting you. Come away through.' She led the way into the light living room. Only from the inside was it possible to see that the ceiling – and the floor above – were also made of glass.

Jason gawped. 'That's one glass ceiling you wouldnae want to smash,' he breathed.

Stella gave a wan smile. 'You'd have a hard job. It's metallic glass. Pretty much unbreakable.' She gestured at the squashy blue velvet sofas. 'Take a seat.' She looked to be in her mid-thirties, but it was never easy to tell with women who could afford to cheat the eye. Mid-brown hair with clever highlights pulled back in a loose ponytail. Dark blue eyes set wide apart and a generous mouth, giving her face an open appearance. A T-shirt with a faded logo Karen vaguely recalled from a first-person shooter Phil used to play on the Xbox. Loose-fitting yoga pants with a logo she recognised from a designer shop on George Street she'd once gone into by mistake. One thing Stella Leitch didn't appear to be was distraught.

'I'm sorry about your sister,' Karen said. 'People drive so badly around cyclists.'

Stella's eyelids flickered in a set of fast blinks. 'I'm gutted,' she said, sounding as if she meant it. 'We weren't what you'd call close, me and Susan. Different paths, different choices. But we met up every few weeks for dinner, always had a good laugh. Our parents died in the Boxing Day tsunami back in 2004 when we were only teenagers, so I know what it takes to deal with loss. I'll miss her like hell every single day, but she would have been furious if she'd thought I was going to fall apart.' She sighed. 'I save that for when I'm on my own.'

'I understand. Are you Susan's executor, then?'

'That's why I went to the house yesterday. I've been working up to it. I couldn't face it before the funeral. I got her PA to go round and collect the clothes to dress her in. But I knew that I had to get to grips with sorting out the house.

Better sooner than later. If you don't face these things head-on, they drag out forever. It took one of my team three years to clear his mother's house and put it on the market. I get that, I really do. But there's part of me thinks it's immoral to leave a house standing empty all that time. I mean, we're in a housing crisis, right?'

Somehow Karen didn't think Susan Leitch's house was going to play a significant role in alleviating homelessness. But she supposed it might end up as part of a chain whose bottom link might make a difference to someone. At least grief didn't seem to have rendered Stella monosyllabic. Time to capitalise on that while it lasted. 'It can't have been easy. Can you tell me, why did you go through to the garage?'

'I wanted to do a walk-through, so I could start making a plan. It's sort of what I do professionally. Transferable skills, you know?'

'What is it that you do?'

A flash of whitened teeth. 'I'm the creative director of a games company. We're based in Dundee and New York.'

Out of the corner of her eye, Karen saw Jason sit up straight. No mean feat in those sofas. 'What games have you made?' he asked.

'We're probably best known for the Core Survival series,' Stella said with another of her swift smiles. 'But personally, I love the WilderNess open world games. Do you game?'

Jason nodded. 'I like the FIFA games best.'

Karen interrupted the fanboy moment. 'So when you walked into the garage, what struck you?'

Stella drew her brows together in a tiny frown. 'Well, obviously the presence of something big under a tarpaulin. I mean, Susan didn't even have a regular *car*. She belonged to a car club that only has electric vehicles. Anywhere she could cycle, she did cycle. That's why she had the two bikes – the road bike, the one she was riding when she—' Stella stopped abruptly, looking shocked. Then she cleared her throat. 'And a top-of-the-range mountain bike.'

'I'm sorry, but I've only come to this a couple of hours ago. What was it that Susan did for a living?'

'She was a tax accountant. She had a practice in Perth. All those rich toffs with their country houses and estates, she took a slice of their money to stop the taxman getting a bigger slice.'

'And did she live alone?'

Stella nodded, her mood shifting. 'For the last three years. She had a partner, but they split up. Amanda moved out because she wanted to be a free spirit. She thought she was an artist.' She scoffed. 'Let me tell you, DCI Pirie, I work with artists all the time.' She gestured towards the upper floor. 'Though most of that stuff is Duncan's. Duncan, my partner. He actually makes a living creating game worlds.

'Me, I enjoy painting. It's my form of relaxation. But I know I'm not an artist. And neither was Amanda. Of course, like so many wannabes, she couldn't accept her lack of success was to do with a lack of talent. So she decided it was living with Susan that was stifling her creativity.' She shook her head wearily. 'She wanted Susan to give up her practice so the two of them could move to the Highlands and Amanda would support them both with her "art".' Emphasised with air quotes.

'And Susan preferred to let her go?'

Stella unfastened the clip on her hair and shook it free. 'It was a false choice. Susan's good – *was* good at what she did. She loved the job, she loved her clients, bizarre though that always seemed to me. She'd have gone crazy in a wee craft shop by some scenic Highland roadside. She tried everything she could think of to change Amanda's mind, but she was dead set on following her star. So she moved out.'

'Was it acrimonious?'

Stella considered. 'I'd say it was characterised more by sadness than acrimony. They'd been together nearly ten years, Susan thought Amanda was the love of her life and, from the outside, it looked like Amanda felt the same. But you know, relationships get into a rut, and Amanda had started hanging out with a bunch of aspiring artists who'd done their courses at Duncan of Jordanstone's in Dundee and all thought they were going to make a living with their brushes. She drank the Kool-Aid, Chief Inspector. She said it was breaking her heart to leave Susan behind, but that didn't stop her.'

'Where did Amanda go?'

'Some woman had inherited a run-down old house somewhere in Angus. The way Amanda spoke, it was a big rambling place with plenty of room for everyone. She asked Susan to visit, but my sister had made her mind up. No matter how sad it made her, she was determined to make a clean break. She didn't want to spend the next five years picking a scab.'

'That's a tough choice.'

'We're both good at tough choices, me and Susan. After our parents died, we could have let ourselves fall apart. But we promised each other we'd do our best to be the kind of women they'd have been proud of.'

'That's quite a target to set yourselves.'

'I like to think we were doing OK. Till some idiot still over the limit from the night before ploughed into my big sister on the A9.' Stella's voice trembled with anger.

'And now this. What the hell is a skeleton doing in my Susan's garage?'

Karen let her words hang for a moment to take the immediate sting out of them, then said, 'That's what I'm determined to find out. Do you have any idea whose VW camper this is?'

'If I had to guess, I suppose I'd say Amanda. Amanda McAndrew. I mean, most of Susan's friends were entirely conventional. They're more likely to go to Dubai for their holidays than to potter around the Highlands in an old-fashioned camper van. I can't imagine any of them *owning* a van like that, never mind parking it in Susan's garage. Unless somebody saw a report of Susan's death and thought that was a good opportunity to get rid of it?' She sighed. 'I'm clutching at straws, amn't I?'

'The tyres are flat,' Jason said. 'It's been sitting there for quite a while. No getting away from it, I'm sorry.'

Stella bit her lip. 'I knew that, really.'

'Do you have any photos of Amanda?' Karen asked gently.

'You'll need to do some sort of facial reconstruction, right? Like they do on those forensic documentaries? To help you figure out who that ... who that used to be? In the van?' Stella was already on her feet. 'Give me a minute, I'll get my iPad.'

'What do you think, boss,' Jason said softly as the door closed behind her. 'You think it's Amanda? You think she came back and they had a fight?'

'What have I told you about jumping to conclusions, Jason?'

He looked crestfallen and flushed. '"Jumping to conclusions leaves you with a long way to fall," boss.'

Stella walked back in, studying her tablet. 'These are

from a few years ago . . . But people don't change that much, not the basic structures.' She paused, fingers moving on the screen. 'They were taken here. We had a wee family party for Duncan's fortieth, so that'll be four years ago.' She passed the tablet to Karen. 'That's Amanda and Susan. Amanda on the left.' She hadn't needed to make the identification. Susan Leitch was Stella with a conventional bob and a squarer jawline. Amanda had a gelled quiff that Karen thought matched the colour of the hair on the floor of the camper van. But then so did millions of people.

It was a start. Something for River to work with in establishing biological identity. 'Can you send those over to me?' Karen produced a card from her wallet and passed it over. 'Do you happen to know if Amanda has any family? Parents, siblings?'

'She's an only child. She grew up in Selkirk and moved to do a degree in painting at Glasgow College of Art. She used to say her parents had a recycling business but the truth was her dad was a third-generation scrap merchant.'

'Are they still in Selkirk, do you know?'

She shook her head. 'They sold the business ahead of the 2016 referendum. They were planning to buy an olive grove and a villa so they could qualify for residency in Greece. I've no idea whether they went through with that.'

'Do you know their first names?'

Stella stared out of the window, eyebrows furrowed in thought. 'I only met them once. He was Barry, I'm pretty sure about that. I want to say she was called Freda but I think I'm getting confused with that Victoria Wood song. You know?' She sang a few bars. '"I can't do it tonight." Wait a minute, I've got it – Nita,' she announced triumphantly.

It shouldn't be impossible to track down the McAndrew

parents, but it would doubtless take time. Even though this was clearly a cold case, Karen did not subscribe to the notion that this meant she could drag her heels. 'Do you know if there's anything in Susan's house that might provide us with Amanda's DNA?'

Stella pulled her hair back from her face and refastened the clasp while she thought. 'Surely there will be DNA all over the things in the van?'

'It might not be Amanda's DNA. We can't be certain it's her van.'

'Amanda took all her stuff with her when she left.' Stella stared out of the window, frowning in concentration. 'The only thing I can think of, and I don't know whether you'd get DNA from them . . . There's three framed watercolours in the hall. Glencoe in three different lights. Amanda painted them and framed them herself for Susan's thirtieth birthday. Is that any use?'

'To be honest, I'm not sure. But I'll pass that on to our forensic technicians. Did Susan ever mention Amanda coming back? For a visit? Or for good?'

'No, nothing like that. Susan was insistent that Amanda was a closed chapter.' She paused, thoughtful. Karen waited. Then she continued, 'Though I always had a sneaking suspicion that, if Amanda had come back with her tail between her legs, my sister would have opened her heart to her again.'

'Would that have extended to letting her abandon a camper van with a body in it in her garage?'

Stella shrugged. 'I'd like to think not. But when it comes to love even the most sensible of us do stuff we look back at with total bewilderment.'

Karen let that sink in, then, aware she was setting off a

small bomb, said, 'Is it possible that Susan and Amanda got into a fight that ended badly?'

Stella looked astonished. She shook her head, bemused. 'You didn't know Susan.' She scoffed. 'Obviously, you couldn't have. She was . . . No, I can't imagine her in a physical fight. Even when we were kids, she just didn't. She'd walk away. It was like she only had the flight half of the adrenaline response.'

It was hard to argue with such vehemence. But they'd have to check it against someone else who knew Susan. 'And since Amanda? There's been nobody else in Susan's life?'

'Not that I'm aware of. And believe me, Chief Inspector, I'd be aware. We didn't keep secrets from each other.'

Back in the car, Karen stared moodily at the silvery Tay as they headed down the hill. '"We didn't keep secrets from each other." Apart from the camper van with the dead body in it. In my book, that's a pretty big secret.'

8

The paperwork from the French Ministry of the Interior wasn't much of a starting point for Daisy to worm her way into the past of James Auld. But her online research into the Foreign Legion had revealed that they only checked for serious crimes in the background of their applicants. Murder, rape, or armed robbery would all disqualify a recruit. But not a string of minor offences. So it was worth checking UK criminal records to see whether he had any form.

She drew a blank.

Her next port of call was DVLA. Did he have a current driving licence or was there a vehicle registered to him?

Blank again.

Twitter threw up a dozen James, Jim or Jimmy Aulds. Facebook was worse. There were dozens. But at least Daisy had a passport photograph and a date of birth to work with. Patiently, she worked her way through the social media profiles, swiftly discarding almost all of them in seconds. A few took longer. But ultimately they led to profile photographs that were clearly not the dead man, or else they had an extensively documented photographic history going back five years. You could do a lot with Photoshop, she knew. But who could be bothered to doctor that many terrible photos in bars, restaurants, clubs and parties? Not even MI5 would take things that far.

She was ploughing through the last few names that Instagram had thrown up – and really, throwing up was what she felt like after the seemingly endless stream of bad photographs of unappetising food – when Charlie Todd paused behind her chair. 'Very thorough,' he said. 'I take it you drew a blank on James Auld with mispers?'

Daisy felt her stomach plummet. It was so obvious. How could she be that stupid? If a man had walked away from his life ten years before, the chances were that somebody had probably reported them missing. A mother, a lover, a sibling. 'I was just coming to that, guv,' she said, fervently wishing her treacherous ears were not bright scarlet.

Two desks away, DC Pete Gordon cleared his throat with a smoker's rattle. Gordon was weeks away from retirement after a solid thirty years of reliable but uninspired police work. When Daisy had joined the team, she'd hoped she could learn from his experience. Fat chance, she'd soon realised, unless she wanted to discover all the places you could sneak a fag in the vicinity of the office. 'Did you say James Auld?' he inquired now. 'You sure you don't mean Iain Auld?'

Daisy tried not to show her irritation at Gordon's presumption of stupidity. 'His name was James Auld. No middle name.'

Undaunted, Gordon heaved himself to his feet and sauntered across to look over her shoulder. Even without his bulk, his presence was unmissable. The bitter reek of stale tobacco and pungent aftershave hung around him in a permanent miasma. 'You remember Iain Auld, boss?'

Charlie slowly shook his head. 'Doesn't ring any bells, Pete. When was this?'

'Ten years, or thereabouts. You must remember? It was a big thing at the time.'

'I must have missed it. Ten years ago I was on attachment in Sri Lanka, training their detective branch in homicide investigation,' Charlie said. 'I was out of the country from May to September. So who was Iain Auld?'

Gordon pulled up a chair and settled into it, folding his hands across his paunch. 'Iain Auld was a senior civil servant with the Scottish government. He worked in Edinburgh for a long time, but more recently he'd been mostly based down in London at the Scotland Office. One morning, he didnae turn up at his work. Disappeared into thin air.' Gordon frowned and scratched his chin. 'Wait a minute, though. There was something else. I don't recall the details, but there was something suspicious about it. He'd had a row with somebody . . .' He stared up at the ceiling, leaving them hanging. Then he dropped his head. 'Nope, it's gone. You should google him, maybe there's a connection.' He stood up with an air of satisfied finality and headed for the door. Aiming for a smoke after his exertions, Daisy assumed.

'Ten years ago,' Charlie mused. 'About the same time your James Auld joined the Foreign Legion. A bit of a coincidence, that. Could be that Pete's got a point. Maybe James and Iain Auld are one and the same.'

'I'll check it out,' Daisy said, feeling mutinous and cross with herself. Charlie left her to it, briskly summoning a DC from another case to answer another pointed inquiry. *Bloody Pete Gordon. 'Maybe there's a connection?' My arse.* She typed 'Iain Auld Scotland Office' into her search engine. *Sits on his useless fat backside all morning watching me getting nowhere then waits till the boss appears to produce a dead rabbit from a hat.* She hit return.

Her screen filled with a blizzard of responses. The most recent was a two-year-old report of a judgement of the Court of Sessions, declaring Iain Auld dead. The action had been brought by his wife Mary. She hadn't lingered much longer than she had to, Daisy thought. Not that she could find it in her heart to blame the woman. More than seven years of juggling the practicalities of an absent but not officially deceased spouse must have been a nightmare, never mind the emotional trauma.

The court report was naturally an opportunity for journalists to rehash the story of Iain Auld's disappearance. According to the recap, he stayed in a subsidised Scotland Office studio flat in Victoria when work brought him to London. He'd left the office on Thursday, 20 May 2010 as usual, around 7 p.m. None of his colleagues noticed anything unusual in his behaviour. The last confirmed sighting of Iain Auld had been on the CCTV camera covering the door of Dover House, the Scotland Office building on Whitehall.

But that wasn't the last anyone had heard of him. According to neighbours, he'd been involved in a loud altercation with another man in his flat. Raised voices, furniture knocked over, the slam of a door. And a threat, heard by more than one of the nosy neighbours. 'Give it up, Jamie, or you'll be sorry. I'll make bloody sure you're bloody sorry.'

And then Daisy hit the motherlode. 'Neighbour Janine Kitson said, "I recognised the man Iain was arguing with. I'd met him with Iain and Mary once before. It was Iain's brother James."'

Now she had a chance to shine.

9

The one skill Karen hadn't had to coach Jason in was driving. Although he was reticent about the circumstances, she knew he'd been behind the wheel since his early teens. 'I'm presuming that was off-road, Jason,' she'd said repressively when he'd let slip that he'd celebrated his sixteenth birthday driving a Mercedes.

He'd flushed an unattractive scarlet and mumbled something about forest roads. Karen hadn't pursued it; they had an unspoken agreement that they'd both ignore Jason's brother's involvement with the less straightforward end of the motor trade, provided Ronan kept Jason well out of it. And to be fair to Ronan, he'd made sure his brother was a safe pair of hands on the wheel. Once he'd got past his early trepidation of driving a boss who liked to be in control.

So Karen used the drive back to Edinburgh to make sure all she wanted had been taken care of. The van itself would be picked up in the morning on a low-loader and taken to a police garage. Since the van's registration plates had been removed, the forensic mechanics would have to find its unique Vehicle Identification Number. In the event the VIN plate had also been removed, Karen doubted whether whoever was responsible for the skeleton in the van would have had the nous to get rid of the chassis ID. If they'd tried, they'd probably have failed. Even filing the numbers off or erasing them with acid left traces that could be interrogated. With a little luck, Karen would know the registered owner of the VW by the following evening.

The CSI team messaged her to report that they had lifted the three paintings from the hall and sent them with all the other samples to the lab. They'd taken Susan Leitch's toothbrush, hairbrush and underwear from her dirty laundry hamper to make sure they could distinguish hers from any other DNA they found. They'd checked the van for fingermarks and DNA. All they'd collected was on its way to the forensic labs in the Scottish Crime Campus at Gartcosh.

So far, so good. But Karen had discovered early in her cold case career, back before the eight regional forces had been amalgamated into Police Scotland, that many of her fellow detectives thought what she did wasn't nearly as important as their cases. That live cases should always take precedence over dusty historic files. But Karen knew different. She'd seen enough grief close up to understand that time did not diminish the pain of not having answers to the questions that sudden violent death left in its wake. Finding those answers was just as urgent to Karen as a murder that had happened yesterday. It was the driving force in her professional life and so she'd built her own support system to make sure her cases weren't constantly pushed to the back of the queue.

River Wilde was a key part of that, but her reach didn't extend inside Gartcosh. When the police labs opened there, Karen had sent out delicate feelers every time her paths had crossed any of the technicians'. She'd had to stifle her natural impatience for months before she discovered

Tamsin Martinu. Tamsin was an Australian who looked like a throwback to the punk era, her hair an ever-changing kaleidoscope of spikes, her piercings notorious for setting off metal detectors. She was a digital forensics specialist, but she'd established bridgeheads to every discipline in the lab, making friends and allies across the board. Her currency, as far as Karen could make out, was IT expertise and chocolate biscuits.

And like Karen, Tamsin cared about cold cases. She regarded their unsolved status as a personal affront, a medal of failure hung round all of their necks. So when Karen came calling, Tamsin would chivvy, persuade and sweetly bully her colleagues not only into going the extra mile but also travelling that distance at a sprint. Karen had her on speed dial, and she used that now. Tamsin answered with, 'Hey, girl, how's it going?'

'Like a three-legged greyhound.'

Tamsin snorted. 'That'll be where I come in, then. Leg transplants our speciality. What have you got for me?'

Karen ran through the details. 'You'll be getting Susan Leitch's laptop. I've no idea where her phone is. Probably in an evidence locker somewhere. They'll be hanging on to it till the fiscal decides charges to lay against the driver who ploughed into her bike.'

'I'll chase it down,' Tamsin said. 'What are we looking for?'

'The ex, Amanda McAndrew. They split up about three years ago. Anything between them after the split. Right now, all I've got are question marks. Did they stay in touch? Where was Amanda living? Was she looking for a reconciliation? You know the drill, any recent history between them. Facebook, Twitter, emails, Insta, the usual.'

'And the other stuff?'

'It'd be really helpful to ID the remains. River reckons she can extract DNA from the skeleton and probably the hair. But we need to match that. We've sent three framed paintings from Susan's house. They were painted and framed by Amanda McAndrew. If we can get DNA from them and it's a match, then we can make an assumptive ID.'

'I'll take a wander down there and see what I can do. It's a bit out of the ordinary, getting DNA from a painting, but a challenge like that always pulls them out of their shells.'

'I owe you,' Karen said.

'Chocolate ginger crunch every time for the DNA boys. Catch you later.'

'You think they'll get a DNA match, boss?' Jason risked a quick glance at Karen.

'It's the most obvious answer. If it's Amanda McAndrew, it's a reconciliation gone wrong. Susan Leitch is dead too now, so it's probably the fastest "case closed" in the history of the HCU.'

'What if it's not her?'

Karen sighed. 'Then we struggle.'

Silence while the traffic flowed around them. Then Jason said, 'What I keep coming back to is, what kind of person keeps a skeleton in their garage?'

Judging by the frown screwing up his face, Karen reckoned the answer to that was a leap of imagination too far for Jason. 'My impression is that Susan Leitch was a pretty conventional woman.'

'She was a lesbian. Not that there's anything wrong with that, boss,' he added hastily. 'Just, it's not exactly by the book.'

'The book's changing, Jason. That neat wee bungalow,

that wardrobe with everything colour-coded, hung up or folded neatly? That's my idea of somebody sitting right in the middle of the mainstream.'

'But she had a skeleton in her garage, boss. There's nothing mainstream about that.'

Karen paused for a moment. 'That's kind of my point, Jason. She wasn't expecting to have to deal with a corpse. She was a smart, organised woman. I suspect if she'd set out to commit a murder, she'd have thought it through. A body under the patio, maybe. Or a lovely new rockery at the bottom of the garden.'

'So was it a spur-of-the-moment thing? They had a row, it got out of hand, and the next thing she knew the girlfriend wasn't breathing? I mean, we don't even know if Amanda ever left in the first place. Stella only had Susan's word for it. What if Susan thinks she's persuaded Amanda to stick around? "You can do your painting here, doll, we'll build you a wee studio in the garden," kind of thing. Then she comes home from the office one day and bingo! There's a camper van in the garage and Amanda's loading up her kit. That would piss on your chips.' He gave her an eager grin.

'Maybe.' Karen drew the word out as she considered the options. 'It could have played out like that. And I can't give you a logical reason why that doesn't sit right.'

'Well, what else could it be?'

Karen took a deep breath. 'Maybe she didn't have any choice. Maybe it was foisted on her. And she just didn't know what to do about it.'

10

Daisy was good at digging. Four years of a French and Legal Studies degree at Aberdeen hadn't exactly been vocational but it had taught her a reliable range of basic research techniques. She knew how to use the police databases, but she wasn't afraid to spread the web of her search more widely. By the time the evening briefing rolled around, she was confident she had something solid to report.

More than that, she was pretty sure nobody else would have come close to uncovering what she'd found out.

The team trickled into the incident room, clutching coffees and teas and a cardboard box filled with fragrant offerings from the nearby Greggs. Daisy helped herself to a cheese-and-onion pasty while Charlie Todd called them to order and outlined the morning's events. 'According to the coastguard, he likely went in on the east side of Elie. Probably somewhere around the ruin of Lady Janet Anstruther's Tower. And probably about ten to twelve hours before the *Bonnie Pearl* fished him out. So, round about now, yesterday evening. It would have been getting on for dark, but he'd have had to walk out there. There's not even a Land Rover track, only a network of footpaths linked to the Fife Coastal Path. I organised three uniforms to get over there this afternoon. Talk to dog walkers and the like, see if any-body saw anything.

'The other key issue is that we don't know where he was staying. He lived in Paris, so the chances are he was booked in somewhere local. Keith, hook up with one of the civilian aides and start hitting all the possible – hotels, bed and breakfast, Airbnb. Daisy, what have you got from the backgrounder?'

It was her moment. Daisy stood up to make sure everyone could see her. 'The dead man was legally Paul Allard. But that was a false name he used to join the French Foreign Legion. After he left the Legion two years ago, he had to revert to his real name to get French citizenship. As soon as it was granted, he changed it back officially to Paul Allard. But for a brief window, he reverted to his birth name, which was James Auld.' There were a few impatient nods.

'James Auld's brother was a man called Iain Auld. Some of you might remember him. He was one of Scotland's most senior civil servants and he disappeared without trace in May 2010. There was a lot of coverage at the time. The night before he went missing, a neighbour in his block of flats heard the sounds of a loud altercation coming from Iain Auld's flat. Shouting, banging of furniture. The argument continued on to the stairs and the witness identified the person Iain Auld was arguing with as his brother, James Auld. She'd met James previously, so she was in no doubt. Police questioned James but he refused to say what they'd quarrelled about. Then a search of the communal bins in the basement of James's flat turned up a bloodstained T-shirt. James was questioned about it before the DNA results came back confirming the blood was Iain's. And although Mary Auld, Iain's wife, confirmed he'd owned one like it, James was released. Then James also disappeared.' Daisy paused for effect.

'Surprise, surprise,' Charlie said. 'Not the Met's finest hour, then.'

'They finally pieced it together. He took a ferry to Belfast, then made his way to Cork, where he took another ferry to Santander in northern Spain. Once he was there, he could go anywhere in the Schengen Area without any checks. His trail went cold and now we know why. A few weeks later, he'd signed up for the French Foreign Legion.' A murmur of what passed for congratulation greeted her summary.

'Nice job, Sergeant,' Charlie said. 'So we've got some answers. But we've got more questions. Going back ten years – what was the row about? Did James Auld kill his brother or did he run because he knew he was innocent and the odds were stacked against him? Was he set up? We're going to have to liaise with the detectives who led the investigation down in London. But I think right now we have other priorities.

'James Auld died on our patch, in our timeline. The first question we need an answer to is why did he come back? He'd buried his past life with complete success, as far as we can tell. He was safe in Paris. He had a life. He must have known he was taking a big risk coming back to the UK. He was still a person of interest in his brother's disappearance, all the more so since Mary Auld obtained a declaration of death in respect of her husband. And yet he came back. With fatal consequences, as we have seen. So, any bright ideas? What might have brought him back?'

A long moment of silence, broken by officers shifting in their chairs. 'Maybe he was just homesick,' Daisy said. 'When he was in the Legion, there was plenty going on to keep him occupied. But then, sitting about in his Paris flat between gigs, maybe he started feeling the pull of home.'

Pete Gordon gave a phlegmy chuckle. 'He'd missed too many East Fife home games, you think?'

'People do get homesick,' Daisy retorted with spirit. 'And after the end of this year, now Brexit has happened, it won't be so easy to slip in and out of the country.'

'Good point.' Charlie stood up and pointed at the map on the wall that showed the coastline between Elie and Pittenweem. 'What's his connection to this part of the coast? Daisy, do we know?'

She felt a moment's panic. Another thing she hadn't considered. 'They grew up in Edinburgh,' she said. 'They might have holidayed in the East Neuk?'

Charlie frowned at her. 'We're woefully short on background here. We need to talk to Iain Auld's widow. Where is she now?'

'The address on the file is in Edinburgh,' Daisy said.

Charlie looked at his watch. 'You'll have missed the worst of the traffic. Away you go across the bridge and talk to the Widow Auld. I want everything there is to know about the Auld brothers.'

Driving over the Queensferry Crossing, its cables angled to look like huge sails, always lifted Daisy's spirits. She sang along with Billie Eilish till she hit the outskirts of Edinburgh and had to pay attention. The bossy GPS led her on a route through the city centre made even more convoluted by the roadworks that seemed to have been deposited at random by a malevolent deity. When she finally arrived at Leopold Place it was past seven o'clock and there was of course nowhere to park. 'Fuck it,' she muttered on her second circuit of the nearby streets, and slid into a 'residents only' parking place. The wardens would be long gone for the day.

Mary Auld's flat was on the ground floor of a grand sandstone tenement building, separated from the street by iron railings and a gate with an unforgiving latch. Daisy wrestled it open and climbed the steps to the front door. It was answered by a tall blond man with a suspicious look. 'Yes? Can I help you?' he said grudgingly.

Daisy produced her ID and introduced herself. He peered even more suspiciously at her. 'I don't understand,' he said. 'I haven't called the police.'

'I'm looking for Mrs Mary Auld,' Daisy said.

'Then you're looking in vain,' he said. 'Mrs Auld hasn't lived here for more than two years.' The door began to close.

Daisy tried not to let her frustration show. 'Do you know where she moved to? Presumably she left a forwarding address?'

'I honestly can't remember. She may have done, but she had a mail redirect on her post, so we never had occasion to use it. Now, if you'll excuse me—'

'Just a minute.' Daisy raised her voice. 'This is a murder inquiry, sir.'

His eyebrows shot up. 'How extraordinary. But it doesn't change the fact that I don't know where Mary Auld is living. You've wasted your journey.'

'She never mentioned where she was moving to?'

He shrugged. 'She may have, but frankly, I wasn't interested. So I have not retained that information.'

Pompous git. 'Do you know if she was friendly with any of your neighbours?' The last throw of the dice.

He considered for a moment. 'Iris Blackford, in the basement. She's on her own too, I think they used to chum each other to the theatre and the like. Very Edinburgh.' The words set Daisy's hackles rising but his smile was surprisingly sweet. 'Now, if that's all?'

'Thank you for your help, sir.'

His suspicious look was back. Maybe he'd actually come off his high horse long enough to notice her sarcasm. He scowled and closed the door firmly in her face. With a sigh, Daisy made her way down the steep stone stairs, worn treacherously away in the middle by two hundred years of feet. The basement area was a maze of plant pots, their contents looking sad in the February cold. Daisy threaded her way to the door, almost blinded by a security light. No doorbell, just a heavy brass knocker in the shape of a dolphin.

The woman who answered the door looked ancient to Daisy, though she conceded to herself that she was probably only in her late sixties. Untidy grey curls sprang from under a purple beret, and her figure was draped in an assortment of layers in shades of purple and pink. But her eyes were sharp and raked Daisy from head to foot. 'I don't buy at the door and I have no need of Jesus,' she said, her accent revealing her West Coast origins.

Daisy smiled and produced her ID. 'I'm sorry to bother you,' she said. 'The man upstairs thought you might be able to help me.'

A wide grin stripped twenty years from Iris Blackford. 'Did you annoy him? I bet you did. Well done. How can I help you, officer?'

'I'm trying to make contact with Mrs Mary Auld, who used to live upstairs. But your neighbour didn't—'

Iris Blackford's hands flew to her face, fingertips pressing on her soft cheeks. 'Is there news of Iain? Finally? After all these years?' Her distress was obvious.

'I'm sorry, no,' Daisy said hastily. 'He's not the subject of our inquiries. I'm afraid I'm not at liberty to say more, but I can reassure you on that point.'

Her hands fell from her face and she folded her arms across her chest, hugging herself. 'Then it must be ... But it can't be, his wee brother vanished in a puff of smoke.' She took a deep breath. Then, suddenly businesslike, she said, 'You'll be wanting Mary's address. She moved over to Fife, her family came from there. Just a minute, I'll get it for you.' She turned away, pushing the door almost closed, in contrast to her earlier friendliness. Daisy wondered what she'd said to cause such a rapid change.

She didn't have long to wait, however. A couple of minutes later, Iris Blackford returned with a sheet of paper torn from a hotel bedside phone pad. The address was in block capitals with a phone number beneath. 'There you go. Lovely view over the golf links across the Forth.'

'Thank you. I really appreciate your help.' The door was already closing.

'You're welcome.' And now it was closed. *So much for Edinburgh good manners.* But at least her journey hadn't been a complete waste of time. She now knew where to find Mary Auld. And if her memory served her well, she wasn't far from a chippie. A fish supper with extra crispy batter on fresh haddock and a mound of chips fragrant with beef dripping would set her up nicely for the drive home.

There was almost always a bright side to be found, in Daisy's experience.

11

The faint promise of spring that had brightened the morning sky had dissolved by home time. Rosebank Cemetery provided no protection against the bitter north-westerly wind cutting across Pilrig. Muttering curses against the weather, Karen turned up the collar of her baggy winter coat and shoved her hands in the pockets just in time to feel the vibration of an incoming text. No way was she going to stop here. She'd wait till she'd crossed at the lights. She might even nip into the Bonnington for a helping of their chilli beef nachos to warm up. Her mouth watered at the thought. All she'd had since breakfast had been a wrinkled apple she'd found at the bottom of her bag.

Once she was in the lee of the buildings, she pulled out her phone to find a message from Jason.

Sorry, boss. In all the excitement earlier, I forgot to pass on what you asked me for. Registered owner Luke Gray, 7 Bughtlin Grove.

Karen caught her breath, all thought of food gone. Now she knew who had picked up Merrick Shand. And if he wasn't at 7 Bughtlin Grove, there had to be somebody else there who could point the finger at his location. Almost without thinking, she took the few steps back to the busy junction, scanning the traffic for the orange glow of an available cab.

Ten minutes later, she was opening her front door and heading straight for the desk where her laptop sat. Karen flipped it open as she shrugged out of her coat and let it fall over her chair. As her browser came alive, she typed in the address. The map revealed that Bughtlin Grove was a small crescent set back from a wider street that bred a dozen narrow thoroughfares of tightly packed houses. Street View showed her a strip of almost-detached houses, connected via their garages. They looked like standard 1970s boxes, their pale grey harling clean and well-kempt. Three small bedrooms, she thought. Open-plan lounge through to a kitchen tacked on at the back. A lot less fancy than the big house Merrick Shand used to live in before he killed Phil Parhatka.

She fished out her wallet and added five credits to her account at a search app she used when she wanted to investigate under the radar of Police Scotland's scrutinised systems. Sometimes it was better not to leave a trace. She headed for Edinburgh City Council's voters' roll. It was a document that was theoretically in the public domain, but you had to be really committed to track it down in a public library. Given how those institutions were shrinking in the name of austerity, it was a moot point how long that would be feasible. Much easier to pay a few quid and search online. If you had a few quid to spare, of course.

When the entry for 7 Bughtlin Grove came up, Karen couldn't repress a tight little smile. There was Luke Gray. And right below him, Jennifer Shand. At a guess, Merrick Shand's sister. Lucky Merrick, to have somebody to take him in on release. Not many convicted killers had that to look forward to.

Karen took the time to change out of her work suit. There was nothing unobtrusive about a woman in a suit on a street or a pub in the Edinburgh suburbs in the evening, even under a shapeless coat. She settled on a pair of jeans, thick socks under flat-soled ankle boots, a long-sleeved T-shirt under a sweatshirt, topped off with a down jacket. Warmth, but layers if she ended up somewhere with decent heating. Standing sweating at a bar was never a good look.

Bughtlin Grove was deserted. A dozen houses curved round a half-moon of downtrodden grass and a handful of dilapidated shrubs. There were lights showing behind drawn curtains on most of them, cars parked up against garage doors. Nobody used their garages for cars these days, Karen thought. They were pressed into service for all sorts – storage, workshops, illegal spare bedrooms, studies. She wondered whether Merrick Shand had been relegated to the garage at number seven. She hoped he'd be shivering the night away on a cripplingly uncomfortable futon.

Karen found a space on the street on the far side of the grass. She could see the house clearly. A narrow sliver of light downstairs, thinner curtains in one of the bedrooms creating a pale panel of dark red. The car in the driveway didn't match the registration number Jason had checked; that one was parked on the street, a five-year-old silver BMW. She settled into her seat, breaking open the guilty pleasure of the cheese savoury sandwich she'd picked up at a service station on the way.

Time trickled by, accompanied by a Marian Keyes novel she'd downloaded on audio. Karen liked the way Keyes wrote characters who had learned to survive, without ever being po-faced or making you feel like a failure if you couldn't always crack a smile at the hand life had dealt you. There had been times in recent years when Karen had stared down the barrel of depression, wondering how she was going to put herself back together after losing Phil in what had felt like a random act of mindless violence. He'd gone out one morning to do his job, working with the Murder Prevention Squad, taking steps to close down domestic violence perps. By the end of the day, he'd been in intensive care, crushed by wife-beater Merrick Shand's monstrous 4 × 4. Two days later, he was dead.

She'd forced herself to carry on. Not because 'Phil would have wanted it,' as everyone kept telling her, but because she was determined not to let Merrick Shand claim a second victim. She'd fantasised often about vengeance. Considered ways to destroy him the way he'd almost destroyed her, then rejected them because she knew that wouldn't make her feel any better.

In her more rational moments, walking the streets of Edinburgh in the small hours of the morning to make the night pass, she couldn't help acknowledging that Shand had lost too. With him behind bars, it had been safe for his wife to divorce him. She'd changed her name and moved to one of the big cities in the north of England. He'd never legally see his kids again, not with the evidence that had been presented at the family court hearing. His business had collapsed without him at the helm, and his legal bills had all but bankrupted him.

She wondered whether he'd ever accepted his responsibility for the disastrous outcome of what in court he'd called, 'a moment of madness'. Not, 'my moment of madness'. He couldn't even own that. Karen thought he probably blamed

70

Phil for standing in front of his car when he tried to make a getaway. Or his wife for provoking him into the actions that had caused the trouble in the first place. Or his kids for being annoying and not leaving him in peace. Anyone but the face he saw in the mirror.

A car arrived home two doors down, the driver hurrying inside, head tucked into his coat collar against the wind.

The chapter ended. A new chapter began.

Her phone buzzed with an incoming call. 'Hamish', the screen told her. She rejected the call; what part of 'Don't call me, I'll call you' had he not understood? But second thoughts followed swiftly. The honest part of her knew she didn't want to cut Hamish out of her life. So she texted him:

Working not ignoring. I will be in touch but I need time.

The front door of the end house opened and a gangly teenager emerged, hoodie up, shoulders hunched. On the end of a leash, one of those poodle crosses with the daft names. She'd heard that poodles were supposed to be intelligent. Not so any of the cross-breeds Karen had come across. It was quite an achievement to breed stupidity into an entire strain of dogs. Watching the teenager trying to control the dog was a trade-off that was almost worth the boredom of the stake-out.

A few minutes before ten, when she was on the point of admitting this was a ridiculous way to spend an evening, a wedge of light spilled out from number seven. Two men emerged and walked across the front lawn. She recognised Shand even in the poor glow from the streetlights. His features were burned into her memory. He'd lost weight in prison. His gym bunny muscles had wasted into something leaner but he moved awkwardly, as if he'd spent too long cramped in the same position. He folded himself into the passenger seat and Gray drove away almost before the door had closed.

Karen squinched up in her seat and set off in cautious pursuit. Gray wove confidently through the maze of streets then, less than half a mile from home, turned into a short road with a late-night supermarket. Gray took the first parking slot, ignoring the disabled signage. Karen committed to the turn and parked further down. She watched the two men get out of the car and walk back the way they'd come. Now she spotted their destination – a long single-storey building with a pub sign. It was an improbable location, in the middle of a housing estate, and the exterior resembled a wing of a care home. The picnic tables on the patio looked out on a roundabout, two blocks of flats and a bus stop.

Karen gave them a few minutes' start then she followed them in. The interior was a pleasant surprise. It was brightly lit, wood panelling painted white and pale grey, booths and benches clean and well-maintained. Somebody took pride in this place. There were only a dozen or so people dotted round the big room, most of whom didn't give her a second glance. The clientele looked to be predominantly in their forties, the women with glasses of wine, the men with pints. There were some chalkboards scattered round the walls with the kind of lines that were supposed to be witty – 'Toilets: Men to the left because Women are always right' and 'Let the Fun beGIN'.

Shand and Gray were leaning on the white bar top, waiting for the barmaid to finish pouring their lager. Karen walked past them and round the corner, where she stood and waited to be served. Gray gave her a cursory look, dismissed her and turned back to lift his pint. Shand handed over a twenty and raised his glass to his lips. He scanned the room with the wary sweep Karen recognised in other prisoners she'd seen over the years. When his eyes reached hers, he fumbled his glass and tipped some beer down his chin. The barmaid had to clear her throat noisily to return his change.

Karen gave him a level stare then turned to the barmaid, who was now moving towards her. She ordered an alcohol-free beer, conscious of Shand's gaze. When the drink came, she raised it towards him in an ironic salute.

He put his glass down a little too firmly. Gray turned, alarmed, as Shand rounded the bar and stopped a little too close to her. 'What the fuck are you doing here?' he demanded in a low voice.

'Having a wee drink,' Karen said, mild as milk. 'Have you got a problem with that, Merrick?'

'I've done my time. You need to leave me alone.'

Karen could hear real venom in his voice. 'You're the one bothering me, Merrick. I'm just standing here minding my own business.'

Then Gray was at his side, a hand on his arm. 'What's going on, Merrick?'

'She's fucking harassing me, that's what.'

Karen spread her hands in a peaceful gesture. 'Like I said, I'm having a wee drink.'

'She's a fucking cop,' Shand spat. 'She was at the trial.'

Karen smiled. Her heart was hammering but she was determined not to show it. 'Every day. You know the bit I enjoyed most? When they took you down.' As calmly as she could manage, she swallowed a mouthful of beer.

'I think you should get lost,' Gray said, trying to pull

Shand away from her. The atmosphere in the pub had changed. There was a stillness in the room.

Now the barmaid was getting in on the act. 'What's going on? Luke? Are you boys bothering this lassie?'

'I just wanted a quiet drink,' Karen said, placing her glass on the bar, moving her hand quickly in case it was shaking. 'I thought this was a nice pub. I didn't know you let convicted killers drink in here.' Then she turned and made for the door. Out of the corner of her eye, she saw Gray grabbing Shand's arm and holding him back.

She pulled the door open and turned back, taking in the shocked faces, Gray's look of panic, Shand's snarl. 'Bye, Merrick,' she said. 'I'll be seeing you. You might not see me, but I will definitely be seeing you.'

As soon as she was through the door, Karen broke into a run, racing down the steps and across the road to her car. She streaked away from the scene, just in time to see Merrick Shand standing on the pub patio, fists clenched, face livid.

Karen drove home sedately. She'd done what she set out to do. She'd planted unease in Merrick Shand's heart. She didn't need to stalk him, as Jimmy Hutton had feared. All she needed to do was to turn up in his peripheral vision every few weeks. Cross his path, apparently by chance. He'd never quite relax again.

It was a start.

12

Tuesday, 18 February 2020

It was hard for Daisy not to feel slighted that her boss had decided to accompany her to interview Mary Auld. He had a reputation for restlessness but knowing that didn't improve her mood. Just because Charlie Todd hated sitting around waiting for the next development in a case didn't mean he had to undermine her. It hadn't been her fault that Mary Auld had flitted to Fife. If Daisy had been good enough to fly solo the night before, how come she needed a babysitter this morning?

Mary Auld had left the Georgian grandeur of north Edinburgh for an unassuming modern bungalow overlooking the golf course at Lundin Links. On a frosty February morning with a brilliant blue sky and a shimmering grey sea beyond the green links, it was easy to see why. 'You'd never tire of waking up to that,' Charlie said, as satisfied as if he was personally responsible for it. 'Different every day.'

Daisy was more ambivalent. There was, in her opinion, a limit to the amount of time you could spend staring at any panorama, however entrancing. 'You'd have to enjoy it,' she said. 'I don't think there's much else to do around here if you don't play golf.'

Charlie chuckled as they walked up the path. 'You've obviously never lived in a village. Don't be fooled by the sleepy surface. Most of this lot will have a busier social life than you do.' Charlie rang the doorbell and fished out his ID.

The woman who opened the door had an ageless quality. Brown hair streaked with silver and cut in a long bob framed a striking face, high cheekbones emphasising beautiful dark blue eyes. Even in jeans and a fisherman's smock there was something elegant about her. She immediately took in Charlie's ID and bit her lip. 'Iain,' she said. 'You'd better come in.' She moved aside to let them pass.

'It's not your husband we're here about, Mrs Auld,' Charlie said hastily.

She frowned. 'Not Iain? Then what? Who?'

'Can we come inside?' Daisy spoke gently.

'Of course.' She led the way into a sitting room that made the most of the spectacular view. 'Please, sit down.' Daisy was used to living rooms where a TV was the main focus. Here, there was no blank screen to be seen. Five comfortable chairs were arranged in a semi-circle around the window, each with its own side-table. The pale fitted carpet was scarcely visible beneath a collection of shabby but beautiful rugs. The walls were covered with paintings, all of them figurative in a slight sort of way that took some working out. 'Can I get you something to drink? Tea? Coffee?'

'We're fine, thanks,' Charlie said. He waved vaguely. 'I think we should all sit down.' He waited till Mary Auld was seated, perched uneasily on the edge of a deep armchair. 'I'm afraid I have some bad news. A man we believe to be your brother-in-law has been found dead not far from here.'

She reared back in her seat, gripping the arms, her fingers like claws. 'Jamie? You don't mean Jamie?'

'James Auld, yes. I'm sorry.'

Now she leaned forward, hands clasped tight. 'Are you sure? Only . . . ' Her voice trailed off.

'I don't think there is much room for doubt, though we would like you to make a formal identification. He was carrying a French passport and driver's licence in the name of Paul Allard, but our inquiries have led us to believe his true identity is James Auld.'

Mary had nodded several times as he spoke. 'You're right, that's Jamie. But what happened? How can he be dead?'

'His body was pulled from the sea off St Monans by a local fisherman. He'd suffered a blow to the head before he went into the water.'

'An accident?'

'We think it may be a suspicious death.'

Mary covered her eyes with one hand and pressed her lips together so tightly they lost their colour.

'We're very sorry,' Daisy said.

Mary dropped her hand and drew in a noisy breath through her nose. 'I can't believe it. He was coming to see me this week.'

'This week? When?' Charlie leaned forward, alert as a pointer waiting for the gun.

'He didn't say what day. He told me he had some things to see to, then he'd drop by. We left it that he'd text me.' Now her eyes were shiny with unshed tears and she dashed an impatient fist across them.

'Why was he coming to see you?'

'Why wouldn't he? He was family.' Her tone was dismissive.

77

Charlie gave Daisy a pained look.

'He was also a person of interest in your husband's disappearance,' Daisy said. 'We know they quarrelled.'

'Oh, for heaven's sake,' Mary said scornfully. 'I said at the time you were all crazy. Just because they had an argument. Have you never shouted the odds at anyone in your family? Jamie and Iain loved each other. Jamie would never have harmed a hair on Iain's head. I told those idiots in the Met till I was blue in the face. But they were so focused on Jamie, they never investigated Iain's disappearance properly. No wonder Jamie ran off to join the Legion. The police made his life hell.'

'In fairness, there was the evidence of the T-shirt stained with your husband's blood that they found in a bin in the basement of your brother-in-law's block of flats,' Charlie pointed out. 'That's not nothing.'

'I'm no lawyer, but I know that's circumstantial. I can imagine half a dozen scenarios where it would be possible to set that up to frame Jamie.' Her chin came up. Nothing they could say was going to change her mind.

'So did you stay in touch with Jamie?' Daisy asked after a moment. 'When he joined the Legion?'

'Why wouldn't I? I was almost as worried about him as I was about Iain. I'd lost the two men in the world I thought would always be there. I was filled with fear at the thought of what might have happened to them. Nothing made any sense. So when a letter arrived from him about six months after he left, I burst into tears. I was so relieved.' Mary gave a shuddering sigh. 'It felt as if I still had hold of a part of Iain.'

'You didn't think to report his whereabouts?' Charlie asked.

An expression of haughty scorn crossed Mary's face. 'Why on earth would I do that? Why would I expose him to more accusations from your dim-witted colleagues?'

'It must have been a comfort for you. Did you exchange letters regularly after that first contact?' Daisy tried to recover the lost ground.

Mary nodded. 'Every few months. He'd tell me what he was up to. Mostly about music. We'd always had that in common. Jamie was a saxophonist in the Legion band, but he'd formed a jazz quintet too.' She sighed again. 'And I told him what I'd been listening to, what I'd been doing. Nothing of any great importance, just a way of staying in contact.'

'Did he visit you then?' Daisy asked.

Mary shook her head. 'It was impossible. He didn't have a French passport yet, and his UK passport would have been flagged up if he'd come home.'

'Did you visit him?' Charlie butted in.

Daisy glimpsed a flash of shrewdness in Mary's face as she replied. 'We met in Paris two years after he joined up. He was on leave and I went over to see him. It was a great support for both of us. To be able to talk about Iain, to discuss our ideas of what might have happened to him.'

'Did you come to any conclusions?' Charlie asked.

Mary managed a wan smile. 'We had all sorts of mad notions. But mostly we ended up back in the same place. A random mugging, his body in the river, torn up by a boat propeller.'

'Did you continue to meet?' Daisy asked.

'We did. Once a year, we'd get together. Paris, Lyon, Marseille. We even met in Berlin one year. Iain loved Berlin, we often went there for city breaks. Then when Jamie left the Legion and got his Paul Allard French passport, he was able to come to the UK in safety. He was still wary, though. When I was living in Edinburgh, he only came and went after dark. He was concerned about the nosy neighbours spotting him and calling the police.' She wiped an eye with her fingertips.

'Did he come often?' Charlie again.

'A couple of times a year. The first time, I had a specific reason for asking. I was working up to selling the Edinburgh flat. I had to wait for the official declaration of death before I could actually put it on the market, but I started the process of downsizing once that was in train. So I asked Jamie to come for a few days, to choose some things to remember Iain by. Books, paintings, photographs, that sort of thing.'

'That must have been a painful experience for Jamie,' Daisy prompted.

'It was for both of us.' Mary stared at her hands, now folded in her lap.

'What did he take?' Charlie asked.

'Half a dozen books. Iain's sketchbook from a holiday we'd all been on in Switzerland. A small oil painting, a seascape. A pair of cufflinks that had belonged to their father.' Another wan smile. 'So very Jamie. He could have plundered the place, but all he took were a few things that had sentimental value to him.'

'A sketchbook?' Charlie again.

'It was what Iain did to relax.' Her face softened at the memory. 'He wasn't much good, bless him. But he enjoyed it. Jamie said the sketchbook was more than a souvenir of the holiday, it was a reminder of Iain at his most chilled, when he left the pressures of work behind him.'

'Do you think there was any special reason why Jamie wanted to visit you this week?' Daisy asked.

'He didn't say. There didn't have to be a reason, you know. Do you always have a reason when you go to see family?'

Daisy thought of all the reasons she found for *not* going to see family. 'I just wondered. If there was a birthday, or an anniversary of some sort.'

Another shake of the head. 'Nothing. He'd arrive, we'd eat together, share a bottle of wine and we'd talk.'

'What did you talk about?'

'What I'd been up to, what he'd been up to. Music. Scottish independence. Life in Paris.'

'Your husband?'

Mary looked down at her hands. 'At first, yes.' She raised her eyes. 'More recently, no. We'd pretty much exhausted the subject. The one thing that was clear to both of us was that Jamie was not responsible for his disappearance.'

'Did he ever tell you what they'd quarrelled about that night?' Charlie cut in. Daisy hid her irritation at her boss breaking the line of communication she'd been building.

'Politics. Jamie's a passionate supporter of Scottish independence. Iain wasn't. And Jamie saw Iain's position in the Scotland Office as ultimately shoring up the position of the Westminster government and Unionists.'

'And that led to a shouting match? Furniture being overturned?' Charlie sounded incredulous, but Daisy thought he was being disingenuous. Passions had been running high over Scotland's future for years now. It was one of the reasons she avoided her own family.

'You forget how frustrating the political climate was after the Tories won the election in 2010. Jamie despaired of Scots ever having a chance to decide their own future.' A sad smile. 'The irony was of course that when the Indy Ref happened in 2014, Jamie couldn't vote.'

'Did he stay long when he visited you?' Daisy tried to steer the interview into less controversial waters.

'Sometimes he stayed for a day or two, more often he

took off again at the end of the evening. He left everything behind when he went to France. Friends, colleagues, people he played music with. Everything. I was the only link he maintained with his past. Understandably enough. He knew he could trust me. And it looks like he was right, if what you're saying is correct. That his death was suspicious.'

'We're waiting for the definitive autopsy report,' Charlie said. 'Did Jamie ever mention anybody who had it in for him? Anyone he was afraid of?'

Again that wry smile. 'Jamie wasn't much given to fear. When things looked black, he took action. He never mentioned being afraid. And why would anyone have it in for him?'

'Soldiers sometimes do things in the heat of battle that provoke acts of vengeance.'

'Jamie didn't see any front-line action,' Mary said firmly. 'He spent most of his Legion career attached to Operation Sentinelle. They're stationed all over France at sites of potential terrorist attack. He wasn't waterboarding anybody in Iraq, Chief Inspector.'

'What about after he left the Legion? Did he say anything about falling out with anybody?'

'No. He played with his jazz quintet. They got a lot of gigs all over the country because they're good at what they do. One of the reasons for that, Jamie always said, was that they were each other's best friends. There was no ill-feeling.'

'What about girlfriends? Was Jamie seeing anyone?' Daisy smiled. 'People always say being a musician is a bit of a babe magnet.'

Mary smiled back. 'Pascale. They've been seeing each other for about a year. She lives in Caen, she owns a jazz club there. They saw each other two or three times a month.

I had the impression that it was fairly casual. There didn't seem to be any question of them moving in together. I suggested he bring her over sometime, but he said it wasn't the kind of relationship where you got introduced to the family. He certainly didn't seem tense or stressed about her at all.'

Charlie and Daisy exchanged a look. Something else to chase up. 'Do you have a surname? Do you know how to contact her?'

'It never came up. But the other band members will know, with them being regulars at her club.'

'Can you give us the names of the other band members? We will need to talk to them.'

'Dom, Patrice, Jean-Claude and Hugo,' Mary said, digging her phone out of her pocket. 'They've got a website.' She tapped the screen then turned it to show Daisy. 'CommeDesEtrangers.cde.fr. It's a pun on their service in the Legion. *Légion Étrangère*, it's called in French.'

Daisy scribbled down the URL. Five men stared out at her from a moody black-and-white shot. She couldn't make much sense of it on a phone screen, but she was sure she could manage to track them down once she got in front of her laptop. 'Brilliant, thank you.'

'You're welcome.' Mary's face crumpled, the realisation of loss returning without warning. 'I don't think there's anything else I can help you with,' she said, her voice cracking.

'If you could assist with the formal identification, that would be a great help,' Charlie said.

With a piteous look in her eyes, Mary slowly nodded.

'I'll make arrangements with the mortuary and get back in touch with you. I'll organise it as soon as possible.' Charlie stood up. 'In the meantime—'

'If my shrivelled old brain suddenly recalls Jamie's bitter

enemies, I'll let you know,' she said, grief shifting towards outrage. 'The truth is, Chief Inspector Todd, the only enemies Jamie ever had were your colleagues. But they won't be on your list of suspects, will they?'

13

Tamsin had worked her magic yet again. When Karen booted up her laptop in the office that morning, there was an email from one of the DNA technicians:

> We've got two substantial deposits of DNA in the main cabin of the camper van. One is a match to the sample Dr River Wilde sent us from the skeleton. The other significant deposit – which is also present in the bloodstains on the carpet of the cabin – does not match the samples that were taken from Susan Leitch's house (which are putatively her DNA). There were traces of Leitch's DNA on the steering wheel and on the driver's seat but nothing in the main cabin. None of the samples shows up on the database, so no serious recent criminal activity. We haven't had time to look at the paintings to see whether we can isolate DNA. I'll get back to you as soon as we know more. Happy hunting.

Karen leaned back in her chair, considering. It seemed clear from the DNA evidence that Susan Leitch had nothing to do with the body in the van. It was hard to see how she could have killed someone in that confined space or even simply placed the body there without leaving any trace of her presence. Unless something extraordinary turned up in the house, the evidence exonerated Susan Leitch.

Unfortunately, not all forensic information was created equal. A question mark still hung over the identity of the corpse. But one thing seemed incontrovertible. Susan Leitch knew what was in her garage even though she wasn't the person responsible for the body that had been left there. Karen wondered how long it had been there, and whether Susan had had a plan for dealing with it. Or had she simply covered it with a tarpaulin and chosen to pretend it wasn't there, like a toddler who covers their own eyes and shouts, 'You can't see me.'

The opening door interrupted her thoughts. Jason shouldered his way in, clutching the cups of coffee that signalled the start of the working day. He plonked Karen's in front of her and said, 'I just got a text from the police garage. The licence plates and the separate Vehicle Identification Number plate had been removed from the VW but the chassis number was still intact.'

'Good to know the criminals aren't getting any smarter,' Karen said, savouring her first sip. The few minutes it took to walk from the nearby coffee shop to the office was the perfect interval for her brew to reach drinking temperature. 'So where does that get us?'

'Well, your car registration document has your chassis number on it. And DVLA can search their records by chassis number. That gives them the name and address of the registered keeper.' Jason grinned and raised his cup. 'Cheers, boss.'

'Did you not make friends with somebody from the DVLA last year? On the Wester Ross case?'

'I did. Kayleigh, her name was. And I put her direct line in my phone contacts. I remember Phil always said never throw away a phone number.' A momentary shadow darkened his pride.

Karen vaguely remembered saying the same thing to Jason more than once, but that didn't fit the battle cry he had adopted – 'What would Phil do?' She didn't mind; anything that raised his game was fine by her. 'What are you waiting for, then?'

He shrugged out of his jacket, stuck his earbuds in and tapped his phone. 'Hi, is that Kayleigh? ... Don't know if you remember me? Jason Murray. DC Jason Murray. From Edinburgh? ... That's right, Historic Cases. How're you doing? ... What's happening down in Swansea ...'

Karen mentally rolled her eyes and tuned Jason out. She opened her email account and sent a message to Tamsin at Gartcosh:

Any joy in tracking down Susan Leitch's phone? If it's not come to you yet, let me know and I'll knock some heads together. K.

She glanced across at Jason and was gratified to see he was scribbling something on his pad.

'That's brilliant, I can't believe you got that so fast ... I know, but usually you guys have got a massive backlog ... Aw, thanks. My mum always says, "It's nice to be nice, Jason." Cheers for your help, you're a real pal.' He pulled out his earbuds and gave Karen two thumbs up. 'Top info, boss,' he said, obviously pleased with himself.

'What did Kayleigh have to say for herself?'

'The registered keeper of the van is Amanda McAndrew.' He paused, expectant.

'Susan Leitch's ex.'

'She acquired it just over three years ago. And she made a SORN declaration less than a year later.'

'What? She took it off the road officially?' As soon as she spoke, Karen realised she shouldn't have been surprised. A vintage VM camper van would have to pass its MOT test every year. But even the most lax of garages would not certify a vehicle as roadworthy if it had a human skeleton and a pile of maggot cases in the cabin. 'Well, that narrows the time frame. Did McAndrew register the van at Susan's address? Or did we get lucky?'

Jason grinned again. 'We got totally lucky. The address she gave was Tullyfolda House, Milton of Glenisla. Wherever that is.'

'Let's go and find out.'

It had taken the best part of two hours to get to Milton of Glenisla. Motorway to Perth, then on country roads through a landscape of rolling hills, fields and woodland stripped bare of summer lushness. It was the kind of grey February morning that made Karen feel as if daylight had taken a duvet day. The normally impressive distant outline of mountains was blurred beyond recognition.

The officious voice of the GPS system invited them to turn off the main road through the glen on to a narrow track that cut between two dense copses. There were no buildings in sight. 'Doesn't look very promising,' Jason grumbled. But about half a mile in, the road took a sharp turn to the left and ahead of them stood a ramshackle house in the Scottish baronial style. One of its corner turrets appeared to have sheared off, leaving a pile of stone on the ground and a gap covered with corrugated iron cemented into place. As they drove through the dilapidated pillars that flanked a gravel drive that managed to be choked with weeds even in midwinter, Karen saw the paint on the window frames was cracked and peeling.

Two elderly caravans squatted near a long stone outbuilding with tall double doors, one of them slightly ajar. When Jason brought the car to a standstill, a pair of mad-eyed collies came rampaging round the corner of the house, tails wagging, barking hysterically and leaping around their doors. 'Jeez,' Jason muttered. 'You think they're safe?'

Karen got out without answering. The nearest dog butted against her leg and licked her hand. The only obvious risk was being loved to death. As she looked around, wondering where to find signs of life, a woman appeared from the same direction as the dogs. She was dressed for outdoors – a waxed jacket over a heavy jumper, jeans tucked into wellies, long socks cuffed over their tops. A tweed hat with earflaps covered most of her head. She frowned at the pair of them. 'Did you take a wrong turning?' she asked.

'Not if this is Tullyfolda House,' Karen said, producing her ID. 'I'm DCI Pirie from Police Scotland and we'd like to talk to the people who live here.' No need to mention which unit of Police Scotland, not yet. As she spoke, a stocky man with a thatch of auburn hair emerged from the outbuilding. He wore a much-stained pair of bib-and brace overalls over a checked flannel shirt. A bright saw hung casually from one hand.

'What's the matter, that you need to talk to us?' he demanded, taking a few steps closer.

'We're trying to make contact with somebody we think used to live here,' Karen said. 'I'm sorry, I don't know what the set-up is here. Is there somebody in charge, or ...?'

The woman gave a soft whistle and the dogs came to her side, lying down at her feet. 'Nobody's in charge. We're a creative community. People come here to live and work. Potters, artists, sculptors, musicians, writers, weavers. We've been host to all of them at one time or another.'

'Do you own this place?' Jason asked.

'It belonged to my family,' she said. 'Now it's held in a trust. The people who choose to come and work here contribute what they can to its upkeep.'

'Not enough, by the looks of it,' Karen said mildly.

'It meets our needs,' the woman said briskly.

'How many live here?' Karen asked.

'Currently, there are five of us—'

'Seven, if you count the bairns,' the man butted in.

'I don't think the police are very interested in Thomas and Dinah,' the woman said. 'Five adults. Declan here—' She waved a hand towards the man with the saw. 'Declan makes beautiful furniture. I'm a tapestry weaver. Charis and Donald are both potters. Thomas and Dinah are their children. Thomas is seven and Dinah is nine. And finally Jessie, who is a painter and collagist.'

'Is there somewhere a bit less Baltic we can talk?' Karen hunched into her coat to emphasise the cold.

The woman glanced at Declan, who shrugged. 'Come in here, I've got the stove on.' She smiled her approval and they all trooped into the outhouse. Rough-hewn stone walls were neatly whitewashed. A rack filled with planks of assorted woods occupied most of the back wall. To one side was a pair of workbenches and on the other, a table saw and some other machines Karen couldn't identify. In the middle of the room were three works in progress: a desk, a free-standing bookcase and a long slender dining table. Each had an easy elegance that Karen envied.

'Beautiful,' she said.

Declan nodded, as if that were his due. 'So what's this all about? You kind of started and then you stopped.'

'Before we go any further, can I take your names? Just for the record.' Karen gave her practised look of rueful reassurance. 'Paperwork's the bane of our lives.'

'I'm Declan Burns.' His scowl was sulky, as if something had been dragged out of him.

'And I'm Camilla Gordon-Bruce.' Her smile was open and generous, in contrast.

Jason had his notebook out and scribbled the answers.

Karen wandered across to the workbenches and studied two pieces of wood clamped together. 'We're trying to make contact with Amanda McAndrew. We believe she was living here about three years ago.' She turned in time to catch the rise of Camilla's eyebrows.

'She was, yes. A reasonable watercolour artist, I thought. Talented enough to produce work that would sell. We have a good relationship with a lot of the local craft and gift shops, they're always on the lookout for what the tourists will go for.'

'Thank God I don't have to worry about that,' Declan muttered.

'Declan works to commission via his website. Why are you looking for Amanda? Has she gone missing?'

No need to tell this pair more than necessary, Karen decided. 'Her former partner died in a road accident recently. We need to make contact with Amanda as a result.'

'Why?' Camilla looked puzzled. As well she might, Karen thought. Usually she could get away with non sequiturs, but this woman wasn't having any of it.

'It's complicated,' Jason said firmly. 'We just need some information from you and then we'll be out your road.'

Karen was impressed. 'As I said, we have reason to believe Amanda was living here three years ago. We wanted to check whether she was still here, and if not, whether you have any idea where she might be living.'

'I remember Amanda,' Declan said. 'She was only here for a few months, though.'

'Why did she leave?' Karen asked.

Declan looked at Camilla. 'You'd know better than me,' he said, turning away and busying himself with some technical drawings on his workbench.

Camilla sighed. 'Not everyone is suited to living collectively. Amanda seemed to fit in at first—'

'Tell them the truth, Milla. After she seduced Dani, everything went to shit,' Declan said angrily. He swept the drawings to the floor and stamped out, nailed boots clattering on the stone flags.

'Sounds like quite the story,' Karen said. 'Who's Dani?'

'Dani Gilmartin's a very talented silversmith,' Camilla said. She pulled a stool from under a bench and perched on it, like a born storyteller. 'She had a difficult childhood – her parents split up very acrimoniously when she was a child and she spent most of her teens being shuttled from one branch of the family to another. She told me she always felt in the way. But she turned it to her advantage. She persuaded her father to pay for a silversmithing course then convinced her mother to bankroll her setting up in business.'

92

'Making the best of a bad job, I suppose?' Karen said.

'Exactly,' Camilla scoffed. 'Then she told both of them to fuck off.'

A long moment. 'I bet they weren't expecting that,' Karen said.

'She meant it, though. Dani arrived here . . . let me think. Just over four years ago. The end of the summer. She wasn't always easy. She was quite volatile – prone to argue over trivial things. But she could be very endearing too. Declan was a bit sweet on her, but she wasn't interested and, in fairness to him, he didn't push it. Then Amanda turned up and the chemistry was obvious, right from the start.'

'And then Amanda seduced Dani?'

Camilla looked pained. 'Look, what Declan said? He's a bit biased. As I said, he was keen on Dani himself. If anything, it was the other way round. Dani made a bee-line for Amanda, but it was evident that her interest was reciprocated.'

'So Amanda and Dani became lovers?'

Camilla nodded. 'Dani was pretty much obsessed with Amanda. She couldn't leave her alone. When Amanda went off to paint, Dani would go too. She'd say she was looking for inspiration for her work in natural forms. But she never followed through. The only time she made any new work was when Amanda sat in the workshop with her. She was, I think, quite needy. And Amanda rather liked being needed.'

'You said Dani was volatile. Was their relationship volatile too?'

Camille frowned, considering. 'It's hard to say. I'd sometimes catch a look on Amanda's face – hunted, panicked, something like that. But they were clearly in thrall to each other. It was a very exclusive, excluding relationship.'

'So what happened?'

'They'd been talking about finding a place of their own. Dani wanted Amanda to herself, I thought. Amanda was quite keen on renting a croft or a cottage where they could grow their own food.'

'Bollocks, if you ask me,' Declan said from the doorway, where he'd reappeared. 'Hippy-dippy bollocks. The kind of nonsense people spout that have never worked anything bigger than a flower bed.'

'You're probably right, Declan, and I did gently try to steer them away from the idea. But in the end, they just left. Amanda came into the kitchen one morning. She looked dreadful, as if she hadn't slept. She said Dani had decided she couldn't live like this any longer and was determined that the two of them should find a place of their own. They'd packed up the van and they were on their way. Amanda was very apologetic. She said she loved it here, but she couldn't say no to Dani.'

'Did you try to persuade them to stay?'

Camilla chuckled. 'Oh no. To be honest, it was something of a relief by that stage. Amanda's easy to get along with, but Dani was always a disruptive energy. This place only works if everyone is pulling in the same direction, and Dani could not help going against the grain. I told Amanda if she ever wanted to come back, she'd be welcome. She realised I meant without Dani. And she just shook her head and said that wasn't going to happen. And it hasn't. She walked out of the kitchen and they drove off in her VW. Not a trace left behind.'

'You didn't stay in touch with Amanda?'

'What would have been the point? I don't live in the past, Chief Inspector. Draw a line and move forward, that's my policy. I've no idea where they ended up.'

'What about the others? Would they have stayed in touch?' Karen asked.

'None of them were here then. Jessie only joined us a few months ago. Charis and Donald arrived several months after Amanda and Dani left. So you see, we can't help you, I'm afraid. Amanda and Dani are a closed book to us.'

Declan spoke decisively. 'Not to me, they're not. Dani's got a website and a blog now.'

14

Charlie had been unusually grumpy all the way back from Lundin Links. Daisy wasn't sure what he'd expected from Mary Auld – a confession? An outpouring of hatred? A denial of having had anything to do with James Auld since he'd fled the jurisdiction? Whatever he'd hoped for, it hadn't materialised. That much was clear.

'At least we'll get a positive ID now,' she'd tried.

'We pretty much had that anyway,' Charlie grumbled. 'The ID in his pocket plus the info you got the French consulate to dig up.'

'And now we've got the name of the girlfriend and the website for the band. Maybe somebody needs to go over to Paris and talk to them? See if we can get a warrant to search James Auld's flat?'

Charlie grunted, his mouth a sarcastic twist. 'Fancy a wee jaunt, do you, Daisy?'

She gripped the steering wheel more tightly and controlled the urge to snap. 'Not me necessarily, sir. I thought you might like to go?'

'I need to keep on top of what's happening at this end. I can't go off gallivanting at the drop of a hat. It's not like the crime happened in Paris.'

'I get that, but since Paris was where his life was, isn't it more likely that the root of his murder lies there?'

'Daisy, he was the prime suspect in the murder of a senior civil servant, close to the heart of government—'

Daisy couldn't stifle a snort of laughter. 'The Scotland Office? Ten years ago, under David Cameron? Even its own mother wouldn't have called the Scotland Office the heart of government.'

It was, of course, the wrong thing to say. It just made Charlie even more huffy. 'If you ask me, what happened to James Auld happened because of his history here, not his blameless life as a jazzman in France. So if anybody's going to Paris, it's not going to be me.'

Then he turned away and made a call to the incident room. From what she could gather, the officers who'd been questioning the dog walkers of Elie hadn't turned up a single witness who'd seen James Auld walking out to the headland where the tower stood. Hardly surprising; it had been dusk, or more likely dark. And there was more than one direction from which to approach the promontory. Daisy made a mental note.

Nor had anyone tracked down where he'd been staying. Daisy thought that had always been a tall order. The East Neuk was saturated with accommodation for visitors, and now short-term lets were so easy to manage online, many of those were officially invisible. Unlicensed, unknown to the authorities. Virtual existence made them virtually impossible to track down.

Matters only got worse when they arrived back at the incident room. Standing with her back to the door, apparently intent on the progress board, was the unmistakable figure of Assistant Chief Constable (Crime) Ann Markie.

Nobody at any rank wore a perfectly tailored uniform that fitted with such flattery. Daisy thought she heard Charlie breathe, 'Fuck,' but she might just have been projecting.

'ACC Markie,' Charlie said, a layer of bonhomie slathered over his grumpiness. 'Good to see you, ma'am.'

She turned slowly, making her presence felt. Daisy, who had never seen her close up, marvelled at the perfection of her make-up. And literally not a hair out of place. She looked as if she'd stepped out of some fashion shoot for men who perved about women in uniform. She wasn't going to be running down the street after some skanky druggy who'd mugged a lassie at a bus stop any time soon. Not in those non-regulation heels. 'DCI Todd,' she said. The unspoken, 'at last' hung in the air. 'And this must be DS Mortimer.'

'Ma'am.' Daisy inclined her head. There was something unsettling about being on Markie's radar. The woman had a reputation for chilly incisiveness when it came to covering her own back. When the shit hit the fan, it slid off Ann Markie as if she were made of Teflon. Heaven help whoever was standing next to her.

'Not much forward movement so far, then,' Markie said, waving a casual hand at the board. 'I'd have to call that a "lack of progress" board.' The four other officers in the room all became completely fascinated by their computer screens. Fingers tapped keyboards. Nobody wanted to be part of this.

'The body only turned up yesterday morning,' Charlie protested, but mildly. 'We're just back from speaking to Mary Auld. The dead man's—'

'—sister-in-law, yes,' Markie cut in. 'As you may have deduced, that's why I'm here. The disappearance and presumed death of Iain Auld still remains unresolved. Now his brother resurfaces in mysterious circumstances. Did Mrs Auld shed any light at all on what's happened?'

'She was expecting to see him this week. James Auld, that is. They'd stayed in regular touch.'

Markie's lip curled in a sardonic smile. 'After he ran away to play at soldiers with the Foreign Legion?'

'Yes.' Charlie narrowed the distance between him and Markie to conversational rather than confrontational.

'And did that correspondence take us any further forward?'

Charlie shook his head. 'Mrs Auld said neither of them had any idea what had happened to her husband. And she was convinced his brother had nothing to do with it.'

Markie turned away and studied the board again. 'And you believe her?'

'At this point, we've no reason not to.'

'Except that her brother-in-law comes to visit and ends up dead. It's quite clear to me that whatever happened to James Auld must be connected to his brother going missing. And that's a cold case.' She picked up one of the marker pens sitting on the ledge below the board and wrote, *'Iain Auld = cold case'*.

Markie perched on the edge of a desk and considered Charlie. 'You don't have much experience with homicide. And you certainly don't have a track record in cold cases. As soon as the Iain Auld element entered this case, you should have consulted his case files, where you would have discovered that DCI Pirie from the Historic Cases Unit carried out a routine review two years ago, including an interview with Mrs Auld. There was nothing fresh to move the matter forward, but she is very familiar with the file. And she has a better idea of how to manage a historic case than you do. So I'm going to assign her to lead on this case.'

Charlie looked as if he'd been slapped. Which of course he had been, Daisy thought. But Markie was still talking. 'Someone has to go to France and check out James Auld's other life. We're going to look very bloody stupid if Iain Auld turns out to have been playing vibraphone in a jazz funk band in Paris for the last decade.' She fixed Daisy with her cold blue gaze. 'Your degree is in French, am I right?'

'French and Legal Studies, yes, ma'am.'

'You can go to Paris with DCI Pirie. I don't imagine conversational French is in her skill set. And DCI Todd can see whether his team can actually come up with something useful to progress the case at this end. Somebody must have interacted with James Auld. You need to find them. I'll send Pirie over so you can bring her up to what passes for speed here in Fife.' Markie picked up her gender-neutral baseball cap and set it straight on her perfect coiffure, shouldered her bag and nodded farewell.

The door had barely closed behind her when Charlie slumped into a chair. 'Well, that's me put in my box,' he muttered.

'Is she always like that?' Daisy asked.

'Only to lower ranks.' He looked mournfully at the board. 'We've hardly had time to get started.'

'It doesn't seem fair. Oh, by the way, I had a thought. From what Mary Auld said, it sounded like James Auld was kind of twitchy about covering his tracks. Maybe he didn't approach the tower from Elie at all. Maybe he came down the coastal path?'

'There would be even less chance of running into a dog walker after dark on the coastal path,' Charlie said.

'But he had to get there from somewhere. I reckon he must have hired a car when he was over here.'

'He could have got a bus.'

'This is a man who was still so worried about being recognised after ten years that he always turned up at Mary's
after dark. I think he'd want to be in control of his exit strategy. And he had a perfectly legitimate passport and driving
licence. I was looking at the map, and you could easily walk
along the coastal path from the Ardross Farm Shop to the
tower. It's only a mile and a half. Is it worth getting one of
the local officers to check whether there's been a car left
there overnight?'

'That's a good thought, Daisy.' Charlie stirred himself and
started towards one of the other officers. Over his shoulder,
he said, 'Better away home and get your passport, though.
Looks like you're off to France with KP Nuts.'

'KP Nuts?'

'Karen Pirie. KP Nuts. They call her that for a reason.'

15

They'd left Tullyfolda House with a URL for Dani's website and a promise that Camilla Gordon-Bruce would search her digital photo archive and forward what photographs she could find of Amanda and Dani. 'What did you make of that?' Karen asked.

'It's hard to know,' Jason said. 'I mean, I wouldn't behave that way, but who knows what passes for normal with folk like that? They didnae seem to think there was anything funny about Amanda and Dani just taking off all of a sudden.'

'We need to find out what happened next. Or indeed, previously. We've got no eye-witness evidence that Dani Gilmartin was still alive when Amanda drove out of Tullyfolda.'

'You think that's Dani in the van, boss?'

Karen filled her cheeks with air and puffed it out. 'That would make sense. If it was Amanda, why would Susan do any favours for Dani? On the other hand, according to Declan, Dani has an active online business. Maybe we're looking for somebody else altogether. It could be that Dani and Amanda split up and Amanda took up with someone else and it ended as badly as it could.'

'Right enough, we don't know how long the van was parked in Susan's garage. But what if Dani hid the van someplace else with Amanda's body in it? Then when she saw the reports of Susan's death, she could've moved the van and left it in the garage.'

It felt far-fetched to Karen but she was pleased that Jason had found the confidence to float his own theory, however unlikely. 'How would she have got into Susan's garage, though?'

Jason frowned. 'That's the sixty-four-thousand-dollar question, eh.'

'I can think of one possibility. If Amanda still had a set of keys, Dani might have hung on to them.' Karen imagined a woman moving swiftly up North Woodlands Crescent, keeping in the lee of those high hedges, latex gloves covering her hands. Then slipping down the driveway and letting herself into Susan Leitch's house by the back door, out of sight of any insomniac neighbours. Into the kitchen, through into the hall, unlocking the door into the garage. The moment of relief when she sees there's room, as she expected from the stories Amanda told her about Susan's neatness. She finds the switch that raises the garage door. More noise than she'd like, but she waits and no lights snap on in the nearby houses.

Then back to the van, parked a few streets away. Drive straight into the garage, minimising the opportunity for anyone on North Woodlands Crescent to hear the distinctive cough of the VW engine. She closes the door, covers the van with the tarp she's already been using in the barn or shed or garage where she's been stowing it, lets down the tyres. Then out into the night again. Walk through the sleeping city and arrive at the station in time for the first train out.

And then she remembered the distressed rubber of the flat tyres. They'd been beyond redemption for a lot more than three weeks.

'Boss?' Jason startled her from her imaginings.

'What?'

'I said, are we heading back to the office or what?'

'Back to the office. Hammering the keyboards, staring into the screens. Tedious, I know, but we need to find what happened to those two women.'

Within minutes of arriving in Gayfield Square, Karen would have paid hard cash for tedium. 'You've got a visitor,' the desk officer told her as soon as she crossed the threshold.

'Who is it?'

He pulled a face. 'Three guesses.'

Karen grinned. 'I'm a detective, not a psychic. Give it up, son.'

He gave a quick glance to either side then lowered his voice. 'The Dog Biscuit.'

Karen rolled her eyes. Ann Markie had gained her soubriquet from a brand of dog treats. Clever and disrespectful, it had spread through the force faster than a head cold, as the best nicknames always did. 'Thanks for the heads-up.' She turned to Jason. 'Away and get yourself a sandwich or something. I'll deal with her majesty.'

On her way down the long corridor to her office, Karen slipped into the toilet. Past experience had taught her she would never rival the Dog Biscuit's impeccable appearance but at least she could make sure she didn't have crisp crumbs down her jacket or mud on her trousers. She ran her fingers through her hair, trying to smooth it down, wondering how it was that some women never looked as if they'd slept in a hedge. She squared her shoulders, took a deep breath and muttered, 'Take no snash.'

Ann Markie was sitting at Karen's desk, tapping with a perfectly manicured nail on a mini-tablet. She barely looked up when Karen entered. 'Sit down,' she said, her voice chilly, and carried on typing. Karen sat in Jason's seat and waited.

Their last encounter had not ended well. Markie had given Karen an explicit order not to do something, which Karen had ignored without a single misgiving. In her book, justice would always trump politics. She imagined Markie would claim the greater good of Police Scotland, but for Karen, her duty to the dead and their families came first, second and last. Even though Karen's insubordination had ended in a murder conviction, she didn't imagine it had pressed 'pause' on Markie's contempt for her. So what could be today's reason for ripping her a new one?

A slow couple of minutes passed while Karen stared out of the window at the wall opposite and thought of lovely things. Like the bottle of Arbikie Nàdar gin that Jimmy Hutton had promised to bring along to their next Gin Monday. Made from peas, with a negative carbon footprint, she thought it was right out there on the margins of mental gins. Who knew what it would taste like?

The tapping had stopped and Markie cleared her throat. Karen drew her eyes from the non-existent view and looked across at her boss. 'What can I do for you?'

'Have you been following the case of the man pulled out of the Forth yesterday morning?' As always when addressing lesser mortals, Markie was abrupt to the point of rudeness. Nobody was ever allowed to forget who was in charge.

'Sorry, that one passed me by. I've been dealing with a

skeleton in a camper van in prosperous Perth. That's been occupying all my time since yesterday morning.'

'If it's a skeleton, it's about as cold a case as it gets. So there's no rush, is there?'

'I like to think we bring the same urgency to historic cases as we do to current ones.'

'Don't virtue-signal to me, Pirie. Even you aren't so naïve as to think all murders are created equal. You can put Perth to one side for now. I need you to take over as SIO on this case in Fife.'

Karen seethed but she kept the lid on by digging her fingernails into her palms below the level of the desk. 'Surely that doesn't come into my remit?'

'Obviously not, as far as yesterday's body is concerned. But it's closely connected to a missing person case that you reviewed two years ago. You made no progress, but at least you know the file.'

A two-year-old review didn't narrow it down. Whenever Karen wasn't pursuing a live lead, she was sifting through the evidence from serious unsolved crimes. But these were not the sort of headline-grabbing cases that Markie craved. These were the dusty and unloved cases that mattered only to the bereaved. Even the original investigating officers didn't love those monuments to their failure. 'Which file would that be?' Cautious now, wondering where this was going.

'Iain Auld.'

The name hung between them like a motionless pendulum, waiting for a push to set it in motion.

Now Karen understood. 'Senior civil servant in the Scotland Office,' she said, nudging the pendulum towards Markie. 'Is this him, then?'

'No. It's the prime suspect in his presumed murder.'

Karen sighed. 'I don't presume. In my book, it's still a suspicious disappearance.' Markie opened her mouth to speak but Karen held up her hand and kept talking. 'His brother. Can't remember the name. But he was a person of interest and he did a runner.' She tapped her fingers on the edge of the desk. 'Went to . . . Spain, was it? Via Ireland?'

'Well done. Your memory for details is impressive.' In Markie's mouth, it sounded like an insult. Karen imagined the unspoken half of the comment running something like, 'But then you've nothing else to occupy you, have you?'

'So the brother turns up dead in Fife. And that concerns me, how?'

'It seems likely that the key to Iain Auld's disappearance lies with his brother. Don't you think? They had a fight the night before he disappeared, the Met found a bloodstained T-shirt in James Auld's bin, then he fled the jurisdiction. I want you to reopen the investigation into Iain Auld's disappearance. And the best way to do that is for you to take overall control.' Markie sounded as if the words were being dragged out of her.

'What's wrong with me working the cold case alongside the existing SIO?'

Markie pursed her lips then said, 'He's never done a murder before. And whatever your faults, your track record when it comes to results is hard to fault.'

Light slowly dawned on Karen. 'It's the politics, isn't it? The people at the top of the power pyramid here in Scotland now were around then too, only not so important. And with the prospect of a second independence referendum, they don't want anything to frighten the horses. They want somebody they trust running the investigation.' She couldn't help a dark chuckle. 'Somebody who's low enough down the totem pole not to have any skin in the game, but far enough up it to deflect any criticism in the media.'

'Think what you like, Pirie. This is about efficient policing. Not politics. I want you to go straight over to Fife to meet the team there and get up to speed. I've arranged for DS Daisy Mortimer from DCI Todd's team to be your bag carrier. You'll be setting off for Paris on tonight's sleeper.'

'Paris?'

'That's where James Auld's been living. Lucky you, Pirie. Just think of all the shitholes he could have shacked up in.' Markie turned back to her tablet then looked up again. 'Why are you still here?'

16

Where are you?

Nando's in the Omni Centre

Of course he was in Nando's. What was it about guys and Nando's? You'd think Scottish chip shops hadn't been serving fried chicken and chips with curry sauce since Karen had been a child. At least he was near at hand.

Wait there. I'll be right over. Get me some peri-peri fries.

She found Jason at a table as far from the door as possible, obviously in the hope that no passing senior officer would notice his flaming red hair hunched over the remains of half a chicken. 'Chips on the way, boss,' he said.

'What do I owe you?' Karen was ever scrupulous about money. They both paid into the office coffee kitty and though Jason always fetched it, she made sure he took what he was owed.

'It's OK, boss, you can treat me to one of they Portuguese custard tarts. How come you're here? You hate Nando's.'

Karen breathed heavily through her nose. 'The Dog

Biscuit chucked me out of my own office. I'm under orders to go to Fife to take over a day-old murder that's tied to a cold case we reviewed two years ago.'

Jason frowned. 'Did we not get anywhere with it?'

'It didn't even get as far as "we". I NFA'd it.' Karen hated writing No Further Action on a file, but when it came to historic case reviews, it happened more often than not.

'I don't get it. Why is there not a Major Incident Team on a day-old murder?' Jason ripped the last of the flesh from his chicken and shoved it into his mouth.

Karen greeted the arrival of her fries as a welcome distraction. 'There is. Sort of. There's a DCI Charlie Todd leading the team over in Fife, but this is his first murder. So Markie's using that as an excuse to get me to pick up the ball.'

Jason wiped his mouth with the back of his hand then wiped his hand with his napkin. 'I don't get that either. Because, like, Markie hates us.'

'This is a win-win for her, though. It's a case with a political dimension. You're probably too young to remember, but ten years ago, a senior civil servant in the Scotland Office disappeared without a trace. It was round about the time that the engines of IndyRef started revving up and the politicians got well poked by the media about it. Now it's surfaced again because the dead man who turned up in the Forth yesterday was the number one suspect. The dead man's brother, just to complicate things. If I manage to sort it out this time around, the Dog Biscuit will take the credit. And if I don't? It'll be another black mark against me.' Karen picked listlessly at her chips, wondering why she'd bothered to order them. They always sounded better than they turned out.

'So you've to go to Fife.'

Karen nodded. 'And then I've to go to Paris.'

'Paris?'

'That's where the brother's been hiding since he did a runner before he could be charged with anything.'

'I've never been to Paris. Never fancied it, to be honest. Eilidh went for the Scotland Argentina game in the Women's World Cup, but that was before we started going out properly.'

Karen hadn't realised Jason's occasional night out for a film or a pizza or an afternoon at the football had graduated to 'going out properly'. 'When did that start?'

He flushed a dark red, his freckles like pale stars in a troubled sky. 'Kind of got serious at the New Year,' he said. 'She's a nice lassie.'

Karen didn't doubt it. She had Mrs Murray's seal of approval, and not much got past Jason's mum. 'Good for you. But while I'm in Paris, I need you to keep plugging away at the skeleton in the van. Make a list, Jason.'

He looked startled. 'Could you not just email it to me?'

'No, I haven't got time.' Reluctantly, he took out his notebook and a pen. 'What I will email you is these.' Karen took out her laptop and pulled up the photographs Camilla Gordon-Bruce had sent her. The first one showed two women sitting at a table covered with the detritus of a meal. They were looking at the camera, toasting the photographer with glasses of white wine. Karen pointed to the one on the left. Shoulder-length light brown hair, a heavy fringe like Claudia Winkleman, sparkly blue eyes and a cheeky grin. 'That's Amanda McAndrew. And that' – she tapped the other woman, whose straight dark hair was cut in a severe angled line from the back of her head to the corner of her jaw; she had round glasses with fashionable thick black frames and a slightly less enthusiastic smile – 'is Daniella Gilmartin. Dani to you and me and Amanda.' She swiped down and there was Amanda in three-quarter profile, studying a painting on her easel with fixed concentration. The final pic was of Dani, caught unawares, turning in surprise towards the lens, in the throes of arranging a display of silver jewellery. 'I think it's fair to take as a starting point that one of them is our skeleton.'

'Might not be, though,' Jason said. 'We know Dani's still out in the world.'

'Do we?'

'She's got a website. She's still selling jewellery.'

'That could be anybody. It doesn't mean she's the one making it, does it? We'll keep an open mind. The key thing is establishing an ID for our victim. We should get the full DNA results from the van and, hopefully, the paintings from Susan's hallway tomorrow or the day after. That could answer the question for us. If the skeleton DNA matches the painting DNA, we can presume it's Amanda. If not, we presume it's Dani, but that's hanging on a shoogly peg until we can find a definitive source of her DNA. This is where you get to play to your strengths, Jason. You know you're good at researching databases.'

He gave Karen a suspicious look, as if he didn't quite believe the praise. 'Am I?'

'You know you are.' She grinned. 'And when you get stuck, you're very good at persuading women to help you out. Must be their mothering instincts. Thank God it doesn't work on me.'

'So what have I got to do?'

'We need to trace family members for Amanda and Dani. Get on to Tamsin and ask her to check whether Susan has contact details for Amanda's parents on the laptop. Get their birth certificates and backtrack to the parents' identities, then track forward to where they are now. Use DVLA, council tax records, Google, phone numbers. You know the drill. Parents, siblings, whatever. I'm counting on you, Jason.'

His face betrayed minor panic. 'I'll do my best, boss.'

'And you need to look into that website and talk to whoever is producing the silver jewellery that's being sold under Dani's name. It could be Dani. But it could be a completely different person.' She pushed her fries towards him and he took a bunch without hesitation.

'OK.' He chewed and swallowed. 'I'll keep you posted, yeah?'

'You better had. This is the kind of case that we're all about, Jason. Never mind saving the politician's arses from the fire. We're here to give folk the answers they need about the people who have disappeared from their lives.' She pushed back her chair. 'I'll talk to you tonight.'

A heavy drizzle misted the street and Karen hurried towards the cab rank. Back home, she packed a bag that would see her through three days. She didn't imagine she'd need longer than that in France. She stuck in a book Hamish had bought her about the race to the top of the Himalayas in the 1930s. It wasn't the sort of thing she normally read, but she was conscious of a faint background hum of guilt because she hadn't contacted him. Even if it was only to tell him to do one, she should have had nerve enough to reach out.

She managed to get out of Edinburgh just ahead of the clotted traffic of rush hour and as she drove, she trawled her memory for what she could recall of the cold case review. Iain Auld had been a career civil servant. Well respected by his colleagues as a safe pair of hands. He had a reputation for being courteous and self-contained. She hadn't stumbled on a single witness statement that accused him of losing his temper.

Karen had been particularly interested in the comments of his political bosses. Who among them might have had something to hide that Iain Auld could have become privy to? Those he'd worked with most closely had risen further through the ranks since then. A couple had disappeared, disgraced in the usual manner of politicos – mismanaging either sex or money. But there were still plenty who would not want to be touched by this new inquiry. No wonder the Dog Biscuit had been so keen to hand it on a plate to her.

The afternoon was fading as she arrived at the familiar building where she'd been based for years when Fife had its own distinct police force and a Historic Crimes Unit that consisted of Karen, a very wet-behind-the-ears Mint and Phil Parhatka. The thought stirred up her anger against Merrick Shand afresh. He'd robbed her of the man who'd given her a sense of self-worth after years of conviction that, when it came to relationships, she was a non-starter.

'Not now, Karen,' she muttered angrily as she slammed the car door and headed for the front entrance. There would be plenty more things to rage about before the end of the day. She could feel it in her bones.

17

Karen could see why Ann Markie was feeling frustrated. A murder inquiry that didn't produce a solid lead in the first twenty-four hours invariably proved problematic. Most murders were straightforward. They happened when a man – and it was almost always a man – lashed out in rage or fear or humiliation or frustration. Usually the object of his fury was the woman who'd been unfortunate enough to form some sort of bond with him. Mostly, she was his partner, but sometimes that bond was as inconsequential as the wrong look across a bar or a transaction with a sex worker that inadvertently provoked the worst possible response.

Those cases were easy to solve but hard to deal with, even if, like Karen, you had never had a relationship with a man whose potential for violence was disturbingly close to the surface. Harder still were the ones who lashed out at children – babies, toddlers, small frightened kids who had no hiding place. Especially when those men manipulated the mothers into privileging them over their children.

Still, those horrific crimes were easy to solve, though sometimes impossibly difficult to prosecute successfully. The hardest cases were the ones where there was no immediately perceptible connection between killer and victim.

Listening to Charlie Todd and Daisy Mortimer bringing her up to speed with the inquiry into the death of James Auld, aka Paul Allard, all Karen's instincts were screaming that this was going to be a very bad one indeed. She felt sorry for Charlie, his hangdog expression not one that came readily to a face that looked as if it would be more comfortable with determination.

'I'll be honest, I'd be well and truly pissed off if I was you, having this snatched out from under you by the ACC. I can't fault what you've done so far,' Karen said. 'I wouldn't have done anything differently.'

'Thanks,' Charlie said listlessly. 'We're only two days in and already all I'm seeing is dead ends. We don't even know when he arrived in the country or how he got here. We're assuming he hired a car, but without knowing where he started from, we're not going to get anywhere.'

'Agreed,' Karen said. 'He sounds cautious – he's not going to have used one of the big firms. He'll have gone to some wee local garage.'

'Daisy thought he might have parked his car at the farm shop and walked along the coastal path from there. But we drew a blank. No cars there overnight.' Charlie sighed.

Karen closed her eyes momentarily, conjuring up the local geography in her mind's eye. It was a place she knew well. She and Phil had often driven along to the East Neuk on a summer evening, walking sections of the coastal path, ending up with fish and chips in Pittenweem or Crail. 'There's car parking at the top of St Monans,' she said slowly. 'He could have walked along the main road to the farm shop then cut through to the coastal path. Judging by what we know about the time of death, even at the latest there would still have been half an hour or so of daylight when he set off. Get a patrol car to take a look and PNC any vehicles in the car park. I don't imagine there'll be many tourists in February. It should be easy enough to eliminate the locals.'

'You really think it's worth it?' Charlie was still despondent.

'It'll take no time. Gotta be worth a go, guv,' Daisy said, geeing him up.

She'd begun to impress Karen with her energy and attitude. She reminded Karen of what she'd been like ten years before, only with the polish that a different background and a university degree provided. 'Daisy, I need you to talk to your pals at the French consulate about how we get access to James Auld's flat. I've no idea what the procedure is, whether we need to get a sheriff to request it or what. But whatever that turns out to be, I think we should head to Paris tomorrow regardless. There's his bandmates to talk to, and we can go over to Caen to see the girlfriend too. I'm proposing we take the sleeper down tonight then walk across to St Pancras and catch the Eurostar. We'll be in Paris for lunch without any airport nonsense.'

'And it's better for our carbon footprint,' Daisy observed. Both Karen and Charlie looked as puzzled as if she'd spoken in Swahili. Carbon footprints were not the ones that interested detectives.

Karen cleared her throat. 'Quite. Charlie, can you get one of your civilian aides to sort that out? I'll be boarding the sleeper at Dundee. I need to go and talk to River Wilde, the anthro, about a different case. Daisy, I presume you'll be getting on at Kirkcaldy?'

Daisy looked startled. 'I didn't know it stopped there.'

'Round about midnight,' Karen told her. She got to her

feet. 'Right. I'm off. I'll leave my car here, Charlie. Daisy, can you drop me at Markinch station so I can get a train to Dundee?'

Daisy sprang to her feet. 'No problem, ma'am.'

Karen winced. 'Don't call me ma'am, Daisy. Chief, boss, guv, any of those. But ma'am makes me feel like a fraud.'

Daisy grinned. 'Right you are, guv. Car park in five?'

Karen nodded, and Daisy left them. 'How did you leave things with Mary Auld?'

'All right, I think. She was a bit chippy about our failure to find her husband, but otherwise OK. Why?'

'Might be worth asking her whether she knows how Auld usually travelled when he visited? There's no guarantee that's what he did this time, of course.'

'Good thought. Thanks, Karen. And for the record, I'm not holding this against you. We've both been stiffed by Markie. She'll have her reasons. From what I've heard, she always does.'

Karen's smile was wry. 'It's how she got where she is. Me, I'm just grateful I'm not cursed with that kind of ambition. Think how radged she must feel when one of us lot doesn't deliver.'

Charlie laughed, his face lighting up for the first time that afternoon. 'Almost makes you want to fail.'

Karen shook her head. 'Never that, Charlie. I know what loss feels like. And how important the answers are for the people left behind. I never want to fail. Not even to piss on Ann Markie's chips. I'll find other ways to do that.'

River was waiting for Karen in the bar at the Malmaison, two cocktails in front of her. 'I checked your train was on time and ordered you a rhubarb and ginger gin. Comes with

Mediterranean tonic, slivers of apple and rhubarb. I thought that might be tart enough, given how pissed off you sounded on the phone.'

Karen kissed the top of River's abundant auburn hair and sat down opposite her, shrugging out of her coat. 'I could not love you more,' she said. 'What's that you're drinking?'

'It's as weird as it gets. Gin Mare, rosemary and black olive tonic, green olives, rosemary, orange. I'm really not sure. I'm leaning towards Jay Rayner's view that too many gins are good vodkas ruined.' River sniffed suspiciously and took a sip. 'Might be better with a pizza. So, have you spoken to Hamish?'

Karen rolled her eyes. 'Pleasure first. What can you tell me about the skeleton from Perth?'

'You're a hard taskmistress.' She raised her glass. 'Here's to solving crime.' They clinked their glasses. 'So, your skeleton. Definitely female. All the bones are present and where I'd expect them to be, which tells me that if the body was moved it was before the process of decomposition began – either that or it was arranged by another highly skilled forensic anthropologist.'

'Which seems unlikely.'

'Which seems unlikely. I looked at the pubic symphysis. Which is what, Chief Inspector?'

Karen grinned. She had learned her lesson well. 'At the front of the pelvis, where the two sides of the pelvic girdle meet above the pubic area, is a joint called the pubic symphysis,' she chanted. 'It changes in identifiable ways with the passage of time, Dr Wilde.'

'Correct. I could give you an inferiority complex and talk about ventral ramparts and the pectinate outline of the dorsal margin?'

'Or you could cut to the chase and tell me how old she was when she died.' Karen tipped her glass towards River and took another swig.

'Somewhere between thirty and thirty-five. Does that help?'

'At this point, we think the victim is one of two women. Three years ago, one would have been thirty-one, the other thirty-four. So no, it doesn't help with ID, but it does confirm that we're in the right ballpark when it comes to victims.'

'If you can get a dental chart, you could make a positive ID. At some point, she's lost one of her front teeth and had a titanium implant. It's a good one. You probably wouldn't have been able to spot it when she was alive.'

Karen nodded in satisfaction. 'That might make all the difference. What about the injury to the skull?'

'I would say she's taken a heavy blow to the back of the skull.'

'Baseball bat? Pipe?'

River shook her head. 'I'd estimate something with a more clearly defined edge.'

'What? Like a metal bar or a chair leg maybe?'

'You know it's not my job to speculate.' She held up a hand to still Karen's protest. 'But yes, either of those things would be consistent with the injury. If I was a CSI, I'd check the work surfaces in the van. It's possible that her head hit a sharp edge accidentally.'

'Or it was hit against a sharp edge.'

River shrugged. 'I need to examine the injury more scientifically to give you clarity on that one. The only other thing I have for you is that we've extracted DNA from the skeleton and the hair and they match each other.'

Karen scoffed. 'Why would they not?'

'No reason, but I like to be sure. Now, what's all this about Hamish?'

Karen groaned. 'I can't do this on an empty stomach. I'm catching the sleeper tonight and I need solid food and a belt of red wine before I get on that train. What about that Neapolitan pizza place round the corner?'

'You're putting this conversation off.'

Karen wasn't willing to admit her friend was right. 'No, I want a proper run at it, and I'm starving. Let's finish our drink and get some food.'

The restaurant was busy, and Karen muttered darkly about not sitting at a shared table. Luckily, a couple were leaving as they arrived and the waiter shoehorned them into the last table in a row of twin-tops. They both knew what they wanted – double mozzarella with spicy salami for Karen, gorgonzola, artichoke and Parma ham for River, a bottle of Primitivo between them.

As soon as the waiter had taken the order, River leaned forward. 'So, now I want the whole story. No more, "he'd crossed the line this time". Chapter and verse, Karen.'

Second time of telling, Karen's anger had cooled some-what. But not her unease at Hamish's behaviour. 'It's the way he assumes he knows what's best for me. Even if I've specifically said something different. When we first got together, I was wary because of the whole earring thing.' That had been the first crack in Hamish's facade. Karen had lost an earring down the sink of the holiday let he'd lent her on the case where they'd first met. She'd asked him if he could look for it in the drain. Days later, he'd turned up at her office with the missing earring. She'd been delighted until Anders, his barista, had let slip that Hamish had ordered a replacement pair online.

'Not that again,' River sighed. 'He did a generous thing, Karen. He fancied you and he wanted to make an impression. Is that such a bad thing?'

Karen fiddled with her napkin. 'Not in itself, no. I get that he saw I was upset about the earrings and he wanted to make it better. But for him it was no big deal to lash out hundreds of pounds on a pair of earrings just to impress a woman he'd barely met.'

'Exactly. No big deal. So why is it such a big deal for you?'

'Because Phil gave me those earrings. And for him it was a big deal. Cops don't earn a fortune, for him to spend that much on anybody was something considered. Something that carried weight. Not just clicking a button on a website.'

'I thought you'd given Hamish the benefit of the doubt on that? You can't punish a man for his generosity.'

'Can you not? You and Giorsal, you're singing from the same hymn sheet on this one. But sometimes there's a kind of tyranny in generosity. A man is that good to you, you should be grateful. How can you not want to be with him?' She twisted the stem of her wine glass between her fingers till River gently covered them with her hand.

'You enjoy his company, right?'

'Right.'

'You have good sex?'

'We're good together, no question.'

'And he treats you well?'

Karen scoffed. 'Except when he tries to run my life by his rules. Turning up like that at the prison, that showed no respect for me. For my judgement. For my ability to take care of myself. I'm a senior police officer, River. I'm used to taking responsibility for myself.'

'I think you're reading it wrong. I don't think it was a lack of respect or a lack of confidence in your ability to handle yourself. I think his motives were a lot closer to Jimmy Hutton's. He cares about you, Karen. He was there as backstop. In case something completely unpredictable happened. Don't shoot him down in flames for wanting to help.'

Whatever mutinous response Karen was about to deliver was cut off by the arrival of the pizzas. Both women exclaimed in delight and treated the waiter to beaming smiles. 'Ya dancer,' Karen said. She cut a slice and folded it over, taking a hearty bite. 'Oh,' she groaned through a mouthful of pizza. 'Died, gone to heaven,' she added when her mouth was empty. 'What about the other stuff though? Venice, when I wanted Wester Ross? Tasting menus full of ingredients I've never even seen before when I'd be delirious with this?' She waved a hand at the pizza. 'It's hard for me to accept all the privilege that goes along with being with Hamish.'

'I get that,' River said. 'But did you ever stop to think it's maybe just as hard for him to adjust to your expectations?'

18

Jason had always liked to feel useful. He'd been an obliging child, which had made him his mother's favourite. The downside was that it had also made him his brother's patsy. Ronan had dumped Jason with the sticky end of childhood misdemeanours at every opportunity. His unlikely saviour had been football. He'd had an instinct for positional play, a good left foot and a gifted coach. A few talent scouts had taken a look at him when he'd been in his early teens. Then a bad tackle had left him with a complex ankle fracture and all hope of a professional career in the game gone.

Through it all, his coach had been there for him. And his coach's day job had been the police. He'd missed out on his dream of playing professional football too, though in his case it had been lack of talent rather than injury that had scuppered him. He'd been heartbroken, just as Jason was. He'd explained that joining the police had been the perfect answer for him. 'You've been dedicated to football, Jason – you've never missed a training session, you've worked hard and you've never let your team down. These are transferable skills. You'd make a good polis and it would make a good man of you.'

His brother had been outraged. His father had mocked

him, saying his mining grandfathers would have disowned him. But his mother had supported him and still told him regularly she was proud of him. Jason had no difficulty meeting the physical criteria, but reading the specimen entrance test papers had filled him with horror. His mother had come to the rescue, taking him through the questions and explaining how to approach them. She'd done it every Sunday afternoon for six weeks and in the end, he'd somehow managed to scrape through.

While Jason had been a probationer, he'd helped Phil Parhatka on a missing child inquiry. They'd already known each other vaguely from the South Stand at Raith Rovers and he'd worked hard to make an impression. But still, Jason had been surprised when he'd got the call from Phil to join the Historic Cases Unit. And that had been that. He'd slowly discovered a dogged persistence that compensated for not being particularly bright. He earned his berth because he ground away at the stuff that drove Karen to distraction. He might not have been as quick to the answers as some, but she could always rely on what he came up with.

And so instead of spending the evening on his IKEA sofa watching Netflix with Eilidh, Jason had been hunched over his desk in Gayfield Place searching records of births, marriages and deaths. He'd soon confirmed that Amanda had been born thirty-seven years previously in Selkirk in the Borders. Selkirk might as well have been the moon for all Jason knew about it.

From her birth certificate, he learned that Amanda's father Barry had been a businessman and her mother Anita had been a housewife. Soon, he knew their dates of birth and where they'd been married. If they were dead, it hadn't happened in Scotland. Thanks to the security paranoia of

Tony Blair's government, Jason was able to access all sorts of data that had previously been unavailable without a court order, as long as it related to a criminal investigation. And a skeleton in a van in someone's garage definitely qualified on that count.

There was no official trace of Barry and Anita McAndrew in the UK after 2015. Google revealed a short item on a local paper website about the sale of their scrap-metal business. Jason grinned at the notion of a scrappie describing himself as a businessman. He'd known scrappies, mostly through Ronan, and that wasn't the word he'd have used. The newspaper article confirmed what Camilla Gordon-Bruce had told them about buying an olive grove in Greece. That was doubly useful – it lent more weight to the idea that she was a credible witness.

But it was Facebook that yielded solid gold. Jason tutted. He'd been on Facebook like everybody else until the boss had pointed out a handful of years ago that he was a police officer responsible for catching serious criminals. Maybe it wasn't a good idea to be quite so easy to find? He'd deleted his account and when he'd started going out with Eilidh, he'd persuaded her to put in place all the privacy measures she could. 'Next time you go for a job, do you actually want them to see pictures of you off your face at your cousin's hen night?' had been the clincher. She'd grumped about being the only one of her mates with no visible life on the socials, but she'd done as he'd suggested.

Clearly nobody had given Barry and Nita McAndrew the same advice. There were dozens of photographs of them in their olive grove on a Cretan hillside. As well as the stunning views of the sea, the sunset and the olive trees, Jason was astonished to see videos of mechanical harvesting. He'd expected Greek grannies swathed in black, faces leathery and lined, gap-toothed smiles gurning at the camera, filling ancient baskets with hand-picked fruit. Instead a huge machine drove down regimented lines of trees, appearing to swallow them whole, leaving behind a row of symmetrical squared-off trees and a hopper filled with olives, leaves and bits of twigs. It was as brutal as the giant compressors Barry would have had in his scrapyard.

Jason put together a memo with the details of his research and sent it to Karen. It would be up to her how to proceed. Somehow, he didn't think she'd just DM them and ask for a DNA sample. Thankfully, working that one out was beyond his pay grade.

But he'd only completed half the job. With a sigh, Jason typed 'Daniella Gilmartin' into the search box and began the tedious process all over again.

Across the Firth of Forth in Glenrothes, Daisy Mortimer was also working late. She'd gone home to collect her passport and pack a bag, then returned to the office with a paper-wrapped parcel of white pudding and chips, heavily seasoned with salt and sauce. The intense aroma filled the office, but since everyone else had already left, there was nobody to complain or attempt to steal her chips. She had a few hours to set things up in Paris before she had to catch the sleeper and she was determined to make the most of them.

A flurry of emails with Verancourt had yielded the name of the officer at the commissariat de police in the Sixth Arrondissement who was to be their liaison. She now knew that murders were investigated by the Brigade Criminelle who divided their squad into teams of seven. Commandant

Jean-Claude Gautier was the *chef de groupe* of the team that had been assigned the suspicious death of the man lying in a mortuary in Fife. According to Verancourt, Daisy and Karen should pitch up at the police headquarters on Rue Bonaparte and ask for Les Gautiers.

The team is named after the senior officer? she'd queried, wondering whether she'd misunderstood something.

It is the custom, the answer came back. Daisy decided she'd enjoy telling Karen they should introduce themselves as Les Piries.

She finished her pudding supper and turned to the internet. She knew the French judicial system was very different, but she needed to find out just how different. The more she read, the more she realised it had at least some common ground with the way things were done in Scotland. In Scotland, the police worked closely with the procurators fiscal, who received case reports from the police then determined the course of investigations into serious crime, as well as deciding which cases should go to court. In France, they had *procureurs*, who seemed to do roughly the same thing, except that they also worked with a *juge d'instruction* who was more like an investigator than a judge. It was very confusing; she hoped it didn't mean the French cops would use the system to shut them out. Somehow, she thought Karen Pirie wouldn't let that happen.

At last, she began to compose an email to Commandant Gautier. She read it back, ticking off the points on her fingers. They needed access to the dead man's apartment and they'd also want to talk to his bandmates and his girlfriend. Had they been informed of his death? Would Les Piries need to be accompanied by Les Gautiers? Could Commandant Gautier smooth the way with the *procureur* and the *juge d'instruction* ahead of their arrival, to avoid wasting time?

Daisy took a deep breath, copied in Verancourt and Karen and pressed send. She'd done her best. She hoped it was good enough for KP Nuts. She checked the time and realised with a shock that she had less than half an hour to get to Kirkcaldy station in time for the sleeper. She jumped up, grabbed her coat and ran for it. If she missed the bloody train, it wouldn't matter how good a job she'd done. She'd be finished before she'd even started.

The sleeper pulled out of the station and wound its slow way through the outskirts of Dundee and across the Tay. Karen tugged the worktop from under the sink in her cabin and set her laptop down. She footered about on the internet, checking her email and the news headlines, pretending she was doing something useful. But there was only so long she could postpone what she had to do.

Hi Hamish

She stared at the two words. Should it be 'Dear Hamish', or was that too distant? On the rare occasions when she'd emailed rather than messaged him, she'd definitely not used anything so formal. Maybe just his name, without any salutation? Or did that sound too challenging?

'Oh, for fuck's sake,' she muttered in exasperation. 'Get over yourself and get on with it.'

Hi Hamish.
I don't enjoy being at odds with you. I really value the time we spend together. You make me laugh, you

129

challenge me to look at things differently. I think we're good together in lots of ways and I don't want that to come to an end.

That took ten minutes and a lot of hammering of the 'delete' key. Karen opened her bag and rummaged for the can of gin and tonic she'd bought earlier. She took a hearty swig, winced at its sweetness and frowned at the screen again.

But even though we've got a lot in common, there's a lot of differences between us. We grew up with very different expectations. I find it hard to adjust to your sense of privilege and I know you think I'm sometimes chippy. I realise you think you're being kind and generous and protective, but to me, that sometimes feels like you want to change me into somebody I'm not. We think of control as being about telling somebody what to do and what not to do, but kindness can be just as controlling.

I mean it when I say I don't want this to end. But you've got to stop deciding what's best for me. When you turned up the other morning, I was outraged. What I was doing was none of your business. Even though it wasn't an official police operation, the last thing I needed was to be distracted by a civilian.

This is me, the way I am. Thrawn. But also gallus. Do you even know what those words mean, growing up in America like you did? Look them up, Hamish. You're not going to change me, and if you're determined to keep trying, we've got no future. I'm sorry if that sounds harsh but there's no point in pretending I'm going to turn into somebody different.

I suspect you're sometimes anxious that you can't stand comparison with a dead man, but in my head, it's not a competition between you and Phil. The person I'm in a relationship with is you. I see you, not Phil. I don't want to lose what we have.

I'm on a train to Paris right now. I'll be away for a few days. I'm on a case. I do want to talk to you (if you still want to talk to me) but I need to focus on what I'm doing, so can we leave it till I get back? Probably just as well if we both have a wee bit of time to work out what we want. I'll let you know when I'm back.

Take care of yourself. Kx

Karen stared at the 'x'. She picked up her can and went to take a swig. To her surprise, it was empty. She had no recollection of drinking it in the pauses between sentences. She read her words again and couldn't see a way of improving their stark message. Shaking her head, Karen pressed send.

She had a difficult few days ahead. Getting one complication out of the way was a step in the right direction. She contemplated walking down to the restaurant car and buying more drink, but she knew that wouldn't make anything better. Solving a murder, though? That beat a gin and tonic hands down, every time.

19

Wednesday, 19 February 2020

Karen stared at Daisy across the café table in St Pancras station. 'You're kidding me? *Les Piries*?' She swallowed a mouthful of coffee as if it would return her to the land of sensible.

'Honest, boss. The teams get called after the SIO.'

'Like we don't suffer enough from brass who think they're God. Don't anybody tell the Dog Biscuit about that.' She smashed the contents of her egg pot together with a fork and scooped up a mouthful. 'You've not heard back from this guy Gautier?'

Daisy shook her head. 'It's early doors yet.' She stifled a yawn. Her night in a reclining seat, the only accommodation left from Kirkcaldy, had delivered less comfort and less sleep than Karen's narrow berth. Still, she was managing to make inroads into a bacon, egg and cheese muffin with a side of hash browns.

'OK. Once we've eaten, we'll get checked in for the Eurostar, then I need to catch up with Jason on the other case. And you can give your mysterious Monsieur Verancourt a wee nudge.' As she spoke, she opened her email on her phone and read properly the message from

Jason that she'd already skimmed. Amanda McAndrew's parents were based in an olive grove in Crete. Dani Gilmartin's mother had died from breast cancer just over a year before and her father was apparently living in a village in the Borders. He was the obvious choice for a DNA sample that might confirm who had been in the VW and whose skeleton was lying in River's morgue.

Jason answered on the second ring, sounding as if he was speaking through a mouthful of doughnut. He cleared his throat, coughed, spluttered and eventually managed, 'Sorry, boss, crumb got stuck in my throat.'

'Sounded more like a boulder. Have we got anything back from the lab yet on the DNA from the camper van?'

'Not a word, boss. I gave them a bell first thing, but they're backed up to buggery. Half the lab staff are off with some kind of bug. Apparently they went on a stag do to Milan last weekend and they picked it up there.'

'Milan? That's not very rock and roll, is it?'

'They got tickets for the football. Some big game.'

'Ended up as a bit of an own goal.' Karen sucked her teeth in irritation. 'I'll call Tamsin and see if she can rattle some cages. In the meantime, you need to hotfoot it down to the Borders and talk to Dani Gilmartin's father. And get a DNA sample from him.'

There was a pause. 'What do I say to him, boss? Do I let on that we think his lassie's dead?'

It was a tough call. 'I think you have to level with him. We have an unidentified body and we have reason to believe it might be Dani. It's a hard thing to hear, but any kind of fudge could come back to bite us down the line. You'll be fine, Jason. Just put yourself in his shoes and think about how you'd prefer to hear a message like that.'

'I'd prefer never to hear a message like that, boss. Poor sod.' He sighed. 'I'll do my best. Oh, and one other thing.' He sounded brighter. 'I don't know if it's got anything to do with anything, but you've always told me to look out for stuff that's out of the ordinary. And I kind of think this is?'

Karen rolled her eyes. Her idea of 'out of the ordinary' was often very different from Jason's. He had led a surprisingly sheltered life, all things considered. 'What's that, Jason?'

'I was poking about online. The way you do. And I thought I didn't really know very much about Mary Auld, because it was you that dealt with her when you did the case review, and this time it's been the other team that talked to her. So I had a wee look to see what I could maybe find out about her. And you know what? Her house is on the market. All very discreet, there's no board up and you have to dig past the flashy photos on the estate agent's website. But it's definitely there. It's been up for sale since the New Year.'

He was definitely getting better at this. 'Well done, Jason, that is interesting. Not least because this isn't the best time of year to sell properties out towards the East Neuk. It's way more sensible to wait till the spring when the tourists arrive and decide they need a place by the sea.'

'So maybe she needs the money? Do you think she'll inherit from the brother-in-law?' He sounded eager now.

'That's something we'll have to check out in Paris. It's certainly a possible motive. And she's right on the doorstep.'

'Nobody ever thinks of women when it comes down to brute force, do they?'

Karen gave a dark chuckle. 'I do, Jason. Trust me, I do. Now away down to the Borders while you're still on a roll.'

Daisy looked up from her phone. 'Sounds like you're making some progress?'

Karen shrugged. 'Not really. Just a loose thread.' She stared into the middle distance, considering all Jason had told her. The DNA hold-up was a pain in the arse. They'd become so dependent on the quick and reliable answers the technology provided that they'd forgotten how to explore other possibilities. And, she reminded herself, there were other possibilities.

She keyed the shortcut for River into her phone and tutted when she was shunted on to voicemail. Karen got straight to the point. 'There's a delay on DNA at Gartcosh because half the team are off sick with some bug they picked up in Italy. In the meantime, I have two words for you: Buck Ruxton. We'll talk later, I'm on my way to France.'

River finally escaped from the eager questions of her nine o'clock class and turned her phone on while she made her way through bustling corridors to her office. She had a terrifying mountain of work to get through; the long-running intermittent strike of university teachers had bitten chunks out of her schedule. This wasn't a strike day, but even if she worked flat out there was still no chance of clearing her desk. Her partner, a senior police officer based in the Lake District, was bemused by her commitment to the strike. 'We don't even have the option of striking, we have to put up and shut up,' he'd grumbled as she'd set off at the beginning of the week for her four days in Dundee.

'I'm not striking for myself,' she'd said, weary of the rerun conversation but still determined to make her case. 'I'm striking for the River Wilde who's just finished her doctorate and is trying to build a career. I walked straight into a proper job as a junior lecturer and moved steadily up the ladder. I had security and stability. If I was starting out now, I'd be lucky to get a ten-month contract. Then maybe six months at the other end of the country. Could you run a police force like that? No, I thought not.' Point made yet again, she'd set off and spent half the train journey suffering a kind of heartburn. In all the years they'd been together, there had never been a bone of contention between them that had proved so stubborn.

She spotted the voicemail from Karen right away but waited till she was at her desk with the door closed before she listened to it. Momentarily, she frowned in puzzlement. Then her face cleared and she grinned. She immediately checked her email, and, as she'd hoped, she found a message from Karen with photographs attached. Then she was out of the door and headed for the mortuary.

She pulled on her protective gear then passed through the dissection room, pausing on the way to answer questions from students working on their assigned cadavers. At the door to the locked mortuary where she worked on police cases, she slowed and invited the four students at the nearest bench to join her. A teaching opportunity should never be wasted, after all.

They followed her in and waited while she flicked on the lights and set the video cameras running. Their excitement was palpable, as it always was when they were asked to watch River working on a live case. 'You know the drill,' River said. 'Touch nothing. Eyes and ears only.' They nodded, staring down at the skeletal remains on the table before them.

'We have here the skeletal remains of a young woman. She has sustained a large depressed skull fracture which is the proximate cause of death, in my opinion. The problem we have is ID. There are two likely possibilities for the identity of the deceased. I've already extracted sufficient material from the skeleton to establish DNA, and that would normally resolve the matter.' Heads nodded.

'However. The issue we are faced with is that there is a delay at the DNA labs at the Gartcosh Campus. But even in cold cases, time can be of the essence.' As she spoke, she turned to the computer that was connected to a large screen angled downwards on one wall. She brought up the photos Karen had sent her. 'In the long run, we'll have DNA evidence. But right now it would be helpful to have something that has investigative value, as opposed to probative. In other words, something to help the officers managing the case, rather than solid evidence to present in a courtroom. Any suggestions?'

'We could do a facial reconstruction.' From the student on the left, a gangly young man with a strong Glasgow accent.

'We could. But that's an expensive option for something that's only being used for investigative purposes,' River said.

'Plus it takes quite a long time.' This from a small, neat young woman from the south of England.

'That's right.' River looked up at the photographs. 'Who can tell me about the Buck Ruxton case?' They were far enough into their courses; they should know the landmarks in forensic anatomy by now.

Samira, whose name River remembered because she was the brightest of the bunch, spoke up. 'Buck Ruxton was a doctor in Lancaster in the 1930s. He murdered his wife and their maid. He dismembered them and removed any distinguishing features like fingerprints and teeth. Then he dumped the bits of their bodies in the Scottish Borders.'

'Thanks, Samira. He made such a good job of it that the pathologist and the anatomist thought at first they were looking at a man and a woman, because Bella Ruxton had a strong jaw and features. Then a lab technician found three breasts among the remains. A bit of a giveaway ... So how did they go about identifying the victims?'

Samira smirked. 'Craniofacial photographic super-imposition.'

'Try saying that after a few pints,' the Glasgow lad muttered. But his admiration shone through his apparent nonchalance.

'That's right. They had a good recent studio portrait of Bella Ruxton, a three-quarter profile. They arranged the skull in the same position and X-rayed it. They printed a copy of the photograph in the same scale and superimposed the X-ray on the photo. It was close enough to convince the detectives. It was an important brick in the wall of evidence that convicted Ruxton.'

'So is that what you're going to do?' The Glaswegian again. 'How reliable is that?'

'That is what I'm going to do, yes. When we also use craniofacial morphanalysis, it's over ninety per cent reliable.'

'What's "craniofacial morphanalysis?"' Samira asked.

'It's a set of algorithms that apply an anthroposcopic method to evaluate the shape correlations between the skull and the photograph. Basically, it assigns probabilities to the apparent congruences.' River grinned. 'It's one of the many ways we get to confuse investigators whose only knowledge of statistics is vital ones. So, we've got photographs here of the two potential victims. I'd like you each to take one of the four images and set up the skull in the appropriate position, X-ray it, scale the photos to match the X-ray size and deliver your findings to me by the end of the day. I'll get one of the technicians to bring in the mobile X-ray machine.'

They exchanged looks. 'What? Work on a real case?' the Englishwoman asked, nervous.

'It's not going to end up in court,' River said. 'Remember what I said? Investigative, not probative.' She smiled. 'Now demonstrate that I've not been wasting my time. Show me what you can do.'

20

Jason had driven through Whitbridge and out the far side before he'd actually registered he was there. He'd shot past a huddle of cottages and a farm vehicle showroom, expecting to arrive at something he thought of as a village, and it took him a moment to realise he'd blinked and missed it. He turned round in a farm gateway and headed back, paying more attention to his satnav this time.

There was no place to park outside the row of low-slung dark red sandstone houses so he drove on to the grass verge outside Ettrick Cottage, the home of Thomas Gilmartin. He'd anticipated something much grander. This cramped wee cottage with its tiny windows and a porch the size of a sentry box didn't look like the home of a man who could afford to send his daughter on a silversmithing course. The house was neat enough, but it was Jason's idea of hell. Where was the nearest takeaway? How far did you have to go to get a pint of milk, never mind a pint? What did people *do* out here in the back of beyond?

The path was three short strides from road to doorstep. No doorbell, just an ugly iron knocker. He lifted it and let it fall. No response. He tried again, and this time, from somewhere on his left, he heard a squeak of a voice. 'Are you looking for Tam?'

Jason stepped back, turning to find himself looking over a low wall at an elderly woman stooped over a walking frame, a hand-knitted tam-o'-shanter in rainbow stripes sitting jaunty on her short silver hair. He couldn't believe how fast she'd made it out the door.

'I saw you pull up in the car,' the woman said, peering at him through surprisingly fashionable glasses with heavy black rims.

'I'm looking for Mr Gilmartin,' he said.

'Are you needing some work done? He's awfu' busy at the moment. It's aye the same in the winter. The weather finds a house's weakness every time.'

'No, I just need to talk to him. Do you know where he works?'

She cocked her head, suspicious now. 'How come you need to talk to him and you don't know where he works?'

Reluctantly, Jason fished out his ID. He couldn't help thinking Karen would have got all the information she needed without resorting to showing her hand. 'I'm a police officer.'

She peered at his Police Scotland warrant card. 'There must be some mistake. Tam Gilmartin's a good man. A good neighbour and an honest tradesman. You lot are always down on the working man.'

'He's not in any trouble. I need to talk to him, that's all.' Jason tried to keep his voice level. What was it about old people? His gran was the same. Every simple question turned into an interrogation.

'He'll be at his work.'

'And where might that be?'

She shrugged, a movement that rippled from one shoulder to the other. 'Could be any place. He's a joiner, he goes where the work is,' she said, as if explaining to a small child.

'Do you have a number for him? A mobile?'

'I've got it written down in the house. But you can look it up yourself on your clever wee phone. T. Gilmartin, joiner.'

Jason squeezed out a smile. 'You've been very helpful.' Her look told him she knew she hadn't, and didn't care. Back at the car, he struggled with one bar of signal and eventually found Thomas Gilmartin's number. He had to drive three miles down the road before he had enough reception to make a voice call. Rubbish like this never happened to the boss, he thought bitterly as he waited for Gilmartin to answer. She'd have had that torn-faced crone wrapped around her little finger in no time flat.

'Tam Gilmartin.' At least this one sounded cheerful.

'This is Detective Constable Jason Murray of Police Scotland,' he said. 'I need to speak to you about a case I'm working on. Can I come and meet you?'

A moment's pause. 'Polis? Am in trouble?'

'You're not in any trouble, Mr Gilmartin. I just need to clear something up that I think you can help me with.'

'Oh Christ,' he sighed, all the cheer gone. 'This is Dani, isn't it? What's she gone and done now?'

'If we could just meet?'

'Bairns, eh. Nothing but trouble. I'm in Hawick, fitting out a shop. You can't miss it, it's right opposite Lidl car park.'

The shop in question was a low brick building with boarded-up windows. It didn't look much like a shop to Jason, but the door was open and the sound of a power tool shredded the nerves of anyone passing by. He stepped inside and found a stocky man in dark blue overalls and a tweed flat cap cutting a sheet of plywood. When the saw stopped, he said, 'Mr Gilmartin?'

The man looked up. 'You the polis?' His face was creased and lined from years of frowning at timber and tools.

Jason nodded. 'I spoke to you on the phone.'

'What's the matter, then, son?'

'Is there somewhere we can sit down?' Apart from piles of building material and a sawhorse, there was nowhere obvious.

'Whatever you've got to say, I can hear it standing up. Nothing Dani could get up to would shock me any more. I take it that it's Dani that brings you to my door?' He stepped towards the street, taking a packet of cigarettes from his pocket. He took one out and cupped his hands round the flame of a plastic lighter. He looked up. 'I know it's against the law to smoke at your work, but I don't think you're going to arrest me, right?'

'Right. Mr Gilmartin, what I have to tell you isn't easy to explain. We've discovered human remains that we think might be your daughter.'

His mouth fell open, spilling smoke. All his confidence went with it. 'No,' he breathed. Then, 'No!' he shouted.

The pub was a barn of a place, the sort of dive that was jumping late at night thanks to cheap beer and a range of activities from karaoke to quiz nights based round TV shows. But at this hour of the day, it felt like the zombie apocalypse had arrived. A few shrunken old men lurked on bar stools and the indifferent barmaid restocked the fridges. Jason and Tam Gilmartin huddled over a chipped table in the far corner, Jason with a Coke and Gilmartin with a whisky. His face had fallen in on itself, his eyes like blue stones polished with unshed tears.

'It's not definite, Mr Gilmartin. Like I said, we believe the remains are either those of your daughter or of the friend she was travelling with.'

'Girlfriend,' Gilmartin corrected Jason. 'It'd be a girl-friend. She was never without admirers. She was bonny, but she was wild with it. It's a combination that's hard to resist. I know because her mother was the same.' He sighed. 'You know what they say? Can't live with them, can't live with-out them? That was Lizzie. I was besotted with her, right from the get-go. But she near drove me demented. She loved company. She loved dancing, drinking, taking drugs, taking chances. It was like she couldn't get enough of anything. She was a useless mother. She'd disappear for days at a time, leaving me with the bairn.' He spread his hands in a helpless gesture. 'I had to work, to keep a roof over our heads, food on the table. I used to leave Dani with whoever could take her – my mother, my cousin, the next-door neighbour. And Dani blamed me for Lizzie not being there.' He shook his head and sipped at his drink.

'I'm sorry,' Jason said. 'That must have been hard.'

'It cut me to the bone, son. Soon as she was able, Dani started to run wild like her mother. She'd stay out late, sometimes all night. She announced she was a lesbian and all men were rapists. That didn't go down well in a wee town. We were living in Galashiels back then and some nights I'd walk the streets looking for houses with lights on, just on the off-chance I might see her. It was round about then that Lizzie got sectioned. She'd finally tipped over the edge with the drugs. Got hooked on something that turned a corner in her head and left her in a place where she didn't recognise herself any more, never mind the rest of us.' He dashed his hand across his eyes perfunctorily then drank some more.

So the line Dani Gilmartin had spun to the people in Tullyfolda about her mother bankrolling her had obviously been a lie. There were things Jason wanted to ask but when he consulted his mantra – 'What would Phil do?' – he reckoned he should let Gilmartin talk himself out. 'I don't know how you get past something like that,' he said.

'I moved out of the town and into Whitbridge,' he said. 'Lead us not into temptation, eh, son? And it kind of worked. Dani was shocked into calming down. For a while at least. She decided she wanted to be a silversmith. God knows where she got that idea from. She set her heart on a college course, cost a rake of money I didn't have. Lizzie had burned her way through every penny I'd earned, and then some. But I managed to scrape it together. Sold some antique tools I'd had from my granddad. Off she went to college and she never came back. The last I heard from her was about four years ago. She heaped the blame for Lizzie's state on me and told me she hated me. It was like having the heart carved out of me for a second time.' He swallowed the last of his drink.

'Would you like another one?'

'No thanks, son. I'll need to get back to work and you need a steady hand with a power saw.'

'Her mother died last year, is that right?'

'Aye. Breast cancer. It took her quick in the end. But she'd not been living in her own head for years.'

'And Dani didn't come back for her funeral?'

'I doubt she even knew about it. I'd no idea how to contact her. The phone number I had for her was out of service.' A deep sigh shuddered through him. 'I always hoped she'd come back. Even if it was only to rub my nose in how well she'd done.'

'Don't give up hope, Mr Gilmartin. It may be that this is not Dani. That's why I need a DNA sample from you. So we can compare it.'

He rolled his empty glass back and forth in his strong, scarred fingers. 'I'm not stupid, son. If you're taking this much trouble to find out whose body this is, I'm guessing they didn't die in their sleep. You think they've been murdered, am I right?'

Jason squirmed. 'It's what we call a suspicious death. That doesn't mean it's criminal. If your old granny dies in her sleep and she's not been to the doctor in a while, then it's treated as suspicious till we establish what happened.'

Gilmartin shook his head, a sad smile on his lips. 'You're a kind lad. But we both know this isn't anybody's granny. Either this is my Dani or my Dani had a hand in it. This'll sound harsh, but I think I'd rather mourn her than visit her in prison. It'd be like walling up a cat. Or a raven.'

Jason had no idea what to say. Instead, he took the DNA testing kit from his inside pocket. 'There's only one way to find out for sure,' he mumbled. 'Can we do this, is that OK? It's not intrusive, I just wipe this big cotton bud inside your cheeks.'

'Why not?' There was a resignation in Gilmartin that filled Jason with pity. The man had endured years of suffering and, one way or another, there was more to come. The joiner opened his mouth wide.

Jason glanced around but nobody was paying them any attention. He swabbed Gilmartin's mouth, trying to ignore the sour fumes of whisky and tobacco, popped it into the tube, sealed it and carefully inscribed the details. 'Thanks, Mr Gilmartin. I'll get back to you as quickly as I can, but I should tell you there's a hold-up in the lab. They're short-staffed at the moment.' He took out a card. 'But if you want to talk to me, you can reach me here.' Then he remembered. 'One other thing. Did Dani ever have a dental implant that you know of?'

Gilmartin's face betrayed the answer. 'When she was sixteen. She tripped on the outside stair at her granny's and broke one of her front teeth. She was raging, she thought she'd have to have a plate. But the dentist managed to swing it that she got an implant.' He swallowed. 'You don't need that DNA now, do you?'

There was nothing more to be said. They stood up and shook hands. Now a single tear slipped from Gilmartin's left eye and trickled down, taking a wrinkle as a watercourse. 'The hardest thing, watching her and her mother both, was that they weren't bad people. Just different from the rest of us. Like animals that can't bear captivity.'

21

Driving through Paris in the back of a police car reminded Karen of that Marianne Faithfull song. What was it? 'The Ballad of Lucy Jordan'. Being whisked through Parisian streets had never been on Karen's bucket list, but it was nevertheless one to cut out and keep. They'd been escorted through the chaotic Gare du Nord by one of Les Gautiers whose name she'd failed to catch. He'd hustled them into a car parked right outside, watched over by a gendarme in uniform. They dodged through the traffic with lights flashing and occasional blasts of the sirens. She thought the driver was having the time of his life.

Karen stared out of the window, fascinated by the strangeness of it all. Everything was alien – the shops, the outfits of the pedestrians, the signage, the apparent randomness of the traffic flow. She'd been to Paris once before, for a long weekend with two of the girls from work not long after she'd joined the Historic Cases Unit back in Fife. She remembered mostly peching up hundreds of steps – the Eiffel Tower and Sacré-Cœur – and trailing round some supposedly discount clothes shops rammed with clothes she would never have worn even if they'd had them in her size. She and Phil had talked about coming over for a proper break but, like most of their plans, it had been snatched from them. Which reminded her of Merrick Shand, triggering a bubble of rage to burst inside her head.

The man who had met them was sitting in the front passenger seat and he turned to speak to them in rapid French. Daisy responded in kind. 'Tell him I don't speak French, Daisy. And remind him that I'm the boss.'

Daisy nodded and came out with another stream of French.

'Ah, OK,' the flic said. 'I am sorry, I did not know. I am Giles Chevrolet. Nothing to do with cars. It means "goat farmer". I am one of Les Gautiers, so, the team of Commandant Gautier. I am like a sergeant, I think?'

'I'm a sergeant,' Daisy said. 'DCI Pirie is the same rank as your commandant.'

All very lovely, Karen thought, but time to get a sense of what was happening here. 'Is there a plan of action?'

'Naturally. We have information from your investigation and it seems clear that while we must work hand in hand, this is a Scottish crime. So we are willing to give you full support here in Paris.' He gave her a boyish grin that Karen felt sure he'd practised over the years.

'And that means, what? In practical terms?'

'I know you wish to see Paul Allard's apartment. But before you can do that, we must obtain permission from the *juge d'instruction* – you know this thing, the *juge d'instruction*?'

Karen nodded. 'We have something similar in Scotland. How long will that take?'

'The commandant will see him this afternoon. I think there will be no obstruction. I was also told you have a desire to speak with his colleagues? The men in his jazz group?'

'That's right. But where are we going right now?' Karen asked.

'We meet with his colleagues. They have a … practice room?'

'Rehearsal room,' Karen said. 'Do these guys speak English?'

Chevrolet shrugged, 'I don't know. Maybe. Maybe not.'

Karen tried not to show her frustration. 'But Commandant Gautier, he speaks English?'

Chevrolet gave the charming grin again. 'Better than I do. He has studied with the Metropolitan Police anti-terrorist brigade.'

'So, wouldn't it make more sense to hook me up with the commandant and we can sort out the warrant for the apartment while you whisk Sergeant Mortimer away to talk French to the people who maybe don't speak English?'

Daisy said something rapidly in French which Karen presumed was lending weight to what she'd said. Chevrolet ran a hand through his already perfectly tousled hair. 'This is not my orders.'

'Then maybe you need to speak to your boss and get new ones?' Now it was Karen's turn to smile sweetly.

He turned away and spoke rapidly into his phone. Daisy was frowning intently and she gave Karen a covert thumbs-up. Chevrolet ended the call and said, 'OK. It is not how we do it normally, but Les Gautiers, we make our own rules. It seems that the commandant is about to speak with the judge, so I will take you to the *parquet* – the place of the court. Then we will go to the room of rehearsal and talk to the musicians, no?'

'Thank you. That seems to be the best use of our time. And when you've finished, perhaps Sergeant Chevrolet could bring you back to meet me at Allard's apartment, Daisy. I don't think it'll be a quick search.'

Chevrolet seemed taken aback. She wasn't sure whether that was because he wasn't accustomed to being told what to do by a woman or because he assumed their visit was going to be perfunctory. 'OK,' he said, drawing the word out. He said something to the driver, who muttered something under his breath and threw the car into a terrifying U-turn.

A few minutes later, they stopped outside a small café. Chevrolet jumped out, opened the back door and gestured that she should leave. 'Please, Commandant Pirie, go inside,' he said. 'My boss, he is with the judge, just round the corner. He told me he will meet you here.'

'How will I know him?'

Chevrolet looked her up and down. 'He will know you, madame. You do not look French.'

And with that, he was back in the car. The last thing Karen saw was Daisy's anxious face looking out of the rear window. They'd talked on the train about the approach they'd take to the witnesses. But their preparation had been limited because they had little idea of what they were looking for. Karen was about to find out what kind of cop Daisy was. More to the point, so was Daisy.

Karen managed to order a café au lait. She wondered if she'd have long to wait and whether she could risk something off the menu. She thought a croque monsieur was some form of toastie but she didn't want to chance it. Not that she was particularly conservative about food – she absolutely didn't want to be wrestling with something complicated when Gautier showed up.

She'd been staring at her empty cup for ten minutes or

so when a shadow fell over her. She looked up to find a tall man in a grey suit studying her. He had a thin ascetic look, his neatly parted hair streaked with iron grey at the temples. 'Madame Commandant Pirie?' he said, his voice surprisingly gentle.

Karen stood up hastily. 'Commandant Gautier?'

He nodded courteously and gestured to her cup. 'I see you subscribe to the coffee tendency. Can I order you another?'

'Always,' she said. He ordered their drinks at the counter then returned.

He crossed one long leg over the other and smiled. 'This is a tradition in the French homicide brigades. Every day, we take coffee together. When we can, we eat lunch together. We are friends and we are loyal like a family.' His English was clear and precise, his accent faint. Not for the first time, Karen felt ashamed of her monoglot self.

'The cops I know are more like a real family. Feuds and arguments and rivalries. But my team is very small, and it sounds more like yours.'

'The thing I found hardest when I was seconded to the Met was the execrable coffee in the office. The camaraderie only happened in the pub. I felt very uneasy there.' He raised his cup in a mock toast. 'Here's to coffee.'

'Thank you for your cooperation in this,' Karen said.

He lifted one shoulder in a half-shrug. 'It's your case, really. Allard was a French citizen, it's true. But he was also British, and he was killed in your country. The roots of his murder may be here in France but I think it is more likely that they lie in his past and present connections in Scotland.'

'To be pedantic, we're still calling it a suspicious death. Though my instincts all tell me it was the result of criminal violence, we've not had the final report from the pathologists. But I agree with you that the reason behind Allard's death probably lies in Scotland. I don't know how much you've been told about him, but when he left the UK, he was a person of interest in the disappearance of his brother, Iain Auld.' Gautier leaned forward, twin frown lines appearing between his brows. 'Iain was a senior civil servant, and the two brothers had a violent quarrel the night before Iain vanished without trace. The Met thought he'd probably been murdered. His brother was their prime suspect. Pretty much their only suspect, to be honest. They fixed on him and stopped looking. When he did a runner – sorry, when he left the country, the investigation more or less came to a halt. Did you know about this?'

Gautier shook his head. 'This is news to me. It is surprising. The Legion checks for involvement with crime before it accepts recruits.'

'He was only a suspect, though. He hadn't been arrested or charged. The Met didn't have enough evidence for an arrest warrant. So he'd have come up clean.'

He shrugged. Karen had a moment of delight at the sight of a genuine Gallic shrug. 'This sounds lazy to me. If they had reason enough to stop looking for anyone else after he disappeared, they should have had reason enough to issue a warrant for his arrest, no?'

'You'd think so. But for whatever reason, they didn't. Iain Auld was a very senior Scottish civil servant, so maybe some political pressure was applied? I didn't find any evidence of that when I reviewed the case two years ago.'

Gautier gave a cynical smile. 'If they did their job properly, you would not have found any evidence, though.' Another shrug. 'However he arrived, I understand your man had a blameless career in the Legion, and there is nothing known against him since he left. But what you say reinforces what I already believed. The answers you seek are, I agree, in Scotland. Or maybe London. But not here.'

'Nevertheless, I need to see his apartment. I've got no leads right now. It's my best hope.'

'I understand that. And you can have carte blanche to explore his apartment. I have the permission of the *juge d'instruction*. I will take you there as soon as we have finished our coffee. One of my officers will meet us there and I will leave you in his hands. I have other business to conduct, I hope you are not insulted by this?'

'Not at all. I don't imagine this is high on your list of priorities.' Karen managed not to look as pleased as she felt. She didn't want an officer of her own rank and experience looking over her shoulder. In spite of all her assurances of cooperation and sharing, she preferred to be in control of the case information. She'd let Gautier know when she'd put the pieces together. She didn't want him taking over, casting his own interpretation over her findings. In one respect, ACC Ann Markie had been right about her – she didn't always play well with others.

Paul Allard's apartment was in a narrow street leading down the hill from the Place de l'Odéon. Karen caught a glimpse of the impressive portico of the theatre, took in the restaurant on the corner and thought this looked like a neighbourhood it'd be pleasant to live in. The buildings were clean and well-maintained, the shops at street level were small businesses selling everything from second-hand books to imported Chinese porcelain. A uniformed gendarme stood outside a pair of massive wooden doors halfway down the street, and Gautier double-parked outside, effectively blocking the street.

He led Karen over to the officer, who had a similar air of haplessness to Jason. Gautier fired a stream of swift French at him and he nodded like a clockwork toy. He stammered a reply and the commandant said something in return. He turned to Karen. 'OK. This is Officer Henri. He has the key from the concierge. He will escort you to the apartment and wait with you. He will not interfere with your search.' He gave a mischievous smile. 'Unless there is something you cannot reach.' He held out a hand and they shook.

'I appreciate your assistance. I'll make sure you get a full report.'

He winked. 'Full enough to cover both of us will do fine. And if there is something you need us to follow up, let me know. Good luck, Madame Commandant Pirie.' And he was gone, waving casually at the trapped driver glaring murderously at his car.

Karen followed the silent officer through the doors and into a small courtyard. He unlocked a door that led to a stairwell and they climbed flight after flight, passing a pair of doors on each landing. Finally there was nowhere further to climb. He unlocked the far door and gestured to her to enter.

She breathed in deeply, and not just from the climb. She caught the staleness of air undisturbed for days, the faint smell of cooked food, and a hint of lavender which she traced immediately to a bunch of dried flowers stuffed haphazardly into a vase on a table by the door. So far, she'd only known James Auld as a corpse. Now she had a chance to discover the living man.

22

Hand-delivering the DNA swab from Tam Gilmartin might just move things along more quickly. It was, Jason thought, worth a try. He could give them his best hangdog, put-upon look and maybe one of the remaining technicians would take pity on him. Especially if they'd had an encounter with Karen in the past.

In the event, he didn't get near a human being. There was a sign sellotaped to the door of the DNA lab: samples through the slot please. He tried ringing the bell but there was no response.

Despondent, he was about to leave when he remembered that Tamsin had Susan Leitch's laptop. He wondered whether she was making any headway with it. He found her at her desk, an open packet of Jaffa Cakes by her left hand. She glanced over her shoulder and stuffed them into her desk drawer. 'Don't tell,' she said. 'It's against the law to have biscuits next to keyboards.'

'But are they biscuits?'

Tamsin swung round on her chair and grinned. 'The perennial question. The VAT tribunal decision of 1991 was supposed to settle that. Cakes, they said. But Jase, can you in your heart of hearts agree with them?'

He wished he'd kept his mouth shut. Tamsin terrified him. He never knew when she was serious and when she was joking. The fact that her hair made a different statement every time he saw her only made it worse. Today the top of her head was dyed blue and white, the saltire of the Scottish flag. Was it ironic? Or a post-Brexit slap-down? 'I don't actually like them,' he said.

'So why are you here, if not to steal my biscuits?'

'I was passing and I wondered if you'd found anything interesting on Susan Leitch's laptop?'

'Depends on what you find interesting. There's some cool cycle routes in Perthshire and Grampian. And some recipes for taco fillings that had my mouth watering.' His face fell and she took pity on him. 'Karen said you were looking for emails between Susan and Amanda McAndrew.'

'That's right. Have you found anything?'

'Yes and no.'

'What does that mean?'

'You know how you found a skeleton in the VW camper? And that told you there had been an entire body there? Well, I've found the skeletal traces of a whole wedge of emails between the pair of them. But somebody has deleted them at some point. So what we have left is fragments scattered round the hard drive like confetti.'

'That doesn't sound good.'

'I'll be honest with you, Jase. Putting that together is like doing a jigsaw when the dog's eaten half the sky. It'd be beyond most techies.' She turned back to the screen. 'But I am not most techies. I am a fucking genius. I've got a long way to go with this but I can tell you, for example, that Susan sent an email to Amanda somewhere around five years ago that contained the fragment, "toilet rolls and balsamic vinegar". Which I'm guessing is one of those, "Can you pick up on the way home?" messages, not some coded message about obscure sexual practices. Though I could be wrong. There's no telling with Scottish lesbians.'

Jason hated that he could feel a scarlet flush creeping up his neck. 'Any idea how long it'll take?'

'Hard to say.' Tamsin was serious now. 'I've got a program running in the background. Could be tomorrow, could be six weeks, could be never. Depends how good a housekeeper Susan was when it came to her computer. On the plus side, most people are completely rubbish at it. If they let their houses get in the state they leave their hard drives in, you wouldn't visit without a hazmat suit.'

'OK. Thanks. Sorry to bother you.'

'I'll try to remember not to tell Karen,' she said absently, already lost in her screen.

It had never occurred to him that she would. Now he had one more thing to worry about.

On the other side of the Channel, Daisy wasn't faring much better. James Auld's fellow jazzmen were clearly distressed at the news of his death. They all protested that they'd do whatever they could to help catch whoever had done this to him. But none of them could shed any light on who that might have been. Two of them had been friends with him since they'd served in the Foreign Legion together. Yes, sometimes Paul had argued with other men, but it had come to nothing. 'He was an easy kind of guy,' the drummer said. 'Some guys in the Legion, they're always looking for a fight. He wasn't like that.'

'Don't get the wrong idea, he wasn't a coward,' the bass player chipped in. 'He'd stand up for himself. But he was good at taking the sting out of a row, you know?'

'No enemies that you can think of?' Daisy was almost pleading. They looked at each other and shook their heads. She thought they were genuinely stumped. 'What about his love life? Did he upset anyone? Steal someone's girlfriend? Have an affair with somebody's wife?'

The drummer laughed. 'He was like all of us when he was in the Legion. Like a monk except when he wasn't. We all used hookers when there was no choice. And we all had one-night-stands and meaningless interludes from time to time.'

'But he wasn't in the Legion any more,' Daisy pointed out.

The keyboard player gave her a shrewd look. 'He has a lover. But not here in Paris.'

The drummer again. 'Pascale Vargas. She's quite a catch. She owns a jazz club in Caen. A nice little earner. And she's a good-looking woman. Her and Paul, they hit it off from the first time we played there.' He scoffed. 'Fucking sax. It's like catnip to women. Should be called a sexophone.' Suddenly he looked alarmed. 'Not that I care about Pascale, don't get me wrong, I have my own woman.'

'Paul didn't cut anybody out,' the keyboard man insisted. 'Pascale was single when they got together.'

This was going nowhere, Daisy thought. The only thing she was getting out of it was an extensive revision session in colloquial French. 'Did he ever talk about his life before the Legion?'

The drummer laughed. 'There are two kinds of men in the Legion. The ones who never stop talking about how hard their lives were before they joined, and the ones who never start. I don't know anything about Paul's reasons for signing up. All I know is that he was Scottish and when he arrived he had a dog of an accent and not a curse word to his name. He soon fixed both of those.'

The keyboard player leaned forward earnestly. 'We really want to help. We loved the guy. But we didn't talk about why somebody might want to kill us. We talked about music and football and movies and whether we were going to drive or take the train to next week's gigs.' He spread his hands in a shrug. 'Sorry.'

'Did he say anything about what he was going to do back in Scotland? Who he was going to see?'

The bass player frowned. 'I asked him if he still had family back there. He didn't answer. He just said he was hoping to see somebody he hadn't seen for years.'

Daisy's instincts sprang to attention. 'He didn't say who?'

'I didn't ask. It was none of my business, after all. If he wanted me to know, he would have told me.' He gave her a crooked smile. 'I think men and women are very different when it comes to sharing their lives. Maybe you should go to Caen and talk to Pascale. If he said more to anyone, I would think it would be her, no?'

Daisy bloody hoped so. It was a long way to come to find themselves stuck in a cul-de-sac.

23

No one had ever accused Karen of being tidy, but even she would have been driven mad by James Auld's flat. Every surface in his living room was covered with teetering piles of books, sheet music and music magazines, a pile of concert ticket stubs. The only exception was a laptop-sized space on a small table in one corner. The shelves were crammed with CDs and vinyl. Three gleaming saxophones stood in a line on stands. Glasses that had once obviously held red wine perched in random spots. Either Auld had been rebelling against all those years of a spartan military regime or else it had simply failed to knock his natural hoarding tendency out of him.

Where there was wall space between the shelves, there were framed photographs. Auld in action with his quintet. Auld in his Foreign Legion uniform, smiling knowingly from underneath the peak of his kepi. Other jazz musicians she didn't recognise. And by the window, with its view of roof terraces and tiles, a photograph of the Auld brothers in their twenties, arms slung round each other's shoulders, grinning at the camera. Beneath it, a wedding photograph. Karen peered at it. Iain and James Auld were groom and best man; the smiling bride, a younger version of the Mary

Auld she'd interviewed during the case review. No sign there of the sort of animosity that led to murder. Not that there was any significance in that. Too often she'd seen what happened when love twisted and turned into shapes of rage.

The kitchen that led off the living room was tiny. It looked as if James Auld had done little more than make coffee and store bottles of red wine here. Who could blame him? There were cafés and bars on every street corner. There was no need for a man to cook for himself if he lacked the inclination. She opened the fridge. Two bags of coffee beans; a Tupperware box containing three half-consumed cheeses she couldn't name; a half-empty jar of artichokes in olive oil. Five bottles of beer.

She moved back to the cramped hallway. Between the coats hanging on the wall and the young gendarme, there was barely room to turn around. She gestured to him to move aside so she could go through the pockets. Three pairs of gloves, some crumpled receipts for a few euros, two tubes of lip salve. Karen sighed and stuck her head into the bathroom. It looked clean and surprisingly neat. Toiletries sat on a long shelf, towels hung folded on a rail on the door of the shower.

The final door led from the hall into a bedroom. Karen had expected the same chaos as the living room but she was surprised to find the same neatness as the bathroom. The duvet had been shaken out over the double bed, the pillows plumped up. One end of the room was curtained off, acting as a wardrobe. Jackets, shirts and trousers in shades of black and dark blue hung neatly and a small chest of drawers contained a couple of sweaters, underwear and T-shirts. Five pairs of shoes sat in a line along the bottom. He didn't have many clothes; it looked as if he spent his money on music.

On the wall opposite the bed was a long mirror and next to it, a small framed oil seascape. She took a quick photograph with her phone. Presumably this was the one he'd chosen from his brother's possessions but she'd better check at some point with Mary Auld. Just to dot the I's and cross the T's. And find out where it was, in case it might have some relevance. Though what that might be, she had no idea.

A chair sat tucked beneath the dormer window, a light sweater thrown over the back. The only other furniture in the room was a bedside table. A fat paperback sat under a goose-necked lamp. Karen picked it up. *Norman Granz: The Man Who Used Jazz for Justice* by Tad Hershon. She'd never heard of either of them, but that wasn't surprising. Once you got past Ella Fitzgerald, it was like a foreign language to her. Idly she opened the drawer, expecting nothing, merely putting off her return to the chaos of the living room.

A buff-coloured cardboard document wallet lay underneath a pair of earphones. Karen stretched out a gloved hand and eased it out. She opened the flap and took out the contents. At first glance, they made little sense. A photograph, a newspaper article printed off the internet, a cryptic scribble on the back of it, an article about art prices and an old hardback of Ian Fleming's *On Her Majesty's Secret Service*, complete with a pretty battered dust jacket.

She sat down on the bed and studied them more closely. The photograph showed two men from mid-torso upwards. They were in a close embrace, arms around each other, nose to nose, eyes locked, smiles mirroring each other. And they were naked. There was no mistaking the nature of the moment. Lovers, caught in the act of affection.

One of them was Iain Auld. There was no mistaking that either. She turned it over. In faint pencil, she read, *This* between the endpaper and the back board of OHMSS. Now I know who the man was.

'That's more than I do,' Karen muttered under her breath. She picked up the book and opened it at the back. She could see the endpaper had been carefully separated from the board. She guessed it had been done with a scalpel, or something similar. She could see the faint outline of the photograph on the endpaper, around ten by fifteen centimetres. That must have been what alerted James Auld to its presence.

So it appeared Iain Auld had a secret male lover. That hardly made him unique in the ranks of British civil servants. But seriously, she thought, how could it have anything to do with his disappearance? It might have been embarrassing but it wasn't criminal, unless the other man was a Russian spy. Even then, what would a foreign power want with an insider's view of the Scotland Office?

She put the book down and picked up the printout. It was a four-year-old news story from the *Guardian* about a fire destroying an art gallery in Brighton. The article said it had housed the best and most extensive collection of contemporary British art outside London. Art worth tens of millions of pounds had gone up in smoke and police suspected arson. The words were accompanied by photographs of the blaze, flames shooting into the night, splashing the sea with scarlet and gold. A third picture showed a crowd of spectators, as excited as children on bonfire night. There was a headshot of billionaire industrialist Simon Goldman, whose collection had formed the core of the museum's contents. He was an elderly man who bore no resemblance to the stranger in the photo. Karen had absolutely no idea what it all meant. As far as she knew, neither Iain nor James Auld had any connection to Brighton. Maybe that was where the mystery man lived. Maybe he'd worked in the gallery? And where exactly would that take her, if it were the case?

'Bloody nowhere,' she muttered. She turned over the cutting. In the same neat hand as the writing on the photograph, she read:

12 NT
Ouds
Hilary 92/3

Karen rolled her eyes. '12 NT' looked like one of those obscure notations you got in newspaper descriptions of bridge games. She'd never played anything more complicated than whist, so she had no idea whether it was anything to do with cards. She googled 'Oud' and discovered it was a thirteen-stringed instrument like a lute that hailed from the Middle East. For all she knew, it was a mainstay of Lebanese jazz. And who was Hilary? It could be a man or a woman, a first name or a surname. Back in 1992, Iain Auld must have been in his very early twenties, James a couple of years older. Was this someone Iain knew from university? He'd done his first degree at Edinburgh, then a masters at Oxford. She didn't remember the name Hilary cropping up in the files she'd pored over two years before.

What the hell was going on? She was a good detective, she knew that. But she wasn't Sherlock Bloody Holmes. Cryptic clues and the French Foreign Legion? This was the kind of bollocks she and Phil used to rip the piss out of, curled up on the sofa with Sunday-night television. Standing in a Paris atelier trying to make sense of some sub-Agatha Christie nonsense? That wasn't proper coppering, not the way she understood it.

She put everything back in the folder and stuck it in her backpack. She had no compunction about keeping it to herself. If it meant nothing to her, it would mean even less to Commandant Gautier. But in spite of her inability to make sense of the contents of the document wallet, she felt certain it was connected to what had brought James Auld back to Scotland, and to his death.

That would have to wait. For now, she couldn't ignore that anarchic disarray in the living room.

Karen had barely finished the first pile next to the sofa when Daisy turned up with Chevrolet in tow. He whistled softly when he took in the task before them. 'My wife would kill me if I tried to live like this,' he said.

'But our guy didn't have a wife,' Karen pointed out. 'He lived the way he wanted. He was untidy, not dirty. The kitchen's clean, the bedroom's like a monk's cell.' She turned to Daisy. 'How did you get on with the band?'

Daisy pulled a face. 'Waste of time. Considering how much time these guys spend together, they know amazingly little about each other's lives. It just confirms all the clichés about men being from Mars and women being from Venus. If I'd spent this long with any of my female friends I'd know every detail of their day-to-day, as well as their entire emotional history and their relationships with their parents and siblings.'

Chevrolet shrugged. 'Different priorities. I can tell you who won Ligue 1 every year this century. Ladies, feel free to engage with the life of Paul Allard. I will leave you with my colleague for now. Perhaps we can meet for breakfast? Where are you staying?'

Karen looked at Daisy. 'Where did you book us in?'

Daisy flushed. 'You didn't tell me to book a hotel.'

'So where did you think we were going to sleep? Under a bridge? When I told you to sort out the travel, I assumed you'd have realised we needed somewhere to stay.' Karen shook her head, cross. 'Even Jason can manage that.'

Chevrolet was clearly enjoying the moment. He had a tiny smirk that Karen had a powerful urge to rearrange. 'Maybe something we men do better. Don't worry, Commandant Pirie. There are some hotels in the next street, we use them when we have to make arrangements for visitors. I will go now and find you accommodation.' He gave a small bow from the waist. 'I shall return.'

Karen waited till she heard the front door close. 'He's a very annoying man.'

'Helpful, though,' Daisy pointed out.

'That's part of what makes him annoying. I wish you'd thought things through and not left us any further in his debt.'

'I'm sorry,' Daisy said. 'I've never been part of an operation like this.'

'And there was really nothing of interest from the boys in the band?'

'Right at the end, I asked if Auld had said anything about his trip to Scotland. Apparently, he said he was hoping to see someone he hadn't seen for years. But that's all. Could that mean something?'

Karen shrugged. 'That could mean anything.' Before she could continue, her phone rang. She glanced at the screen and gave a wry smile. 'News, with a bit of luck. But not in this case.'

She stepped out of the room as she took the call, leaving

the young gendarme confused as to who he should be keeping an eye on. 'River,' Karen said, crossing to the bedroom.

'How's Paris?'

'Very French. How's Dundee?'

'Not nearly French enough. So, that was an interesting exercise, doing the superimposition. I set it as an exercise for some of my students. And it turned out to be a bit more complicated than I expected.' She paused for effect.

'How?' Karen asked obediently.

'If you take away the very different hairstyles, the two women actually resemble each other facially. But then, it's not unusual for people to be attracted to someone who looks quite like them. So when the students did the superimpositions, it wasn't entirely straightforward. In the end, it came down to a significant difference in the zygomatic arch.'

Karen sighed. 'I knew you were going to blind me with science.'

'Cheekbone, to the likes of you. Dani's the one with the cheekbones. Amanda's are much flatter and less distinctive.'

'So which of them matches the skull, River?'

'The assumptive identity of the skull in the camper van is Daniella Gilmartin.'

'You can't be more certain?'

'Assumptive, remember? But if it's one of those two women, it's definitely not Amanda McAndrew.'

Karen sighed. 'And that raises more questions than answers.'

'Why? Is there a problem?'

'Dani Gilmartin appears to be very much alive. She's a practising silversmith with a website. It's a bit hard to pull that off from the other side of the grave.'

'I'm sorry it's not the answer you wanted. But remember, *assumptive*. Daniella Gilmartin isn't the only woman on the planet with dark hair and lovely cheekbones, Karen.'

24

Not for the first time, Jason's initial response to Karen's information was, 'I don't get it.' Dani Gilmartin's website showed pictures of her work. There were instructions on how to buy examples of those earrings, bracelets and necklaces. There was a page where you could upload your own designs and Dani would come back to you with how she could incorporate them into a piece. There was a blog, which seemed to be updated every six weeks or so. The last entry had been a fortnight ago. In it, Dani had spoken about a walk through a January wood. There were photographs of skeleton leaves and bare branches against a winter sky which she said would provide inspiration for new work. There were messages from satisfied customers, the most recent dating from just before Christmas.

All this he'd explained to Karen when she'd called him from Paris with the results of River's analysis. She'd thought for a moment, then said, 'Two possibilities that I can see. Either the website is smoke and mirrors and there is no jewellery. Or else Amanda has picked up enough knowledge about silversmithing to assume Dani's identity and her business.'

'So how do we find out? There's no address on the website. Just an email.'

'Did the blog say where she went for her January walk? Any details?'

'I don't think so. I think it was the kind of thing you could write about anywhere.'

'Check it out. And go back through the blog entries and see if there's any clues.' Her voice had slowed, a sign he recognised. A smart idea was about to emerge. 'There's one easy way to find if the website is for real. It's about time you bought Eilidh a wee present, isn't it?'

'You want me to buy something off the website? It's not cheap stuff, boss. I think the lowest priced earrings were something like forty quid,' he protested.

'Surely she's worth it?' He thought he could hear a tease in Karen's voice but he wasn't sure. He waited and was rewarded. 'You can claim it on expenses, Jason. I'll vouch for it.'

'Thanks, boss.'

'And it'll give us an answer, one way or another.'

'I got a DNA sample off her dad, by the way. I took it to Gartcosh myself, because of everything being held up by this bug. Oh, and he told me she had a dental implant. A front tooth. From when she was a teenager.'

Typical of Jason to leave the best till last. With some people, that might be a deliberate choice. With Jason, it was simply because that was the last thing he'd learned. 'That clinches it, then.'

'That's what I thought. But belt and braces, right? That's what we do?'

'It is. Good job, Jason.'

'Thanks. So how's the Paris thing going?'

'Not very productive, to be honest.'

Jason had a moment of gratification at that news, then

swiftly hated himself for it. It wasn't a competition with Daisy, after all. He was Karen's wingman, they were a team. Daisy was just temporary, drafted in because she spoke the language and hers was the team that happened to catch the live end of the case. 'Sorry to hear that, boss.'

'We've got a mountain of stuff to sort through in Auld's living room. That's going to see us through to bedtime, I suspect. And in the morning we're off to Caen, wherever that is. I'd like to get home tomorrow night. It's not that I don't trust you, but I hate working a case at a distance.' He heard a muffled voice in the background. 'Right,' Karen said. 'I've got to get back to work here. Get that blog read and see if you can find any clues as to where our so-called Dani is based.'

'Do you want me to find out where the website's registered?'

There was a pause. 'Don't you need a warrant for stuff like that?'

'No, there's websites you can sign up for and they'll tell you where the URL is registered and you can find out who hosts the site and everything,' Jason said, ridiculously pleased that he knew something she didn't.

'How do you know that?' Karen sounded like she was struggling not to sound amazed.

'Ages ago, I was trying to track down somebody that ripped off Ronan. All we had was the website address. I thought Tamsin would know how to do it, so I asked her and she told me. It's totally straightforward. Do you want me to do that, then?'

Karen stared at her phone. Obviously, 'what would Phil do?' was having the right sort of effect. Not only was Jason

172

using his initiative, he'd found the confidence to tell her as much. Maybe she should adopt the same approach. What *would* Phil do? She twisted her mouth in a half-smile and sent Jason a text of two thumbs-up emojis.

Back in the living room, Daisy was sorting through another stack of sheet music and magazines. She glanced up, glum. 'I think this is a waste of time,' she muttered.

'Probably, but we've got to do it.' Karen hunkered down by a fresh pile of newspapers and books.

'We don't even know what we're looking for.'

Karen gave their chaperone a quick look. 'We'll know if we find it. A letter, a photograph, a newspaper cutting.'

'How will we know if it's important? Or even relevant?'

'We use our common sense. If it's anything to do with his brother, or visits to Scotland, or something that doesn't fit with the rest of his life.' She was, she knew, whistling in the dark herself. But it didn't help junior officers if they thought you were as much at sea as they were. She began to work her way through the pile, tossing over any letters in French to Daisy, who swiftly dismissed them.

'Someone offering to sell him a soprano sax ... An appointment a year ago with his doctor to discuss the results of blood tests ... a reply from an art dealer in Dublin to an inquiry about an artist ... a letter from the Legion about his pension ... ' And so on.

Shortly after nine, Giles Chevrolet returned. They were on the final two piles of papers and had found nothing more interesting than James Auld's tax returns. 'I have two rooms for you in the next street,' he said.

'Thanks. We're nearly finished here.'

'Did you find anything I should know about?'

Karen smiled, shaking her head. 'It's been a complete

waste of time. You should be grateful we were here to do the dirty work for you.'

'I am so grateful that I will take you to dinner. There's a very fine bistro round the corner. The gendarmerie are friends of the house.'

Over a platter of charcuterie and cheese in a wood-panelled bar with low ceilings, Chevrolet interrogated Karen about the Iain Auld case. 'The more you tell me, the more convinced I am that the answers you seek will not be found here,' he said, topping up their glasses from a carafe of ruby red wine.

'Even so, I still want to go to Caen to talk to his girlfriend. It's possible he spoke to her about what he intended to do in Scotland.' Weary though she was, Karen wasn't about to fold. When she dug her heels in, they stayed dug. Chevrolet was smart enough to recognise an immovable object when he found one.

'Very well. We will go tomorrow morning. We'll pick you up at the hotel at nine thirty. There is no point in leaving earlier, not unless we want to deprive Madame Vargas of her beauty sleep. Nightclub owners don't get up much before noon.'

Karen couldn't argue with that. Her body craved sleep now and the thought of an early start made her feel faintly sick. They finished their wine and Chevrolet insisted on walking them back to the hotel, chattering all the way about the charms of Caen and the Normandy beaches. They managed to disengage from him after they'd checked into the small private hotel, only because the ancient lift was barely large enough for the two women.

'I thought he'd never go,' Karen said.

'I know. Who knew there was so much to hear about Caen?'

'"The chateau was built by William the Conqueror before

he conquered your country."' Karen imitated Chevrolet's accent. 'Not my country, pal.'

Daisy laughed. 'Just as well you didn't get into that.'

They peered at the door numbers in the dimly lit corridor. Karen found hers first. 'Dump your stuff in your room and come back. There's something I want to show you.' Daisy looked startled.

Karen tutted and rolled her eyes. 'From the apartment. I didn't want to share it with the French because it's obviously to do with the Iain Auld case.'

Relieved, Daisy hurried off. Karen found herself in a fussily decorated room with a double bed and a wardrobe that was about the same size. An armchair with worn tapestry upholstery and an upright chair tucked under the smallest desk she'd ever seen completed the overstuffed impression. She'd barely tossed her backpack on the bed when Daisy knocked.

'Grab a seat.' Karen took out the folder. 'I found this in James Auld's bedside table. I decided not to share because I don't think it's got anything to do with his life in France.' She spread the contents on the bed and Daisy pulled the chair close to the bed to inspect them more closely.

'Is that James Auld?' she asked hesitantly, pointing at the photograph.

'No. It's his brother Iain. There's a resemblance, I agree, but trust me, I looked at enough pictures of Iain two years ago to know the difference.'

'OK. So who's the other man?'

'I have no idea. There's no name on the back of the photo.'

Daisy continued to stare at it, frowning. 'That's a very intimate photo. I mean, they look like they're together. Don't you think?'

Karen nodded. 'I'd say so. There's definitely something about it that says "lovers" rather than "friends". It's not two guys mucking about on a rugby club night out.'

'Do you think Mary knew about it?'

'Well, that's the question, isn't it? She never gave the slightest hint that there was any issue in the marriage. But who knows what goes on under that smooth, self-contained surface? Very Edinburgh. There's the swan sailing serenely along, no clue that under the surface the feet are paddling away like buggery fuck.' Karen pulled the other chair forward and threw herself into it. 'You've seen her more recently than me. What did you make of the lovely Mary?'

Daisy shrugged. 'She was upset about James. Jamie, she calls him. But she held it all together.' She smiled. 'Like you said. Very Edinburgh.'

'If she did know her husband was leading a secret gay life, some might say it would be a motive for doing away with him. The embarrassment, the insult, the duplicity, the loss of status.' Karen ran a hand through her hair. 'But these days? Even ten years ago? Sure, it would have been humiliating, but only for about five minutes. It's not like they were in the public eye. They could have separated and each gone their own way and that would have been the end of it. I don't see it myself.'

'All the same . . .' Daisy looked thoughtful. 'Where was she the night he went missing?'

'Good question. She claimed at the time she'd been at home in Edinburgh. She'd had a quick drink in the early evening with friends but there was nobody to vouch for her later on. Same absence of an alibi the next day. She worked part-time and the following day was one of her non-working days. She said she'd been at home all day, cooking. Filling the freezer.' Karen's incredulity was obvious. 'Apparently she'd let things get a bit low.' She shook her head. 'All credit to the officer who interviewed her – he checked the freezer. His report said there were a dozen Tupperware containers all neatly labelled with the contents and the right date.'

'That proves nothing,' Daisy said. 'She's a smart woman.'

'Really smart people don't bother with convoluted plots involving freezer labels and driving through the night to London. They push their victim down a flight of steep stairs or off the side of a mountain, or they slip something lethal in the foraged berries. And unless she was in league with James, how could she have set it up so the two of them had a blazing row the night before Iain disappeared? It's way too complicated.'

'Maybe she *was* in league with James? Maybe they wanted rid of Iain so they could be together?'

Karen rolled her eyes. 'That's what divorce is for, Daisy. Whatever this photograph is all about, I don't think it's much of a motive for Mary.'

Daisy frowned. 'He was a senior civil servant, though. Top level in the Scotland Office. Could he not have been blackmailed over this?'

'Twenty years ago, maybe. But ten years ago, in the Scotland Office? It wasn't even a Tory Secretary of State, it was a Lib Dem, and they're not exactly noted for their persecution of the LGBT community.'

'So it's irrelevant.' Daisy looked sulky.

'I didn't say that. I just don't know *how* it's relevant.' Karen moved the photograph aside and unfolded the news-paper offprint. 'A fire in a modern art gallery four years ago. What's that got to do with anything?'

Daisy skimmed the article. 'Mary Auld's got a lot of

paintings on her walls,' she said dubiously. 'They look quite modern.'

'I remember. I don't know much about art, but I don't think the Aulds' paintings were like the ones that went up in flames. This gallery' – Karen tapped the paper – 'seems to be all about contemporary artists. What do they call them? Damien Hirst and Tracey Emin?'

'Conceptual art. But there were paintings here too, it mentions that.'

'Then there's this note.' She pulled out the sheet of paper with the cryptic message.

12 NT
Ovds
Hilary 92/3

'Does that mean anything at all to you? I have not got a scooby.'

'Maybe Hilary's the guy in the picture? That can be a man's name too, right? Maybe that's when they first met? And then they got together again?'

It wasn't a bad idea, Karen thought, disgruntled that she hadn't thought of it herself. This case was messing with her head.

Daisy picked up the final piece of paper. It was a printout from a website that reported the prices paid at auction for a list of paintings. They ranged from a small sketch by Picasso to a swathe of artists she'd never heard of. She frowned. 'One of those letters in the flat was from an art dealer. Remember? In Dublin.'

'Fuck,' Karen exclaimed. 'How did that not set alarm bells ringing?' She groaned. 'This is what happens when I don't get enough sleep. I miss obvious connections. Do you remember the name of the artist Auld was asking about?'

'I didn't pay attention, sorry. It didn't seem important at the time.'

'No reason why you should have thought so. We'll have to go back and get the letter.'

'We don't have the keys. And it's nearly midnight.'

'Not right now, obviously. We'll have to go back in the morning. Which means explaining to Gautier why we want to go back.' Karen stood up and moved restlessly round the room. 'I can't believe I missed that.'

'It happens to all of us,' Daisy ventured. Karen glared at her.

'Maybe if we leave it till after we've spoken to Pascale,' she said slowly, thinking out loud. 'We can always say she referred to something that reminded us of one of the letters in the flat. Then I won't have to admit to walking off with evidence Les Gautiers will think I should have shared with them.' Daisy looked surprised. Karen grinned. 'What? Nobody told you I can be devious when I have to be?'

'They told me one or two things, but not that. You must've been devious enough for them not to realise they'd been had over.'

Karen gave her an appraising look. 'Aye, right. You'll go far, Daisy. But right now, we both need to go to our beds. I'll see you downstairs at breakfast at eight. Get some sleep. I'm going to need you at your sharpest tomorrow. If anybody knew James Auld's secrets, it will have been the lovely Pascale.'

25

Thursday, 20 February 2020

For once, Karen slept long and hard. The insomnia that had plagued her since Phil's death and had turned her into a night walker of whatever city she found herself in had recently begun to abate. It was still unpredictable; going to bed in a state of exhaustion was no guarantee that sleep would come, nor was feeling wide awake an indication that she'd inevitably stay in that state. When she awoke just after seven, she was almost disappointed. It was as if she'd been cheated of the chance to get to know a different Paris from the one she'd traversed in daylight.

But as often happened, she woke to new insights, fresh ideas chasing themselves round her head. Jason's idea of tracking down the source of Dani Gilmartin's website was solid, no getting away from that. It wasn't the only answer, however. There were plenty of other, simpler ways to track someone down if you had the resources of a police officer. Karen shook her head. What was wrong with her? This wasn't the first time she'd juggled more than one case at a time. But this time, she was struggling to focus.

In the shower, she ran through a mental checklist of

instructions for Jason. She went straight to her laptop to compose an email to him, but what leapt out at her as soon as she opened her email program was a message from Hamish. 'Later,' she muttered and began her message to Jason. Was this the underlying issue that was eating away at her concentration? Or had her encounter with Merrick Shand unsettled her at a deeper level than she was willing to acknowledge?

Whatever, she had to get a grip. The last thing she could afford was to screw up either case. Whether Daisy Mortimer knew it or not, she was Ann Markie's fifth column inside the HCU and Karen knew better than to give the Dog Biscuit any ammunition to shoot her down.

She towelled her hair and ran her fingers through it in her usual vain attempt to persuade it to behave, wrapped herself in the towel and started typing before she forgot what she wanted to say.

Hi Jason

Good suggestion yesterday about tracing the website address. When you talk to the site host, keep it very low key – don't mention the seriousness of the case. If you can get away with not even mentioning you're a polis, so much the better. We do not want to ring any alarm bells and have the target of our investigation do a runner before we get close.

There are also other avenues to pursue. If 'Dani Gilmartin' is trading, she'll have to have a bank account. If your attempt at a fake purchase works, you'll get some banking info, even if only from your credit card company. She might be VAT registered, so talk to HMRC.

At some point she will have acquired a National
Insurance number. See where that gets you. Also try
the Passport Office – let's see when her passport
was issued and if it's been renewed. Also DVLA – she
probably has a vehicle registered to her. At least one
of these avenues should produce an address. And I
can't emphasise enough the need to be low key here.
The skeleton appears to be the real Dani Gilmartin,
so someone is using her identity, and the chances are
it's the person who killed her. It's likely to be Amanda
McAndrew but we don't know that for sure.

Keep me posted. I'm hoping to get back to the UK in
the next 24 hours.

Karen

She sent the message and started to close the laptop lid.
But Hamish's name was impossible to ignore. If she didn't
read his response, it would niggle all day. Why could he not
just do as she'd asked and leave it till she got back? Tight-
lipped, she opened the email.

Hi Karen. Got your message. Appreciate your candour.
We can work this out. Let me know when you get
back and we'll talk. Hope you get some quality
French scoff! Hx

If she had to deal with a response, this was a decent one.
She reminded herself that he was good at getting what he
wanted without ever appearing pushy. 'God save me from
reasonable men,' she muttered under her breath.

She found Daisy in the dining room, tucking into
a croissant loaded with butter and jam. Karen helped

182

herself to a chunk of fresh baguette and a selection of cheeses and cold meats. It was like a rerun of dinner, which was fine by her. There was already a pot of coffee on the table; as far as Karen was concerned, this was about as good as it got in the absence of bacon, black pudding and tattie scones.

'I got a text from the drummer in the band,' Daisy said. 'He spoke to Pascale. She'll be in the club from noon onwards, like Chevrolet predicted.'

Karen nodded, chewing the delicious bread, trying not to make happy foodie noises. She swallowed. 'Let's hope she's got something useful for us.'

Chevrolet was prompt to the minute. Karen insisted on taking their bags with them. 'If it's possible, I'd like to get back tonight,' she said. 'I think you're right. The answer to this lies in Scotland, not here in France. The sooner we get out of your hair, the happier you'll be, I suspect.'

Chevrolet chuckled. '*Au contraire*, Commandant Pirie. We don't have many women of your rank in our department. Most of the teams are like Les Gautiers – we don't have any women at all. So for me, it's very instructional to see how women do this job.'

Karen bit her lip, then changed her mind. 'In Scotland, we know women do this job every bit as well as men. Sometimes better. Frankly, most of us, men and women, would consider any single-sex team lacking.' She caught Daisy grinning out of the corner of her eye as the driver set off through the narrow streets of the Left Bank.

'Totally,' Daisy said. 'It's so weird not to have the perspective of half of the human race.'

Chevrolet harrumphed. 'Maybe so. But this is a dangerous

job. It's why we carry guns. I don't think women react so well in life-and-death situations.'

'And yet the unit I lead regularly tracks down killers and puts them behind bars. Without guns or machismo.' Karen didn't bother softening her words with a smile.

Chevrolet half-turned in his seat. 'So what do you do when someone points a gun at you?'

'It doesn't happen very often because our gun control laws are much stricter than yours. It's only happened to me once.' Karen remembered the chill slither of cold sweat running down her spine, the shotgun barrel looking big as a dustbin lid, the slow certainty that it might be the last thing she'd see. She'd tried to keep her voice steady as she said, 'I know you don't want to do this. If you pull that trigger, there's no going back. Your life's over. Same goes for everybody you care about.' By some miracle, they'd been the right words. Kyle Kelman had let the barrel slowly drop till it was pointing at the floor. The air had rushed back into Karen's lungs and she knew she was going to live.

'Once is enough,' Chevrolet said. 'One bullet is enough.'

'And if you find the right words, one sentence is enough.' Karen turned away and stared at the crawling traffic. 'How long till we get to Caen? Are we there yet?'

The city was an intriguing mixture. The centre was dominated by impressive medieval buildings whose pale stone glowed in the winter sunshine, threaded through with squat modern blocks. It was hard to distinguish between apartments with shops on the ground floor and offices with shops on the ground floor. It wasn't unattractive, Karen thought. Just an odd combination.

As if he'd read her mind, Chevrolet said, 'The city paid

a high price for its liberation. Many old buildings were destroyed.'

'I kind of like the look of it,' Karen said. 'The colour of the stone makes it feel quite light. In Edinburgh, where I live, the old town is dark, many of the buildings are pressed close up against each other. There's a sense of space here.'

They drove along a canal then turned into a narrow side street. The driver pulled up by a corner bar. 'This is it,' Chevrolet said. 'Bar Trente-Deux.'

'Bar Thirty-Two,' Daisy said. 'Why that?'

'No idea,' Chevrolet said. The driver said something incomprehensibly swift. Chevrolet grunted. 'He says thirty-two bars is the typical length of a verse of popular song.'

'Every day a school day,' Karen sighed, following them inside. The bar was cosy, fitted out with dark wood that appeared to have come from a previous generation to the building. Chevrolet spoke to the middle-aged man behind the counter, who jerked his head towards a pair of saloon-style doors at the back of the room.

Chevrolet led the way. As if it would have gone down any other way, Karen thought cynically. They found themselves in a spacious room with a compact stage at the far end, a drum kit glittering in the middle. Tables and chairs were arranged cabaret-style, and a long bar ran along one side wall. The house lights were up, and as always, the dim wattage made the daytime bar forlorn, stripped of its nightlife glamour. In a corner by the stage, a woman sat at one of the tables. She appeared to be working her way through a pile of paperwork. She barely looked up when they entered and went back to scrutinising the next sheet on the stack.

They wove their way through the tables, Karen studying the woman as well as she could in the poor light. She had a tumble of blonde hair so bright it must have come from a bottle. As they grew closer, Karen decided with a wry twist that Pascale Vargas was that quintessentially French phenomenon, the *belle laide*. Wide forehead, jutting prow of a nose, a scarlet lipsticked slash of a mouth and a square jaw. An unlikely combination of features generally dismissed as ugly that somehow came together to create a magnetic attraction. She wore a baggy jumper with a boat neck and a necklace made from apparently random chunks of brightly coloured plastic.

'Madame Vargas?' Chevrolet spoke first.

The woman looked up, taking off her glasses with their bright red heavy frames. 'Oui,' she drawled.

Karen worked out that Chevrolet was introducing them. Pascale clearly decided Karen was the one who mattered and fixed her gaze on her. *'Parlez Français?'*

Even Karen could manage that. 'I don't' – she gestured with a thumb to Daisy – 'but she does.'

Pascale grinned, showing an improbable number of teeth. 'Then we speak English. I think it will be easier. Please, sit down. Call me Pascale. Madame Vargas sounds like my grandmother.'

Karen pulled out a chair and sat. 'I'm very sorry about Paul.'

Pascale looked across at the stage, her lips pursed. She turned back, gathering herself, and said, 'He was a beautiful soul. He played with such grace, such inspiration. And I loved him.'

That was something Karen understood. To lose the man you loved in a moment of senseless violence. It was tempting to share but that was seldom a productive way to conduct an interview unless you were a tabloid journalist. 'We knew him by his original name,' she said. 'James Auld. Did he ever talk to you about his past?'

Pascale shook her head. 'I've known many musicians over the years. Most of them play to forget themselves and their back pages. Paul told me about his time in the Legion but almost nothing from before that. I knew he was Scottish, and he had a brother who died, but that's all, I think. We spoke of many things but not much about our history.'

It didn't sound as if Pascale was going to be much more use than the boys in the band. All this way for next to nothing, 'When did you see him last?'

'A couple of weeks ago. He had come back from London. He said he'd been to see someone to check he wasn't imagining things.'

Karen's senses quickened. 'Imagining things? What things?'

Pascale's smile had no joy in it. 'I asked him but he wouldn't say. He said he was chasing a phantom. That he'd tell me about it when he had worked out the truth.'

'Did he say why he wouldn't tell you?'

'He said I would think he was crazy.' A twisted smile. 'He said he thought *he* was crazy.'

'And that's it? Nothing more than that?'

'*Non.*'

'Did he ever talk about having an enemy? Someone who wanted him dead?'

A frustrated shake of the head. 'Why would he? People liked Paul. He wasn't perfect but he wasn't a shit either. He wasn't somebody who would start a fight.'

'Did he have any financial worries? Was he in debt?'

Pascale frowned. 'I don't think so. He lived a simple life. He didn't gamble, he didn't do drugs, he didn't go to fancy restaurants. He had a small pension from the Legion, and the band was always in demand. He wasn't rich but I never saw a sign of troubles with money.' She sighed. 'I wish he'd been here the weekend before he went to Scotland instead of going to Dublin.'

'Dublin?' Karen leaned forward. Out of the corner of her eye she could see Daisy straighten up. 'Paul went to Dublin?'

'*Oui*. Like I said, the weekend before he went to Scotland. The band played here on the Thursday night and on Friday he caught the train to Paris then he flew to Dublin.'

'I'm interested in anything unusual in Paul's behaviour. Did he often go to Dublin?'

'Never. Not since I knew him. We once went to Biarritz for the weekend, but never Dublin. He never mentioned knowing anyone there.'

'Did you see him after he came back? Between Dublin and Scotland?'

'No, but we spoke on the phone.'

'Did he say what he'd been doing in Dublin?'

'He said he'd had a bit of business but he spent most of his time walking round the city. And he found a jazz bar.'

'He didn't say what the business was?' Daisy chipped in.

'I told you all he said about it.'

'And Scotland?' Karen said. 'What did he say about Scotland?'

'Nothing much. He goes to see the widow of his brother. Mary.' She shrugged. 'I know nothing of her. She has never been here, to Caen.'

Now Karen produced the photograph she'd found in Auld's apartment. 'Do you know anything about this photograph?' She handed it to Pascale, who studied it carefully.

'He looks like Paul, but it's not Paul,' she said firmly,

tapping Iain Auld with a fingernail. She turned it over and her puzzled frown cleared. 'This is the photograph he found in the book.' She looked up. 'His sister-in-law let him choose some things belonging to his brother when she was moving house. He chose a James Bond book, because it was a favourite. And he told me he took it down to read it again, and he noticed something about the back of the book. *La page de garde.* I don't know how you say it in English, the inside paper stuck to the back of the book?'

'Endpaper,' Daisy said. 'What about it?'

'There was an outline of something and when he opened it up, this photo was there. He said it was his brother and another man he didn't know.'

'What was his reaction? Was he surprised? Puzzled?'

She raised her eyebrows. 'He sounded angry. Not surprised. I asked him what it was about but he said he didn't want to talk about it.' She gave a wan smile. 'Paul was not a man you could push. If he didn't want to talk about something, that was that.' Pascale handed the photo back.

Karen showed her the newspaper clipping and the writing on the reverse side. 'Does this mean anything to you? "12 NT. Ouds. Hilary 92/3".'

Pascale rubbed the middle joint of her finger up and down her philtrum as she considered. 'I have no idea. It's nothing to do with music, that's for sure. I wish I could help.' She looked at her hands, folded in her lap, and sighed. Then she raised her eyes and met Karen's.

'I want you to find the man who did this. I think Paul did not deserve to die like that. Find him and make him pay the price, Commandant Pirie.'

Karen nodded. It wouldn't bring Pascale's man back, but she knew from her own experience that it gave the heart some ease to know something had been exacted from the person who had taken so much. She stood. 'Thanks for your time.' She handed Pascale a card. 'If anything else occurs to you—'

Chevrolet thrust his arm past her and dropped his card in front of Pascale. 'You will call me, Madame Vargas.'

Pascale's lip curled. She said something curt in French.

'*Allons*,' Chevrolet said, equally curt and annoyed. Karen and Daisy followed a few paces behind. 'Are you thinking what I'm thinking?' Karen said softly.

'Dublin. We totally need to go back to that flat.'

'Oh yes. I think we've finally got our hands on the end of the thread.'

26

Karen said nothing until they were well on the way back to Paris. 'We need to go back to Paul Allard's apartment,' she said to the back of Chevrolet's head.

He half-turned. 'Why? I thought you said there was nothing there of interest.'

'That was before Dublin was mentioned.'

'You found some connection to Dublin?'

'There was a letter from an art gallery in Dublin,' she said. 'Daisy, tell the man.'

Daisy gave her a quick sideways flick of the eyes. 'It said something like, "yes, we do occasionally handle paintings by the artist you inquired about. We have none at present. The ones we have dealt with come from a private collection."'

Chevrolet's eyebrows rose then furled into a frown. 'And you did not mention this?'

'Why would we? You saw the state of that living room. I don't think he ever threw away a piece of paper. If you'd come across that letter, would you have thought it had any significance?' Karen glared at Chevrolet. 'I know my job. Until Pascale mentioned Dublin, that letter was meaningless.'

Chevrolet scoffed. 'You think this was the apartment of an art connoisseur? You didn't think it was out of place among the saxophones and the pages of music?'

'He might not have been interested in art, but his sister-in-law collects paintings,' Daisy said. There was a defiant set to her jaw that Karen liked the look of. 'I thought he might be inquiring on her behalf.'

Chevrolet grunted. 'So now we will go back and you will find this letter and hand it over.'

'Hand it over?' Karen bristled.

'It's evidence. Found on French soil, so here it stays.'

Karen recognised stubbornness when she saw it. She saw it often enough in her own mirror, after all. 'We'll want to photograph it. And video you taking it into custody.'

He rolled his eyes.

'It's the law in Scotland. Evidence has to be corroborated. It's not enough for me to wave a photo on my phone and say, "Look, here's the proof." So I need to film you identifying yourself and showing the letter, in the apartment where it was found.'

'This is a crazy law. How do you ever convict murderers and rapists? These are not crimes with witnesses.'

'We manage,' Karen said with a note of finality. *Badly*, her head said. She'd seen too many sexual offenders walk smirking from court after a judge had explained the law to a jury. And those were the tiny percentage who made it as far as the dock. Successive Lord Advocates had tinkered with the law to try to make it work better for the victims but Karen still burned with rage when colleagues passed on stories of yet more failed complaints.

'OK, we will go to the apartment,' Chevrolet sighed. 'Did you book flights back to Scotland?'

'No, we'll catch the Eurostar. I've business in London.'
Daisy gave her a first-I've-heard-about-it look.

'I hope you are not keeping something from me,'
Chevrolet grumbled in a low voice.

'It's to do with another matter. We don't have the luxury
of working one case at a time.' Karen sounded relaxed. Phil
had always said that was her tell for lies.

They barely made the 17:13 Eurostar back to London, and
only because Chevrolet was so keen to see the back of them
that he hustled them through the boarding formalities,
speeding them through customs and immigration and on
to the train. 'I will keep you informed of any developments
here in Paris,' he said with complete lack of sincerity.

'Of course you will,' Karen said. 'And I will do like-
wise.' She smiled. 'We may be able to help each other. You
never know.'

They had a pair of seats by themselves, the high backs
giving them a degree of privacy. No sooner had they settled
in than Daisy said, 'What was all that about? Business in
London on another case?'

Karen shrugged. 'He pissed me off with his territoriality.
He knows nothing about this case or the background, he
showed zero interest in finding out about it. So I'm not about
to tell him the whole story of what I'm up to.'

'What *are* you up to? Am I allowed to ask?'

'Always. Though I may not always tell you. But this time,
I will. I sent a wee message when we were on the way
back from Caen. We're meeting up this evening with DCS
Ron Beckett. Back in the day, he was the SIO on the Iain
Auld disappearance. I spoke to him when I did the cold
case review.'

'How come you did the review? I mean, it was a Met case, right? Not a Scottish one.'

'Not directly, no. Though Lothian Police, as it was then, dealt with the interviews north of the border: Mary Auld, and the Scotland Office team in Edinburgh. And although it's technically not a Scottish case, our political masters have never been convinced that it was taken seriously enough at the time. If you remember, it was the early days of the coalition government and Iain Auld wasn't high on the agenda of the Home Office, who mostly just wanted Scotland to go away and not be annoying.'

Daisy chuckled. 'That went well, eh?'

'Not in the long run, but it was too late for Iain Auld by then.'

'So the cold case review? That was political?'

Karen grinned. 'You might say that. I couldn't possibly comment. Though I have to admit that, having done the review, I didn't see any indication that there was a political dimension to Iain Auld's disappearance. Unless he was in possession of a secret so deeply buried that it's stayed that way.'

'And that doesn't happen often in politics, right?'

'Things have a way of swimming up into the light. It doesn't matter how far you've clawed your way up the ladder, the bodies never stay buried forever.'

'So you think DCS Beckett knows more than he's let on so far?'

'I doubt it. But on the off-chance, now that we've got something to trade . . . Well, since we're passing through, I thought it wouldn't hurt.'

There was, Daisy thought, some kind of fundamental affinity between cops and curry houses. Detective Chief

Superintendent Ron Beckett had directed them to one of several on a side street near Euston station that was as fragrant as some of the Goan bazaars where she'd eaten on the trip she'd made to India with three friends in the summer before their final year.

Beckett was a big man, broad in the shoulder and the face, running to fat around his midriff, an issue that was disguised by decent tailoring till he unbuttoned his jacket and sat down. His silver hair was still thick, brushed back from a forehead tramlined by years of frowns. He had a short squat nose above a thin-lipped mouth, but it was his eyes that she would remember. They were a warm liquid brown, the kind of eyes that offered reassurance and understanding. Daisy would have bet they'd lulled more than a few people into revealing far more than they'd intended in the interview room. 'Never underestimate the attraction of the confessional,' one of her law tutors had once said to her. 'It kept the Catholic Church in power for hundreds of years.'

'Good to see you again,' Karen greeted him.

'You nipped in right on time, Karen. Another couple of weeks and you'd have got the, "Alice doesn't live here any more" response.'

'How come?' She sounded startled.

'I'm offski,' he said. 'I've got thirty-five years in, it's time to kick back and enjoy my pension. We're selling up and moving lock, stock and two smoking barrels across to Galway. I plan to spend my days fishing and my evenings drinking Guinness.'

'Congratulations.' Karen grinned. 'I bet your team are sick with jealousy.'

'I like to think so. And this must be Daisy Mortimer.' He extended a large hand with surprisingly slender fingers and grasped hers firmly. Just enough to establish confident authority without going for macho dominance. 'Hello, Daisy. I've been speaking to your other boss,' he said.

'Charlie Todd's been in touch?' Karen opened the menu. Daisy thought she was aiming for nonchalance and hitting the bullseye.

'Courtesy call to let me know I could close the file on James Auld,' he said drily.

'That's one way of looking it. Not the way we do it in the Historic Cases Unit, though. Even if the prime suspect is dead, the file's still live till we can prove who did it.' Karen spoke mildly but Daisy knew her well enough by now to know this was an article of faith.

'Can't disagree with you, Karen. But let's get some drinks in. Celebrate the last hurrah of a dying breed. Yours is a different world from the one I joined up in, Daisy. We're drowning in admin and reports these days. Not enough boots on the ground.' He signalled to the waiter. 'What's it going to be, ladies?'

Beers and an abundance of food ordered, they settled down to discuss what had brought them there. 'Sounds like Charlie Todd's team are struggling with this one. They haven't managed to track down where your man was staying, so they haven't got his laptop or any notes or letters.' He scoffed. 'You'd think it wouldn't be rocket science. How many places could he be? It's not like Torremolinos, is it?'

'It's a tourist area, Ron. There's plenty of holiday lets. A lot of them, you have to take a place for a whole week. If that's what Auld did, nobody's going to realise he's not there any more until the turnaround day.'

'Yeah, but surely they can phone round and see whether anybody's rented to a Paul Allard or a James Auld?'

'With the rise of short-term lets like Airbnb, there's a lot of places for rent that don't show up on the tourist board or local authority lists,' Daisy said. 'People rent out everything from second homes to static caravans. It's not straightforward, sir.'

'Hmm,' he grumbled. The poppadums arrived and he attacked them. 'So, how was Paris, Karen? You get anything out of it apart from some decent grub?'

'A few loose ends, though it's hard to say if it means any-thing. Auld made two trips before he went off to Scotland: London and Dublin. But without his laptop and his phone, which is presumably at the bottom of the Firth of Forth, we don't have much to go on.' Pakoras arrived and generated a diversion from conversation.

'These are good,' Karen said at last. 'Really good.'

'This is top,' Beckett agreed. 'So you've got no clue what was going on?'

'All we've got is a letter from an art dealer in Dublin. Auld had apparently been inquiring about an artist, but there's no name in the letter.'

If Beckett had been a dog, his ears would have pricked up. 'That's funny.'

'Why?'

'I don't see how it can be connected, but about four, five years after Iain Auld went missing and James Auld did one, I got dragged into another case involving Dover House. You know, the Scotland Office? It wasn't strictly speaking my beat. But I'd already built bridges with the civil servants, and it was a sensitive matter. And in spite of that they thought it'd be better to let me loose on it.' He grinned.

'That sounds intriguing,' Karen said.

'It was. But the only thing it had in common with Iain Auld's disappearance was that we never resolved it.'

Before Karen could respond, the curries arrived, fragrant and unctuous in their various sauces. There was another pause while they loaded their plates and tore off chunks of naan and paratha. Then she said, 'So what's the story?'

Beckett swallowed a mouthful of saag paneer and washed it down with a mouthful of Kingfisher. He clearly relished the art of storytelling. 'So, you've got all these ministers and senior officials in Whitehall. They've all got offices. That's a lot of wall space to cover, a lot of opportunities to impress the people who come to visit. The way it works is the minister gets to choose what hangs on the walls. He or she gets the pick of the national collections. Theoretically, the junior ministers and the civil servants get to choose, but in reality, you'd be mad to disagree with the boss.'

'OK. I get the picture.'

Daisy and Beckett groaned. 'I see what you did there,' Beckett said, pointing with his fork at Karen. 'So, in 2015, a Tory majority government takes over from that dog's breakfast of a coalition. And straight away, the new Scottish Secretary of State decides to flex his muscles and replace all the art with paintings that suit his Tory taste. The existing ones get sent back to the Scottish galleries they came from. But one sharp-eyed conservator noticed something wasn't quite right with one of the paintings. Apparently the original had had some damage repaired and there was no sign of it now.' He paused for effect and to shovel some lamb pasanda into his mouth.

Karen spooned black dhal onto her plate. 'I'm betting they put the rest of them under the microscope.'

'Spot on, Sherlock. And guess what? Six of them turned out to be fakes. Very good fakes, according to the geeks that know about these things, but as genuine as a nine-bob note.'

His eyes slid towards the ceiling as he recalled the artists whose work had been counterfeited. 'Raeburn, MacTaggart, Redpath, Eardley, Crawhall, Doig.' He grinned again. 'I bet you never thought I had that much culture in me, Karen.'

'How come this wasn't all over the papers?' Karen demanded. 'Why is this the first I'm hearing about it?'

'Well, it was a huge embarrassment. The government borrows some art from the national collection and somehow some faker gets not just one over on them but six. How stupid do you think that makes them look?'

'But surely it would have been the previous government who would have had to take responsibility?' Daisy looked puzzled. 'I'd have thought they'd have been delighted to pass the buck to their political rivals.'

Beckett's brown eyes looked sorrowful. 'You're so young, Daisy.' He shook his head.

Karen took pity. She'd been made to feel like the idiot in the room often enough to be merciful. 'The previous government was the coalition between the Tories and the Lib Dems. The Lib Dems held the Scottish Secretary post, but the Tories were the senior partners in the coalition. Disgracing the Lib Dems would have reflected badly on them. Plus it would have been politically dangerous – the Lib Dems knew where the bodies were buried.'

'Correct,' Beckett said. 'So they kept the lid on it.'

'But you investigated?'

'Of course I did, Karen. But it wasn't that simple. The Lib Dem Scottish Secretaries mostly kept the same artwork on the walls that they'd inherited from the outgoing Labour government. They liked them. And they kind of wanted to maintain a distinction between the paintings that would appeal to a Tory minister and what they appreciated. So we

199

had six paintings that had been in place for varying lengths of time from seven to fourteen years. Those copies could have been made any time.'

'What about forensics?' Daisy asked.

'Didn't get us anywhere. Bloody Dover House. Where police careers go to die.' He speared a lump of lamb and chewed gloomily.

'You've hardly ended up on the scrapheap,' Karen pointed out mildly.

'Oh, I know. I'm not complaining. It's annoying, that's all. I hate unfinished business.' He drained his glass and waved it at the waiter. 'But then, I guess you're used to picking up other people's unfinished business, right, Karen?'

'Right, Ron. And every now and again, we get to finish it.'

'Well, I hope you have better luck with James Auld than I did with his brother. I mean, it was sheer luck that his body got picked up when it did. From what I understand from Charlie Todd, if the body hadn't got tangled up with a lobster pot, it might have ended up a pile of bones on a Norwegian beach. If I was a betting man, I'd put money on something like that happening to his brother.'

Karen tore off another wad of naan. 'You're probably right, Ron. If you couldn't find out what happened to Iain Auld, I don't have a cat in hell's chance.'

Daisy focused on the food on her plate, making sure Ron Beckett couldn't see her face. She didn't want to give away the fact that she already recognised when Karen was lying.

27

Karen and Daisy paced platform 15 of Euston station, waiting to see whether there would be any fairy godparents in the shape of no-shows for the sleeper, rendering their berths magically available. Not even their warrant cards and Daisy's charm offensive could spirit up a pair of empty cabins. 'If this was the bloody Orient Express, they'd have a spare in case of homicidal emergencies,' Karen had muttered, shoving her hands deeper into her pockets against the cold.

'Aye, but then neither of us is Hercule Poirot,' Daisy pointed out.

'Just as well, that moustache would be a bugger with a plate of Scotch broth.'

They both giggled at the vision of Poirot's moustache liberally decorated with bits of barley and carrot. 'That was a great curry,' Daisy said. 'Shame "call-me-Ron" wasn't more useful.'

'I wasn't expecting anything, to be honest. But I thought it would be worth keeping the channels open. Turns out, with him on the verge of retirement, it was probably a waste of time. But there's one important lesson for you there, Daisy. That story about the fake paintings – that only goes to show that anything short of murder can be brushed under the carpet if the politicians want to avoid embarrassment badly enough.'

They reached the far end of the platform, only yards beyond the improbably long snake of carriages that formed the Glasgow and Edinburgh sleepers. 'So what do you think happened to the fake paintings?' Daisy asked as they turned their backs on the red signal lights and walked back into the bleak concrete shell of the station. 'Have they been quietly removed from the galleries' inventories? Or are the fakes tucked away in storage with a note never to display them publicly again?'

Karen shrugged. 'No idea. I know one or two of the conservators at the National Galleries' storage facility down in Granton from a case we were looking at a while back, but this is the first I heard of this. Not even a whisper or a hint. But it's not our problem, thank goodness.' Before Daisy could respond, Karen noticed one of the train crew waving to them. 'Come on, looks like we might have got lucky.'

They jogged back down the platform to where a steward stood clutching a clipboard. Wrapped in a thick coat and muffled in a scarf, she looked like a small animal peering out of a nest. 'Good news and bad news,' she said. 'We've got a cabin free but it's on the Glasgow section of the train. It's five minutes to departure, I don't think we'll get anything else now.'

'Is that a single?' Karen asked.

'It's set up as a single—'

'I'll take it,' she said quickly, anticipating the unwanted offer to prepare an upper bunk. She liked Daisy, but not enough to want to share a tiny cabin with her. 'Presumably you've got seats available on the Edinburgh train?'

202

The steward got it. 'That's right.' She smiled at Daisy. 'If you head down towards the rear of the train, one of my colleagues will sort you out.'

With a gloomy nod, Daisy turned to go. 'Daisy? When you get to Edinburgh, head on home, get a shower and some breakfast. Then you'd better go into the office and debrief DCI Todd. I want to take you with me to talk to Mary Auld, but I've got things I need to do first.'

Daisy looked appalled. 'You're not going to show her that picture?'

Karen shook her head. 'Not the whole thing, not yet. It might come to that, but right now I suspect it will only provoke hostility and a total shutdown. I do want to know if she recognises the other man, though. We can crop Iain out of the pic and show it to her. And I want to see her face when I ask her what she knows about James Auld's trips to London and Dublin.'

'OK.' Daisy didn't sound enthusiastic. 'Do you want me to tell Charlie about the folder?'

Karen raised her eyebrows. 'Of course. I'll scan the material as soon as I get into the office and forward it to you. If he can make more sense of it than I can, he'll be top of my Christmas card list. Now, away you go and get settled in. Try to get some sleep.' She sketched a wave and headed for her coach. As she passed the steward, she winked and said, 'Thank you.'

'No bother, sleep well.'

Karen dumped her bags in the cabin and made her way to the bar. Armed with a miniature of gin and a can of tonic, she settled down on her bunk, laptop open on the pull-out table. She was tired, but not ready yet to attempt sleep. She knew the misery of lying awake longing for sleep when she lacked the option of getting up and wearing herself out with nocturnal walks; better to wait a while than try to force it now. She opened up her email and checked for anything that looked relevant to either of the cases she was working, but both seemed to have gone quiet. Probably just as well, since she wasn't there to steer the direction of travel.

She took an apprehensive sip of her drink and began a new message.

Hi Hamish
  I'm heading for home on the sleeper. If you're free, we could meet up this evening? I'm not sure what time I'll be back from work but if you want to come over, I'll text you when I'm home.

She paused, weighing up the options.

It would be good to see you. Kx

Before she could have second thoughts, she sent it off into the ether then closed her email. Because the new sleeper trains had half-decent Wi-Fi, she headed for the BBC iPlayer site and found a Scandi crime drama she'd not seen before. She got ready for bed, inserted her earbuds – in spite of not understanding the language she wanted the sound effects and the music – and settled down to watch some Norwegian cop figure out an impenetrable serial killer cold case. Ten minutes in and she reckoned she'd have done a better job. Fifteen minutes in and she was spark out, lulled into strange dreams by the meaningless mumble in her ears.

When Karen woke and checked her phone, she realised they were at Carstairs, where the long snake of the night train split in two, half heading for Glasgow and half for Edinburgh. The jolt of separation was what had wakened her. She stretched and yawned, pulling the earphones out as she did so. Deciding there was no point in trying to catch any more sleep, she rolled out of bed and headed for the cubicle that housed the toilet and the shower.

By the time the train pulled into Glasgow, she was clean and refreshed, hair still damp but reasonably tidy. Her brain was working and she was making plans for the day. It was time to grab these cases by the throat and take control.

Karen was gratified to find Jason already at his desk when she walked in shortly after nine. 'Boss,' he exclaimed, nearly knocking over a can of Irn-Bru in his surprise. 'When did you get back? You never said . . . '

'I just got off the sleeper. What's with the Irn-Bru? Standards slipping?' Now she looked at him more closely, she could see the dark smudges under his eyes and a pallor on his skin that turned his freckles into an orange star map.

He sighed. 'Busted. I had a few bevvies last night. One of Eilidh's pals, it was her birthday, we all went out for a pizza, that new place down the bottom of Leith Walk, they do massive jugs of sangria and before you know it, your mouth's stopped working.'

Karen grinned. 'As long as your brain's still working. I'll away and get us some coffee. Better arrange your thoughts and bring me up to speed.'

When she handed over the coffee, Jason took a swallow and shuddered. 'Bloody hell, boss, what's in that?'

'Two extra shots. I thought you needed a wee livener.'

His eyes widened. 'Livener? More like a heart attack in a cup.'

While he worked on his drink, Karen scanned in the contents of the folder from James Auld's bedroom and pinged it across to Daisy. Probably a pointless exercise, but maybe somebody on Charlie Todd's MIT would understand something she hadn't. 'How did you get on with tracking down Amanda McAndrew? Or her alias?' she asked.

Jason couldn't disguise his glumness. 'Not a trace. I tried DVLA with both names. No vehicle registered to either of them since Amanda had the camper van. It was de-registered following the SORN declaration three years ago. But we know where it's been for at least some of that time.'

'I'd say pretty much all of that time. You wouldn't take the risk of driving around in a van that would be picked up as illegal on traffic cams or by any patrol car that bothered to run the plates. Not with a dead body in the back. No, I think the van was already in Susan Leitch's garage when the road tax ran out. So, we're not going to find her that way. What about HMRC?'

He shook his head. 'Nothing. Neither of them is registered for VAT and neither of them has submitted a tax return for the past three years.'

'And the website? How did you get on there?'

'OK, so I went to the site and tried to order a pair of earrings. And the screen said, "Sorry, this item is currently out of stock. Please leave your email and we will message you when it becomes available." Fair enough, I thought. So I had a crack at a nice wee pendant with a tiger's eye stone in it.' He referred to his notebook. 'And this time, the screen said, "Sorry, we are having some difficulty in sourcing stones of sufficient quality to fulfil your order at this time. Please leave your email and we will message you when it becomes available."'

'Interesting,' Karen said. 'Did you try to order a specially commissioned piece?'

'Sure did, boss.' Again he checked his notes. '"Due to an unusually high number of recent orders, we are unable to accept fresh commissions at present. Please leave your email—"'

'"And we will message you when it becomes available,"' Karen finished.

'It's like they don't want to sell you anything.'

Karen tapped a pencil end to end on her notebook. 'I think it's that they don't actually have anything to sell you. Because dead women don't do silversmithing. It's a smoke-screen, Jason. If anybody goes looking for Dani, they're going to find the site and if they try to make contact, they'll get a message that looks like she's doing pretty well. Did you manage to track the website host?'

'It's a one-man outfit in Birmingham. But that's a dead end too. He doesn't know where his clients are based. It's totally anonymised, they pay him in bitcoin. You tell him what you want, he'll set up your site, no questions asked.'

Karen groaned. 'Really? How do we let unregulated stuff like that go on? No wonder the bloody internet is such a sink of horror.'

'The one thing you can say about this?'

'Go on, I'm listening.'

'All this? You don't do this unless you've got something bad to hide. It's like a confession on its own.'

'That's true, but it doesn't help us get any closer to Amanda McAndrew.'

'Maybe we should try to talk to her parents? They might be able to suggest—'

'The parents.' Karen interrupted him eagerly. 'Do we

207

know when they moved to Crete? Get their Facebook page up, Jason. Let's see how far back it goes.' She jumped up and walked round the desk, leaning over his shoulder as his fingers rattled over the keys. He scrolled down the page, clicking on various option.

'I think it was 2015,' he muttered. 'Should we not contact them and see what they've got to say about their daughter?'

Karen pulled a face. 'It's hard to make that sort of contact from a polis seem anything other than a big deal. And it's not how you want to tell someone their daughter might be a murderer. For one thing, you'd want to see the whites of their eyes. For another, we don't want them to alert Amanda to how much we know.'

'Fair enough.'

'There,' she said, tapping the screen with her pencil. 'It goes back nearly five years. Before Amanda and Dani hit the road.' She returned to her seat. 'They didn't just buy a wee holiday home. They bought a business, a way of life. They've got no plans to come back here. They'll have sold their cars. And who knew that better than their daughter? Jason, get back on to your DVLA contact. Check out whether there have been any vehicles registered to Barry or Anita McAndrew in the last three years. I can't believe she's in the wind without a motor.'

28

Friday, 21 February 2020

If Karen had been hoping that Charlie Todd or one of his team would have some brilliant case-cracking inspiration when they were presented with the Parisian information, she'd have been in for a disappointment. But since she'd had no optimism on that score, she'd merely sighed, scooped up Daisy and headed for Mary Auld's house.

They were almost there when Charlie called. 'Good news, Karen,' he said.

'You sound like a man who's won the lottery.'

'Well, five out of the six numbers anyway. We've had a call from a woman who lets out a cottage in Elie. She went in this morning to do the turnaround, but the renter's stuff is still in the cottage. Clothes, laptop. And the fresh food in the fridge is either past the sell-by date or heading that way.'

'You're right, Charlie. We're only ten, fifteen minutes away from Elie now, we might as well head over there before we talk to Mary Auld. Can you text me the address and get the owner to meet us there? And we'll need a crime scene team to check the place over.'

'Aye, OK.' He couldn't keep the disappointed note from

209

his voice. Karen felt like the playground bully, stealing his sweets at playtime.

'If your guys hadn't been all over the holiday lets, we'd have struggled with this,' she said, trying not to sound patronising.

'Right enough, it's all about teamwork,' he said, brightening. 'Good luck in Elie.'

Bayview Cottage did what it said on the tin. It was a low-slung cottage painted coral pink, hunched on the shore where Elie merged into Earlsferry next door. They'd had to park on the main street and head down a narrow vennel that led them to the seafront where an easterly wind threatened to strip the top layer from their skin. The sea was battleship grey, flecked with slashes of white foam. 'This is how we have such great skin in Fife,' Karen observed, tears springing to her eyes. 'We get exfoliated on a daily basis.'

The cottage was well maintained, front door and window frames painted pale grey. Karen barely raised her hand to ring the bell when the door opened. 'Are you from the police?' The woman on the doorstep set Karen's teeth on edge. It wasn't so much the cut-glass English accent as the look that swept over her from head to toe and dismissed her as insufficient. At first glance, she looked in her early thirties, blonde hair arranged in a loose chignon. She was dressed in thigh-hugging jeans tucked into leather riding boots, her upper half swathed in the sort of designer knitwear that Karen knew would turn her into a walking ball of wool. It was only when they drew closer that Karen realised she was nearer fifty than thirty.

'Detective Chief Inspector Pirie,' she said. 'This is Detective Sergeant Mortimer. And you are?'

'Do you people not communicate with each other? I'm Mrs Archibald. Livy Archibald. This is my cottage. You'd better come in.' She stepped back and waved them inside. It was comfortably furnished in a clean but somehow lived-in style. The decor was predictable for a coastal cottage – framed prints with a nautical theme, pottery decorated with stylised fish and bits of boat. A trio of glass net floats sat in the hearth. But there was no sign of a laptop. 'I don't normally do the changeover,' she said. 'But the girl let me down. Some nonsense about having the flu.' She tutted. 'Honestly. As if I've nothing better to do. And now this.'

'Does this sort of thing happen often? People not checking out on time?' Karen roamed the room, looking for signs of occupation and finding none.

'Occasionally they're a couple of hours late. But this guy should have cleared out yesterday. I only got to it this morning because I was busy then.'

'And you called us, why?'

She rolled her eyes. 'Because your people sent an email to all the listed owners of holiday lets asking if we'd let a property to anyone called Allard or Auld. I didn't get round to checking my records until I turned up this morning and found all his stuff in the kitchen and the bedroom.'

'Busy, were you?' Karen's tone was mild but her eyebrows were raised.

'Yes, as it happens. Now, are you going to clear this man's stuff out of my cottage so I can get on with running my business?'

'It's not quite that straightforward, Mrs Archibald. This is a murder inquiry and this is potentially a crime scene.'

'A crime scene?' Her voice rose. 'Look around you.

Nothing's been disturbed. Is this the guy they fished out of the sea off St Monans? How on earth is this a crime scene?'

'There may be evidence of a third party having been here with Mr Auld—'

'Allard. It was booked under Allard. You don't even know the name of the person you're interested in. And I've got another couple booked in here, arriving this afternoon. What am I supposed to do with them? I'm trying to run a business here.'

'I'm sorry, Mrs Archibald. Our crime scene technicians will be as quick as possible, but until they're done, nobody else comes in here. And we're going to need your finger-prints and DNA for elimination purposes.'

Daisy was standing behind the landlady and Karen caught her eye. 'When did Mr Allard book the cottage?' Daisy asked, picking up the hint.

'I'll have to check my records.'

'Perhaps we could go and do that now? Do you live nearby?'

Livy Archibald pursed her lips and frowned. 'Just up the road in Kilconquhar. This is all incredibly inconvenient.'

'I could follow you back there and get the details.' Daisy produced her best smile.

'It would save you hanging around here,' Karen said.

Grudgingly, the woman agreed. She handed Karen the cottage keys and followed Daisy out, grumbling every step of the way. Karen snapped on a pair of nitrile gloves and headed straight across the hall to the bedroom. It was dominated by an unmade king-sized bed. Judging by the single dent in the pillows, only one person had occupied it. A holdall sat on the window seat. Karen rounded the bed and looked inside. A pair of black trousers, winter weight, a

French label she didn't recognise. Four pairs of underpants, three pairs of socks. Two T-shirts and a lightweight crew-necked sweater. A pair of slip-on black leather loafers. One paperback novel in French by Bernard Minier. Not so much as a notebook. As she turned away, she caught sight of the edge of a laptop sitting on the shelf below the bedside table.

'Bingo,' she said, reaching for it. She opened the MacAir. 'And of course it needs a bloody password.' She checked her notebook for Auld's date of birth and tried various combinations coupled with both of his names. No joy. She flicked through the pages until she found her notes on Auld's career in the Foreign Legion. His service number got her nowhere, not with names or dates of birth. 'Fuck,' she muttered, closing the lid. This was one for Tamsin over at Gartcosh. And who knew how long that would take?

The bathroom yielded little. A plastic spongebag, generic supermarket hair and body wash, deodorant, toothbrush, toothpaste and an electric razor. James Auld travelled about as light as a man could get. The laptop was the only possible source of clues to what he was doing here, beyond visiting Mary Auld.

The kitchen was no more informative. A plate, a water glass and a mug sat on the dish drainer alongside a fork, a knife and a spoon. The dishwasher was empty. A loaf with a few slices off one end sat on the breadboard, hard as a brick. The fridge contained a tub of butter, a half-eaten Scottish camembert, two ready meals from the local farm shop, half a carton of milk and most of a packet of ground coffee. Karen thought it didn't look like the provisions of a man having a wee holiday in the East Neuk. These were the basic rations of a man on a mission.

Back in the living room, she stared out of the window at

the wintry Forth. East Lothian was a mere blur on the far side. The view was about as clear as her take on the case, Karen thought. Nothing was going her way, and the spectre of the Dog Biscuit was hanging over her. She'd demanded a swift clean resolution to this case and that was the one thing that was completely out of reach right now.

Karen was saved from descending into gloom by the arrival of the CSI team. She brought the crime scene manager up to speed. 'There's no sign of a struggle, no indication that there was anybody else here other than our victim. But I want to be sure of that. There's a laptop in the bedroom. That needs to go to Gartcosh as a matter of urgency, marked for the attention of Tamsin Martinu.'

The CSM looked bored. He'd heard it all before, but he'd worked with Karen way back when she was still Fife Police's cold case boss and she knew he wouldn't cut corners. She stepped outside to let them get on with their work and turned into the vennel out of the wind. She texted Daisy to come and pick her up as soon as she was finished with the landlady and walked to the nearest pub to wait and brood. It was the part of the job she enjoyed least.

Karen had warmed to Mary Auld two years before. There was something dignified about her, something humane too. But that didn't mean she got a free pass when it came to either her husband's disappearance or her brother-in-law's putative murder. As soon as they walked into the living room, Karen's eyes were drawn not to the dramatic view but to the paintings. They'd been on the walls in the Edinburgh flat, she remembered. But the light here meant they created much more impact. She knew next to nothing about art, but even she could see that Mary Auld's walls exhibited a coherence of taste.

'That's quite a collection,' she said, pausing to admire them.

'Iain and I had similar taste in the visual arts,' Mary said. 'We liked a certain style of painting that was typical of the mid-twentieth century. We kept an eye on local auctions and sometimes we got lucky. They're not very valuable, but we chose them because we liked them. I find it comforting to have them around me still. Are you interested in art, DCI Pirie?'

Karen looked rueful. 'I'm embarrassed to admit I'm one of those people who say, "I don't know much about art but I know what I like."' She wasn't about to explain that what scant knowledge she possessed had come via the expert curators at the National Galleries, thanks to previous investigations into cold case thefts.

'I think liking is the only reason to buy art,' Mary said, steering them to the chairs that looked out at the sea. 'Have you taken over the investigation from DCI Todd?'

'We're working together. Because of my review into your husband's disappearance. There's a possibility the two cases are connected.'

Mary Auld gave a weary smile. 'I can see why you might think so. Two apparently inexplicable events in the same family invites a desire to link them. But I don't see how there can be any connection, not after all this time.' She fiddled with the wedding ring she still wore, turning it round and round. 'But of course I'll help you in any way I can.'

The one thing Karen had paused to do in Edinburgh was to scan the photograph of Iain Auld and the mystery man. She'd cropped the civil servant out of the picture, leaving the other man in profile. Now she took the print from her bag and passed it to Mary. 'Do you know who this man is?'

She studied it carefully, frowning in concentration. 'No,' she said at last. 'I've no recollection of ever having seen him. Why? Where does he fit in to all this?'

'We don't know,' Karen said. 'We found this photograph in a folder in James Auld's flat in Paris. There was a print-out of a news story from the internet about a fire at an art gallery in Brighton—' She proffered the page.

Mary glanced at it and handed it back. 'We never had any dealings with them. Far too rich for our blood, I'm afraid. I don't know why Jamie would have that; he had no interest in art at all.'

'That's strange. Because he also had this.' Karen gave Mary the list of artworks and auction prices.

Mary gave this her full attention, running her finger down the names. 'This covers quite a wide range of styles and periods. You've got half a dozen YBAs – Young British Artists, I should say. Then some European artists running across the second half of the twentieth century. And other odds and sods going back to the 1920s. There's nothing coherent about it. It looks like a report of a general auction. The sort of thing a medium-scale auction house would put together.' She passed it back. 'There's nothing to indicate which auction house. Though you could probably find out quite easily.'

'How would I do that?' Karen asked.

'Google the paintings. It won't take you long to find details of when some of them last changed hands. Are you any further forward in finding out who killed Jamie?' Mary asked. Her mouth twisted, her contained grief momentarily breaking through.

'We're putting together a picture of his life. His world. We've not been able to access his laptop yet, so we're struggling a bit. We did find a name on the back of a print-out of a newspaper article about a gallery fire. Does the name Hilary mean anything to you? Did Jamie ever mention a Hilary?' Karen had picked up on how Mary referred to her brother-in-law and reflected it back at her. It was a simple tactic to build connection. 'It might be a while back, the early nineties, possibly?'

Mary shrugged. 'That doesn't ring any bells.'

'Maybe somebody he knew in connection with Iain? Did Iain have any friends, any colleagues called Hilary?' Karen knew she was grasping at straws, but straws were all she had.

'I wish I could be more help,' Mary sighed. 'I vaguely remember someone called Hilary who worked for the First Minister at Bute House, but she wasn't one of the people Iain had regular dealings with.'

'I'll get someone to follow that up,' Karen said. 'Sergeant Mortimer spent time with the other members of Jamie's band in Paris, and we went to see his girlfriend, Pascale. I'm very keen to follow up something she told us.'

'What did she say?' Mary leaned forward. Her curiosity was obvious but Karen had no sense that she was apprehensive.

'In the week before he came to Scotland, James travelled to London. When he came back, he went to Dublin overnight. He didn't tell Pascale what he was doing. All he said was he had some business there.'

Mary was clearly frustrated. 'He said nothing about either trip to me. Not a word. But it's curious that he went to London. Even after all this time, he was wary of being in London. I told him time and again, nobody would recognise the man he was in the man he had become, but he still worried. He never lost sight of the notion that he was a wanted man. He tried to avoid travelling through London whenever he could. The idea that he'd make a specific trip to London – that seems strange to me. He must have had a pressing reason for it.'

'Any idea what that reason might have been? Was anything bothering him? Was he pursuing anything? Even something apparently innocuous? Maybe something connected to his music? Or this list of artists' auction prices?'

'As I said, he never mentioned anything that connected to those trips. Those places, even.'

'We know he'd been in touch with an art dealer in Dublin,' Karen said.

'That's news to me. Honestly, I don't remember ever having a conversation with Jamie about art or painters. I'm sorry, I'm as baffled as you are.'

'Do you happen to know who the beneficiaries of Jamie's will are?'

The question seemed to affront Mary. 'I have no idea. I don't even know whether he has a will.'

Karen smiled. 'We have to ask these questions.' She got to her feet. 'I hear you've put this place on the market?'

Mary shook her head, a cynical expression on her face. 'What? You think I killed Jamie for his money? No, Chief Inspector. It's much more prosaic than that. Much as I love the view from here, I find life in a village crushingly boring. I want to move back to Edinburgh, where there's some life in the streets. You're very welcome to speak to my accountant if you want to check my financial security.' She rose from her chair and steered them towards the door. 'You people! As if anyone would murder Jamie for his money. I suspect they'd be in for a hell of a disappointment.'

29

After Karen dropped Daisy back at base, she headed to Edinburgh. On the approach to the Queensferry Crossing, Jason rang. 'Hey, boss,' he said.

'What have you got for me, Jason?'

'I think we might have struck oil. According to Kayleigh at DVLA, there was a Skoda Yeti registered in November 2017 to Barry McAndrew.'

Karen whooped with delight. 'God bless Kayleigh at DVLA. Did you get the address?'

'Sure thing, boss. Isherwood Studios, Reddish Road, Stockport.'

She couldn't help groaning. 'Not more travelling. I'm beginning to feel like I'm on the end of a piece of elastic.'

'I could go myself,' Jason said tentatively. 'If you're too busy, like?'

'No, we both need to be there. Corroboration, remember? Even if she's in England, this is a Scottish inquiry. We're a bit stalled at the moment on the James Auld case. If that's still the position in the morning, we'll head down to Stockport and see if we can chase up Amanda. Or Dani. Or whatever she's calling herself. But there's no mad rush. If she's been spooked by the media coverage of the story, she'll have run already. If she's sitting tight, she'll still be there in a day or two.'

'OK. What do you want me to do in the meantime?'

'Take another look at the Iain Auld review files. See if you can find any reference to art or artists in there. And any mention of a connection to Dublin.'

He knew better than to ask why. 'I'll get on to it right now, boss. See you in the morning.'

Karen drove on to the bridge, for once too busy with her thoughts to appreciate the soaring design that resembled giant sails sweeping drivers across the sea. She moused her way through her music, looking for something a bit jazzy, something that might make her feel connected to James Auld. The nearest she had was a playlist of German film composers that River had forwarded to her when she'd complained of not having anything mindless to help her concentrate. It hadn't been the right thing, but she still had it on her phone. She set it playing and promptly ignored it.

Music had never been that important to Karen. It wasn't that she disliked it; more that it didn't fill a need in her the way it seemed to for other people. She didn't need it as a mirror for her emotional state, and she didn't measure the key stages of her life by what was playing on the radio or streaming on YouTube. She'd often heard people talk about particular songs as time machines, how simply hearing them in a bar or in the car would transport them back vividly to a particular event. She wondered what it would be like to be a musician, a life defined by what came in through your ears and went out through your fingers.

With a jolt, the idea occurred to her that for someone like James Auld, the music was at the heart of everything. Lovers, friends, family might come and go, but the music was a constant. So what else would you choose for a password but the music that spoke most sonorously to you?

She'd just crossed Cramond Brig at the end of the dual carriageway so she was able to pull over to the side of the road. She turned back the pages of her notebook until she found Pascale Vargas's phone number. She tapped in the number and waited patiently for the international call tone. It rang out for so long Karen thought she was out of luck but finally she heard, '*Oui, bonjour?*'

Deep breath. '*Bonjour*, Pascale. *C'est* Commandant Pirie. From Ecosse. We spoke yesterday?'

'Ah, *oui*, of course. How can I be of help, Commandant?'

'I have a question for you. Do you know the password of Paul's laptop?'

'*Non, je ne le sais pas*. I don't know, I never needed to. Sorry.'

'OK, that was a long shot. I have one more question. Did Paul have a favourite musician? A kind of hero?

'*Mais oui*. He admired in particular the saxophonist John Surman. You need me to spell that?'

'Please.' Karen tapped out the name on her phone. 'Thank you. You've been a great help. I'm sorry to have troubled you.'

'It is no trouble.' A deep sigh. 'I cannot believe he's gone, you know? When the phone rings, I think it's him. It doesn't feel possible.'

Believe me, I know. 'We're determined to find out who killed Paul,' Karen said. 'It won't take the pain away, but it will give you some answers.'

'There can be no answer that makes any sense, Commandant. He was a good man. A decent man. I don't understand how anyone could hate him enough to kill him.'

I know that feeling too. 'I'm sorry. I'll make sure you're kept informed of any developments.'

'Thank you. Good luck with your inquiry.'

The line went dead. Karen leaned her head on the steering wheel and let her own memories swamp her for a moment. At least she had a focus for her rage at the loss of the man she'd loved. Merrick fucking Shand. She didn't know how she'd have coped without that knowledge. Pascale was trapped in a nightmare with no answers, and that would poison her life in a different way, unless Karen could solve this case.

Karen straightened up and dashed the back of her hand across her eyes. She needed to get a grip. Google was her friend again and she found John Surman immediately on Wikipedia. Not only was he a virtuoso sax player, he also played synthesiser and bass clarinet. Who even knew there was such a thing? She read on and discovered he composed free jazz and modal jazz. She was pretty sure there wouldn't be many catchy tunes in his back catalogue. She was astonished to find that Surman had recorded an album with a Tunisian oud player. Was this nothing more than a weird coincidence or could it have something to do with the words on the back of the newspaper cutting? She couldn't imagine how that might connect to Auld's murder more than twenty years after the recording, but she filed it away for possible further consideration.

What was probably more useful was that his date of birth was 30 August 1944. It was a starting point.

She called a familiar number and was relieved to hear Tamsin Martinu's brash greeting. 'What's up, Karen? Fucked over any bad guys today?'

'I did manage to seriously piss someone off earlier, but the day is young.'

'True, I know I can count on you. So what are you after, sister?'

222

'You'll be getting a laptop from the CSI team in Fife. It's from the James Auld murder inquiry. It's passworded, and I tried the usual name, date-of-birth stuff without any luck. But here's the thing. He was a jazz musician. His hero was a saxophonist called John Surman.' She began to spell it, but Tamsin interrupted.

'Yeah, yeah, I know Surman. He's got this very cool album, *Coruscating*, it's on my late-night heavy rotation. You should give it a try one of those insomniac nights.'

Karen sighed. 'Whatever. Anyway, I think it's probably worth trying some combinations round that. His DOB is 30 August 1944.' Like Tamsin couldn't have found that out for herself in seconds.

'I'll look forward to it. What are we hoping for?'

'I'm mostly interested in emails. Anything about Dublin, London, his brother Iain Auld. And paintings.'

'I like it when you narrow it down. I'll crack it as soon as I can. If we're lucky, he'll use the same password for the machine and the email account.'

'Front of the queue?'

'You know I never promise.'

But you always deliver. Because my cases fascinate you, and you want answers as much as I do. 'Just as well. Because one of these days . . . '

'Not going to happen, Karen. Now go away and ruin somebody else's evening.' She hung up, leaving Karen with the reminder that the chances were high that she was about to do precisely that.

30

Karen swung by Aleppo to collect the selection of mezes she'd ordered from the car. Miran, the manager, had never forgotten the helping hand she'd extended when they'd been trying to set up the business; he nodded in resigned approval when she shoved cash into the refugee charity box after he'd refused her money yet again. 'It's good to see you, Karen,' he greeted her.

'You too. How's the family?'

He smiled. 'We are all well. I put some extras in the box, new dishes Amena is trying out. Let us know what you think.'

Miran's wife Amena was the creative brain in the kitchen. Nothing new had arrived on the menu when she'd briefly been on maternity leave, but normal service was clearly resumed. 'Now that's a treat,' she said. It would give her and Hamish something to talk about, at least.

When she reached home, she texted him before she got cold feet.

I'll be there in half an hour. x

Karen showered in less than five minutes, taking care not to wet her hair. Loose-linen mix capris and a dark green top with black swirls she'd picked up in the Sahara sale. Trying, but not too hard, was the message she was going for. She laid the table, opened a bottle of Shiraz, then stood looking through her floor-to-ceiling windows at the restless sea beyond. Was Hamish a mess of contradictions, or just a man who'd chosen to embrace multiple possibilities?

When they'd first met, right at the start of one of Karen's thorniest cases, she'd taken him at face value – a modern crofter in the north-west Highlands, running sheep and holiday lets on his land. Albeit a bit of a hunk who looked like he'd stepped straight out of an episode of *Outlander*, with his kilt and his work boots, his luxuriant beard and flowing red-gold hair. She'd hoped he was playing it ironically, but a flicker of doubt about who he really was had burst into flames when she walked into the kitchen of his cottage. It wouldn't have been out of place in one of the flats in Edinburgh's West End that had been gutted and refitted with steel and marble so they could be sold for a small fortune. Pride of place in Hamish's kitchen went to a coffee maker that probably had more computing power than the first moon landing. The cup of coffee he'd made her had suckered her in, in spite of her suspicious nature.

Soon, she'd uncovered Hamish's other existence. He owned Perk, a small chain of hipster coffee shops in Edinburgh. He commuted between the two worlds, swapping his crofter wardrobe for skinny jeans, tweed jacket over checked shirts and a ponytail. *A ponytail, for fuck's sake*, she'd chided herself on her first encounter with his city persona.

Then there was his open, hail-fellow-well-met presentation. Just an ordinary guy making a living. Except he'd grown up with the kind of advantages Karen could barely imagine. Both parents high-flying academics. He'd spent his teens in America, shuttling between a private school in New England and his parents' home in California, returning to Scotland to go to university in Edinburgh. It couldn't have been more of a contrast to Karen's working-class background in Fife. She remembered the pride her parents had exhibited when they'd finally scraped together the deposit on the two-bedroomed modern house where she'd spent her teens. There had never been cash to spare in her childhood. Holidays were taken in caravans by the Scottish coast, not on the beach in Mexico or skiing in the Adirondacks.

But he couldn't help that, and in spite of her instinctive mistrust of people she believed hadn't earned their privilege, she warmed to him. And then he'd done the devious thing with the earring, right at the start. That had left her on shaky ground, unwilling to take another step forward. But he'd persuaded her that it had been an uncharacteristically stupid move, one that had appealed purely because he wanted to be more to her than a witness in a cold case.

Karen had let herself be convinced. He was, after all, the first man she'd been remotely interested in since Phil's death. She'd thought she could maybe trust him enough to take the first tentative steps towards a relationship. And so they'd eased into it. She was glad that her job and his double-sided life meant they could only be part-time lovers; she had no appetite for anything more committed, not yet, maybe not ever. She'd already been wary of the differences in aspiration and expectation between them. But the events outside the prison that Monday morning had driven a wedge between them. She didn't know how to get past something so deep.

Nothing like that had ever come between her and Phil. She'd always thought that was a measure of how strong their love was. But maybe all it meant was that they'd never been tested in the fire. Both of her closest friends thought she should try to work things out with Hamish. She shouldn't be afraid to take their advice, should she? And was she being disingenuous when she told Hamish he wasn't in competition with a dead man? Was she holding him to an absurd standard?

The intercom buzzed through her thoughts. Time to put this to the test. Karen pressed the outside door release then went to open her front door. The lift dinged and moments later, Hamish rounded her corner of the hallway. In spite of her misgivings, her stomach gave a jolt at the sight of him striding towards her, hair loose and glinting, carrying a huge bunch of exotic-looking flowers she didn't know the name of. And that said it all, the cynical voice in the back of her head said. Phil would have brought daffodils and she'd have been perfectly happy with that. Hamish had to go one better.

And she had to learn to stop comparing. Because she knew the dead always came out ahead.

Hamish stopped a few feet short of her. 'I was afraid I wouldn't see you again,' he said.

'Hamish, there's no way I'd ever stop buying coffee in Perk.' She gave a mischievous smile. He met it with a tentative one of his own. 'Come on in.'

He thrust the flowers at her and followed her into the flat. Karen put them down next to the sink and turned to face him. Now there was no barrier between them. She gave him a level stare, then stepped forward and put her hands on the lapels of his overcoat. She turned her face up to his and he bent his head. Their lips grazed gently and she drank in the familiar smell of him. Beard oil with its notes of sandalwood and eucalyptus, the faint burned smell of roasting coffee beans and an undertone of undefinable masculinity. It was hard to resist.

Actually, she didn't want to resist. They kissed again, less provisionally this time, then they wrapped their arms round each other in a tight hug. 'I'm so sorry,' Hamish whispered. 'I can't help wanting to make everything right for you.'

'That's not your job,' Karen said. 'You think it's how you show you care for someone. In my world, it feels like a marker for wanting to control me.'

He sighed and screwed up his eyes in frustration. 'I get what you're saying. It's hard for me to put that into practice.'

'How about you wait till I ask for help, rather than breenge in when you decide I need it?'

'The other side of that is you being able to ask.'

A long moment. 'So we both have lessons to learn.' She gave him another quick kiss. 'Now how about you take your coat off and make it look like you're going to stick around for a while?'

Hamish shrugged out of his coat and took it through to the hall to hang it up. By the time he returned, Karen was transferring the meze from the fridge to the table. 'Need a hand?'

'It's fine. It's from Aleppo.'

'Excellent, that's a treat,' he said absently, moving papers aside to lean on the breakfast bar. Glancing down, he said, 'Why have you got a picture of David Greig? And who's the boyfriend?'

'What?' Karen turned swiftly, her tone sharp.

Hamish waved the photograph of Iain Auld and the mystery man. 'David Greig.'

228

'Saying it again doesn't help,' Karen said. 'Who's David Greig?'

He stabbed the mystery man with his finger. 'David Greig. Don't you know who he is? Or rather, who he was?'

'No, I don't.' Now her interest was fully engaged. Was Hamish going to be the source of the answer she'd been seeking?

'So why have you got a picture of a man you don't know? Is this work?'

'Yes, it's work. You know I can't tell you any more about it.' She took the picture from Hamish, who let it go without a fuss. 'Tell me about David Greig.' Urgent now.

'I can't believe you don't know who he is,' Hamish said, sounding properly relaxed for the first time since he'd walked in.

Exasperated, Karen said, 'If I bribe you with a drink, will you stop treating me like an idiot?'

Hamish grinned. 'Deal. A glass of that red will do the trick.'

Karen poured two glasses and returned with them to his side. 'Tell me about David Greig.'

'He was a YBA. One of the second wave, RCA rather than Goldsmiths.'

'Hamish, I didn't understand any of that. I'm a career cop from the back streets of Kirkcaldy. Can we just assume I know fuck all about fuck all?' The relaxed mood of a few minutes before had gone as flat as day-old Irn-Bru.

'I'm sorry. I can't help being a pretentious wanker.' He tried an apologetic grin. Karen replied with a twist of the lips that might have been an attempt at a smile. 'YBA, Young British Artists. Conceptual artists who used shock tactics and understood very well the economic possibilities of making art make money. Damien Hirst, Gillian Wearing, Tracy Emin, that lot.'

Light dawned. 'That lot. Sharks in formaldehyde and unmade beds and elephant dung.' Karen rolled her eyes. 'Seems to me that they didn't create art, they created a whole generation of people like me shaking our heads and going, "what the actual *fuck*?" They were a machine for making philistines out of the rest of us.'

Hamish chuckled. 'I can't disagree with you. I had a few mates who went to art school in the nineties and, honestly, I thought their stuff was the emperor's new clothes, to the max. But I did go and see the Sensation exhibition in New York in 2000.' He shook his head, a bemused look in his eyes. 'I thought a few of the pieces were amazing but it didn't change my mind.'

'So where does David Greig fit in among the condoms and the giant vulvas?'

'So you did take some notice?'

'Red-top headlines notice. What did this guy actually make?'

'Like most of them, he had a gimmick. He did portraits, but in a very weird way. What he did, he started with a landscape or a building that was integral to the subject of the portrait. So, if he was painting me, he'd maybe have gone up to Clashstronach and painted the glen with the croft house and the sea loch in the background. Or he might have chosen the interior of one of the Perk outlets. Then he'd take that landscape and cut it up into little pieces. Slices and triangles and squares and shards. And he'd build my portrait out of those fragments.' Hamish drank some wine and made appreciative noises.

Karen frowned. 'You mean, a collage? Made out of the landscape painting?'

'Exactly. I know it sounds completely mad, but somehow he made it work.' He took out his phone and googled, 'David Greig Tony Blair'. The screen revealed an image of the former prime minister that was almost photographic except that the colours were an odd palette of greys and blues, with the occasional shading of green. 'You can't see it on this scale, but he started with a painting of Fettes, where Blair went to school. Greig would photograph the original landscape painting and exhibit it alongside the portrait.'

Karen shook her head. 'It's very tricksy. But how is it art?'

'I think it's meant to make us challenge our perception. That the context a person occupies shapes our view of them.'

She groaned. 'Talk about simplistic. It's just showing off.'

'Maybe, but showing off a high degree of skill.'

'Seems like a waste to me. You said, "Who he is. Or rather, who he was." What did you mean by that? Has he fallen out of favour?'

'He killed himself,' Hamish said. 'I don't remember all the details, but he threw himself off a cliff. His body never turned up, but it wasn't like the guy out of the Manic Street Preachers who simply disappeared. Greig left his clothes and his wallet on the clifftop. I've got a vague recollection of a suicide note.'

'When was this?' She forced herself to sound nonchalant. Two men in a photograph. The look of love. One disappears, one apparently kills himself but his body never turns up. She didn't believe in coincidences like that. But belief was nothing without evidence.

Hamish puffed out a breath. 'I don't remember. Must be ten, twelve years ago. Is any of this helpful?'

'Identifying Greig is a big step forward. I don't know where it'll take me, but it's a lead.' On an impulse, she picked up

231

the newspaper cutting and flipped it over. 'I don't suppose you know who Hilary is, in the context of the art world?' Her voice was a tease but it disguised a genuine inquiry.

Hamish studied the scribbled lines on the page. 'Did your guy go to Oxford, by any chance?'

Karen stared open-mouthed. 'How the hell did you work that out?'

Hamish pointed to each line in turn. 'Well, OUDS is the Oxford University Dramatic Society, and Hilary's what they call the spring term there. In that context, I'd take a wild guess that "12 NT" stands for a production of *Twelfth Night*.'

He spoke so casually, as if his interpretation was obvious. For Karen, it held the bitter sting of her limited experience. 'I didn't know that,' she said. 'Why do they call a university term Hilary? That's mad. I thought Hilary must be a person.'

'It's probably named after some saint. The patron saint of mortar boards or some such nonsense. I'd have thought the same as you except that I used to go out with a girl who fancied her chances at a career on the stage. She'd done a lot of acting when she was at Oxford. She was always talking about OUDS as if it was the Royal Shakespeare Company.' Hamish pushed his hair back from his face with an awkward smile. She realised he was trying to not make her feel inadequate.

'And did she make it?' Karen didn't really care but it seemed the easiest response.

He grinned. 'She's working in HR in some City law firm.'

'You dodged a bullet there.'

He laughed. 'In more ways than one, Karen. I'm a lot happier here than I would have been in her Docklands flat.'

232

Karen picked up the paper to avoid meeting his eyes. 'So you reckon this is something to do with a production of *Twelfth Night* in, what? Hilary Term 1992 or 1993?'

'Does that make sense in terms of your investigation?'

It did, but she wasn't going to share that. 'Stop fishing.' Karen leaned over and kissed Hamish. She was longing to dive into researching David Greig, but she knew that could wait. Nobody was going to die before morning. She told herself that the important agenda for the evening was to make things right between her and Hamish. So she pulled him to his feet. 'Time for food. I've hardly eaten all day and, now you're here, I need to keep my strength up.' She stood on tiptoe and kissed him, then took his hand and led him to the table.

He hesitated at his chair. 'Are we all right? Am I forgiven?'

Karen met his eyes. 'I don't want this to be over, Hamish. But we need to be honest with each other when either of us is uncomfortable with what the other one says or does. That goes for you as much as me.'

Hamish stared at the table. 'I'll try.' Then he looked up and gave her the disarming grin that always stirred her. 'The trouble is, I don't mind when you get stroppy. I love the challenge.'

'Then stop trying to placate me. Now sit down and eat your dinner.'

'Don't you want to get on the laptop and research David Greig?' He sat, giving her a mischievous look.

He knew her better than she generally liked to admit. Karen pulled a face. 'Dead men can wait. Especially when I've got a living one to take advantage of.'

31

Saturday, 22 February 2020

Karen's eyes snapped open. The low light from her bed-side clock read 4:27. Next to her, Hamish snored softly, but that wasn't what had woken her. She'd been dreaming, something about the sea. Looking down at the sea? Whatever it had been, it had slipped out of her conscious-ness now, gone too fast to grasp. She eased herself out of bed, shivering at the night air on her naked skin. She grabbed her dressing gown on the way out of the bedroom, knowing there would be no more sleep for her that night. There was only so much oblivion she could earn from good sex.

Closing the door softly, she made her way back to the living room and turned on the heating and the desk lamp by her laptop. She'd have liked a cup of coffee, but there was no possibility of grinding beans without waking Hamish, and there was no need for both of them to be sleep-deprived. She settled down with a can of sugar-free Irn-Bru; any hit of caffeine was better than none.

Karen sat for a long moment contemplating the blank

screen, indulging herself in the buzz of anticipation. It had only been a couple of days since she'd discovered the photograph of Iain Auld and David Greig, but it felt as if the puzzle had been nagging at her for much longer. Now she had an answer, she wanted to savour this moment before the hard work started.

She booted up and typed 'David Greig artist' in the search box. It might have been around a decade since Greig had disappeared but the internet had not forgotten him. Approximate 1.25 million hits. Wikipedia was the first port of call. Pinch of salt needed, of course, but although the entry could be underpinned by malice or adoration, there would be something to get her teeth into.

David Greig (1969–2010) was an English conceptual artist, considered a member of the Young British Artists movement. His portrait of Ali Smith was shortlisted for the 2002 Turner Prize.

Early Life
Greig was born in Manchester and raised in a single-parent household by his mother. He attended Burnage High School for Boys. He was awarded a BA in painting from Edinburgh College of art and an MA from the Royal College of Art.

The Edinburgh connection piqued her interest. She made a note to check whether anyone who had taught Greig was still in post. That would definitely be worth an hour of her time.

Art Practice

His primary interest was portraiture and he very quickly developed a unique practice involving landscape painting, collage and multimedia to construct portraits of his chosen subjects. The environments of the landscapes always had an intimate connection with the portrait subjects. His intention was to demonstrate how our personalities are integrations of many fragments. His work was considered to be more accessible than many of his YBA contemporaries, not least because he generally chose subjects who were in the public eye – politicians, pop stars, actors, writers. From early in his career, his work achieved some of the higher prices paid for contemporary art. Balanced against that was the relative modesty of his output, given the time and intensity his method required. He seldom produced more than three or four paintings per year.

Karen skimmed the details of exhibitions, galleries and critical responses to Greig's work and scrolled down to the part that really interested her.

Death

Greig committed suicide on 10 June 2010.

That sentence stopped her in her tracks. Three weeks after Iain Auld's disappearance, the man pictured in an intimate moment with him had also vanished. Excited, she read on.

He had complained to friends of feeling depressed at the ending of a relationship. His clothes, shoes and wallet were found neatly folded on the top of the Gogarth cliffs on Anglesey. In his jacket pocket was a suicide note which

236

was read out at the inquest into his death. In it, he said he had lost his creative impulse when his lover had left him and that he did not want to live if he could not paint. His body was never recovered.

Reputation

His work is still held in critical esteem and remains popular with collectors, achieving good prices at auction, particularly since several of his portraits were destroyed in the catastrophic Goldman Gallery fire of 2017. Many of his portraits were sold privately and from time to time they emerge on to the market. In the past decade, eight previously unrecorded works have appeared. Their authenticity has not been doubted because of Greig's unique method of validating his work. He would affix a selection of nail clippings to the back of his canvases. 'My agent has legally verified examples of my DNA. If anyone doubts my work, they can have one of the nail clippings tested to clear the matter up,' he told a journalist who was investigating the nature of authenticity in a contemporary art world that had come to rely heavily on the concept of the 'factory' production of artworks, which its proponents compared to the studio system of renaissance masters.

How must it feel, Karen wondered, to work in a job where what you achieved was worth more when you were dead? Phil Parhatka had been one of the most committed cops she'd ever served with. The work he'd done, particularly in his last post with the Murder Prevention Unit, had transformed lives and prospects. But who even remembered his name, apart from her, his family and a few close friends? Ten years on from his death, would she still be grieving?

Would she still be turning over the pages of memory, seeing even more value in the things he'd done? Would the women and kids whose lives he'd saved even remember his name? And yet David Greig, a man who'd never saved a life, was revered and referred to in dozens of reference books and articles. Where was the justice in that?

For a moment, she buried her head in her hands. Thinking this way was the quickest route to guilt over the man asleep in her bed and that wasn't fair to Hamish. Or to her own future. Karen growled deep in her throat and sat up straight. She had the basic facts lined up. Now it was time for whatever spin the media had put on Greig's death.

She went for the trashiest tabloid first. BRIT ART BAD BOY IN CLIFF PLUNGE screamed the headline.

> Multi-millionaire artist David Greig has thrown himself off a cliff to his death, police believe.
>
> Notorious for his drug-fuelled partying, gay David, 41, left a heartbroken suicide note on top of the sheer cliffs in Anglesey, North Wales, it is claimed.
>
> A friend said, 'He had a bad break-up and he'd lost his mojo. Without his art and his lover, he just couldn't go on.'

Karen would have bet her flat on the fictitious nature of the 'friend'. She skimmed the rest of it and gleaned the information that Greig's car had been found unlocked in the nearby South Stack lighthouse car park and that Anglesey had been the scene of childhood holidays.

One of the red-tops had dredged up an ex. Among the scurrilous tales of drug-taking and sexual misbehaviour was an admission that Greig had calmed down in the past few years after a health scare. '"He more or less stopped partying hard,"' she read. '"I know he was seeing someone, but he'd started to keep his personal life very private. Then a couple of months ago, the news all over town was that he'd been dumped and he was completely devastated."'

Karen frowned. The timing was interesting. If the ex-boyfriend's timeline was right, Greig had been left broken-hearted at least a fortnight before Iain Auld had disappeared. If Auld had been his secret lover, a distraught Greig moved neatly into the prime suspect slot. A spurned lover driven wild by grief and rage was a much better fit. And it made sense of Greig's suicide. Overcome by remorse, he'd gone back to a place where he'd been happy and taken his own life. Textbook, she thought.

And yet. And yet . . . In her experience, textbook was usually an excuse for lazy investigation. Settling for the obvious without probing for the hidden truths. In the back of her head, she could hear Phil's voice. 'Where's the evidence, Karen? A single photograph. That's all you've got. How does Oxford University fit into this? You don't even know whether OUDS performed *Twelfth Night* in 1992 or 1993. And what has any of that got to do with an art gallery fire twenty-five years later?' They'd often tested their evidence like that. Challenged each other, unpicked the assumptions and stripped them back to the bare facts.

If this convenient explanation of what had happened to Iain Auld was true, it had a profound effect on the investigation of his brother's murder. It meant that this second death was completely unconnected to what had happened to Iain. By rights, she should concentrate on trying to find some evidence that would prove her hypothesis and hand the current case back to Charlie Todd. Tell the Dog Biscuit it had nothing to do with politics, that everybody in the

Scottish establishment could breathe a sigh of relief. That was the obvious course of action.

But for some reason, she didn't want to let go yet. 'You're so bloody possessive,' she muttered. Because she'd already done the legwork, part of her felt she was entitled to follow the thread through the labyrinth. It certainly wouldn't hurt to pursue the Edinburgh College of Art connection, though she had no idea how to find someone who had taught Greig thirty years before.

Karen stretched and yawned. The clock on the computer said 6:43. Time always slipped away once she started chasing down the rabbit holes of the internet. She was about to open her email when she heard the door open. She swung round to see Hamish in the doorway, tousled and yawning. She wasn't surprised; his dual lives running a croft and a chain of coffee shops had made him an early riser. 'I didn't hear you get up,' he said.

'I'm glad I didn't wake you.'

'Are you working? Shall I make coffee?'

'You know me so well. Let me check my email and I'll be right with you.' Karen turned back to the screen, the familiar grumbling and hissing of the coffee machine an accompaniment to a slew of routine messages.

'We could go down to the Malmaison for an early breakfast,' Hamish said, handing her the fresh brew.

'I've got too much to get through today.' She softened the rejection by putting down the coffee and kissing him. 'It's your own fault,' she added, tickling the curl of hair behind his ear. 'You handed me such a great lead.'

He gave a rueful chuckle. 'I've always been my own worst enemy.'

32

Jason swivelled round in his chair when Karen walked into the HCU office. 'So, are we going to Stockport, boss?' he asked, cheery as a small child on the first day of the school holidays.

'Maybe later,' she said. 'I've got a few things I need to sort out first.'

He looked disappointed. 'Oh. OK. What do you want me to get on with in the meantime?'

'We know where the car was registered to Barry McAndrew. That's our best lead right now. Let's see if we can save ourselves some running around when we get down there and maybe find our missing person turning up anywhere else. Check electoral rolls and council tax registers for Daniella Gilmartin, Barry McAndrew and Amanda McAndrew. Go back to HMRC, try the Department of Health and Social Care, see if Dani's signing on for the dreaded Universal Credit.' It was make-work, in all probability, but making Jason feel useful was always a positive.

'OK.' He turned back to his screen then swung back to face her. 'Boss?'

'Jason.'

'See, if somebody was going to buy somebody a ring, how would you know what size to get?' His ears pinked.

'Are you planning on asking Eilidh to marry you?' Karen hoped her surprise didn't show. Eilidh was a nice enough lassie; however, she hadn't thought they were that serious. 'Is that not a bit soon?'

'We've known each other the best part of a year. And I really like her,' he said. The blood was rising from his neck to his cheeks. 'And I think she really likes me and we get along great. I've never met anybody that I wanted to be with like I want to be with her.'

Karen felt a genuine surge of happiness. Her initial frustration with Jason's limitations had mellowed into a real warmth and a respect for his willingness to work hard. He never complained even when she loaded him with tasks that would have made her weep at their prosaic repetitiveness, and she couldn't deny he was a far better cop than he'd been when he'd first arrived on the team. But most of all, he'd looked up to Phil and loved him like the big brother he wished he'd had instead of the feckless and amoral Ronan. How could she not be pleased for the good fortune of someone who had cared that much for Phil? And if he brought that same loyalty to Eilidh, who was she to say 'too young'?

'All good reasons to want to put a ring on her finger. Does she wear other rings?'

'Not when she's working. She says she has to be careful not to get them tangled in her clients' hair. If she was a barber, it wouldn't be a problem. But being a ladies' stylist, she could easy get a fancy ring caught in a tangle.'

'What about when you're going out and she gets dressed up?'

Jason's brow furrowed in thought. 'Sometimes, yeah,' he

said at last. 'She's got some of those big rings. Kinda bling, you know what I mean?'

Karen smiled. 'Then all you need to do is sneak one of them out of her jewellery box and take it to a jeweller's. They can tell you what size it is. And that's a pretty good guide. If it ends up being a bit too big, it's easy enough to get it taken down a size. Just make sure it's not a pinkie ring, though.' With Jason, it never hurt to state the obvious.

His face lit up. 'Thanks, boss. That's a brilliant idea.'

'Good luck, Jason. I hope she realises she's already got a diamond and says yes.'

Beaming, he said, 'I don't know about that, but I'll tell her you said it.'

'And, Jason?'

'What?'

'You should also tell her that if she breaks your heart, I will break her legs.'

His eyes widened in shock. 'You're joking, right?'

'You think?' She let a tiny smile creep across her lips. 'Now get on with your work.' She turned her attention to her screen. She wondered whether there was any point in trying to find someone at the College of Art who would remember David Greig as a student. She suspected it wasn't the sort of institution where they'd have yearbooks or matriculation photos. Still, nothing ventured, nothing gained. A quick search revealed an email address for their alumni organisation, so she fired off an email asking them to contact her. Not that anyone would read it before Monday morning.

Now Hamish had made sense of the notations on the back of the newspaper printout, her next task was to see whether Mary Auld could shed any light on them. She toyed for a moment with the idea of sending Daisy to see her, but Karen had to acknowledge she wanted to gauge Mary's reaction herself.

Mary's phone rang out several times before she picked up. 'This is Mary Auld,' she said, oddly formal.

'DCI Pirie here. I'm sorry to bother you again but there's something I wanted to ask you about.'

'It had better be useful rather than a bother, Chief Inspector,' she sighed. 'How can I help?'

'Did you know your husband when he was at Oxford?'

'No, we didn't meet till he came back to Edinburgh. Why do you ask?'

'I know it sounds a bit bizarre, but we have to follow up every thread of an investigation. I wondered whether Iain did any acting when he was a student?'

A pause. Karen interpreted it as stunned silence, but she was wrong. 'It's very odd that you should ask that,' Mary said slowly. 'Yes, he did. He was quite keen on am-drams at university and afterwards. Well into his twenties, in fact. But you asking isn't what's odd.'

Sometimes the timbre of a conversation shifted and Karen knew that something important was coming. She didn't always recognise why it was significant at the time, but the feeling always made her mark it with a mental asterisk. 'What is it that's odd, Mary?' she asked cautiously.

'I had a phone call a few weeks ago from a woman called Verity Foggo. She's an actress. She pops up on TV some-times, but she works primarily on stage. Iain knew her from Oxford, they were both in a Shakespeare production.'

Karen realised she was holding her breath and slowly let it out. 'What play, do you remember?'

'It was *Twelfth Night*. Verity played Viola and Iain, Antonio.'

'And she called you out of the blue?'

'Yes, it was a surprise. We'd met up with her for drinks a few times, in London. But we hadn't been in touch since Iain's funeral.'

'Why did she contact you?'

Another pause. 'It was quite peculiar. She asked if I was still in touch with Jamie. I explained that the police had been treating him as a suspect in Iain's disappearance so he'd gone on the run because he couldn't bear it. She said she knew all that, but she didn't believe Jamie would have cut himself off from family. She said she wanted Jamie's email so she could get hold of him.' Mary sounded puzzled.

'I don't understand. Why did she want to be in touch with Jamie?'

'Well, that's the thing. I'm not entirely sure. She said she'd got to know Jamie when Iain was at Oxford. They'd gone out together once or twice, she said, though that was the first I'd heard of it.'

'Fair enough, but why did she want to get back in touch with him now?'

'She told me some tale about a burst pipe in her storage unit. Apparently she'd lost a whole archive box, including all the photographs from the *Twelfth Night* production. Jamie had taken the photographs of the production and she wanted to contact him on the off-chance that he still had the negatives, or at least some of the prints.'

'So what did you say to her?'

'I said that even if I did know how to contact Jamie, I'd be a fool to give his details to anyone. As far as I knew, the police still thought he was a person of interest in Iain's disappearance. And besides, why would he have gone on the run with her photographs?'

Karen could make no sense of any of this. It didn't fit any of her theories about the case. And it certainly didn't shed any light on James Auld's death. 'So how did you leave it?'

'I told her I couldn't help her.'

'Did you tell Jamie?'

'Oh yes, there was no reason not to. I mentioned it the next time we spoke on the phone. He was as baffled as I was.'

'Did he follow it up, do you know?'

'He didn't mention it, so I assume he didn't. I mean, why would you? Some self-obsessed actress who thinks he'd been carting round her picture for the last thirty years? I know it's a cliché, but really, actors ... It's always about them, isn't it?'

What little experience Karen had had with actors had left her thinking their egos were no more monstrous than average. If anything, they were more fragile because their living was dependent on the good opinion of others. But she wasn't about to get into that with Mary Auld. 'You're right, I'm sure Jamie would have told you if he'd reached out to her. I expect the notes we found were what he scribbled down when you were talking on the phone.'

'That would make sense.'

'I'm sorry to have bothered you with something so trivial. But in a murder inquiry, we have to eliminate everything, no matter how trivial it seems.'

'I understand. I only wish your colleagues had been so thorough when Iain disappeared,' she said tartly.

And that was the end of that conversation. Karen stared at the name she'd written down. Verity Foggo. Where did she fit in? Did she fit in at all? Or was she the equivalent of a rogue piece from another jigsaw altogether? Her head was nipping with the disparate elements of the case, not to mention the ongoing matter of the skeleton in the camper van; she needed a sounding board whose judgement she could trust. Once that would have been Phil, and this was one area where Hamish could never replace him.

She sighed, and googled Verity Foggo. Judging by the results, she worked more than most actors. She appeared to be one of those jobbing performers who never gets the lead role but often turns up in the middle of the cast list. Karen clicked on 'images'. Verity Foggo looked vaguely familiar, and Karen recognised some of her TV credits as episodes in series she'd watched. But she wouldn't have been able to pick her out of a line-up. She checked her out on Twitter and discovered she was currently appearing in Glasgow in a touring production of something called *Hyde and Seek* by a playwright she'd never heard of. For once the stars were aligned in her favour, it seemed.

But before she could act on her discovery, her phone rang. It was an unfamiliar Edinburgh number. 'DCI Pirie, Historic Cases Unit,' she recited.

'Oh, hello? This is Sonja Hall from Edinburgh College of Art's alumni office? You emailed us earlier?'

Unsure why someone with a Glasgow accent felt the need to make every sentence a question, Karen said, 'I did, yes. Thanks for getting back to me.'

'No bother, really? I'm not usually in on a Saturday, but we're about to launch a big fundraising appeal and I had to make sure the "giving" page was running right? So, here's the thing? We have a strict GDPR policy at the College of Art so I can't personally give you any details of alumni?'

'I thought that might be the case. But—'

'See, what I can do, and what I have in actual fact done,

is contact former students on the painting course from those years that we've got details for on file and asked them to get in touch with you?'

Karen unravelled the sentence. 'That's great, thanks, I appreciate that.'

'I don't know how much help it will be? Because we didn't have such good contacts with graduates back then? So there's only half a dozen on our list?'

One would be enough, if it was the right one. 'Hopefully that'll do.'

'Sure but see, one of the lecturers who taught that course, he's still on the staff? I thought maybe he would be able to help so I asked him?'

'He's still there from twenty-eight years ago?'

A giggle. 'I know, it's incredible, isn't it? Anyway, he remembers David Greig really well, he was kind of his mentor?'

'Can you put me in touch with him?'

'He's going to call you, if that's OK? I just wanted to give you a wee heads-up, so it wouldn't come at you out of the blue, like? His name's Alasdair Darnley?'

'Sonja, that is brilliant. I can't thank you enough.' *Now get off the line and let me talk to the man who is going to make David Greig come alive for me.*

'No worries, it's great to get such an interesting query, mostly it's dead straightforward, you know? Your job must be totally fascinating?'

'It has its moments. Thanks again.' Karen ended the call, then sat drumming her fingers on the desk. Seven minutes dragged by before the phone rang again. She grabbed it on the first ring. 'DCI Pirie, Historic Cases Unit,' she gabbled.

'This is Alasdair Darnley,' a slow sonorous voice intoned.

'I believe you wanted to talk to someone who knew the late David Greig.'

'I do, sir. Thanks for calling. I wonder if we might meet?'

'I don't see why not. Are you in Edinburgh?'

They settled on the Perk branch on George IV Bridge, midway between his Marchmont flat and her office. Having something to do energised Karen. She grabbed her coat and her bag as Jason looked up. 'Are we going to Stockport? Only—'

'Later, Jason. I've got to go and talk to a man about a painter. And then you and me are going to Glasgow.'

'Not Stockport?'

'It's on the way. Well, kind of. Two birds, one stone, sort of thing. Trust me, Jason.'

As if he'd have done anything else.

33

Karen emerged from the dystopian fluorescent gloom of the Gayfield Square station into sparkling sunshine on Leith and the rest of the city. Even though the trees were still bare and the weather crisp, it almost felt as if winter was on the retreat. It was enough to lift her spirits in spite of what felt like an amassing of information without any forward movement on either case. She took so much pleasure in the day that she was entirely oblivious to the man who kept pace with her all the way across North Bridge, up the High Street and on to George IV Bridge. When she turned into the coffee shop, her pursuer cut across the street and found a window seat in a café opposite.

Anders the barista greeted Karen with a friendly smile and finished making an espresso for a painfully thin young woman clutching an armful of textbooks. Then he turned his attention to Karen. 'Flat white?'

'As usual. You busy?'

'So-so. Hamish isn't in, if you were looking for him?'

One of Hamish's virtues was that he wasn't the kind of boss who hovered. He hired people he trusted and if they let him down, there were no second chances. All his team understood that, but because he treated them like adults and paid better than the going rate elsewhere, it seemed to work, if the low turnover of staff was anything to go by. 'No, I'm meeting somebody,' Karen said, looking around and failing to spot anyone who looked like her idea of an art teacher. 'I'll go and sit in the window and try to look like a cop.'

She'd barely made a start on her coffee when a little barrel of a man waddled in. He was the epitome of a certain Scottish type: short, rotund, bald, with a face that looked like it had been formed from modelling clay – button nose and double chin, round cheeks and fleshy brow. A pair of gold-rimmed glasses dug into his nose. He was wearing a fisherman's smock straining at the seams under a volu-minous raincoat. He looked around with the air of a man attempting to act as if this was his natural environment. He caught Karen's eye and frowned. 'Are you waiting for me?' he asked. 'I'm Alasdair Darnley.'

Karen stood up. 'And I'm DCI Pirie. Can I get you a coffee?'

He bustled into the seat opposite her, bellying up to the table. 'An Americano with soy milk, please. I'm lactose intolerant.'

Karen ordered the drink then returned to her seat. 'Thanks for meeting me.'

'I'm intrigued,' he said. 'David Greig. Now there's a name from the past. Why would a detective chief inspector be interested in talking about the late David Greig?'

There was a condescension in his manner that she found irritating, the more so since she'd have to disguise it. But that was the nature of the job sometimes. 'As I said on the phone, I'm with the Historic Cases Unit and David Greig's name has come up in connection with a case I'm currently reviewing.'

'That sounds very tantalising. Is he suspected of having committed some heinous crime?'

Karen hoped her smile didn't look as weary as it felt. 'Nothing so exciting. Following up some loose threads.'

'Well, David could certainly be loose,' he said archly. Anders came over with his coffee. Darnley didn't even thank him. 'Perhaps you'd give me a clue as to what precisely interests you?'

'I'm trying to find out what he was like. Since I'm based in Edinburgh, I thought I'd make a start here. You taught David painting, is that right?'

He gave an affected chuckle. 'I don't teach artists like David to paint. I point out the deficiencies in their work and suggest directions they might choose to take in order to make it better. But yes, David was one of my students.'

'What was he like? As a person?'

'Full of himself and convinced he was God's gift to painting. Loud, opinionated and ambitious. But he was also handsome and funny and charismatic. He was popular with most of his fellow students, which naturally made him very *un*popular with others. And of course he was flamboyantly gay, which was not unproblematic in the days of Section 28.'

Karen knew Darnley was fishing for a reaction but she couldn't be bothered. She didn't know what she was looking for but she was pretty sure its roots didn't lie in Greig's student days. 'And as a painter? What was your opinion of him?'

Darnley sipped his coffee and pursed his lips. 'I'll be honest. At first, I wondered whether we'd made a mistake in admitting him.' A self-satisfied smirk. He was like a puppy, performing for the next treat. Or in this case, the next prompt.

'Why was that?'

'In his first year, his work was startlingly derivative. He could copy any style, from Bellini to Bacon. For the first term, in the life class, his draughtsmanship was superb but there was nothing original about it. One week he sketched like Dürer, the next like Picasso, then like a Michelangelo cartoon. Whatever he'd been looking at most intently in the immediate past, there it was on his easel. But when we sought his own creativity, there seemed to be a vacuum. It was worrying, Detective Chief Inspector. We're a college of art, not a college for copyists.'

'Something obviously changed?'

'He had a Damascene moment.' He paused, assuming she'd have to ask for a translation.

'And what was his revelation on the road to Damascus?' All those Scottish Presbyterian Sunday mornings did sometimes pay off.

'He went to an exhibition where they were showing some works by the German collage artist Kurt Schwitters. Something in those works spoke to him and he came back halfway through his third term fired up with enthusiasm for the form. It was a complete transformation. As if someone had flicked a switch marked "imagination" in his head. He brought all that technical skill to bear on this revelation.'

'So that was when he came up with the idea of making a portrait collage from the landscape?'

'Not quite that specific at first. He started with a more conventional approach. He made portraits from magazine clippings. But at some point over that first summer break, he hit on what he called "Mode: Landscape to Portrait". A kind of pun, you see? From the idea of computer printing, which of course was still in its early days back in the early nineties. I thought it was a remarkable idea.' He peered over his glasses and pursed his lips again. 'It was the only original idea he ever had. But people loved it and he milked it. Every celebrity, every politician wanted a David Greig portrait. They didn't all like the end result, though. He became very good at seeing past surfaces.'

'So when did he take off, in terms of reputation and collectability? When did the money start rolling in?'

'Not for a few years. Not till after he went down to London to the Royal College and was taken up by the patrons of the Brit Art phenomenon. No, David was like the rest of his crowd, a poor student. But he did manage to avoid having to take holiday jobs in places like this.' He waved an insouciant hand towards the counter.

Karen bit back the obvious retort about the skills involved in making what she considered a good cup of coffee. 'How did he do that?'

'He used his skills as a copyist to produce versions of famous paintings with faces chosen by the people who commissioned him.' Again, the pregnant pause.

'I'm not sure I understand,' she admitted reluctantly.

'If you were getting married, he'd do you a version of Van Eyck's Arnolfini Portrait but replacing the original faces with those of you and your bride. Only, probably not pregnant ... Or if it was your wife's birthday, he'd do you a version of Vermeer's *Girl with a Pearl Earring*. Your husband in his rugby kit in the style of Holbein. A Gainsborough family portrait including the family dog. He knocked them out with alarming speed. There are probably dozens scattered round the bourgeois drawing rooms of Edinburgh. All very tongue in cheek, of course. But what can this possibly have to do with whatever it is you're investigating? I

254

mean, you do know that David has been dead for nearly ten years?'

Karen gave him a long hard stare. 'Were you surprised to hear that David had committed suicide?'

Darnley had the grace to look abashed. 'Yes, I was,' he said after a moment, his voice soft. 'If you'd asked me, I'd have said David was not a man plagued by self-doubt. He came back to the college a couple of years before his death to give a lecture, and he seemed much calmer and happier than I remembered. His work had become highly collect-able, his critical reception was generally good. He used to be what I'd term a risk-taker, but by then he wasn't even drinking. He told me he'd had a dose of Hepatitis B and it had been a wake-up call. So yes, I was shocked when I heard he'd committed suicide.'

'When he came back to give his lecture, did he say any-thing about being in a relationship?'

Darnley shook his head. 'Not a word. A group of us went out to dinner afterwards and someone asked in a jokey sort of way about his love life. He closed right down and said his private life was exactly that – private. So we all moved on to other gossip.'

Karen couldn't think of anything else to ask. Alasdair Darnley had filled in some of the blanks in her understand-ing of David Greig, but his knowledge of the man had been neither intimate enough nor close enough to when he'd died to be of any more use. To wind up, she said, 'Does his work still command high prices?'

'Oh yes. Most artists get a positive bounce when they die because there's not going to be any more work. But David has benefited from two things. There was a fire at the Goldman Gallery in Brighton a few years ago that destroyed a whole swathe of YBA works, among them some of David's portraits.'

'And that bumped up his value?'

'Correct.' He gave her an indulgent smile.

'And the other thing?'

'Yes. There was a private collector who amassed a substantial number of David's paintings. He – or indeed, she – has been releasing them on to the market at a rate of one every fifteen months or so. They're previously uncatalogued, so there's always a lot of excitement when one comes up at auction.'

'So if they're unknown works, buyers presumably have to rely on something else for proof of provenance? I read about David's thing with the nail clippings, does the dealer actually certify the DNA?'

'I believe so. The Scottish National Portrait Gallery bought his portrait of Gordon Brown back around 2015 and they were satisfied that it was the real thing. One of the curators told me it came with an original bill of sale signed by David. I've spent some time looking at the work, and I'm in no doubt at all that it's an authentic David Greig.' He drank some more coffee and pulled a face of distaste. 'Why are you interested in this?'

'I'm naturally nosy,' she said. 'You never know when a random bit of knowledge will win the pub quiz.' She pushed her chair back. She wasn't sure what she'd hoped for from their encounter, but at least she now had more of a sense of the man Iain Auld had fallen for. 'I won't take up any more of your time. I do appreciate it.'

He shrugged one beefy shoulder. 'You're welcome. Though I'm still none the wiser as to what you were after.'

She stood up and smiled. 'That makes two of us.' She was

still enjoying his look of befuddlement as she walked briskly down George IV Bridge.

She was also still oblivious to the man who had emerged from the café opposite Perk and was following in her wake. He stayed on her tail as she crossed the Royal Mile and cut through St Giles' Street to the steep descent of the News Steps. Lost in thought, she took her time, gazing out over the city as she went. Then, at the turn of the stairs, where there was a kind of landing, she heard a scuffle of footsteps at her back and looked round just in time to realise she was trapped.

34

Adrenaline fizzed and surged through her body, amping up as Karen realised this was no random encounter. Merrick Shand loomed over her, unshaven, hair tousled and breath a blast of decay. Automatically, she was on the balls of her feet, her hands curling into fists.

'Step away,' she barked, not a tremor to betray the fear making her heart pound.

He held up his hands, palms facing her. 'I didn't mean to scare you,' he said, taking a step back. 'I'm not here to give you a fright.'

'Then why are you creeping up on me like a fucking assassin?' Karen raised her voice, hoping someone coming up or down the cut-through would hear her and show their face.

'I wanted to speak to you. I wanted to say sorry I reacted like I did in the pub. It was a knee-jerk.'

'Like all the knee-jerk times you slapped your wife around?' Karen's fear had changed gear to rage and she inched closer to him. 'You don't scare me, Merrick Shand. I've never been scared of bullies.'

'You've nothing to fear from me. Look, I'm a different man now. I was shocked the other night, I didn't expect to see you, I wasn't ready to face you.' His hands dropped and his face twisted into an expression of miserable frustration. 'I didn't want it to be like this.' His hands moved over each other as if he were washing them.

'What did you think it would be like? You killed my man. And they took a pathetic three years of your life away in exchange for all of his. What did you expect? Forgiveness?'

He took another step back. 'I didn't want anything from you. I don't want anything from you. I wanted to apologise. I've spent two years in group therapy learning to face what I did to my wife and to your man. To Phil Parhatka.'

'Don't even speak his name.' The low throb of anger in her voice.

'I have to. I have to name the people I've wronged. I have to own the weight of what I've done. I can't take any of it back, but I can refuse to repeat the wrongs I've committed.'

'That's easy said. I expect the parole board loved that. Recommended your release because you learned to say the right things.'

He shifted uneasily from foot to foot. 'I understand why you'd think that. There's nothing I can say that will convince you that I'm genuinely remorseful for what I did. But I wanted to say it. I'm sorry for your pain, and you can be as angry with me as you like but I'm never going to retaliate. See, the rest of my life? I have to live it like it's an atonement. I lost my wife, my kids, my home, my business. I'll never get that back again. I have to rebuild my life from the ground up, and I need to do it in a different way. Maybe if you take a look at me in a few years, you'll see the truth of that. Not in what I've said but in what I've done.'

'Nice wee speech. Perfectly calculated to make me leave you in peace. Been practising it, have you?' The sneer on her face as well as in her voice. 'Here's a tip. Don't creep up on folk in quiet places if you want them to believe you're Mr Nice Guy. Now get out my road before I arrest you for threatening a police officer.'

He instinctively recoiled, hands up again defensively. 'I'm sorry, I only wanted to talk to you privately. Honest, the last thing I wanted was to scare you.'

'Epic fail.' She pushed past him and moved swiftly down the steps. Two young men in the court uniform of lawyers headed for the Court of Session were climbing the steps, deep in conversation. *Too late for the action, guys.* Karen paused and looked back. Shand was leaning against the wall, head in hands. Was it possible he'd been sincere?

Pushing the thought away, Karen picked up speed and shoved past the lawyers. When she got to the bottom of the flight, the adrenaline deficit kicked in and she found she was trembling. She made it down the hill and dived into the Gordon Street coffee shop. For once, she avoided a blast of caffeine and ordered a hot chocolate instead. A sugar hit was what she needed to get her back on an even keel after the encounter with Shand.

Taking him at face value seemed impossible to accept. It felt as if he was somehow trying to cheat her out of a legitimate anger. What was she to do with her grief if she had to acknowledge Shand's remorse as a genuine state? Where could she focus her sense of outrage and loss then? If he was prepared to absorb her pain like he said, there would be nothing to feed it.

She was truly going to have to find a way past her anger. Karen squeezed her eyes tight shut and clenched her fists. She couldn't deal with this now. She had work to do. Other lives to answer to. She rummaged for her phone and messaged Jason.

'You all right, boss?' Jason greeted her as she got into the passenger seat. 'Only, you look kinda pale.'

'I'm fine,' Karen said, sharper than he deserved. She took a breath. 'I'm fine, really.'

'Where are we headed?'

'Glasgow. We're going to talk to an actress called Verity Foggo. She's in a play at the King's Theatre.' As they drove out of the city and headed down the motorway, Karen brought Jason up to speed with the James Auld investigation. Doing a briefing always helped her organise the material in her head and often threw up possible avenues to explore. Sometimes, it even prompted links that hadn't quite joined up previously. Now, as she took Jason through the steps she and Daisy had taken, her voice tailed off mid-sentence.

'What is it?' Jason asked, concerned again.

'When Daisy and I had our curry with Ron Beckett, he went off at a tangent. Another case he'd been involved in connected to Dover House.'

'What's Dover House?'

'The Scotland Office HQ in London, where Iain Auld worked. A few years after Iain disappeared, Beckett got hauled into another inquiry. They brought him in because it was a sensitive case and he already had the contacts.'

'What kind of sensitive? Politicians getting up to the usual shenanigans?'

'Hard to say, since they never made an arrest. This was art forgery, Jason. Somebody copied paintings on loan from the Scottish national collections and had it away on their toes with the originals. And this morning I was talking to a lecturer from the College of Art about a former student who had a remarkable knack for copying other people's work.'

'You're kidding?'

'No, but I'm slow. I didn't put it together right away because the forgeries weren't discovered until years after David Greig was dead. But the substitutions could have been made long before then because those forged paintings had all been hanging in Dover House for years.' Karen smacked one fist into the other palm. 'Shit. What if David Greig and Iain Auld weren't lovers? What if they were co-conspirators? Setting up a racket to rip us all off by stealing valuable paintings?'

'But how would they sell them? I mean, you can't just take them down the saleroom if they're well-known paintings, can you?' Jason sounded dubious.

'There's a black market in art. Private collectors who don't care where a painting comes from as long as they can be assured it's the real thing.' Karen shook her head, despairing of her own stupidity. 'How did I not make that connection the minute Alasdair Darnley started on about Greig's gift for imitation? I'm supposed to be a detective, for fuck's sake.'

'To be fair, boss, you didn't have any reason to connect up the dots. I mean, why would you think an upstanding guy like Iain Auld would be up to his neck in that sort of nonsense? There was nothing that came up in the case review to say he was anything other than a straightforward kind of guy.'

Karen sighed. 'I know. Still, I should have been open to any indication of criminal activity. I should have known about the art thefts, somebody should have brought it up during the case review.'

'You're not psychic, boss. If nobody bothers to tell you, how are you supposed to know? And even if it had come up at the case review, how would it have meant anything? You didn't know that David Greig even existed, never mind that he was involved with Iain Auld,' he protested.

'I suppose so. But I need to reassess my whole approach to this case.' She ran a hand through her hair, frustrated.

'Maybe this Verity Foggo will shine a light, boss?'

Karen grunted. 'Let's hope we can find somebody at the theatre who can tell us where she's staying. She'll not be very thrilled if we turn up right before she's due on stage.'

For the second time in one day, Karen got lucky. The company manager of the touring production was backstage, making arrangements for the get-out on Monday. 'We're in Manchester next week,' he explained, leading them out of the wings and into a tiny windowless office that smelled of stale bodies with an undertone of sickly sweet vape smoke. 'Two months into the tour, you'd think they'd have it down to a fine art, but every bloody time, it's like teaching small children the two times table.' He dropped into the sofa that occupied about a third of the room. 'Now, what can I do for you? The only cops we ever see are uniforms giving us a hard time for where the trucks are parked.'

'I need to speak to Verity Foggo.' Karen held up a hand to still the worried protest she could see coming her way. 'She's not in any trouble. We think she might have some information pertaining to our investigation. Where will we find her? Where is she staying?'

He licked his lips, clearly not mollified by her words. 'You're not going to screw up my show tonight, are you?'

Karen shrugged. 'It's just a few questions. Nothing upsetting.'

He shifted his weight and pulled his phone out of his back pocket. He thumbed through the screens and said, 'She's in a flat on the other side of the motorway.' He read off the address. 'I'm going to call her, let her know you're on your way. I don't want her upset and unsettled.'

'That's fine. But if she's not there when we knock her door, we'll be back.' She smiled with her mouth but not her eyes. 'You should bear in mind that police obstruction is an offence.'

Out in the street, Jason said, 'That was a bit harsh.'

'You think? I don't like it when people have such a shit sense of priorities. Why would a performance of a play be more important than a criminal investigation?' As the words left her mouth, Karen heard herself and wondered when she'd become so self-important. This case was messing with more than her head.

They found the flat in a tall sandstone tenement in a side street a few minutes' walk from the theatre. Karen pressed the intercom button and the door release buzzed without the occupant even checking who was there. 'How is it always the top floor?' Jason grumbled as they toiled up the worn stone steps.

'Life,' Karen said.

Verity Foggo stood in the doorway of the flat, face clean of make-up, hair tied up in a topknot. She wore yoga pants and a baggy cotton sweater that came almost to her knees. Even so, Karen recognised her from a drama about surrogacy that she'd watched a few months before. 'You'll be the police,

264

then,' Verity said, the warmth in her voice matched by her smile. 'Steve told me you were on your way. Come on in.'

They followed her into a characterless living room that had clearly been furnished in an assault on IKEA. 'Bloody Airbnb,' Verity said. 'Less personality than a chain hotel. Take a seat.'

Karen made the introductions as they settled down. Verity's perfectly shaped eyebrows rose at the words 'Historic Cases Unit'.

'I didn't think I was old enough to qualify as historic,' she said. 'What is it you want to talk to me about?' There was something guarded about her. Karen wasn't sure whether she genuinely had no idea why they were there or that she was already holding back. That she was a professional actor was only going to make this interview harder to read.

'I believe you were recently trying to get in touch with James Auld?'

Verity didn't look as surprised as Karen thought she should. 'That's right, how did you know that?'

'His sister-in-law told us you'd asked her to pass your email on to him. Did he contact you?'

She cocked her head to one side slightly. 'He did. Why is this a police matter?'

'Why did you want to reactivate your connection to James Auld?'

'What an odd turn of phrase, Chief Inspector. Look, why are you asking about him?'

The subtle approach wasn't getting her anywhere, Karen realised. Time for the direct approach. 'James Auld's body was pulled out of the Firth of Forth at the beginning of the week. He'd been brutally attacked and thrown into the sea to drown.' A bit of poetic licence, but not much.

Verity's mouth fell open and she clapped her hands to the side of her face. 'No,' she gasped. Karen waited. 'Oh my God. That's awful.' Verity took a deep breath and hugged herself. 'Ask me anything you want, anything that could help. Oh my God, poor Jamie.'

Karen noted the use of the family nickname. 'Why were you so keen to be in touch with him after all those years?'

Verity cocked her head and looked up from under her eyebrows. 'I don't know where to begin. If I start at the beginning, you'll think I'm mad.'

'Trust me, Verity, I've heard plenty of strange stories. The order doesn't matter, as long as it makes sense to you.'

Another deep breath. 'I thought I'd seen a ghost.'

35

It wasn't what she'd expected, but still Karen didn't flinch. 'Where did this happen, Verity?'

'On Facebook. Except it goes back further than when I saw it this time. You know how Facebook throws out these random memories? "Five years ago you liked this picture that Fred Bloggs posted"?'

'I know what you mean, yes.'

'So, a few weeks ago, one of those popped up. It was a photo, and the message was, "Four years ago, you commented on your friend Megan's post." And I vaguely remembered it; she'd posted a link to load of photographs someone had taken of an art gallery fire in Brighton. She'd paid attention to it because she's got a shop that sells candles and crystals and tat like that to tourists, and her shop's just down the street from the gallery. She was having a rant about the ghouls who turned up to watch the place burn. And I'd said, yes, people loved a bit of schadenfreude and a bit of spectacle and never thought about its impact. All those works of art, up in smoke.' She gave a wan smile. 'I suppose because I'm a creative artist myself, I felt a sort of kinship.'

Karen's antennae were twitching. Another reference to the gallery fire in Brighton, so hot on the heels of the earlier one. She didn't like coincidences. Too often the links turned out to be the opposite of accidental. But she knew better than to jump all over it before Verity had told her all she could. 'So, when this picture turned up again, you thought you'd seen a ghost?'

Verity nodded slowly. 'When I saw it the first time, I didn't pay much attention to it. I think I only glanced at it on my phone. But when it reappeared, I was on my laptop and it was much clearer. And there, in the middle of the crowd, I saw him.' Dramatic pause. 'I saw Iain Auld. But I knew it couldn't be him. Because he disappeared ten years ago and he'd been declared dead. I saw that in the papers.'

'If Iain Auld's picture was all over the papers and social media four years ago, I don't understand why nobody else identified him.'

'Because it wasn't Iain as everybody else knew him. It was Iain the way he looked when we were in *Twelfth Night* together at Oxford. I was Viola and he was Antonio. He let his hair grow for the part. And he grew a goatee beard and a moustache. He looked quite different. Honestly, if you didn't know it was him, you wouldn't have recognised him,' she said eagerly. 'I've got some pictures of the production, I looked them out to show Jamie.' She jumped up. 'Let me get my laptop, I'll show you.'

Karen and Jason exchanged a startled look as Verity hurried out of the room. 'I wasn't expecting that,' Jason muttered.

'Me neither. I've no idea where this is going.'

Verity returned, opening her laptop and typing in her password. She fiddled with her keypad and keyboard, then turned it so they could both see it. A bunch of actors in approximate Elizabethan costume grinned at the camera.

'Look,' she said. 'This is us in May 1993. In the Oxford University Dramatic Society.' She tapped a long nail over a young woman in breeches in the centre. 'That's me.' A second tap. 'That's Iain.'

She was right. Karen would never have spotted Iain Auld. His hair was swept back from his forehead and fell in curls around his face, skimming his collar. The facial hair transformed the shape of his face, making it longer and narrower. 'He does look quite different,' she said.

Verity took the laptop back and clicked on something. Then, triumphant, she showed them what she'd done. 'I did this so Jamie wouldn't think I was completely mad,' she said.

Karen looked at the screen. On one side, Verity had cropped Iain from the OUDS picture and enlarged him. On the other side, she'd isolated the man in the crowd outside the Brighton gallery and done the same. The resemblance was startling. She'd want to confirm it with River, who could calculate the proportions of the two faces and see whether they were an exact match. But to her eye, it looked like two images of the same man. Still, it was hard to swallow such an unexpected correspondence. And newspaper photos were never clear enough for certainty. 'I can see why you thought you'd seen a ghost,' Karen said. 'You said you wanted to show this to Jamie. Am I right to assume he'd made contact with you?'

'Oh yes,' she said. 'He sent me an email the day after I spoke to Mary. Like you, he wondered why I wanted to get in touch with him, and when I explained, he got quite excited. I emailed him copies of the photographs, but he said he wanted to see the original of the Oxford photo for himself. He was living in France – but I expect you knew that?' Karen nodded and Verity continued. 'He came over to London a couple of weeks ago. We have Sunday and Monday off, and so I met up with him in London. I couldn't believe the change in him. He was so grown-up, so in command of himself. He told me all about his years in the Foreign Legion and about his music.' Her expression had become wistful and she sighed again.

'When I first knew Jamie, he was such a restless soul, he wanted to travel and have adventures. Being with him was fun, it was unpredictable. But the man who came to see me was completely settled, content with his life. The only ambition he seemed to have left was to find out what happened to Iain. He got excited when he saw what I had to show him. Like me, he was convinced it was his brother. He wanted to take the Oxford photo with him, but I said no, I'd have it copied and send that to him. Sadly, I hadn't got round to that yet.'

Karen butted in. She'd spotted an inconsistency. 'I thought Jamie actually took the photographs of the Oxford production? That's what you told Mary Auld. Surely he had the negatives?'

Verity gave a tinkle of laughter. 'You've caught me out, Chief Inspector. I did tell Mary a white lie. I knew Jamie had gone on the run, but I didn't believe he'd have broken his contact with Mary. They were such a tight-knit family. But still, I needed to come up with a plausible reason for wanting to get in touch with Jamie. And everybody thinks that actors are incredibly vain, so I thought she'd fall for a story that sounded as if all I was interested in was myself. I remembered Jamie liked to take photographs on his Olympus Trip, so I spun her a yarn about needing copies of photos Jamie had taken for my archives. I'm sorry if that was misleading.'

'I understand. What was Jamie's reaction? Did he really believe the man in the Brighton picture was his brother?'

'He went very quiet.' Verity sat back in her chair, legs folded beneath her. 'I didn't want to push him, so I waited. Finally, he got up and started pacing to and fro across the room. He was really quite agitated. Then he said he'd almost begun to believe his brother actually was dead, but he'd recently discovered another photograph that had made him question everything. I asked what it was, but he refused to tell me. He said he had someone else to see before he'd be able to understand what had happened but that he hoped he'd finally solve the mystery of what had become of his brother.'

'And he didn't give any indication of who that person was? Or where they were? Or what he thought they could tell him?'

She shook her head, the very picture of regret. 'I've told you all I know, Chief Inspector.'

'One last thing – I don't understand why you didn't tell Mary Auld about your suspicions. Surely it would have been more straightforward to ask her to look at the picture?'

Verity gave a fine representation of sympathetic innocence. 'In case I was wrong. How could I have lived with myself if I'd built up her hopes and then had to watch them fall apart? I thought Jamie would be better able to handle the whole thing. If I was wrong . . . '

Karen couldn't be bothered pandering to her. She took out her card and handed it over. 'Can you email me those images, please?'

'Of course, I'll do it right now.' She unfolded her legs and grabbed the laptop.

As she typed, Karen said, 'And we'll need the original of

the Oxford photograph. You'll get it back in due course, but it's now evidence in a murder inquiry.' Stretching it slightly, she knew, but she wasn't about to take no for an answer. 'Are you going back to London tomorrow?'

'Yes, I'll be there till Tuesday morning when I have to head up to Manchester.' She made a *moue* of distaste. 'Two months is about my limit for enjoying touring. I'll be glad when this one is over. I'm on stage for almost the whole thing, it's exhausting.'

'Still, it must be good to be in work in your business,' Jason piped up.

'Sweet of you, but I'm never short of offers,' Verity said, turning the beam of her charm on him. He blushed.

Karen broke the moment. 'I'll arrange for someone from the Met to come round and pick up the photograph. You'll get a receipt.'

Verity sighed. 'Fine. But do be careful with it. It has sentimental value.'

Not to mention what the media might pay for it if this case was ever resolved, Karen thought. But she smiled and agreed as she got to her feet. 'Thanks, Ms Foggo.'

'Not at all, you're very welcome,' the actress said. 'I've picked up lots of tips for the next crime drama I'm cast in.'

There was barely enough time on the short train ride from Glasgow Queen Street to Gartcosh for Karen to message Tamsin to tell her she was on her way to the forensic department in the crime campus. In the light of what she'd learned that day, she'd decided she needed to remain in Scotland to pursue the various lines of inquiry that had emerged in the Auld brothers' investigation. She was also conscious that she hadn't stayed on top of the forensics in either of the cases she was working. And experience had taught her that even with the following wind of Tamsin's support, you had to keep chasing or you'd find yourself bumped to the bottom of the queue by officers who were making the scientists' lives a bigger misery.

There was no point in Jason going to Stockport on a Saturday evening, The chances were good there would be nobody around at the Isherwood Studios till Monday morning. So she'd sent him home with explicit instructions to drive down to Stockport the following evening. 'Book into a hotel, treat yourself to a decent dinner and an early night. First thing in the morning, head round to Isherwood Studios where the McAndrew car is registered. It's all we've got to go on. Be discreet but try to get a lead on where "Dani" or Amanda is hanging out. Do your best to get eyes on her and when you do, keep your distance and call me. Do not approach her till I'm with you.' She couldn't have been clearer. And clarity was what Jason liked best. So she could shove that ingredient of their full plate to one side for now.

Gartcosh station was as basic as it could get. Two concrete platforms separated from the rest of the world by a fence of wire mesh and concrete posts. Two primitive metal and Perspex shelters and a pair of ticket machines. The bitter westerly wind swept a few scraps of litter ahead of Karen as she set off for the distinctive black-and-white edifice of Police Scotland's nerve centre. On a summer day, dawdling in the sunshine, it would take about eight minutes. Today, she did it in under five.

She was still feeling chilled when she tracked down Tamsin at her desk. As she approached, Karen took out the packet of dark chocolate mint biscuits she'd picked up in the convenience store by Queen Street station. Tamsin was

273

engrossed in what was on her screen, but as soon as Karen waved her offering in her eyeline, she swung round and snatched her prize. 'Good move, KP,' she said.

Karen pulled up a chair. 'I was passing. And I thought, "who will save me from myself and share these lovely biscuits with me?"'

'You saved me a phone call. You're on my to-do list for this afternoon.'

'I'm disappointed to be so far down it.' Tamsin grinned, showing a new gold crown on a canine tooth. 'How's it going?'

'My dad's a big Motown fan. One of his all-time favourites sums it up – "Ball of Confusion (That's What the World Is Today)". I've got a ragbag of bits and pieces where my brain should be.'

Tamsin made a sympathetic noise. 'It's a shame you can't defrag your brain like a hard drive. But you're smart, girl, you'll figure it out. And I have some more bits and pieces to shove into your ragbag. Who knows, maybe they're exactly the bits you need?'

'A lassie can hope. Did the DNA guys get any further with the paintings?'

'I gave them a few words of encouragement.' A wicked grin. 'And they finally got back to me at lunchtime. Most of what they found was pretty fragmentary. Not definitive enough for the courtroom. But on two of the paintings, they did find enough to stand behind. Both samples match one lot of DNA from the van, but not the DNA from the skeleton. Does that help at all?'

Karen ripped open the biscuits and took one. 'It's a negative confirmation. We know there were two people sharing the van. Now we definitely know who the skeleton isn't.

And who our prime suspect is. What about the sample Jason dropped in the other day?'

Tamsin nodded. 'Father and daughter. The dead woman is Thomas Gilmartin's daughter.'

'You were teasing me, not telling me that up front, weren't you? That puts it beyond doubt, then.'

'I'd say so. And I did manage to pull out a bit more from the emails that Susan Leitch trashed on her laptop. I'll ping over the fragments I have. They might mean something to you, but don't get overexcited. They're pretty scant.'

'What about Susan Leitch's phone? Has that turned up in the system?'

'No. I've got a shout out for it, but so far it's a no-show.'

Karen tutted. 'It'll be sitting in some evidence bag somewhere, some bottom-feeder paying no attention to their inbox. Luckily I'm not expecting much from it. What about James Auld's laptop?'

Tamsin groaned. 'Gimme a break, Karen. We only got it this morning. I've not had time to fire the bloody thing up yet. Trust me, as soon as there is anything to pass on, you'll know about it.'

Karen held her hands up in a placatory gesture. 'Sorry. I know I'm a greedy cow.'

'That's not a character flaw in my world. You're like me, you can't be doing with slow progress. I'm not in tomorrow, but I'll make it a priority when I come on shift on Monday, OK?'

'Thanks.' She glanced at her watch. 'I'd better make a move.'

'Good to see you. Thanks for the biscuits.' As Karen headed for the door, Tamsin called her back. 'One thing. This virus thing in China? You might want to stock up on hand gel and wipes. And get yourself a box of face masks.'

'Are you kidding me? It's only like the flu, right?'

Tamsin pulled a face. 'That's not what I'm hearing online. Just do it, Karen, it's not like you can't afford it.'

Karen shook her head in amusement. 'OK, I'll go to the chemist on the way home. Anything to get you off my case.'

'You'll thank me if it turns out to be the big one,' Tamsin said absently, already lost in her computer.

On the train back to Edinburgh, Karen messaged Nora Brooke, the National Galleries of Scotland curator she'd worked with on a cold case series of art thefts.

I know your working week is as ridiculous as mine, but can we meet for brunch? I need to pick your brains. (Though I think you might find it quite interesting too . . .)

Nora messaged her back immediately. Make it Monday, I'm in Aberdeen till then, God help me.

Karen smiled in satisfaction then turned to the email fragments Tamsin had salvaged from Susan Leitch's deleted email conversations with Amanda McAndrew. Much of it made no sense on its own and most of it dated from the period before they broke up. It seemed to be about diary dates and domestic arrangements. After the break-up there was almost nothing. But one telling fragment from Amanda to Susan had survived . . . can trust . . . trouble to your door . . . help . . . pick it up when things . . .

Karen was wary of reading too much into the gaps, but she couldn't resist wondering whether the message had gone something like, You're the only one I can trust. I'm sorry to bring trouble to your door but I need your help. I'll pick it up when things calm down. It made sense, both in terms of what was there and the rest of the evidence. Slowly but surely they were beginning to make sense of the skeleton in the camper van.

She had another call to make but she was conscious of other people's ears on the train. As soon as she reached the platform, she found a quiet corner and called Fiscal Depute Ruth Wardlaw. Swiftly, she outlined the web of evidence she'd spun around Amanda McAndrew. 'Can you get in front of a sheriff and get me an arrest warrant if I ping the details over to you right now?'

Ruth chuckled. 'For a cold case detective, you always manage to inject a high level of urgency into your requests.'

'It's a talent. What do you think? Can you fix it?'

'Let me look at what you've got and I'll decide if it merits a warrant.'

'Harsh, Ruth.'

'Maybe. But you are a chancer, Karen.'

It was a judgement Karen couldn't disagree with. Nor did she want to.

36

Monday, 24 February 2020

Karen loved brunch at Aleppo. It was just what she needed to lift her spirits after a long evening grinding through the details of the James Auld murder case. She'd spent the day with her parents in Kirkcaldy, taking them out for a pub lunch then for a brisk and bracing walk round Ravenscraig Park. She knew she could have been with Hamish instead, but that still felt like a step too far after the complications of the previous week.

She'd passed the whole evening fretting at what she knew like a child picking a scab. Was Verity Foggo's identification reliable? And if so, what did it mean? Did the Dover House forgeries even have anything to do with her case? She'd eaten the leftovers from her picnic with Hamish while she covered the ground from every direction and still Karen felt there was something she was missing. The one thing that had lifted her frustration had been the arrival in her inbox of an arrest warrant, courtesy of Ruth Wardlaw.

She'd woken with a surge of excitement at the prospect of Aleppo. She always chose the baked eggs with mushrooms, spicy nduja and aubergine, accompanied by feather-light flatbreads.

When she arrived, Nora opted for a basket of pastries with butter and fig jam. 'I've never enjoyed a savoury breakfast,' she said, her round pink face evidence of her love of sweet treats. She swept her long wavy brown hair back from her face and wrapped it into a loose knot on the back of her neck. 'Don't want to get jam in it,' she muttered. 'This is a real treat, Karen.'

'You don't know what I want from you yet.' Karen burst an egg yolk with her fork and mixed it with the rest of the dish.

'Is it another cold case? More paintings stolen from castle walls?'

'It's a cold case that has a very warm element to it. A murder this week that ties into a suspicious disappearance ten years ago.'

'Ooh, that sounds like an episode in that series where Trevor Eve gets all shouty.'

Karen chuckled. 'If you have to get that shouty, you're not doing it right.'

'So what's all this got to do with the wonderful world of fine art?' Nora broke apart a croissant and moaned softly. 'Oh, my lucky stars.'

'A bunch of paintings came back to the galleries from the Scotland Office in London that turned out to be fakes. Do you know about this?'

Nora froze with a chunk of pastry halfway to her mouth. 'How do you know about it? It was all hushed up. We were told not to talk about it on pain of death. Well, maybe not *actual* death, but you know what I mean?'

'I think it might have a connection to the case I'm investigating. What can you tell me about it?'

'We never had this conversation, Karen. I mean it, I can't be associated with this.' Nora put down the piece of croissant, all ease gone from her face.

'You have my word, Nora. This is background, there's nothing that will come back on you. Tell me what you know.'

Nora gave a sharp glance to either side then focused on Karen. 'There were, I think, six paintings. They were all Scottish artists, which is why they'd been chosen for the Scotland Office. But they covered a wide range in terms of period and style. They were all quite valuable – low six figures, mostly. Apart from the Peter Doig, which would sell at auction for upwards of five or six million. None of the originals has turned up, which means they'll be sitting in some rich bastard's private collection. Whoever painted the copies will have made a killing.' Her hand shot to her mouth. 'I didn't mean that literally.'

'I know. Tell me, how good were the copies?'

'Now, that is possibly the most interesting question you could have asked. People talk a lot of guff about knowing instinctively that a piece is a fake. Me, I think that's pretentious nonsense. What they attribute to instinct is actually subconscious knowledge acquired from a lifetime of studying a lot of art very closely. Now, these six paintings were, from a technical point of view, very skilful. Looking at them by itself didn't set off alarm bells. Whoever did the copies managed perfect matching on colour and brushstrokes. But they weren't designed to stand up to close scrutiny. When they came back to the galleries, we could see right away that they were not the originals. The materials were all wrong. A forger whose principal aim is to get away with it will research their materials painstakingly. They'll source canvas of the right age. They'll grind their own pigments so that they match what was available when the work was made. They'll make their own glue so even that matches. These copies weren't like that. They looked authentic but they didn't examine authentic.'

'How does that make sense? If you can make something look that good, why would you take all those other shortcuts?'

Nora readdressed her croissant. 'Because they weren't intended to convince. They were placeholders while the criminals disposed of the originals. It bought them time.'

Karen drank some coffee and pondered. 'It's almost as if they're thumbing their nose at you,' she said slowly. 'As if they're saying, "You see, I can fool you. And if I wanted to, I could completely fool you, but I can't be bothered."'

Nora frowned. 'Maybe. Or maybe they're just lazy. Doing it thoroughly is time-consuming and difficult. Knocking off superficially convincing copies is pretty straightforward.'

'Nobody's ever been arrested, have they?'

'Not as far as I know.'

'Were there any suspects? Any names come up?'

'The Scotland Yard Art and Antiques squad did look at a few people. But the squad was disbanded in 2017 after the Grenfell Tower fire. Their work was deemed non-essential and the Met needed all the bodies they could lay hands on. We haven't heard anything since. I think the stumbling block was access to Dover House. We were of the view that not all of the copies were of the same age. The availability of different paints at different times made it possible for that judgement. And wholesale replacement of six canvases in one go would have been a very risky enterprise. Much safer to take six small risks than one massive one.'

'I guess. So no names in the frame? Not even hints?'

Nora shook her head then brushed crumbs from her generous bosom. 'I'm not holding out on you.'

'What kind of value are we talking about here? Millions? Tens of millions?'

Nora laughed. 'Not tens of millions, Karen. Added together – and this is a rough estimate – the Raeburn, the MacTaggart, the Redpath, the Eardley and the Crawhall would probably fetch somewhere between quarter of a million and three hundred thousand. The cherry on the cake is the Peter Doig. At auction, like I said, north of five million. Maybe as much as ten.'

'For one painting?'

Nora nodded. 'Doig is a star.'

'So, they could have made upwards of ten million for their not-so-little scam?'

'Not on the black market. They'd be lucky to make half of that.'

'Maybe not enough to retire on, but still a pretty good payday.'

'I don't know, I think I could cheerfully retire to some lovely Caribbean tax haven on five mil. Getting to that point would be high risk, though. You'd have to trust whoever was dealing the paintings for you.'

'You wouldn't do it yourself?'

Nora picked out a raisin whirl and took a bite while she considered. 'I don't think many fakers would have those direct connections to collectors.'

'What if it wasn't someone known primarily as a fraudster?'

'What do you mean?'

'OK. I've promised to keep your secrets. Now I need you to promise to keep mine. I want to talk to you about something that you absolutely can't share with anybody.'

Nora raised her eyebrows, intrigued but also pleased. 'I promise on my cat's grave.'

'You'll be familiar with David Greig?'

'Wow. If I'd made a list of the top one hundred possible artists we'd be talking about this morning, I doubt David Greig would have made it. You do know he's dead?'

'Yes, Nora, I know he's dead.' Karen rolled her eyes and scooped some more baked eggs into her mouth, deliberately keeping Nora on tenterhooks. 'Do you know how David Greig paid his way through art college?'

'Are you talking about his witty portraits? Oh yes, I know all about them! There's a very famous painting in the Louvre called *Gabrielle D'Estrées and One of Her Sisters*, where they're sitting in the bath, naked from the waist up and one is pinching the other's nipple. Greig did a version of that for one of the Portrait Gallery curators and her girlfriend who commissioned it. It was one of those moments where everybody pretends to be scandalised when they're really highly entertained. But you're surely not suggesting David Greig had anything to do with the Dover House frauds? He'd been dead for years before they turned up.'

'They'd been hanging there since well before he actually died. The timeline wouldn't be a problem. What I want to know is whether you think David Greig could have perpetrated that fraud.'

Nora stared at Karen, open-mouthed. She expelled a long breath, puffing out her cheeks, then said, 'Fuck, yes.'

37

Jason had done exactly what he'd been told, with the single addition of a long FaceTime chat with Eilidh, mostly consisting of a detailed discussion about which box set to binge next. They'd eventually settled on *Narcos*. Jason had argued that it might be a bit like bringing his work home, but Eilidh had pointed out, not unreasonably, that the Historic Cases Unit didn't involve a lot of shoot-outs, stake-outs and high-octane car chases.

Isherwood Studios looked as if it had been designed in the sixties by an architect exacting revenge on the neighbourhood. Built from concrete panels, steel struts and glass, it squatted between an imposing red-brick church and a row of undistinguished local shops. A signboard announced ISHERWOOD STUDIOS: STOCKPORT'S ARTS AND CRAFTS HUB. Jason couldn't think of anything he'd seen that was less hub-like.

The entrance was around the back of the building, through a pair of shabby maroon doors. They led into a large square foyer where a young woman in paint-stained overalls, hair in a tie-dye turban, was working on a mural of what appeared to be an urban landscape seen through a fish-eye lens. Jason cleared his throat. 'Hiya,' he said.

She turned and gave him a friendly grin. 'Hiya yourself. Are you looking for somebody?'

'I was wondering if Dani was around. Dani Gilmartin. Scottish lassie.' He gave her his best smile.

'Not this morning, mate. What were you after her for?'

'I just wanted to look her up.' Inspiration struck and his face brightened. 'We used to share studio space back in Scotland. At Tullyfolda? She maybe mentioned it.' She gave him an incredulous look. Jason supposed he didn't look much like an artist, even though he'd taken off his tie.

'I don't know her that well. I'm Orla, by the way.' Although it appeared as a friendly gesture, it was clearly a demand.

'Jason. Look, I'm only around for the weekend, do you know where I can maybe find Dani?'

Orla sized him up again. 'She runs a class on Saturday mornings. Watercolours for beginners. In the church hall up by Morrisons. You'll catch her there until noon.'

Jason grinned. The boss would be proud of him. 'Thanks,' he said. 'Really appreciate it.' He sketched a wave and headed back to his car.

He was completely unaware that before the door had swung shut behind him, Orla was already making a phone call. Whoever the Scotch guy was, she'd have bet her Norton that he wasn't any kind of artist. Except maybe a con artist.

'Up by Morrisons' covered an annoying number of side streets, Jason discovered. But at the third or fourth try, he found what he was looking for. The hall was a long brick building with a pitched roof and diamond-paned windows with protective metal gratings. He watched as half a dozen women and one man of indeterminate age gossiped their way inside, then cautiously followed. He paused by the noticeboard which announced, among Brownies, Cubs, Slimming World and Senior Choir, 'Watercolours for Beginners with Professional Tuition from Dani. Saturdays 10-12. All welcome. £5 on door.' He'd found the right place.

He walked the length of the street to consider his next step. He couldn't just assume he'd found the right person. He'd need to see her, to compare her with the photographs. Nothing less than absolute confirmation would do for the boss. He turned back in time to see another trio of women enter the hall. He followed, but not too close. As he approached the tall wooden doors that stood open, he could see far enough inside to spot a pair of interior swing doors with small windows at head height. If he waited till the class started, he could peer through and with a bit of luck, get a good enough look at the teacher to make a positive ID.

He killed a few more minutes by walking to the end of the street again. Seven minutes after ten, he cautiously made his way back to the hall. This time he entered the stone-flagged vestibule and crept towards the windows in the door. He'd barely reached them when an elderly woman appeared at his elbow. 'Don't be shy, lad,' she exclaimed. 'We don't bite, you know. Everybody's nervous the first time.'

Jason stepped back, panicked. 'I'm not ... I didn't ... '

But the woman was not to be put off. Now she had a hand in the small of his back, pushing him towards the door. He didn't know what to do. He couldn't wrestle a pensioner, and already she had one half of the doors open and was shoving him firmly forward. 'We've got a new recruit,' she called out. 'A nice young lad, he's going to give you a run for your money, Tony!'

Every head was turned towards him. Jason felt the heat

rising in his face. He half-raised his hand in greeting and said, 'Hello,' in a squeak that surprised him. It wasn't warm in the hall, but he could feel sweat springing out on the back of his neck. He looked around and saw a dozen people standing in front of simple easels with sheets of paper fixed to them. Sitting on the edge of the stage with a sardonic smile on her face was the teacher. Her hair was longer than in the photos, but there was no doubt in Jason's mind that he was in the presence of his target.

'Welcome to the group,' she said, her Scottish accent still evident. 'I'm Dani.'

No, you're not. You're Amanda. 'I'm Jason,' he said. 'I've never done this before.'

'You're in the right place. Watercolours for beginners,' she said, pushing off from the stage and heading towards him. She steered him through the group to a free easel at the opposite end of the room from the entrance. No chance of slipping out unnoticed, he thought gloomily. 'OK, every-body, let's get started. As usual, I've laid out a selection of images on the stage plus a still-life arrangement. Choose the one you want to have a go at and lay down your base wash while I get Jason here sorted out.'

'Thanks,' he muttered as the room broke into action.

'You haven't brought any paints or brushes with you,' she observed. 'The class costs £5 a session but for an extra £20 I supply a basic starter kit with some paints and brushes. It'll get you going and when you get bitten by the bug, you can sort out what you prefer. Are you up for that?'

He nodded dumbly and took out his wallet and handed over £25, oblivious to the momentary shockwave that crossed her face when she spotted his Police Scotland ID. While he fretted over whether he'd be able to claim the money back without a receipt, Dani fetched a plastic box and a jam jar from a blue IKEA bag at the side of the stage.

'You can fill up your jar in the kitchen, on the left through the door there.' Dani opened the box of paints and selected the largest brush. 'Go and choose an image to have a crack at, get some water and I'll show you how to start.' A brisk smile and she was off to tour the other easels.

Jason took off his jacket and hung it on a stack of chairs behind him. Then he headed for the stage. Almost everyone had picked their preferred picture but two of the women still hovered. He stared haplessly at half a dozen photographs, a mixture of landscapes and still life. One of the women nudged him and pointed to a bunch of party balloons against a blue sky. 'If I was you, I'd make a start with that. It's less of a bugger than the other ones.'

He studied it then gave her a pained smile. 'Thanks. I'm really not sure this is for me.'

'You don't know until you try, lad. You're Scotch, aren't you? Like Dani?'

'That's right.'

'Are you new around here?'

He found her questions oddly reassuring. He was used to nosy old women; they made up half of his extended family. 'I've been here a few months, but I thought it was time to get out and meet some new people.'

The other woman gave a filthy chuckle. 'You'll not find a likely lass here, son. We're all knocking on heaven's door.'

'Speak for yourself, Irene. I've still got a spark in my firebox.' They elbowed each other and giggled like teenagers.

'I've got a fiancée,' he said quickly, before the banter got out of hand. It was almost the truth, after all. He grabbed the picture of the balloons and headed back to his easel. The next two hours dragged past in a nightmare of smudges and drips. Dani visited often with plenty of advice and tips, but it was soon clear to Jason that, whatever talents he possessed, painting wasn't one of them.

Finally, the class came to an end. There was a corkboard in the hallway by the kitchen. It was already covered in paintings, but Dani swiftly took them down and replaced them with that morning's offerings, still damp. The class picked out their own past offerings, then gathered coats and bags. Jason was about to make a break for the door when Dani snagged him.

'Would you mind giving me a hand with the easels? I usually do it myself but I'm in a bit of a hurry today and I can't really ask the oldies.' She sounded apologetic and her smile was charming.

'Sure.' He watched her fold one of the easels then copied her as everyone else bustled out of the hall, full of chatter and laughter.

When he'd done three, Dani said, 'I'll show you where they go.'

He followed her down the hall past the kitchen and round a corner. Dani paused by an old-fashioned heavy wooden door and flicked a light switch. She unlocked the door and drew back bolts at top and bottom. She pulled it open to reveal a steep flight of stone stairs lit with a single bulb. 'Down there,' she said, stepping back to let him pass.

Jason felt a sharp push in his back, then he was tumbling down the stairs in a tangle of easels. And everything went black.

38

Nora stared at Karen across the table. 'You think David Greig was behind those fakes?'

'I wanted to know whether you believe it was possible that he could have painted them.'

'But you said it would have to be someone who had access to the Scotland Office headquarters. From everything I know about Greig, he didn't move in those sorts of circles. Some artists, they let themselves become darlings of the establishment. They turn up at parties and openings like lapdogs, they're totally tamed. Greig wasn't like that. He was subversive and dangerous.'

'Mmm.' Karen didn't want to show too much of her hand in spite of Nora's promise to keep her counsel. 'He does seem to have a reach beyond the grave, though. From what I understand, new paintings of his keep turning up.'

'It's not that surprising. He was very collectable even while he was still alive. Exactly the sort of artist who would attract a patron with deep pockets. The sort of person who views art as an investment as much as a pleasure. Greig wasn't hugely prolific, so his value has held.'

'And then there was that fire in Brighton,' Karen said. 'Some of Greig's work went up in smoke there, didn't it?'

'That's right, I think there were three or four of his portraits lost that night. Which would have been a bonus for anybody who had a stash of his work. The fewer surviving paintings there are, the more valuable the remaining ones become, so long as an artist's rep doesn't decline.'

'So if he was making such good money, why would Greig conspire to perpetrate a fraud like this?'

Nora spread her hands in a shrug. 'Karen, when it comes to money, for some people no amount is ever enough. And Greig was a notorious bad boy. He might have done it for fun, rather than greed. From what I've heard about him, he'd have loved to have put one over on the art establishment. The more I think about it, the more I reckon he did it for a lark.'

Karen took out a copy of the list she'd found in James Auld's Paris apartment. 'There's a Greig listed here. *Jarvis Cocker in the Year 2000.* Almost three-quarters of a million dollars. Is that about the going rate for one of his?'

Nora shrugged. 'I'm not an expert on valuation. But I wouldn't be surprised.'

'How do I find out who sold that painting?' Karen showed her the list. 'There's no gallery name here.'

'If you look online, you should be able to find out quite readily.'

'And they'd be able to tell me who they sold it on behalf of?'

'If the seller wants to remain anonymous, they won't tell you. Can't you get a warrant for something like that?'

'I'd have to have pretty good probable cause,' Karen said.

'And do you?' Nora gave her a coquettish glance.

'Don't fish, it's not a good look. So, there's no easy way of finding out who's benefiting from these newly released paintings?'

Nora took a large bite from a pain au chocolat and chewed vigorously. She swallowed hard then said, 'Well, it's not direct as such, but there might be a way. When a work of art is sold on in one of the countries in the European Economic Area, the gallery or the auction house has to pay what's called the Artist's Resale Royalty. It's a percentage of the purchase price and it goes to the artist or, if they're dead, to their estate. So the ARR from all of these David Greig paintings will be passed on to his estate. Whoever the beneficiary is, they might well know who the seller is. Because they might have been contacted about any documentation or personal knowledge that supports provenance.'

Karen seized on this. She immediately sensed it could be crucial in putting the pieces together in the right order. 'How can I find that out?'

There are specialist organisations that administer the programme, I'll find the details when I get home and pass them on to you. I've no idea whether they'll hand over the info, or whether you'll have to get one of those troublesome warrants again.'

Karen ate the last mouthfuls of the brunch she'd amazingly let grow lukewarm. Her brain was motoring as she tried to process this latest information. 'Maybe not. Presumably that information will have been in his will? He'd have had to designate whoever benefits from the ARR? Or at least have a residuary legatee?'

Nora's eyebrows rose again. 'I imagine so. You'd know more about that than me.' She reached slyly for a piece of baklava.

Karen spoke slowly, thinking aloud. 'Greig lived and died in England. He'll have owned stuff in his own right even if it was work in progress. So whoever his executor was will have had to get a Grant of Probate and that means the will is public.'

'Really? You can see anybody's will? Who knew?'

'Thank you, Nora, you've given me lots to think about.' Karen pushed her chair back. 'I'm sorry but I'm going to have to go and do some online trawling. Take your time, order more coffee, whatever. When all of this is over, we'll have dinner, I promise.' And she was gone, pausing only to stuff two twenties in the charity box by the till.

It was so dark when he first came round that Jason thought he'd gone blind. He tried to get up but the pain in his leg made his head swim and nausea gripped him. Gradually the agony subsided. As long as he didn't move, he could bear it. He wanted to run a hand over his leg, to isolate the source of the pain but he was too afraid of what he might discover there.

At first he couldn't work out where he was or what had happened to him. But slowly his head cleared and he remembered being at the top of the cellar steps and feeling a hand in his back. Then tumbling. Then nothing.

There had been a light on the stairs. There had definitely been a light. But now he was in pitch darkness. And something was pinning him down. He'd been carrying easels, that was it. They'd been light enough to manage three of them, but they were a lot more cumbersome now they were lying across his body.

Slowly, gingerly, gasping as fresh waves of pain shot through him, he managed to push the easels to one side. He lay there, panting. He had no idea how long he'd been down there on what felt like – his fingers explored – a stone floor. He was cold enough for it to have been a while. What chilled him even more was the realisation that nobody knew where he was, and his phone was in the pocket of the jacket he'd left draped over a pile of chairs in the church hall.

Jason groaned. Reflexively, he tapped the fitness tracker on his wrist. It said 12:46. He'd been out for around half an hour. Maybe there was still someone upstairs. Ever the optimist, he took a deep breath and shouted, 'Help,' as loudly as he could. There was no echo; whatever was in the basement had swallowed the sound whole. 'I'm so fucked,' he whispered.

He shifted slightly, whimpering at the pain from his leg. Broken, he had to admit it. When he'd broken his ankle, it had been exactly this kind of excruciation. But this was bigger, deeper. It was worse.

The movement made something dig into his thigh. His keys, he realised. There was a wee LED torch on his keyring, wasn't there? Eagerly, he shoved his hand in his pocket and managed to fish them out with only one moment of panic when he felt them slip. He swallowed hard and fumbled with the button on the torch. A slim beam of white light illuminated a slice of the cellar. Trestle tables were stacked along one wall. Beyond them was a tall stack of cardboard cartons. Toilet rolls and paper towels, according to the box sides. A pile of what looked like velvet stage curtains occupied the far corner. And to one side, the easels he'd shifted off his body. What he could see of the walls was whitewashed brick. There was nothing resembling a toolbox or anything useful.

Jason craned his neck and moved the slender cone of light so he could see the flight of stairs. He could see more than a dozen steps leading up, but not as far as the door. He'd have to try and drag himself up there if he was to have any chance of being rescued.

Why had this happened? Obviously the art teacher wasn't Dani Gilmartin because Dani Gilmartin was dead. And the only person who could have assumed Dani's identity and who had a motive to shove him down a flight of stone steps with no regard for the consequences was Amanda McAndrew. Besides, he'd recognised her from the photos Karen had shown him. But how had she known who he was? He hadn't identified himself either at the studios or in the art class. Was it that obvious that he was a polis?

The only thing he could imagine was that the woman he'd spoken to at the studios had called Amanda and told her a guy called Jason that she used to know was looking to catch up with her. And when he showed up at the class, she knew that was a lie. And that was enough to send her into full-on flight mode. She must have been waiting for something like this for three years now. She probably had a bag packed ready to run. Even if he did get out of here, she'd be long gone.

But why had she done this to him? She could have let him walk out with all the oldies and then done a runner. She must have been terrified he was going to arrest her then and there. And that meant she definitely did have something to hide. And that was pretty much proof that she'd killed Dani. So he'd managed to let a killer get the better of him and escape.

The boss wasn't going to like this one bit.

But even if all he was facing was the worst bollocking of his career, he still had to get out of here. Jason checked where he was in relation to the bottom step then turned off the torch and put his keys back in his pocket. He needed both hands for this. With infinite care and glacial slowness, he put his palms on the floor, straightened his arms and inched backwards. He screamed but he didn't stop his efforts. At last, sweating and swearing, he got his backside on the bottom step.

It was a start.

39

As Karen turned up Leith Walk, the rain came sheeting down in what would have been a tropical downpour had it not been a bare degree or two above freezing. She ran for the nearest bus stop and huddled beneath its limited shelter. She'd barely boarded a 25 when her phone rang.

The last person she wanted to talk to, especially on a crowded bus. She accepted the call and jammed her phone tight to her ear. 'Ma'am?'

'Where on earth are you, Pirie?' Markie was in her usual default state of imperiousness.

'I'm on the bus.'

'How quaint.'

Karen stared out at the grey tenement buildings, dozens of flats piled above takeaways and pubs and cramped shops with eclectic wares. Somehow they survived the onslaught of retail parks and online shopping. She couldn't imagine the Dog Biscuit willingly crossing any of Leith Walk's thresholds. 'Ma'am,' she said.

'I have a meeting at St Andrew's House on Wednesday morning at eleven. I require a briefing from you beforehand. I presume you do have *some* progress to report?'

'My office is on your way. I'll make a point of being there.' Just on the right side of insolence, Karen judged.

'Ten a.m. Prompt, DCI Pirie. And I expect to have something positive to report to our lords and masters.'

'You know me, ma'am. I let the chips fall where they may.' Karen couldn't help herself. Giving the Dog Biscuit something to fret over was some small satisfaction for the mountain of unpaid overtime work she'd already put in over the past week.

She got off the bus and ran across Elm Row and into Gayfield Square nick, shaking the rain from her hair on her way to her office. 'Should have picked up a coffee,' she muttered, shrugging out of her coat and settling in at her desk. As her computer warmed up, she noticed the time. Almost one o'clock, and Jason hadn't checked in. That wasn't like him. He still didn't trust his own initiative; if he had any key decisions to make, he'd still always call first. On the other hand, her instructions had been clear. Find the woman and ring when he had her in his sights. But maybe he was growing more confident? Maybe she should stop acting like a mother hen?

Maybe next week. She keyed his number into her phone and listened to it ring out. Three, four, five times, then voicemail. 'Jason Murray here. Leave your number and I'll call you back.'

Karen waited for the beep, then said, 'It's Karen here. Just wondering how you were doing. Give me a call when you can.'

Then she put Jason from her mind and concentrated on the next task in hand. Find the last will and testament of David Greig. The government probate site was helpfully called Find A Will. It asked for a surname and a year, and up popped almost a hundred names. She scrolled down and almost at the end of the third page, she found him. She had to register with a password and then, for a modest £1.50, David Greig's last wishes would be at her fingertips.

Except of course it wasn't quite that simple. The message on the screen confirmed her purchase and told her that, when the will was available, she'd get an email. And of course there was no phone number to connect her to a minor bureaucrat who might be persuaded to make the wheels turn a bit faster. What were the chances of getting an answer before Markie arrived in her pomp? 'Oh, for fuck's sake,' she exploded.

Perhaps she'd have better luck with the gallery who were selling the apparently never-ending supply of David Greig originals. This was the sort of tedious work she'd normally delegate to Jason, but he was fully occupied tracking and tailing Amanda McAndrew. And Daisy wasn't coming over till the middle of the afternoon. She might as well crack on with it.

The art world was bewildering to Karen. There seemed to be dozens of sites online that all claimed to track auction and gallery sales. Some listed the same works with different prices. Some were opaque in the descriptions of the work for sale; a piece that seemed a bargain turned out to be an overpriced signed print. After more than an hour, she had what seemed to be an exhaustive list of the previously unknown Greigs that had come on the market since his death. *Jarvis Cocker in the Year 2000* she knew about already. The others were, unsurprisingly, new to her. *Rihanna Disturbia*, *Barack/House Black/White*, *Madonna of the Celebration*, *Dame Judi*, *Time Out for Stephen Hawking*, and *Passing Divine* were the others.

Karen pulled up images of the collage paintings and marvelled again at the skill and imagination that had translated
the colours and shapes of buildings and landscapes into
such recognisable versions of iconic figures. There was no
obvious link between Greig's choice of subjects. Karen wondered whether it had been nothing more complicated than
chancing on a suitable inanimate image to break down into
components that could be translated into a portrait. That
was as coherent an organising principle as anything else
she could come up with.

Tracing the pictures back to their original source had
been less than straightforward. But the connective tissue
in all of their pasts seemed to have been the same Dublin
dealer that James Auld's letter had come from. Surely it
couldn't be coincidence that Auld had discovered the photograph of his brother with David Greig and then contacted
the gallery that sold his work? There was something going
on here, just beyond her grasp.

Francis Flaxner Geary had a gallery off Merrion Square.
Karen didn't know Dublin at all, but looking at the satellite
map and the street view, it seemed to be a prosperous part
of town. Gallery Geary had a small frontage but from the
aerial view she could see it went back a fair way. Francis
Flaxner Geary was obviously doing all right for himself. The
sales of David Greig's paintings alone had garnered almost
$12 million. Given the cut that intermediaries took in the
art world, the dead man must have been keeping Geary in
some style.

Karen always preferred to conduct potentially difficult
interviews in person, but for once her impatience got the
better of her. This was going to be one of those occasions
that called for little white lies. Even if she got nothing from

Geary, she would at least have a sense of the man. And she wouldn't have screwed it up for a face-to-face approach.

Finding a number for the gallery was the work of seconds. Before she could have second thoughts, Karen tapped it into her phone. It rang for so long she thought she'd be cut off, but just as she was about to give up, the line opened and a man said, 'Gallery Geary. And how may I help you this damp February afternoon?' His tone was genial, his voice tinged with an Irish accent.

'Can I speak to Francis Geary?'

'This is Francis Flaxner Geary at your service. To whom am I speaking?'

'My name is Karen Parhatka,' she said. Stealing Phil's name in a good cause was no sin. 'I'm working with the exhibitions team at the Edinburgh Art Festival. I understand your gallery represents the estate of David Greig?'

'Lovely to meet you, even if it's only on the phone, Karen. You're quite correct. We were David's gallery when he was alive and we've had the very great privilege of continuing that relationship with his estate.' His style was genial and florid, a man with apparently nothing to hide.

'The team here are very intrigued by the amazing array of his work that's emerged in recent years. You clearly have a connection with someone who has built an extensive collection. What we were wondering is whether it would be possible for us to display a previously unseen Greig at this year's festival?' She thought it wasn't a bad attempt on the hoof.

A fruity chuckle. 'We've had similar requests before. All I can do is pass them on. But don't hold your breath, Karen. These paintings are very closely held.'

'It'd be a great showcase for a future sale,' she tried.

301

'We do a pretty decent job of that ourselves,' Geary said. 'Having said that, of course, being David Greig's work, they more or less sell themselves. I'm sorry to disappoint you.'

'Is it the estate that holds the paintings? Or is it an individual collector?'

'We deal directly with the estate,' Geary said. 'I couldn't say what their relationship is with the owner of the works in question.'

'Could you put me in contact with them?' Karen tried for coquettish. 'So I could try to persuade them myself?'

'Charming as you are, Karen, I can't do that. We have a duty of confidentiality to our clients. I had the exact same conversation with someone a few weeks ago, and he'd come all the way from Paris.'

'From Paris?' She couldn't help herself.

'That's right. As I said, David Greig's work sells itself. He's a major figure, as I'm sure you're well aware. Now, it's been grand talking to you, but I can't help. Do stop by if you're ever in Dublin, I'd be very happy to buy you a coffee and explore ideas about forming a relationship with the Edinburgh Art Festival.' And the line went dead. Clearly, she'd exhausted Francis Flaxner Geary's charms.

But she knew more now than she had before. It was beyond credibility that the man who had visited from Paris was anyone other than James Auld. Irresistibly, Geary was the next link in the chain. Was he a crooked link? Hopefully, once she'd heard back from the probate registry, she'd be a crucial step closer to understanding the mystery that surrounded the Auld brothers.

Before she could complete her written summary, the phone rang. Praying it would be Jason, she snatched it from under the scribbled sheets of rough notes that covered it.

She wasn't sure whether to be pleased or disappointed when she saw River's number on the display. 'Are you in Dundee today?' she said.

'I am. Ewan's off to Brussels for a conference on post-Brexit cooperation so I thought I'd come back a day early. Besides, I've got a backlog you wouldn't believe.'

'Trust me, I know all about backlogs. I'm in over my head right now. So is this call an excuse to skive or have you got something for me?'

'I've been taking another look at the Perth skeleton. Daniella Gilmartin, as you're assuming.'

'It's the only credible assumption. We know she was living in the van with Amanda and we know the skeleton's DNA isn't Amanda's.'

'I supply the science, I leave the case-building to you.'

'Aye, right. So what have you got for me now?'

'I went back to the van to see whether I could identify what she might have collided with to create the fracture. There were a few possibilities – the edge of the countertop by the stove, the side of the tall cupboard, the edge of the door. But either they would have shown traces of the impact or they weren't sturdy enough or there wasn't enough space for an accidental fall to have built up enough momentum. The only possibility I was left with was the edge of the sink unit. Stainless steel, a right-angled edge. And unlike the rest of the interior, it's been cleaned of any fingermarks or other residues.'

'OK, so it was the edge of the sink. Where does that take us?'

River sighed. 'It takes us straight to homicide. The only way for Dani's head to have built up enough momentum to generate so deep and wide a fracture in the space available

303

was for someone to have smashed her head against it with far more force than an accidental fall could have created.'

A long silence. 'So Amanda did kill her.'

'Someone killed her, Karen. It's up to you to prove it was Amanda.'

The call with River had pricked Karen's conscience about Jason again. What the hell was he doing? It was unheard of for him not to make contact with her for this length of time on an active investigation. Even if he was getting nowhere, he'd have called her, if only in the hope that she'd have a suggestion for him to pursue. She tried his number again but this time it went straight to voicemail. Surely he hadn't let his phone run out of juice?

Frustrated, she crossed the office to Jason's desk and opened his top drawer. She lifted the pen tray and took out the post-it note he had squirrelled away with all his passwords. Karen went back to her desk and got her mini iPad. She logged out of her Apple account and logged back in as Jason. From there, she made short work of connecting to Find My Phone. She zoomed in on the map and was puzzled to see that Jason appeared to be at an east-bound service area on the M62 between Manchester and Leeds. Hartshead Moor Services offered a petrol station, a motel and a nearby golf course. No houses to stake out. Unless Amanda McAndrew was playing a round of golf, the only reason to be there was to fill up with fuel and a Starbucks coffee. If he was on her tail, that made sense. But still, it wasn't like him to go dark on her.

When he did turn his phone on, she'd make sure he knew never to do that again. Not without a copper-bottomed excuse.

*

Jason leaned against the door at the top of the stairs and wept. It had taken him the best part of four hours to drag himself up the steps, one by agonising one. He was pretty sure he'd fainted at some point, only because he'd become conscious of a line of drool running from the corner of his mouth to his chin. He'd talked to himself, sung tunelessly and practised marriage proposals to Eilidh to hold panic at bay. And every step had driven sharp rods of pain down his left leg and left him trembling.

Before each one, he'd craned his neck to look upwards. About halfway up, he'd had a moment of elation when he realised he could see a faint thread of light outlining the door that stood between him and rescue. The sight had kept him going as he'd gritted his teeth and moaned his way up the stairs. His mouth was dry and periodic waves of nausea stopped him in his tracks.

The hope that had sustained him on the climb was dashed almost as soon as he reached the door. He'd squirmed round to reach the handle, but when he depressed it, nothing happened. He put his eye to the crack and he could see two breaks in the line of faint light. One for the door catch and another for the lock whose keyhole sat beneath the handle. He shone the slender beam of the torch into the keyhole but it was almost completely obstructed. Jason realised he couldn't even attempt the sort of nonsense that worked in comics. He couldn't poke the key out of its hole because the bitch who'd done this to him had given it an extra half-turn to take it beyond the vertical.

He let out a sob of frustration. He banged the back of his head against the solid door and gave a cry of rage. 'I'm not gonna die here,' he shouted defiantly. But it was bravado and he knew it. He was locked in the cellar of an empty church hall and nobody was going to come and let him out. Not tonight. Maybe tomorrow, though? It was obviously a hall that was used regularly. Surely there would be some group or class using it soon? A slimming club, or a mother and toddler group? Surely?

He knew you could do without food for weeks. But water? That was a matter of days. Next to no time, wasn't it? With a broken leg and no water, how long would he last? How long would it be before the boss came looking for him?

More to the point, how long would it take her to find him?

40

Karen was pleased to see Daisy was a quick learner. She turned up at Karen's office with two cartons of coffee and a couple of Belgian chocolate chip flapjacks and all the bounce of a puppy who's just been offered a walk.

'How's the investigation on the ground going?' Karen asked.

'We're really struggling. Still no witnesses who saw James Auld heading out to the tower. And strangers are ten a penny around there, even in the dead of winter. They come over for the snowdrop festival at Cambo then wander around all over the East Neuk. To be honest, until we get something back from James Auld's computer, we're dancing in the dark.'

'I stopped by Gartcosh yesterday, their top digital analyst promised me she'd get to it tomorrow. Hopefully that'll give us some new leads. I could do with a following wind right now – I've got ACC Markie on my back. If I don't have a bone for her to throw to the politicians, she'll make do with me instead.'

Daisy raised her eyebrows. 'She's quite something, isn't she?' It was a diplomatic response.

'She's a nightmare, Daisy. You know that feminist notion

that successful women give a hand up to the ones coming up the ladder behind them? Not the Dog Biscuit. She would stamp on your fingers till you let go the rungs.'

'You're not a fan, then?' Daisy was grinning now.

'Let's just say we have a different concept of the point of policing. Now, let's see where we're up to.'

Daisy took out her phone. 'While I was on the train, I drew up a timeline, as far as I could. Shall I send it to you?'

Karen pulled up the timeline on her screen. It was clear and concise, with the level of detail she'd probably have chosen herself. It wasn't Daisy's fault that she hadn't been in possession of all the facts. 'You've done a good job with the information you have,' Karen said. 'That's really helpful. I've managed to make one or two steps forward since we got back from Paris. Let me fill you in and then,' she gave Daisy a wry smile, 'you can add them.'

She walked Daisy through every step she'd taken since they'd parted. Daisy's expression grew more incredulous then admiring as the information sank in. 'That's wild,' she breathed. 'So what Superintendent Beckett didn't know was that David Greig was a brilliant copyist.'

'Turned forger, we assume.'

'When you tie that to his relationship with Iain Auld—'

'Again, assumptive.'

'But it makes so much sense!' Daisy was excited now. Karen could see she was desperate to add this new information to her timeline.

'And it also makes sense of Iain Auld's disappearance and David Greig's suicide,' Karen said, realising how her new information fitted the bigger picture. It was true that two heads were better than the sum of their parts. 'The 2010 General Election was in May. Auld knew that a Tory

Scottish Secretary would make very different decisions about what paintings to have on the Dover House walls. The messages would all be about the Union, Edinburgh as the Athens of the North, Scottish soldiers going into war. Not a celebration of art for art's sake.'

'So Auld and Greig knew the ball was on the slates. The forgeries would go back to Scotland where some eagle-eyed curator would spot the difference and there would be trouble.'

Karen nodded. 'And a lot more of a stooshie than there actually was in 2015 when the forgeries were discovered. In 2015, the new Tory government had a vested interest in keeping it quiet because they didn't want to accuse their former coalition partners of robbing the national heritage. It would have blown up in their faces. There were too many recently buried bodies that the Lib Dems knew all about.'

Daisy was actually bouncing in her chair. 'Whereas, in 2010, the Tories would have loved to have yet another stick to beat Gordon Brown's government with. It would have been all over the media and they'd have left no stone unturned to uncover the culprits.'

'Auld was afraid the finger would point to him. And back in 2010, it might well have done. I imagine there might have been some CCTV coverage. Some record of who he'd brought into the building after hours. He wasn't to know that it would be another five years before anyone would discover his and Greig's little game.' Karen unwrapped her flapjack and took a thoughtful bite.

'That all makes perfect sense but it still doesn't explain what happened to Auld. And why Greig killed himself,' Daisy said, crestfallen.

'I think whatever happened to Auld is the reason why

Greig killed himself. If Auld panicked and ran, maybe he and Greig had a fight that turned bloody? Or maybe Auld finally saw himself for what he was – a liar and a thief who'd betrayed the trust of his wife and his country. And killed himself. Greig couldn't live with the guilt and took the same way out?' It felt more tentative to Karen than it had sounded when she said it. And then she found the flaw.

'But that doesn't fit either.' She frowned, cross with herself. 'According to the reports in the papers, Greig had been telling friends about a broken love affair well before Iain Auld disappeared.'

'That doesn't mean it didn't go the way you suggest. I was only a student back in 2010, but I remember nobody expected Gordon Brown's Labour government to be re-elected, even before the election campaign started. The writing was on the wall, surely? What if they had split up, then the election came along and Iain Auld freaked out and told Greig they had to come clean? They could have got into a fight and it played out the way you suggested.'

It was plausible, Karen thought. But was it plausible enough to build a case on? She needed to get to David Greig's executor. Someone close enough to be responsible for administering his estate must have known the details of his private life. Except that she wasn't factoring in Verity Foggo's evidence. Was it possible she'd been mistaken? That the 'discovery' that had set the ball rolling was a misapprehension after all?

Karen massaged her temples and sighed. 'Let's go and get something to eat. There's a decent Thai and a good Indian up the street.'

'Sounds like a plan. Have I got time to put this new stuff into the timeline before we go?'

'Sure. I need to try to get hold of the Mint.'

Daisy looked up. 'The Mint?'

'You've not met Jason yet, have you? My wingman. DC Jason Murray, aka the Mint.'

Daisy looked baffled. 'The Mint?'

'You're too young, aren't you? "Murray Mints, Murray Mints, too good to hurry mints."'

'Oh. OK.' She shook her head. 'Cop nicknames. They're so convoluted.' She turned her attention back to the screen. 'Where is he?' she added absently.

'Good question, to which the answer seems to be AWOL.' Karen scowled at her phone and put it to her ear. Straight to voicemail again. This was beyond a joke. She reached for her iPad and ran the Find My Phone app again. And there was Jason's phone, still right in the middle of the Hartshead Moor service area. 'I don't like this,' she muttered. Even if Jason had tracked Amanda McAndrew to the nearby golf course, it was already after six. It would be dark, and as far as Karen was aware, people didn't play golf in the dark.

'What's the problem?' Daisy asked.

'I'm not sure.' If Amanda had been playing golf, she might have stopped for a drink after the game. But surely Jason would be in the golf course car park? Or even in the bar. She zoomed in and turned to satellite view. The service area was separated from the clubhouse by two lines of what looked like trees and dense shrubbery. Even Jason wouldn't think that was a reasonable place for a stake-out. And why was his phone turned off? If he was in the car, he'd be able to charge it up, no problem. 'Let's get something to eat and worry about Jason later.'

They settled on the Thai restaurant round the corner on Union Street. 'Mmm, a pre-theatre menu,' Daisy said. 'I love a bargain.' She made a wry face. 'Must be all those years in Aberdeen.'

'So it's true, Aberdonians are tight?'

'Just as true as what they say about you Fifers. "One generation away from the caves."'

Karen laughed. 'Aye, but that's true.' She chose what she always had – crab in rice paper wrappers, then pad khing. She loved the crispy ginger that ran through the dish and woke up her taste buds. Daisy was more conservative, going with fish cakes and pad Thai. She was young, Karen thought. Give her time.

They agreed not to talk about the case while they were eating. Instead they talked about holidays. Daisy, it turned out, was in love with the Greek islands. With her friend Tori, she was working her way round the smaller ones, avoiding the tourist trap seafronts lined with tavernas packed with holidaymakers determined to get wasted on beer and ouzo. 'We love those villages where you rock up to a taverna that's basically somebody's patio and you go in the kitchen and choose your fish. And they throw it on the grill for you. Bliss.'

Karen had never been to Greece. She'd heard stories of the plumbing and had decided to give it the body swerve. But what Daisy described sounded like her sort of place. Maybe she'd been too hasty. Maybe it could be a future compromise destination for her and Hamish.

'Are you heading back to Fife?' Karen asked as she waited for the bill.

'Are we done?'

'For tonight anyway. I can't see anything much happening until we either get something from James's computer or the copy of David's will. And I'd like you to follow up the Artists' Resale Register angle on Monday too.' It was the kind of task Jason did well. But Jason wasn't here and Daisy was.

'What about you?'

'First I'm going to have one last attempt to get hold of the Mint.' Karen tried her phone. Voicemail again. And the iPad's Find My Phone was giving her the same location.

Now she was seriously worried.

Obviously concerned, Daisy said, 'Still nothing?'

'His phone's been going to voicemail since late morning. I did Find My Phone right before you arrived at the office and it says he's been at a motorway services in Yorkshire ever since. There's something wrong. Jason never goes dark. He's so anxious about getting it wrong, he's the opposite of going freestyle.' The waiter arrived with the bill and Karen paid with her card.

'What's he doing down there?'

'It's another case we're working. We think a woman called Amanda McAndrew killed her girlfriend then stole her identity.'

'Why would she do that?'

'I'm not sure, but I think it might be to muddy the waters. If you can pull it off, it's a very good way to obscure the time of death. She knew her lover was estranged from her family, and she'd established that they were going on the road, so nobody was going to report the girlfriend missing. After enough time had gone by, McAndrew could re-emerge as herself, free and unencumbered.'

'That makes sense, I suppose.'

Karen's smile was wry. 'It's the best I can come up with. We did a bit of fancy footwork and connected her to an address in Stockport. I sent Jason to track her down. I gave him explicit instructions not to make an approach. All he was supposed to do was find where she's living or working and stake her out till I could join him. And now this. I've heard nothing from him since last night. And we think this woman is a killer.' Karen's face had taken on a pinched look.

'Can't you get the local boys to swing past the services and see whether they can spot him?'

'They've got no skin in the game, it's not going to be high on their priorities.' Karen sighed deeply. 'Why do I always feel responsible for him? I'm not his bloody mother.' Then she had a thought. She grabbed her phone and searched her contacts for Eilidh. 'The girlfriend,' she muttered in response to Daisy's questioning look.

Eilidh answered on the third ring. 'Hello, DCI Pirie,' she said. It didn't matter how often Karen told the lassie to use her first name, she followed Jason's example.

'Hi, Eilidh. Sorry to bother you, but I think there might be a problem with Jason's phone. I wondered if he'd been in touch with you today?'

'Yeah, he spoke to me first thing this morning. He was fine, he was going off to some art studio or something. He'll call me later on, we always speak at bedtime if we're not together.' She sounded unworried, which Karen was pleased about. She didn't want to panic her.

'OK, no worries. He's maybe just in a black spot.'

'Or else he's out of juice. You know what he's like, head in the clouds.'

That was one way of putting it. Karen ended the call and stared glumly at her phone. There was nothing else for it. She was going to have to find her wayward wingman.

Sitting on a cold stone step had been bearable earlier in the day. But the sun had gone down hours ago and whatever heating had been on in the hall had turned itself off too. A thin shirt and a pair of suit trousers were no match for the drop in temperature. Jason could barely feel his fingers. He was going to die here, he was convinced of it now. If the lack of water didn't get him, the cold would.

He kept having spasms of shivering that racked his body with more pain as his broken leg juddered. And then he remembered the pile of velvet curtains in the corner of the basement. The thought of them made him tearful all over again. What was worse? To stay up by the door where there was a chance he could make himself heard whenever people came back to the hall, always supposing he hadn't frozen to death? Or drag himself through the agony of descending the stairs and wrapping himself in the curtains, too far from the stairs to be heard when he called for help?

It was no choice. He scouted out the descent with his feeble torch and this time he spotted a handrail. If he pulled himself up on the handrail, he could move his good leg down step by step. It would still be agonising but hopefully it would take less time than working his way down on his backside.

By the time he reached the bottom, he was drenched in cold sweat. Worse still, he needed to piss. He was determined not to wet himself. Not because it would be embarrassing when he was found, but because he knew it would only make him ever more cold. Balancing on one leg, gripping the banister with white knuckles, he undid his zip and direct the flow towards the stack of tables. He felt bad about it, but he didn't have an alternative. Exhausted by the effort, he lowered himself to the floor and lay there for a few minutes until he'd gathered a little strength.

More than ever, he craved the soft warmth of the

curtains. He crossed the stone floor in a crippled commando crawl and, with an impressive stream of swearing, dragged himself on to the curtains and wrapped one of them round his suffering body. Whimpering quietly, he managed to find a position that was almost free from pain. If this was going to be his last night on earth, at least he'd be warm.

41

Daisy had refused to take no for an answer. Karen had protested that there was no need, that it wasn't Daisy's case, that the whole thing was crazy and that she'd be fine on her own. Though she owned to herself that she wouldn't mind back-up. And to Karen's secret relief, Daisy had simply insisted. 'From everything you've said about Jason, I'm sure he'd do the same for me.'

'Aye, if he thought of it. He sometimes needs a wee nudge but his heart's in the right place.'

And so they'd gone back to Gayfield Square and commandeered a marked police car. 'That way we can put the blue lights on and hammer down the road. That should shave a fair bit of time off the journey,' Karen explained as they set off. 'Plus if we need to intimidate anybody, we look very bloody official.'

They said little while Karen drove out of the city to join the A1 heading south. Once they were on the dual carriageway she put her foot down and soon they were doing over a hundred miles an hour, the blue lights washing the carriageway around them. The traffic was light, and Karen rarely had to touch the siren. She was in the zone, focused on handling the car at speed. But the dual carriageway ran out after thirty miles and she had to adjust her speed accordingly.

'Wow, this is quite a drive,' Daisy said.

'There'll be a lot more flashy-dashy driving to come. Can you read in the car?'

'Yes, I don't get car-sick, if that's what you mean.'

'OK. Can you check something out online? The fire at the Goldman Gallery in Brighton four years ago? Can you see whether it was arson? What was the word at the time? And how many of David Greig's paintings went up in smoke? I was planning to follow it up, but bloody Jason got in the way.' Karen hit the siren to force her way past a couple of cars dawdling on the outskirts of Eyemouth.

Daisy searched the web, her face illumined by the phone screen. Karen drove on regardless, concentrating on covering the miles at the maximum speed she felt was safe. Eventually, Daisy spoke. 'The police and the fire service both believed the fire had been started deliberately. There's a quite detailed piece in the local paper. They reckon somebody poured petrol through a delivery slot in the back door and set fire to it. The room where the blaze started was displaying four David Greig portraits plus landscapes, a conceptual piece by Tracey Emin, a series of Damien Hirst Spots paintings and half a dozen works by people I've never heard of.'

'Any arrests?'

'Nope. Not a one. Lots of speculation about the motive. Was it a spurned artist who was jealous of the ones on display? Was it a protest against contemporary art in general? Was it a firebug who wanted to see a good blaze? Or was it something personal against Simon Goldman? He'd recently closed down a factory in Kent, which didn't go down well with the workers who'd lost their jobs.'

'Plenty lines of inquiry there. But I suppose the insurance company coughed up and nobody was hurt, were they?'

'No loss of life, no injuries reported. So that would have taken the pressure off, right?'

'Right. The media don't generally get overexcited about some rich bastard's pet project getting torched once the first excitement's over. So if that was Iain Auld standing in the crowd watching his lover's paintings burn, maybe it was Iain Auld who started the fire?' Karen sped up as they reached a short stretch of dual carriageway.

'Why would he do that? I mean, if he was still alive, why would he want to destroy his lover's art?'

Karen zipped past a clutch of lorries lumbering along in the inside lane. Then she said, 'What's the first question we always look at when a case isn't open and shut?'

'Who benefits.'

'And who benefited from this gallery fire?'

'The gallery owner? He'd just closed a factory. What if he needed the insurance?'

'He's a billionaire, Daisy. He'd have plenty of ways to resolve a cashflow problem without burning down his art collection. He could have sold it, if he was that desperate.'

Daisy sighed. 'Sorry, I didn't think that through.'

'The main beneficiary of that fire is whoever has the stash of uncatalogued David Greig portraits. And who's most likely to have those?'

'Iain Auld? He's not dead? Verity Foggo was right?'

'I've asked River Wilde – you know, the forensic anthropologist at Dundee – to compare the photographs with each other and with historic pix of Auld. If she confirms it, then yes, we have to work on that assumption.'

Daisy frowned, pondering the implications. 'So when

David Greig killed himself, Iain Auld had access to a secret supply of his work?'

'That's one possibility. But there's another one that I like a lot better. What if David Greig didn't commit suicide? What if the uncatalogued paintings are ones that Greig completed after he was supposed to be dead? What if they're *both* still alive?'

It was Daisy who broke the silence. 'How could they have got away with it? Why would you even think of a scam like that?'

'I've been thinking about it, trying to make sense of it. Imagine you're Iain Auld. You're a highly respected senior civil servant and a supposedly happily married man. Nobody we've spoken to has suggested otherwise. And then you fall catastrophically in love with a man. Not just any man, but a notorious bad boy. He's got a reputation for promiscuity, drug-taking – excess of all sorts. It's not going to play well in your professional life. And it's going to cause immense pain to your wife, who you still care for.'

'And maybe the last thing David Greig wants is to be publicly linked with somebody who's the soul of respectability. He'd have been a laughing stock among the YBA crowd, I bet,' Daisy chipped in.

'I hadn't thought of that, but yeah. It's not exactly avant-garde, is it? So they get together in absolute discretion. I imagine Iain wanting to show off Dover House to his lover – it's an architectural gem, after all. And David, who is a brilliant copyist and a man who loves taking risks, checks out the paintings on the walls and comes up with the idea of replacing the originals with copies. I can imagine how he'd sell it – it's subversive, disruptive. And it's also the emperor's new clothes – how long will it be before anybody notices what he's done? And he talks Iain into this.'

'As a sort of elaborate practical joke, you mean?'

'Exactly. But David is a properly bad boy. The joke isn't enough. He knows enough about the world he moves in to know that there are crooked dealers out there who supply private collectors, no questions asked. Now this is me going out on a limb here, but I suspect David had sold those original paintings on. Otherwise, he could have replaced the copies with the originals when the government changed. But they couldn't do that if he'd already disposed of them. They must have known the moment of discovery wasn't far off. They didn't know how watertight they were once the deception was discovered. And besides, they'd reached the point where they were tired of a part-time secret relationship. They wanted to be together.'

Karen was on a roll now as they raced down the M1 forty miles an hour above the speed limit. 'So the first thing that happens, in the run-up to the election, is that David plants the seeds. He confides in his friends – his lover has dumped him, he can't work, he's falling apart, he's never been so depressed. Then soon after the election, Iain disappears, apparently without trace. I think he sneaked out of the country. I wonder whether David's dodgy contacts extended to supplying false passports? That would have made it a lot easier. Anyway, however they managed it, Iain goes off to wherever they're going to start their new life.'

Daisy scoffed. 'You have such a devious mind.'

'I've learned from some very devious people. Not all of them in the polis.'

'So once Iain's safely out of the way, David waits three weeks then fakes his suicide?'

'Spot on. I'm interested in his choice of location as well. Those Anglesey cliffs are only a few miles from Holyhead. And from Holyhead, it's easy as pie to jump on a ferry to Dublin.'

'And that's where Geary is. Presumably his dodgy dealer?'

'It all fits, doesn't it?' Karen hit the siren to force a day-dreaming lane-hogger to swerve into the middle lane. 'They hook up and set up home somewhere nobody knows them and establish a new life. Paid for by the new work that David makes. Paintings that are genuinely authenticated, given the provenance of a private collector. They pass through Geary's gallery, which has always handled David's work, and they get the proceeds.'

'And then somehow James starts to put the pieces together?'

'I wonder about the row that the brothers had the night before Iain disappeared. Maybe he told his brother he was having an affair. With a man.'

'Why would he do that?' Daisy wondered.

'They were close. If he was genuinely tired of living a lie, Iain might have thought James was the one person he could trust with the truth.'

'But surely he'd have told the police when David Greig hit the headlines as a suicide?'

'Not if Iain didn't reveal the identity of his lover. And James seems to have been genuinely fond of Mary Auld. He wouldn't want to cause her any more grief than she was already going through, would he?'

'Maybe not.' Daisy sounded doubtful. 'But if it got him off the hook?'

'Who knows? He'll never be able to tell us now. What we do know is that when he found the photograph of his brother and David Greig, he must have recognised Greig. I imagine he'd have been looking at the papers for some time after his brother's death, to see if anything turned up. And Greig's picture was all over the front pages when he supposedly killed himself.'

'So that answered one question for him. And he started researching the market in Greig's paintings and discovered new ones were still showing up.'

'And then Verity Foggo enters, stage left. Confirming what James had maybe started to work out for himself.'

'I love the way you get all the pieces to fit. So who killed James?'

'Logically, either David Greig or Iain Auld.'

'And we don't know which one?'

'And there's one other problem.' Karen scowled at the road ahead. 'Like Jason, we don't know where the fuck they are.'

'The only sticking point for me is the gallery fire. I don't know much about artists, but I can't imagine somebody who was serious about their art agreeing to burning their work.'

'If their bank balances were running low, they'd have to sacrifice something. The alternative would be taking the chance on their deceptions being uncovered, which would expose them to a whole raft of charges. And Greig knew he could make more art whenever the mood took him.'

'I suppose. I kind of assume all artists are totally precious about everything they create.'

'Maybe they don't want to be judged by their earlier work? I remember watching some film or other where they talked about Michelangelo taking a hammer to one of his statues because he didn't think it was good enough.'

'Makes sense, I guess.' Daisy studied the map on her

phone as they approached the Hartside Moor Service Area on the M62. 'We're coming at it from the wrong side,' she said. 'And there's no link road. We'll have to go past to the next junction and turn around there.'

Karen growled. 'Typical.'

When they finally arrived at the eastbound services, Karen cruised slowly round all the parking areas. 'His car's not here.' She pulled up as close to the main building as she could and checked the location of Jason's phone again on the iPad. The detail was remarkable. 'It's behind the main building,' Karen said, getting out of the car and heading off at a jog. She held the iPad out in front of her as if that would lead them to the phone more quickly. Daisy followed her round the side of the building. There was a staff entrance, and beside it, a litter bin.

'It looks like it's in the bin,' Karen said. She tapped the icon that would instruct the phone to make a sound. She waited, poised on the balls of her feet. And then a series of beeps issued from the bin, rising in volume.

'Shouldn't we—?' Daisy said anxiously.

'Bollocks to that,' Karen said, thrusting the iPad into her hands and grasping the outer skin of the bin with both hands. Grunting with the effort, she lifted it up and staggered backwards with it, dropping it on the tarmac as she cleared the internal container. She fished a pair of nitrile gloves out of her jacket pocket and hauled the black bin liner on to the ground. It was only half full; clearly it had been emptied earlier that day, judging by the state of the contents. Karen ripped the bag open and rummaged through fast food containers, coffee cartons, chocolate bar wrappers and leftover food.

In less than a minute, she had Jason's phone in her hand. 'He's not here,' she said. 'I don't think he's ever been here.'

42

Because she needed something physical to do, Karen gathered the sides of the bin liner together and shoved the contents back where they'd come from. She glared at the bin as if it that would somehow ease the fear and frustration gnawing at her heart.

'We could have a cup of coffee while we figure out what to do next?' Daisy's suggestion was tentative but Karen knew it made sense. Apart from anything else, it was almost eleven o'clock and she was feeling drained from the drive. She needed sustenance and even shitty motorway coffee had life-saving caffeine on board.

'Should we get the local police to go round to the art studios to see whether Jason's there?' Daisy asked once they were hunched over their hot drinks and dispiriting motorway sandwiches.

Karen sighed. 'I thought about that. But they wouldn't do it on my say-so from some random mobile. They'd want to check that I am who I say I am, which means phoning Police Scotland and finding someone to verify my ID. It would be so cumbersome at this hour. I think we'd be as quick to drive to Stockport. It can't be much more than half an hour, forty minutes from here at this time of night.'

'Then what?'

'Watch and learn, Daisy. Watch and learn.' There was nothing patronising about Karen's delivery. She simply couldn't be bothered explaining. She was too tired and too anxious. For some reason, a line from a Bob Dylan song popped into her head. Something about having to pay to get out of doing things twice. She was certainly paying forward tonight.

Back on the road again, the swirl of blue light their accompaniment again as they crossed the Pennines, the darkness of the moors suddenly giving way to the distant orange glow of Greater Manchester as they crested the last rise. As they turned on to the orbital motorway, Karen said, 'Find the nearest police station to the Isherwood Studios.'

Daisy busied herself with her phone. 'There's one on the main drag. It starts off as Gorton Road then turns into Reddish Road. It's open twenty-four seven. You need to come off at the next junction, on to the A57 heading for Manchester.'

A few minutes later, they rolled to a stop outside a single-storey brick building. 'It looks more like a health centre than a nick,' Karen muttered, unclipping her seat belt. She stretched her back as she got out, rolling her shoulders and groaning. 'God, I'm starting to sound like an old woman.'

The foyer was as spartan as she expected. Vinyl tiles, brick walls, half a dozen chairs, public information and missing person notices on the walls, and a glassed-in counter opposite the door. Karen crossed the room and pressed the white plastic bell mounted by the glass. She drummed her fingers impatiently but knew better than to ring again. She needed goodwill here tonight.

A few minutes passed then a uniformed PC who looked

too young to be shaving came in through a side door. He slid back the reinforced glass and said, without enthusiasm, 'Can I help you?'

Karen already had her ID to hand. 'Detective Chief Inspector Karen Pirie from Police Scotland. I need your assistance.'

He looked startled. 'What kind of assistance?'

She smiled reassuringly. 'The easy kind,' she said. 'One of my officers was in the area today on routine inquiries. He's not checked in since last night. I need to retrace his steps. You know the Isherwood Studios? Just down the road from here?' She spoke with casual familiarity. 'I need you to get me the phone number of the keyholder.'

'I'm not sure I understand?' he stammered.

'It's straightforward. I need to find out who my officer spoke to and where they might have directed him to. And I can't wait till tomorrow morning because, as I explained, my colleague has disappeared from the radar.' She added conversationally, 'Did I mention this is a murder inquiry? So there really is some urgency here.'

'I need to speak to somebody.' He backed away and disappeared through the door.

'Of course he does,' Karen sighed. She leaned against the wall, letting her head drop. As long as she'd been driving, she'd had to concentrate so hard there had been no room for her imagination to roam over the possible fates that Jason had endured. She should never have sent him off in pursuit of a woman who could well be a killer, a woman who had already demonstrated an imaginative resourcefulness when it came to wriggling out of the problems created by having a dead body in the back of her camper van. Karen silently berated herself for her impatience. This could have waited

327

till she had time to concentrate on it properly, instead of trying to shoehorn it into the interstices of a much wider investigation. If something had happened to Jason—

But before she could go down that road, a grizzled uniformed sergeant came through the door. Karen returned to the partition and managed a tired smile. 'PC Armitage tells me you're looking for a contact for the keyholder of the Isherwood Studios? Something about a colleague of yours on the missing list?'

She nodded. 'That's right.'

The sergeant cocked his head, sizing her up. 'You're a bit off your patch, aren't you? You sure he's not just gone for a night on the ale?'

'He wouldn't dare,' Daisy chipped in. Karen flashed her a surprised look. 'DCI Pirie runs a very tight ship.'

'Can I ask why you didn't let us know you were running an operation on our ground?' His tone was mild but his eyes didn't move from hers.

'Because we weren't. DC Murray had orders to track down the suspect and make no approach. Once we'd confirmed we had the right address and we were ready to move, we'd have informed you.' Matter-of-fact, no big deal.

'Armitage says it's a murder?'

'A cold case.' That usually reassured them that it wasn't going to kick off in their back yard. 'Just following up a lead on a witness.'

He pursed his lips and shook his head. 'I probably shouldn't do this, but what the hell.' He drew a folded piece of paper from his pocket and pushed it across the counter. 'There you go. She lives a few streets away.'

Karen opened it out and read, 'Patience Cameron,' followed by a phone number. 'Thanks, skip,' she said.

'Step lightly, Chief Inspector.'

They made their way back to the car. Karen glanced back into the station and saw the sergeant behind the counter, his eyes still following her. 'Nothing to see here,' she murmured, getting back behind the wheel. She took out her phone and keyed in the number on the paper. One, two, three, four, five, six. 'Come on.' Seven, eight—

'Hello? Who is this?' The voice was wary. Only to be expected this close to midnight.

'Ms Cameron? I'm very sorry to bother you. I'm Detective Chief Inspector—'

'Jaden! Has something happened to Jaden?' Urgency, fear. Karen understood that.

'No, it's nothing to do with Jaden. There's nothing to worry about, honestly.'

'So why are you calling me up at this hour?' There was a faint lilt of the Caribbean beneath her Manchester accent.

'You're the keyholder of the Isherwood Studios, is that right?'

'Has there been a break-in? What's happened?'

'No, no break-in. There's no reason to panic, Ms Cameron. If I can explain?'

'OK. OK, explain away, Miss Chief Inspector.'

'One of my colleagues was due to go round to the studios first thing this morning. But he's not checked in since then, and that's not like—'

'What was he wanting at the studios?'

Whoever had christened her Patience had got it badly wrong, Karen thought. 'We're trying to make contact with Dani Gilmartin.'

She made a noise with her teeth that sounded like 'Tchaw'. 'He wouldn't have found Dani there this morning.'

Her tone was dismissive, as if any fool would know that. 'Only person he'd have found there first thing was Orla, working on her mural.'

'And would Orla have known where to find Dani?'

'Everybody knows that. Monday mornings, Dani runs Watercolours for Beginners in the church hall down by Morrisons.'

Karen felt her breathing return to normal. 'And that's where Orla would have sent him?'

'I said so, didn't I?'

'What street is that? Sorry, I'm not local.'

'No, you don't sound it. It's on Lingard Fold Lane. But there won't be anybody there this time of night, it'll be all locked up till the slimming class tomorrow afternoon.'

Please, God, just one break ... 'Do you know who has the keys?'

'Well, we have a set at the studios, but Dani will have them with her, she'll have locked up after her class. Now, can I get back to my film?' She was starting to sound irritated, and who could blame her?

'One last thing – do you know where Dani lives?'

'Do you know where everybody you work beside lives? All I know is that she lives somewhere over Gorton way. Now, goodnight, Miss Chief Inspector.'

The church hall was set back from the pavement, a black shape against the sky. They parked at the end of the street and walked back. Karen stopped so abruptly that Daisy couldn't help bumping into her. 'Fuck,' Karen said, pointing across the street. 'That's Jason's car. If he left here, he didn't do it under his own steam.' Her chest hurt, fear a physical grip.

Five minutes was all it took to demonstrate there was no easy way into the building. Doors locked, front and back. Windows all covered with grilles. 'I should have done this earlier,' Karen said, pacing the path and taking out her phone. She dialled her Area Control Room back in Edinburgh, and gave her authority for a 'stop and detain' on the car that had been registered to Barry McAndrew. 'There's a live arrest warrant for Amanda McAndrew, alias Daniella Gilmartin. I'll email it over to you as soon as I come off this call. But I need you to pass this on as an urgent request to other forces in the UK,' she insisted. 'And I want an all-points alert on passports issued to Daniella Gilmartin and Amanda McAndrew. Ferry ports and airports. Are we clear on that?'

The duty officer read back the details to her.

'Thanks. And can you pay particular attention to the Hull ferryport? They have night crossings to Holland and Belgium. She left Manchester on the M62 heading east. If she was aiming to get out of the country, the Hull ferries would be the obvious routes.' It was confirmed in a matter of minutes. Again, Karen wished she'd set up the alert earlier, but she'd been giving Jason a chance to show he could use his own initiative.

Whatever had happened to him was her responsibility.

She turned back towards the church hall to see Daisy leaning nonchalantly against the jamb of an open door. 'What the fuck?' The words were out before Karen knew it.

Daisy waggled a bunch of lock picks as Karen drew near. She was definitely smirking. 'You know how you said earlier, "watch and learn"? Well, I thought I'd just crack on and save a bit of time. I can always teach you another day.'

Karen laughed in spite of herself. 'I'm going to pretend this never happened,' she said. 'Come on, let's take a look inside.'

They walked into the vestibule and pushed open the doors into the main hall. Daisy flicked on a bank of light switches and the fluorescent tubes glared into life. 'I hope the neighbours don't call the cops,' she muttered.

There was nowhere Jason could be hiding. Not unless he'd been folded up toddler-sized and rammed into the Wendy House that occupied one corner. Karen checked it nevertheless, just to make sure.

They crossed the hall and went through the door at the far end. Daisy slipped into the kitchen on the left, looking for signs of a struggle, for blood, for anything that was out of place. She found it in the bin. Gingerly, using a fork from the cutlery drawer, she fished something out from among the rubbish. 'Is this Jason's?' she asked, showing Karen the suit jacket dangling from the fork.

Karen nodded, mute. She didn't trust herself to speak. She turned away and clattered into the women's toilets. She slapped the doors hard so they banged against the flimsy cubicle partitions, swearing under her breath at each empty space. She did the same in the men's.

Daisy held out Jason's notebook. 'That's all that was in there.'

Karen grabbed it and flipped through to the latest entry. 'Church hall, side street, Morrisons,' the last entry read. She shook her head and carried on down the corridor. She followed it round a right-hand corner and nearly walked straight into a stack of easels. Daisy bumped into her, which dislodged the neat pile enough for Karen to realise they were obscuring a door. Adrenaline surged through her.

'Let's get these shifted,' she said, grabbing the nearest one and propping it against the opposite wall.

It was the urgent work of a few minutes to move the easels out of the way. 'He's got to be here,' Karen panted as she grabbed the last one and virtually threw it down the hall.

They were confronted by a solid wooden door, bolts at top and bottom, key in the keyhole. 'Gloves?' Karen demanded. She'd used her only pair at the service area.

'Kitchen.' Daisy scuttled back down the corridor and raked in the cupboard where she'd seen a box of flimsy plastic gloves. She grabbed a handful and hurried back.

Karen slipped a pair on and gently turned the key, careful only to touch the edges of the bow. She doubted Amanda McAndrew would have been so cautious. 'Open one of those gloves,' she demanded, and dropped the key into it. Then she struggled with the stiff bolts till they grudgingly slid free. She noticed the light switch by the door and pressed it. She felt on the verge of tears.

She pulled the door open. 'Jason,' she bellowed, running down the stairs without a pause. She stopped at the foot and looked around wildly. What hit her first was the ripe smell of stale piss. But no Jason to be seen or heard. 'Jason?' It was almost a whisper, a tremble in her voice.

And then, a groan. From the corner where the light barely reached. Karen could see what looked like a pile of discarded curtains. Daisy at her heels, she rushed forwards. At closer quarters, she could see the top of Jason's head, his ginger hair a splash of clashing colour against the plum velvet. Her heart leapt in her chest, relief momentarily overcoming fear. And then the terror was back. What had happened to him? How badly was he hurt?

Karen crouched beside him and cautiously pulled the

edge of the curtain back from his head. He was drip white, dark shadows under his eyes and a long bruise forming on one side of his face. His eyelids flickered and he frowned. 'Boss?' he whispered through cracked lips. 'I'm sorry.' His eyes rolled back and he breathed heavily.

'Call an ambulance, Daisy.' Karen laid a hand on the side of his head, careful not to move him. 'And the police. Where does it hurt, Jason?'

'Leg,' he groaned. 'Left leg. Broken.'

'OK. Help's on its way, hang in there.' He mumbled something she couldn't make out. 'What?'

'Water,' he said loudly.

Karen waited till Daisy had finished with the emergency services then shouted, 'Get a cup of water, Daisy.'

'Should you give him something to drink?' Daisy said, anxiety overcoming her reluctance to contradict Karen. 'I mean, if they have to operate on his leg?'

'Good point. But bring some water and a paper towel. I can at least wet his lips, for fuck's sake.'

The ambulance seemed to take forever, but Karen knew that was an illusion. The paramedics were efficient and kind, getting a drip into Jason before they moved him. 'It's the tibia,' one explained. 'It's either a displaced or a comminuted fracture. Hard to tell. We need to get him to hospital and get it X-rayed.'

'Will he have to have surgery?' Karen asked. She didn't relish telling Mrs Murray her boy had been broken on her watch.

'Not for me to say, love,' he said. 'We're taking him to Stepping Hill hospital, down the A6. Are you coming with?'

Karen shook her head. 'I need to wait for the local police. This wasn't an accident. This is a crime scene.'

43

Tuesday, 25 February 2020

It was after three in the morning when they checked into the same hotel where Jason had stayed the night before. They'd left him at the hospital, sedated and awaiting a surgical procedure to screw his tibia back together. The local police had swung into action with commendable enthusiasm; it was, Karen thought, as if he was one of their own. They'd rousted Patience Cameron from her bed and stood over her while she phoned round the other tenants of the Isherwood Studios till she found someone who had an address for 'Dani'. They'd invited Karen and Daisy to join them when they kicked in the door of a maisonette on the third and fourth floor of a strip of housing in nearby Gorton that looked like a barracks.

'Last time I was round here, they were using it as a film set for East Germany during the Cold War,' one of the local lads had remarked. Karen could believe that with no effort at all.

The flat held little of interest. Karen assumed Amanda had swung by to strip the place of anything that might either have been incriminating or have given a clue to her

335

destination. No family photographs, no letters, no laptop or tablet. Just large watercolours of the Scottish Highlands drawing-pinned to the walls. Karen recognised Schiehallion and the Buachaille. Maybe Amanda wasn't as tough as she'd thought; the mountains she'd missed showed a degree of homesickness. It spoke of a more vulnerable side than the apparent coolness with which she'd got out from under Dani Gilmartin's death.

Although she was bone-weary, sleep eluded Karen once she'd crawled under the covers. Intellectually, she knew that what had happened to Jason had been Amanda McAndrew's fault, not hers. But emotionally she felt responsible. It hadn't occurred to her that she was sending Jason into trouble, but it probably should have done. Walking back the cat to the origins of disaster was pointless yet somehow she always found it hard to resist.

Her phone rang at 03:39 and she nearly fell out of the unfamiliar bed in her urgency to take the call. It was the Area Control Room. 'Hey, DCI Pirie. Sorry to wake you but I thought you'd want an update.'

'You thought right,' she said. 'Has she been picked up?' She squirmed round to sit on the edge of the bed, elbows on knees, phone to her ear.

'Not as such. But we know where she is. The local lads in Hull found her car two streets away from the ferry terminal. We got them to check the ticket sales and she bought a berth yesterday afternoon on the overnight Rotterdam run. It gets in around half past eight in the morning, their time.'

Karen rolled her eyes. 'So I've got less than five hours to sort out a European Arrest Warrant?'

'Less than four hours. They're an hour ahead of us, remember?'

Karen groaned. 'Leave it with me.' She hauled herself out of bed and set herself up at the table with her tablet and her phone, earphones plugged in to give her hands-free. The number she called was Fiscal Depute Ruth Wardlaw. Karen knew Ruth well enough to be pretty sure that she'd answer her phone even if she wasn't the depute on call. Like Karen, she couldn't resist the siren call of an interesting case, and nobody would dare ring her in the middle of the night unless it was an interesting case. Not to mention that she'd be livid if Karen took the case to anyone else in the fiscal's office after she'd done the heavy lifting of securing the arrest warrant in the first place.

The number rang out half a dozen times then cut out. Karen heard a clatter, then a muffled, 'Bugger,' followed by the sound of fumbling. 'Who is this?' Ruth sounded justifiably grumpy.

'Karen. I'm sorry to wake you but it's urgent. Amanda McAndrew is on the night ferry from Hull to Rotterdam. She threw Jason – you remember Jason, DC Murray? She threw him down a flight of stairs and left him for dead, then legged it. We need a European Arrest Warrant and we need it within the next couple of hours.'

Ruth sighed. 'Good morning to you too, Karen. She threw DC Murray down a flight of stairs? Where did this happen?'

'Does that matter? It happened in Stockport.'

Ruth yawned. 'Well, that's good news and bad news. The bad news is we can't add that to the warrant because it happened in a different jurisdiction to the homicide. The good news is we don't have to complicate things by adding it to the warrant.'

'Can you do it?'

'Karen, it's me you're talking to. As soon as we finish

this call, I will contact the duty extradition sheriff of the International Crime Unit of the Crown Office and email them the arrest warrant along with a brief outline of reasons why we need the EAW. Meanwhile you will send me a short report of the assault on your officer. I'll add that in a separate docquet as evidence of intent to flee. And then I will drag my weary body round to the ICU office to make any arguments the sheriff needs to hear and to pick up the EAW.' Karen could hear sounds of movement in the background and the low mumble of another voice.

'Will you send that on to the Dutch police and immigration officials? Or do I need to do that?'

'It'll come from our ICU. I'll send you a copy. If by any chance we're running out of time, we can apply for a provisional warrant. That means they can arrest her when she gets off the boat regardless, but we have a window of either twenty-four or forty-eight hours to formalise the warrant. I'm not sure off the top of my head what the limit is in Holland. We'll get her, Karen. Trust me. These guys at the Crown Office are no strangers to urgency. Even in the middle of the night, you'd be amazed at the turn of speed a sheriff can muster. Now, bugger off and let me do what I do. We'll talk later.' Dead line.

It was almost five a.m. when Ruth called back. 'The warrant's been issued and the Dutch have it in their hands. Police and immigration have been alerted at the port of arrival. They're assuring us she'll not get past them.'

Karen wished she shared their optimism. 'Make sure they understand how devious she is. She's good at getting people to cover for her. She'll not be on foot. Chances are she'll have talked somebody into giving her a lift. They

338

need to check all the cars and lorries as well as the foot passengers.'

'I'll pass it on. I'll keep you posted. As soon as I hear anything, you'll know.'

Karen lay down again and squinched into a comfortable position. She wondered whether Amanda McAndrew was sleeping, or whether the fizz of fear was bubbling in her blood, keeping her edgy and wary. Where would she be heading for? Would she try to reach her parents and hope they'd take her in? Jason had suggested that, from what he'd seen on Facebook, their daughter had visited them two years before, but she hadn't asked him to dig deeper. Another thing she should have done. Presumably they hadn't known their daughter was running around on someone else's passport, so they might have been her backstop. The place where Amanda McAndrew could re-emerge.

The last thought that drifted through Karen's head as she slipped into sleep was, 'Though it would be better to arrest her before it came to that.'

Karen had set her alarm for eight. The ferry was due to dock half an hour before that, but she reckoned it would take some time for the Dutch authorities to lay hands on Amanda McAndrew and some time after that for the news to filter back through the system to Ruth.

The lack of sleep and the stress of the previous day had left her feeling as if she'd had an unwise night on the gin. But before she tried to shake off the sloth and arouse the cotton-wool brain, she had a phone call to make. She'd persuaded the number for the direct line to the ward from the nurse who'd been taking care of Jason and now she dialled it. 'This is Detective Chief Inspector Pirie,' she said sternly to the man who answered. 'I'm ringing to inquire about the condition of one of your patients. We brought him in late last night. Jason Murray.'

'Are you a relative?'

Cheeky bastard. 'I'm the detective chief inspector who rescued him and accompanied him to hospital. It's a simple question. How is he doing?'

'We're only supposed to inform relatives about patients.'

Don't do this, son. Really, don't do this. 'Are you seriously obstructing a police officer in the commission of her duty?' She upped the incredulity level to eleven.

'N-no,' he stumbled. 'It's just—'

Karen heard a firm voice in the background. Then a woman came on the line. 'Is there a problem?'

Karen introduced herself again. 'I'm Jason's boss,' she said. 'I'm the nearest thing he has to a relative in a two-hundred-mile radius and I'm responsible for him.'

'Good point, well made, love. He's in surgery – they put him at the top of the list on account of him being a copper. If you phone back in an hour or so, I can give you an update. Ask for Shirley. Don't worry about him, he's going to be fine.'

Karen thanked her and closed her eyes for a long moment. She breathed deeply then searched her phone for another number. This was the call she was dreading.

'Is that you, Karen?' Surprised and wary simultaneously. 'Are you looking for Jason? He's not here, hen, I'm not expecting him today.'

'I know, Mrs Murray. He's been on a job down south. And there's been a wee accident.'

A sharp gasp. 'Oh no, not my Jason—'

'It's not serious,' Karen interrupted, her voice urgent.

'He's not in any danger, I promise you. He took a tumble down a flight of steps and broke his leg. He's in the hospital now, they're operating on his leg to sort it out.'

'An operation?'

'It's completely routine, I came off the phone this minute with the ward and there's no grounds for concern.'

That's easy for you to say, Karen Pirie. But folk die on the operating table every day of the week.'

She could hear the tears in Mrs Murray's voice. 'If it would put your mind at rest, I could get an officer to drive you down here?' Sod the Dog Biscuit and her budget.

'No, I don't want to sit in car with a stranger, I'll get our Ronan to bring me.'

Finally, the world had found a use for Ronan. 'I'll text you the details. But please, Mrs Murray, try not to worry.'

'Easy seen you're not a mother.' She took a deep breath. 'I'm sorry, Karen, that was uncalled for. You've always been good to my Jason. I'll get Ronan and we'll get on the road right away. Does Eilidh know?'

'I called you first.'

'Aye, well, I'll get in touch with her and we can pick her up on the road. She'll want to be there and I don't doubt he'd rather see her at his bedside than his old mammy.'

It would, Karen thought, be a close-run thing. The hard job over, she turned her attention to the business of working out a plan of action for her and Daisy. But first, breakfast. Nothing would be achieved without coffee and calories.

44

Karen was on her second cup of coffee when the call came from Ruth Wardlaw. 'Good news,' the Fiscal Depute said. 'The Dutch police followed your advice and checked the cars coming off the ferry. McAndrew had tried to give them the slip by persuading a Polish plumber to give her a lift in his van, but they spotted her. She's currently languishing in a holding cell in Rotterdam, waiting to see a lawyer.'

It felt like a turning of a tide that had been running against her ever since James Auld's body had been plucked from the waters of the Forth. 'That's brilliant news. What happens next? What's the timescale?'

'It depends. If she agrees to return to face the charge on the warrant, she'll be back in Scotland within ten days. But if she decides to contest it – and everything you've told me about her would suggest she'll go down that route – the Dutch courts have sixty days to determine whether she should be returned.'

Karen's spirits dipped. 'So she could still walk away from it?'

'Don't panic! The Dutch hearing won't be a trial of the evidence. They'll simply look at whether our ICU were right to issue the warrant, based on the nature of the crime and the legitimacy of the proceedings. And I've got no worries on that score. We're on solid ground here, Karen.'

'What if she tries to argue that it wasn't homicide but an accident?'

'That's irrelevant. The charge on the arrest warrant is homicide and that's what we'll be pursuing. Whatever she argues in her defence when she has her day in court, we'll be ready to knock holes in it.'

'Fair enough.'

'The bottom line is, you don't fail to report a death, hide the body then steal your victim's ID when it's an accident.'

Karen demurred. 'I can see how you might worry about misinterpretation, especially if you were known to have a volatile relationship.'

'You can see that and I can see that, but for the majority of people who sit on a jury, what McAndrew did was inexplicable in anything other than a criminal context. Relax, Karen, you've done the heavy lifting. Dani Gilmartin's father finally gets to know what happened to his daughter, and that's a result, whatever the outcome in court.'

She was right. 'Thanks, Ruth.'

'You're welcome. Now I'm away to my bed. See you soon.'

Lucky Ruth. Karen poked the last couple of mouthfuls of scrambled egg with her fork and decided it had gone too far in the direction of rubber. At some point today, Tamsin would have data from James Auld's laptop. With a bit of luck, the pathologist's report would soon make its way to her and formally confirm that Auld's injuries were consistent with murder rather than accident. There was nothing more she could do for Jason, not now that his mother, his girlfriend and his feckless brother were on their way.

Karen pushed her plate away and gave in to her

impatience. It was time they were on the road. She texted Daisy. See you in the foyer in 15 minutes. Plenty of time to walk back from the café and liberate the car from the multi-storey. The news of Amanda McAndrew's arrest had reinvigorated her. The Dog Biscuit was in for a surprise in the morning.

The drive back to Edinburgh seemed to go on for ever. The constant drizzle and the poor visibility didn't help. Nor did Karen's refusal to go up the M6 like a bat out of hell with the blue lights flashing. 'Abuse of privilege,' she muttered when Daisy asked why they were studiously sticking to the speed limit.

Bringing Daisy up to date with the McAndrew case occupied the first part of the journey. Daisy was clearly fascinated by the step-by-step pursuit of the case, from the garage in Perth to the artist colony in Glenisla and down to the church hall in Stockport. 'But what a bizarre beginning to a case,' she said. 'I mean, if Susan Leitch hadn't had that accident on her bike, it could have been years – decades, even – before Dani's remains turned up. Susan might even have got her nerve up and got rid of her. She could have buried her in the garden, or – I don't know, burned the bones and ground them up. Or taken a hammer to them and driven down to the coast and dumped them in the sea.'

'Or just carried on ignoring them.'

'Could you do that? Could you live in a house knowing there was a dead body in the garage? It's not like she never went in there. It's where she kept her bikes and all her tools and stuff.' Daisy shuddered. 'I don't think I could.'

'You'd be surprised how people manage to block things out,' Karen said. 'I remember one case where a guy was in total denial for twenty-odd years about having shot his own daughter. He waged a campaign to find her killer even though at some level he had to have known he was responsible.'

'That is so weird. You get really interesting stuff in cold cases, don't you?'

'The passage of time turns straightforward murders into convoluted journeys. But sometimes all the undergrowth that obscures the path withers away and you can see things clearly.' Karen scoffed. 'Listen to me, I sound like one of those pretentious tossers on the radio.'

'No, what you said makes sense. You think one day I could maybe get a transfer into the HCU and work with you and Jason?'

Karen flashed her a quick look to check whether she was at the wind-up. 'Seriously?'

'Why not?'

'Most front-line polis think we're a backwater. That the cases we investigate don't matter the way the live cases do.'

Daisy harrumphed. 'That's all swagger. What you do is much harder and much more useful. You put right the mistakes, the inefficiencies, the prejudices that stopped cases being solved in the first place. I think it's cool.'

'That's one way of looking at it. Or you can take the Dog Biscuit's view that we're a thorn in the flesh of Police Scotland precisely because every success we have is also a reminder that the front-line heroes fucked it up. If she had her way, we'd be disbanded. We have to keep succeeding very publicly to survive. Fuck up once, and we're dead in the water.'

'Sounds like you need all the help you can get.' Daisy gave her a cheeky glance. 'We're nearly at the services. Can we stop? I need a pee and they do great home baking here.'

Karen couldn't deny she liked Daisy's gallus attitude. And her understanding of the importance of coffee and cake to the proper running of a case. She pulled off the motorway and parked at a distance from the entrance to the café and shop. 'Could you bring me a flat white,' she said. 'I need to make a call.'

Daisy hurried off and Karen called the hospital again. This time she dropped lucky and Shirley the nurse answered. The good news cycle carried on. Jason was out of surgery and there had been no complications. Karen explained that his family were on their way and wished the nurse good luck.

While she was waiting for Daisy, she checked her email. To her delight, Professor Jenny Carmichael's report had landed in her inbox. Everybody seemed to be working weekends these days. It confirmed the verbal report she'd made to Charlie Todd in the mortuary. The medical evidence pointed to deliberate homicide. And another message from Charlie himself was the clincher. One of the team of officers who'd been making inquiries on the scene had taken it into his head to clamber down the tumble of rocks beneath the tower and he'd found a metal crowbar wedged in a cleft. In spite of the rain and salt spray that had landed on it over the days since the murder, the underside had been protected. The crime scene tech who had recovered it had preserved the surface and there were traces of blood and hair that matched James Auld. Charlie Todd's plods had come up trumps. They're still testing to see whether they can find any other DNA or any prints. Hope this helps. And hope Daisy's doing the business for you, Charlie had finished. She suspected he'd be less than thrilled if Daisy ever got her way and joined the HCU.

Daisy came back with coffees and the biggest sausage roll

Karen had ever seen for herself. 'I didn't have breakfast,' she mumbled through a mouthful of meat and flaky pastry.

'No, you had sleep.'

Karen gave Daisy the latest news while she ate, scattering fragments of pastry down her jacket and into the footwell. 'That's all great,' she said. 'Sorry about the mess, I'll vac it when we get back, promise.'

'You'll be the first,' Karen snarked.

Another twenty miles up the road and Daisy was asleep, head lolling, a thin line of drool sliding from the corner of her mouth. Karen vaguely remembered she'd once had that gift. Felt like a past-life experience. To cover the miles, she turned on her driving playlist. Daisy stirred and groaned in her sleep but didn't wake. For the first time in days, Karen felt the tension easing from her shoulders and something approaching peace invade her mind.

Which was odd, given that soon she'd be held to account.

Karen dropped Daisy at Haymarket and cut across the city to her flat. She'd been gone less than thirty-six hours but it felt much longer. The first thing she did was strip off yesterday's clothes and stand under the shower for as long as it took to sluice the travel stains from her brain. She wrapped herself in a thick bath towel and stretched out on the sofa with a tumbler full of ice, Martin Miller's gin, Fever-Tree tonic and three slim slices of cucumber. Simple but effective, she thought.

She made a call to Sandra Murray. Filleted down to the essentials, the news was that Jason was sitting up and talking, complaining about the hospital food and the uncomfortable stookie on his leg. The doctors wanted to keep him in for another night, not least because of the blow he'd taken to the head. Then his mother and his brother could bring him home. Eilidh was already on a train back to Edinburgh, unwilling to lose a day's pay over something as minor as a broken leg. 'The lassie's got clients that depend on her,' Mrs Murray had pointed out, Karen admired Eilidh for her sense of priorities. She'd have been pissed off if her hairdresser had cancelled on her at the last minute.

She'd barely finished the call when a phone alert told her she had an email from Ruth Wardlaw. Groaning, she got off the sofa and booted up her laptop.

> Hi Karen. I thought this would interest you. I don't think she's had legal advice, because, as I explained, the Dutch aren't interested in trying the case; what matters to them is that due process has been observed, which in this case it clearly has. If she'd spoken to a lawyer, they would have warned her against making a statement to the prosecuting authorities that might be capable of being disproved.

There was an attachment. Karen opened it and read

> *To whom it may concern. I am protesting against the unreasonable demands of the Scottish courts to have me extradited to Scotland. Not only did I not commit the crime on the arrest warrant, that crime wasn't actually committed at all. My name is Amanda McAndrew and I've been accused of murdering my former partner, Daniella Gilmartin. For the record, I did not lay a hand on her. All I am guilty of is panicking after she died in an accident.*
>
> *We had been living in an artist community at Tullyfolda*

in Glenisla, in Scotland. Dani wasn't happy there and she insisted that we should move away and find somewhere on our own. This wasn't difficult to do because we were living in my Volkswagen camper van. We left Tullyfolda in May 2017 and spent a few weeks driving around in the Scottish Highlands looking for the right place where we could make a home. One night we were driving down a single-track road near Glencoe when a deer jumped out in front of me. I slammed on the brakes but we skidded off the road and I had to wrestle with the steering to get back on it again. Dani had been in the main cabin of the van fetching a drink of water, but when I turned to check she was OK, she was lying slumped on the floor. I ran round to the side door and climbed in beside her. She wasn't breathing and then I noticed there was blood on the edge of the sink. I turned her over and her head was caved in. She was dead. I couldn't believe it.

I panicked, I admit it. I knew there was nothing I could do for Dani. But the people we'd lived among at Tullyfolda knew Dani could be volatile and argumentative. I'd had to calm her down very publicly more than once. I thought nobody would believe my version of events. There was at least one person there who would have wanted to blame me for anything that happened to Dani.'

Declan. Karen thought he'd have been happy to rush to judgement.

I didn't know what to do. So I contacted my ex-partner, Susan Leitch. I knew Susan still loved me and I knew she would help me. I begged her for help and she told me to come to her house. I drove to Perth and parked the van in her garage. It was a terrible journey. All I could think of was Dani

349

*dead in the van behind me. I couldn't take it in, that someone I
had loved was dead from such a stupid accident.*

*Susan was always very calm in a crisis. She suggested I
leave the van where it was. She didn't have a car and she
could cover the van with a tarpaulin away from prying eyes.
We agreed that I would come back at some point and we would
work out what to do. I left the next day and I am ashamed to
say I never went back. I covered my tracks because I didn't
know what to do to make things right. I'm sorry I was a
coward. But I'm not a killer and I don't deserve to be sent back
where people can give false evidence against me. I won't get a
fair trial. Please believe me, because I am telling the truth.*

It was a clever massaging of the story, Karen thought. If
not for River's assertion that the force required to cause the
injury was more than could be accounted for by an accident,
it might have given her pause. But there were too many
aspects that McAndrew had wallpapered over. And trying
to lay the decision for hiding the body at Susan Leitch's
door was a low trick. It was far more plausible to Karen
that McAndrew had played on Susan's continued love for
her to persuade her to help in the crisis. And then she'd
run out on Susan, leaving her in possession of a corpse and
a vain hope that her ex would return to sort out the mess.
Let McAndrew come back and argue her case in front of a
properly constituted court. That way the dead might get the
justice they deserved. *The things we do for love.*

And then her phone rang. 'Tamsin,' Karen said wearily.
'I'd forgotten you were due me a call.'

'You got bumped down the to-do list by a raid on a
shonky vitamin supplement company with a court hearing
in the morning. Sorry about that.'

'Believe me, I'm not complaining. I know you go the extra mile for me.'

'So what's this I hear about the Ginger Ninja ending up in a hospital bed?'

'Nothing runs faster or hotter than Police Scotland office gossip,' Karen sighed. 'You know the Mint. A wee bit too trusting. He got pushed down a flight of stairs by Amanda McAndrew. Who promptly went on the run on the night ferry to Rotterdam.'

'Busy weekend for the HCU, then. Did she get away?'

'No, we got her on a European Arrest Warrant. She's tucked up in a cell in Holland. And Jason should get out the hospital today or tomorrow, complete with a stookie. But that's tomorrow's chip papers. Did you manage to get anywhere with James Auld's laptop?'

'Did I manage? Are you forgetting who you're talking to, girl? Thanks to your John Surman tip, I was through the door inside ten minutes. Surman plus Auld's Legion service number in reverse, in case you need to know.'

'That's great news.'

'Well, kind of. Turns out your Mr Auld – or Allard, depending on which email account you're looking at – wasn't what you'd call a Chatty Cathy. He kept pretty tidy inboxes and didn't download a whole shitload of stuff. This guy was to netsurfing what Boris Johnson is to truth. Anyway, I've loaded up a mirror of all his data on the cloud storage, I'll email you the link to get in and you can see for yourself. Oh, and I ran his email exchanges with the girl-friend through the translation software. Enjoy.'

'Your biscuits are in the post.'

Karen abandoned the sofa and fired up the laptop. The link Tamsin had sent took her straight to the contents of

James Auld's laptop and she dived into his email program. As Tamsin had explained, he had two accounts. On the principle of leaving the best till last, she looked first at the Paul Allard one. There were ticket receipts for train and plane tickets, confirming what she already knew or suspected of his movements. London, Dublin, Edinburgh, regular trips to and from Caen. There were a handful of messages about gigs but she reckoned the band probably used WhatsApp for their communications. It made more sense. Most of the other emails were exchanges with Pascale. They dropped each other notes every few days, updates on where they'd been, who they'd seen, what they'd been doing, when they'd meet next. No torrid outpourings, just day-to-day stuff in a tone of affection.

The only other email was one to Francis Flaxner Geary, dated four days before his death:

Dear Mr Geary, I'm sorry you were unable to furnish me with details of the vendor of the David Greig portraits your gallery has sold in recent years. But I do appreciate your duty of confidentiality to your clients. I wonder if I could prevail upon you to pass this email on to the client in question and ask him if he would be good enough to contact me? We have a mutual friend in James Auld. I will be travelling in Scotland over the next few days, but I will be contactable by email. Thank you in advance. Yours sincerely, Paul Allard

Karen drew in a sharp breath. There was no trace of a reply from Geary, but if the dealer had forwarded James' message, and what she suspected was right, it could have led directly to that fatal confrontation on the rocky promontory in Fife. The trail she had to follow had suddenly become a lot clearer.

The James Auld account offered no further revelations. The only people he swapped messages with were his sister-in-law and Verity Foggo. In both accounts, messages only went back a couple of months; as Tamsin had indicated, he obviously cleared out his old mail regularly. Karen worked her way through his messages and found nothing new. The exchange with Verity Foggo confirmed what the actress had told him. All it added to her knowledge was that Verity Foggo's relationship with punctuation was tangential.

His internet history confirmed that he had been in pursuit of David Greig's art and his legacy. There was a long list of sites featuring reports of the Brighton fire, articles about Greig dating from before and after his reported suicide, and many of the same sites about art sales and prices that Karen herself had visited. She'd have loved to have found a set of notes about his conjectures and deductions but there was nothing.

Karen checked the time. Hamish would be there soon, and she still hadn't formulated a battle plan for her meeting with ACC Markie in the morning. There would have to be time enough to work out a strategy in the morning. For now, what she craved was sleep.

45

Wednesday, 26 February 2020

Karen made a second cup of coffee and a slice of toast and thought about the gaps in the edifice she was building. A cold case was a story, constructed piece by piece. Sometimes the pieces arrived in the wrong order, so it made no sense at first. But some stories were like that. They began at the end or in the middle and you had to stay vigilant, making sure you didn't miss the clue that would shape the fragments into a narrative. And at the end, if you found all the pieces, you had a coherent tale.

Sometimes, though, you ended up with a stack of ill-assorted bits that didn't quite fit, no matter how hard you tried. Then it was like one of those novels that won literary prizes, the ones where you got to the end, closed the book and asked yourself, 'What just happened there?' Karen had never enjoyed that sort of novel. She liked ones where the ending made sense of the beginning and all the elements in between.

She wasn't there yet with the story of David Greig, Iain Auld and his poor dead brother James.

And in the meantime she had to compose something to placate the Dog Biscuit. As she considered the cast of characters who still needed to be fleshed out, she realised there was one she could do something about. It was too early to phone Nora, but not too early to text. She was the kind of woman who'd turn her phone to silent when she went to bed, lest it disturb her comfort.

Nora, I need your help again. Francis Flaxner Geary, the gallery owner in Dublin who sells David Greig's uncatalogued work – what can you find out about him? What's his reputation? Gossip? Unsubstantiated rumours? All grist to my mill. Can you see what the grapevine has to say about him?

She polished off a second slice of toast, rich with proper butter. None of that spreadable stuff, not when it came to toast. She'd enjoyed it so much, she carved another slice off the sourdough and dropped it in the toaster. She needed all the sustenance she could get before she faced the boss.

Karen was in the office by nine. She was wearing a suit she'd bought on a rare impulse from a shop on the steep curve of Victoria Street. It wasn't the kind of place she normally shopped but the suit had been in the window and in the sale and she'd liked the look of it. It was a lightweight silk tweed, the colour of a wet Highland moor, with pencil-thin windowpane checks in a dark sapphire. It had been hanging in the wardrobe for weeks, waiting for a day when she felt confident enough to get away with it and nervous enough to need the boost it gave her. The Dog Biscuit was always sharply tailored and ready for her close-up, and in her presence Karen had to work hard not to feel like a tumshie freshly pulled from a farmer's field.

VAL McDERMID

Markie was prompt. She carried promptitude like a slap in the face to the rest of the sloppy world. She kicked off as she came through the door. 'I hope you've got good news for me.' It was a challenge, not a question.

'We're a good way down the road. Far enough for you to tell our political masters that there's nothing here that's going to bite them in the arse.'

Markie gave her a long hard look. 'Would you care to elaborate?'

'The roots of James Auld's murder lie in the disappearance of his brother ten years ago, it's true. It's tied in to the counterfeit paintings that turned up in Dover House. But the buck stops at Iain Auld's door. There's no suggestion that any politician had the faintest idea anything was going on. And nobody in the present Scottish government was within a hundred miles of any of it.'

'That's something, at least. Do we know who killed James Auld? And why?'

'I have some further inquiries to make. If I'm right, we should have it cleared up by the end of the week.'

Markie tutted. 'That's not what I'd call a full report. Nothing like.'

'That's because I don't have a full answer and I'd hate to send you off with a theory that might yet fall to bits. Just think how disappointed you'd be.' Karen produced her sweetest smile to cut through her insolence.

'Not for the first time, where you're concerned. Where are the answers you're looking for?'

This, Karen thought, was where it got difficult. 'I need to make some inquiries in Dublin.'

Markie rolled her eyes. 'Don't tell me you're going to be looking for another European Arrest Warrant? Twice in a week would be something of a record for a front-line officer, never mind Historic Cases. I know exactly what you've been up to.'

Karen wasn't in the least surprised that word had already filtered upstairs about her nocturnal adventures in England. 'Then you'll know that a homicide suspect is in custody in Holland awaiting transfer back to Scotland.'

'I know she's challenging that.'

'Let her. The warrant will stand, I've been assured of that by the Crown Office team.'

'For your sake, I hope you're right, especially since your little adventure has put one of your colleagues in hospital.'

'If anyone has the right to hold that against me, it's DC Murray. And he's fine with it. Ma'am. And speaking of that, I'm a man down. DS Mortimer has been a great asset on the James Auld inquiry. I'd like her formally seconded to the HCU till DC Murray is back in action.'

Markie gave a sharp bark of laughter. 'Your brass neck is almost admirable,' she said with a curl of the lip. 'You preside over chaos, your junior ends up on the injured list and you ask for more?'

'Perhaps DS Mortimer will bring order to my chaos?' Karen said sweetly.

'From what I've seen of her, at least she knows how to get down a flight of stairs in one piece.' She shook her head in a show of despair. 'Fine. For now. You obviously need someone who knows what they're doing. But no more running round the bloody country and demanding instant service from the fiscals without reporting to me first. Is that clear?'

Karen said nothing, meeting Markie's angry gaze with as mild a look as she could manage.

'I said, is that clear?'

Karen wondered if her boss dared to speak to the First Minister like that. Somehow, she doubted it. 'It's clear,' she said nonchalantly.

Markie clenched one fist, then turned and marched out without another word. The door had barely closed behind her when Karen dropped into her chair and covered her face with her hands. She didn't know whether to laugh or cry but, for once, she'd had an encounter with Markie that hadn't reduced her to impotent rage. Maybe she was getting better at this.

Karen had been checking her inbox every five minutes since she'd arrived at the office and within a minute of Markie leaving, she'd refreshed the page again. This time, top of the list was a message from no-reply@probatesearch.service.gov.uk with the subject line *Delivery of Requested Will*. She opened the email to discover her order was available. She clicked on the line and within a matter of moments, she was staring at a scanned copy of David Greig's will.

It could hardly have been simpler. Name and address and the standard revocation of all previous wills. Then the first clause:

I appoint Daniel Connolly of The Hill House Ramelton Co Donegal ROI to be the executor of this my will and is hereinafter called 'my executor'.

I request that my body be cremated and my ashes scattered in the Manchester Ship Canal and the expenses thereof to be borne by my executor.

I give all my property whatsoever and wheresoever to my executor to retain or dispose of as he sees fit and to act as he sees fit in respect of any and all of my artworks that remain in my possession at the time of my death.

And that was that. Not even one of those, 'If my executor does not survive me by at least twenty-eight days' clauses.

So who was Daniel Connolly? Was he the mysterious client of Francis Flaxner Geary? If her theory was right and the two men were still alive, was Daniel Connolly the conduit between them and the money? She googled 'Daniel Connolly' and 'Ramelton' and got not a single hit that included all three. That was weird in itself. She tried the address on Google Maps and it appeared at once. The satellite view showed a good-sized property standing on its own at the end of a few hundred metres of driveway on the outskirts of the town. So the address existed. She zoomed out and checked the route from Ramelton to Dublin, which gave her food for thought. The rudiments of a plan were starting to form in her head.

Between Daniel Connolly and Francis Flaxner Geary, it looked as if all roads led to Ireland. The Dog Biscuit wouldn't like that one little bit. On the other hand, the Dog Biscuit didn't need to know the details till it was all done and dusted. Karen wondered about ferry times from Stranraer to Larne. If she was going to be chasing round the countryside, she wanted her own wheels with her.

She'd barely clicked on the ferry website when her phone rang. 'Daisy,' she said. 'You were next on my list.'

'Oh, OK. Why?'

'You called me, remember? Let's do that first.'

'Mmm, that makes sense. Well, you know the crowbar that one of the uniforms found on the rocks? The lab's managed to get a second DNA trace on it. How amazing is that?'

Karen rolled her eyes. 'Only moderately, unless there's a hit on the database.'

'Oh, I suppose.' Daisy sounded deflated.

'And is there?'

'No.'

'Never mind.' Karen's mind was racing. 'There are other possible avenues. Here's what I want you to do. The UK Missing Persons Unit has a DNA database. Where they've got the confirmed DNA of a misper, they place that on the database. But if that's not available or they can't be a hundred per cent sure, they take samples from close relatives for potential familial matches. I want you to check with Mary Auld and see whether they ever uploaded material to that database, and if they did, we need to run it.'

'You think Iain Auld killed his brother?' Daisy was horrified.

'I'm not convinced. But it happens. So check that out.'

'OK. Oh, one other thing? The ARR thing you asked me to check out? The royalties go to a man called—'

'Daniel Connolly. Of Hill House, Ramelton, County Donegal.'

'How did you—? You beat me to it.' She sounded upset.

'That happens too. He's the executor and beneficiary of the will. When you've checked in with Mary Auld about the DNA, I want you to pack a bag for a couple of nights away and meet me in Edinburgh. Bring your passport and walking clothes.'

'Where are we going?'

'Don't tell Charlie, but we're going to Ireland.'

'Are we going to talk to Francis Flaxner Geary?'

Clearly she was going to have to work on the concept of discretion with Daisy. 'Among other things. I promise nobody will push you down a flight of stairs.'

46

In her wing mirror, Karen could see Daisy returning to the ferry queue with a mutton pie and a fully leaded Irn-Bru. She couldn't work out how the lassie packed away so much crap and still stayed slim. Some folk had all the luck. She quickly got out of the car and wagged a finger at Daisy. 'Not in my motor,' she said.

'But boss, it's freezing,' she whined.

'You should have thought about that. You're forgetting, I've seen the crumbs you leave when you eat in a car.'

'That was flaky pastry,' Daisy protested.

'I don't care. You can eat all the pies you like when it's your own wheels, but I have standards. They might not be very high, but I do have some.' Karen grinned and got back behind the wheel in the warm fug of the car.

Daisy ate her pie in record speed, ostentatiously brushed the invisible crumbs from her coat and got back in the car. 'See when you rang? I was so busy sorting out in my head the implications of checking the misper DNA, and then actually talking to Mary Auld about it and then submitting it after she said yes, she'd given them Iain's DNA from his electric razor, that I forgot all about you saying there was another possibility. What did you mean?'

'When did they say they'd get back to you?'

'Tomorrow. But what did you mean, boss?'

'To be honest, I'd be surprised if it is Iain Auld's DNA on the crowbar. Apart from anything else, our lab would have had big loud bells ringing as soon as they looked at it next to the victim's. His brother, remember?'

'Oh yeah, of course. So why did you ask me to do all that with the mispers?'

'I wasn't wasting your time, Daisy. You always have to bear in mind that the people we think are our parents are sometimes lying to us. Mostly it's mothers lying about who the real father is. But from time to time, every bastard is throwing sand in our eyes. I like to be certain.'

The tail lights of the car in front lit up and the exhaust exhaled a ghostly drift into the cold afternoon gloom. Karen started the engine in time to inch forward as the queue began to move.

'So what is this other possibility?'

'If Greig and Iain Auld are still alive, they're the only two people with anything like a motive for killing James. Now, do you remember me telling you how David Greig authenticated his paintings?'

Daisy lit up. 'Of course! The nail clippings glued to the backs of the canvas.'

'It's the ultimate fall-back if a buyer doesn't trust the paper provenance. I'm guessing there's a certified copy of his DNA lodged with a lawyer somewhere. I bet Geary knows exactly where. So we can compare the DNA on the crowbar to the certified copy and see where that gets us.' Karen drove on to the lip of the ferry ramp and followed the line of cars below decks.

'That's genius,' Daisy said. She was still buzzing from

the news that she was assigned to the HCU for now. It was clear to Karen that the young sergeant thought she'd make herself so indispensable that she'd be kept on even after Jason's return. That would be a result, Karen thought. Which probably meant the Dog Biscuit would see it never happened.

They were halfway across the narrow strait between Scotland and Northern Ireland, the granite bulk of Ailsa Crag a darker blot in the starlit dark, when Karen's phone rang. Nora's cheery voice crossed the distance between them, a lift of the spirits in the gloom. 'Where are you?' Nora asked. 'What's that rumbling?'

'In the middle of the Irish Sea. Luckily it's pretty calm.'

'Ooh, interesting. Heading for Mr Geary, by any chance?' Her voice was a tease.

'You know I can't tell you that. And speaking of him . . . ?'

'Ah yes, Mr Geary. Well, I asked around, very discreetly, among people who have their fingers very much on the pulse. I hinted we were hoping to acquire something from Geary whose provenance I'd been looking into.'

'Nicely done.'

'I thought so myself. Both said much the same thing. They warned me to be very careful that the papers stood up to scrutiny. Geary, it turns out, has a reputation for sailing close to the wind. He's never been charged with anything, not even accused of questionable antics. But there's a feeling that he's not entirely transparent. One of them said he'd heard – and this is the whisper of a rumour, nothing more – that it's been said he will supply private collectors off the books. Cash for paintings whose provenance is, to say the least, dubious.' Nora concluded her report with an air of satisfied finality. Karen could picture her folding her arms across her bosom with an expression of gratification on her face.

'You mean, stolen paintings?'

'Not in so many words, but yes, that's what was being hinted at. There's a significant market in stolen art. Organised crime sees it as a way to launder money.'

'I'd heard that, but I've never understood it. I get that you buy the painting with cash, but how do you sell it on? How do you actually launder the money?'

'The art sits in a Freeport facility and it's eventually sold on to other collectors. If it's a big name, there will always be private obsessives who are happy to acquire something to add lustre to a collection that will always stay behind closed doors. And that's before we even get on to forgeries. That's what's so clever about what David Greig did – authenticating your work with DNA makes forgery almost impossible.'

'Shame the Old Masters didn't think of that.'

Nora chuckled. 'And of course, before everything was available at the touch of a keyboard, if you waited long enough, nobody recognised a stolen painting most of the time. It's a lot harder to get away with it these days, though. Now, is all that of any help to you?'

'It is, Nora. One thing more – presumably all these transactions take place in cash? There's no financial paper trail?'

'Naturally. Otherwise you'd miss the whole point of money-laundering, wouldn't you? I can't imagine Mr Geary would survive unscathed a serious audit by the financial authorities, though.'

Leverage. Just what Karen needed. 'You've been a huge help, Nora. I owe you.'

'After that brunch in Aleppo? I don't think so. That's defo what they call paying forward.'

They spent the rest of the crossing studying a detailed map of the area around Ramelton that Karen had bought in the bookshop across the street from her office while she'd been waiting for Daisy. She'd also brought up the satellite imagery on her tablet. 'This is the house,' she said, outlining it on the map with a black Sharpie. 'It's far enough away from the road that we're not going to see much from there. But look . . .' She pointed to the tablet. 'There's a footpath that passes quite close to the back of the house. And what looks like woodland or shrubbery between the path and this gravel area where the two vehicles are parked.'

'You think it might give us enough cover to stake the place out?'

'I hope so. Because neither of us looks like Jehovah's Witnesses or Gas Board inspectors.' Karen gestured at the jeans and sweater she'd changed into before they'd left. 'Even in civvies, I still look like a polis. I don't know how, but I just do.'

'It's that suspicious look you've got, boss. Like you don't believe a word anybody says.'

Karen raised her eyebrows in surprise. 'Do I?'

Daisy waggled her hand. 'Kind of. Mostly. I think it's how you get people to talk. You make them uneasy when they tell lies or exaggerate.'

'I never knew that. I'll have to practise looking more trusting. Anyway. We'll get up at the crack of sparrowfart and see what's possible. At least it doesn't get light till later this time of year, that gives us more options. We'll stay in Derry tonight – it's less than twenty miles away so it's handy. We can get checked in to a hotel, grab some dinner and have an early night.' Even as she spoke, Karen knew the early night was probably wishful thinking. Not because they'd stay up drinking, as their male colleagues tended to do whenever they perceived themselves as being off the leash. But because sleep was still elusive.

And so it proved. They were back at their hotel by ten, full of buttery rare steak and chips, but Karen didn't even bother undressing. Her mind was racing, the morning's options chasing themselves round her head in a parade of possibilities. She knew she had to walk, and the leaflet in the hotel room provided the perfect option.

The sturdy walls that had circled the city for the best part of four hundred years were the obvious place to start a night walk. Karen found the nearest access point a few streets away and set off on the mile-long patrol of the ramparts. It was a cold night, crisp now with frost, thin gusts of icy air coming off the nearby river. Sometimes in winter, the wind was sharp as a sushi knife, cutting straight through streets and alleys. Other times, like tonight, it swirled around and changed direction, doubling back on itself like a burglar casing the streets, looking for an easy target. The few people on the streets below were hurrying, eager to be somewhere the cold was not. Walking the walls wasn't high on the list of anyone except Karen and she passed nobody on her circuit. Her eyes were on the city, but little of what she was looking at made any impression. Her gaze tonight was inward, working through the permutations of the information she'd gathered, wrestling with the problems she could see ahead if what she believed to be true turned out to be the case. The time slipped by quickly, marked only by the steady beat of her walking shoes on stone, and before she knew it, she was back at her starting point.

Her body was tired but she wasn't drowsy yet. So she walked down towards the river and stood for a while, transfixed by the elegant curve of the Peace Bridge that crossed the River Foyle. It stood as a promise of an end to centuries of the spill of blood and anger across the streets of a city so divided it couldn't even make its mind up what to call itself. She'd watched *Derry Girls* and laughed at its cheek, but she understood that sometimes laughter was the only way to survive wounds that went bone deep.

However things turned out tomorrow, there would be wounds that would cost at least that much damage. No peace bridge could provide an escape route from that.

47

Thursday, 27 February 2020

By half past six, they were on the outskirts of Ramelton. It was hard to form much sense of the town in the dark. The petrol station on the main road was still closed, to Daisy's disappointment. 'I'm starving,' she complained. 'You'd have thought they'd have somewhere I could get a bacon roll.'

Karen scoffed. 'You're a bottomless pit. If there's any-where open, I promise we'll stop and stock up.' They passed a hospital and a Catholic church, rows of white houses opposite like a gap-toothed mouth. Then the bare branches of trees arching over the road, a huddle of houses and a T-junction with the narrow finger of the river a black void beyond it. The house fronts on the main road were painted in assorted pastel colours but in the dim glow of the street lights, they looked sickly. They passed a Spar franchise, shuttered and dark.

'Follow the road round across the bridge,' Daisy instructed her. 'Then turn right and take the first left fork. It's a wee road.'

Karen did what she was told and almost immediately

they'd left behind the streetlights of the small town. She drove slowly along a narrow road that glittered with frost, past a substantial cemetery, the graves ghostly with rime. They'd climbed far enough for her to be able to see across the rooftops of the town below.

'We're nearly here,' Daisy said. 'Those trees up ahead – I think that's their place. We can pick up the footpath just past their property boundary, I think.'

They were beyond the limits of the town now, and across the fields they could see the distant glint of a bend in the river. Karen kept going past the belt of trees and they were rewarded with a pair of stone gateposts surmounted by carved pineapples. A simple five-barred wooden gate was closed across the paved driveway. Not a single light indicated the house against the dark mass of the shrubbery. She drove on, slowing as she spotted the point where the trees gave way to scrubby hedgerow. All at once they saw a makeshift gravelled layby with barely enough room for two cars. Karen swerved into it and jammed on the brakes. 'Not exactly well signposted, is it?' she muttered.

'There's a wee sign there, you can hardly see it in the dark.' Daisy pointed ahead.

Karen peered out but saw nothing. 'Time I got my eyes tested. Right then, let's do it.' She reached behind the seat and snagged her small backpack. She unzipped a side pocket and took out a small suedette bag. Out of it came what looked like a miniature telescope and a clip.

'What's that?' Daisy asked.

'It's a telephoto lens for an iPhone.' Karen fiddled with the lens and the clip and managed to attach it to her phone. 'It's an optical zoom, not a digital one.' She chuckled. 'See how I said that, like I know the difference? All I know is that it

369

works. Perfect for a stake-out. And now it's time to take a look at our so-called Daniel Connolly.'

They left the warmth of the car behind and stepped out into a stiff breeze coming across the fields from the sea lough beyond the estuary. Daisy gave a sharp intake of breath. 'Fuck, it's cold. Let's get moving.' She headed towards the fingerpost that read 'Ramelton'. It pointed the way through a narrow gap in the hedge.

The path itself was a considerable improvement on its signage and access. About a metre wide, it had been surfaced with asphalt. Even in the dark, the way was clear. It cut along the side of a field of coarse grass, following the edge of a low stone wall that separated it from the tree plantation that surrounded Hill House. The path curved round a corner and they continued for about forty metres. Karen stopped and eyed the wall. 'I think it's time we made a move,' she said.

Both women scrambled over the wall. In the pre-dawn silence, every movement sounded cataclysmically loud. But no creature stirred as they pushed their way through the trees and on into a mass of rhododendrons and laurels that hid the house from view. Only by crouching low to the ground could they navigate through the sturdy trunks and whippy branches of the well-established plants. Karen had to stifle a cry more than once as a bent stem sprang back and lashed her face. So tightly packed were the shrubs that they almost emerged from cover before they realised they'd reached the edge.

They'd ended up at one side of the parking area at the back of the house. There was a clear line of sight from the back door to the two cars that sat there, windows crazed with frost. Karen was relieved to see no sign of CCTV security cameras. 'Well judged,' Daisy said softly. 'How do we play this now?'

Karen hunkered down on her haunches and dipped into her backpack again. 'I overcame my phobia of HQ for long enough yesterday to go down to Fettes Avenue and talk to the tech guys.' She took a pair of dull metal boxes no bigger than a matchbox from the bag. She looked up at the house. Still no lights showing. The cold sweat of apprehension crept along her hairline. 'Wait here,' she said, then ran at a low crouch across the gravel towards the cars.

She reached under the wheel arch of the first, a black BMW SUV, and let the magnetised box come to rest against a flat surface. She gave it a tug; it didn't budge. She hurried on to the next car, a silver Mercedes convertible, and repeated the operation. As she completed her task, Karen glanced back at the house and her chest constricted. On the first floor, a light was showing. No curtains, so probably a hallway or a stair, her panicked brain told her.

She made a quick calculation. If she made a dash for it, anyone passing the window would be attracted by the movement. She'd be spotted, for sure. She made a snap decision and instead of heading for where she'd left Daisy, she used the cars for cover and rounded the side of the house.

Karen straightened up, panting, leaning against the wall. There was a twenty-yard strip of lawn between the side of the house and the start of the trees. No cover of bushes here but she could still work her way back to Daisy without being seen. She closed her eyes and took a deep breath then sprinted for the trees, hurling herself to the ground as she reached them. 'I'm too fucking old for this nonsense,' she grumbled under her breath as her shin clattered against a trunk and sent arrows of pain up her leg.

It took an agonisingly long time but she eventually made her way back to Daisy, who had cleared enough space to sit down among the leaf litter. She'd bent a laurel twig to one side so she could see the back of the house and Karen squeezed in behind her. 'I thought you were done for back there,' Daisy said.

'And then you remembered who you're dealing with here,' Karen said, mock-heroically. Now the first light had been joined by another upstairs. As they watched, a cluster of windows along the lower floor burst into light, revealing a kitchen that was about the same size as Karen's flat. Warm wood gleamed and even from that distance, she could make out the shapes and shine of a battery of kitchen equipment. She could also see from behind a tall man in a dark blue dressing gown. He put a kettle on a wide range cooker and took two mugs from a glass-fronted cupboard. Reached for a tray. Picked up a large brown pottery teapot and poured in some water from the kettle. Now he turned to face them as he went to the sink to swill out the pot.

'That's Greig, isn't it?' Daisy said eagerly.

Karen, made more cautious by experience, said, 'It could be. I can't be certain from here.'

He turned away and she watched him spooning loose tea into the pot. He filled it up from the kettle, added it to the tray and carried it out of the room. He left the lights on and they could see him in snapshots as he climbed the stairs and walked along the landing. 'At least we know they're home.' Karen reached for her backpack again and pulled out a folding sit mat.

Daisy looked on open-mouthed as she unfolded it and settled down. 'Is there anything you don't have in there? Trackers, telephoto lenses, something to sit on ... I don't suppose you've got anything to eat?' Karen smiled and her hand disappeared inside the bag again. It emerged with two energy bars. Daisy's face fell. Reluctantly she took the one Karen offered and studied the label suspiciously. 'Dates? Apricots? Carob? Oats? Coconut flour? What have I done to upset you, boss? What's wrong with a Tunnock's Caramel Wafer?'

'You'll thank me later. Slow release, not a quick sugar high and then a come-down. Now, settle down and keep your eyes on the prize. We could be here for hours.'

In the end, it was only two cold hours before the back door opened and two men emerged, each carrying empty shopping bags. Karen, who had been nursing her phone in her lap, woke it up and focused the lens on their faces, grateful now for the daylight that had been making her fearful of discovery. A cluster of shots of them both together, then individually. 'Gotcha,' she breathed.

She could feel the excitement vibrating off Daisy. 'Do you recognise them? Is it them?'

'Hard to tell, but it could be. I need to look at them on a bigger screen.' As she spoke, they climbed into the BMW and drove off. 'Off for the weekly shop, at a guess. Let's get back to the car and take a look at these pics on the laptop.'

Daisy looked behind her. 'Do we have to crawl back the way we came?'

Karen studied the house. The lights were all off and there was no sign of life. 'Let's chance it.' She stood up and packed everything away in her bag, slung it over her shoulder and marched boldly towards the treeline at the side of the property. They pushed through the narrow gaps between the trunks, checked there was nobody else in sight then clambered over the wall. They kept up a brisk pace all the way back to the car, as if it was the most natural thing in the world to be walking through featureless fields shortly after daybreak on a freezing February morning.

Before Karen uploaded the photographs to her laptop, she checked the tracker app on her phone. It revealed that the BMW was parked in a side street in the centre of Ramelton. 'Seems to be working. You'll need to get this up and running on your phone too, just to be on the safe side. But right now, let's see what we've got from the telephoto.'

They both stared intently at the images as Karen scrolled through. Then she pulled up archive shots she'd assembled of both men, including Verity Foggo's *Twelfth Night* picture of Iain Auld. 'That's so them,' Daisy exclaimed. 'We nailed them, boss, we totally nailed them.'

In reply, Karen moved through the pics slowly, one by one. Then she split the screen and placed old and new images side by side, first of David Greig then of Iain Auld. She had not a flicker of doubt about Greig. His once-luxuriant hair was receding, greying and cut much shorter, but the face was unmistakable. Still handsome, still sculpted round the cheekbones and the jawline, still the same arrogant angle of the head.

Auld was a different matter. If she hadn't seen the *Twelfth Night* photo, Karen would have struggled to see the clean-cut, neatly barbered civil servant in this guise. His still-sandy hair brushed his collar, swept straight back from his forehead. His beard was trimmed to a point, his moustache curled at the ends. If it hadn't been for the round glasses, he'd have been a dead ringer for one of the supporting cast in *Shakespeare in Love*. But the more she looked, the more she could see the congruence between the man who had disappeared and the man who had appeared at the back door of Hill House this morning.

'You're right,' Karen said.

'But this is supposed to be Daniel Connolly's house. Where do you suppose he is?'

Karen chuckled. 'I think he's out doing his messages, Daisy. I think we saw him getting into his motor this morning.'

Daisy frowned. 'I thought you thought he was a conduit funnelling the money to Greig and Auld?'

'I did. But I was overcomplicating it. Having a third party involved multiplies your risk exponentially. Why involve somebody else when you can become somebody else?'

'You mean they've got false IDs?'

Karen nodded. 'Exactly. Geary must have dealings with all sorts of dodgy people if he's shifting stolen art and maybe forgeries too. It's not too big a jump from that to knowing people who can create a new identity. I'd bet one of those two is Daniel Connolly on paper. And that they've both got valid Irish passports.'

A moment's silence while they contemplated what Karen had said.

'That's going to complicate things, isn't it?' Daisy ventured.

'Not necessarily. There's always a way round complications, in my experience.'

48

Daisy whinged all the way through Ramelton because Karen refused to stop to buy something to eat. 'And how clever would it be if we walked into a shop and came face to face with Greig and Auld?' Karen had demanded.

'They wouldn't know us from a hole in the ground.'

'True. But if everything I've planned goes tits-up and we have to follow them and they notice us at all, they'll freak out and we'll not see them for dust. So you'll just have to hang on till we get to Letterkenny.'

Daisy sighed, muttered about fainting from hunger and hunched over her phone. 'There's a superstore off the main drag. You'll need to fill up since we're going all the way to Dublin. We can get petrol there as well as food. And coffee,' she added, playing to Karen's known weakness.

As they drove, Karen called Sandra Murray. 'We're getting him back today, hen,' she reported. 'They say his leg's going to be fine if he does what he's told and goes to the physio. And the dunt to his head did no damage.' She cackled. 'You know what they say, where there's no sense, there's no feeling.'

'I'm glad to hear it, that's a weight off my mind.'

'Aye, well, he says you told him not to go near the lassie,

so it's all his own fault. I hope she's going to go to the jail for what she did to our Jason.'

'She's going to go away for a long time, Mrs Murray.'

After the call ended, Daisy eyed her and said shrewdly, 'You dodged answering her when she said about McAndrew going to jail for what she did to Jason.'

'Well spotted. I didn't answer her because she wouldn't have liked the answer. McAndrew won't be charged for what she did to Jason.'

'What? How come?'

'It's a quirk of the European Arrest Warrant. We can only apply for a warrant for crimes committed in our jurisdiction. Somebody who's returned to us can only be tried for the crimes on the warrant and we can't then pass them on to another jurisdiction. And because technically England's a separate jurisdiction, we can't hand her over to the cops in Stockport to prosecute her there. We'll just have to make sure we make the homicide charge stick.'

'That feels wrong.'

'I know. Maybe there's a way for the lawyers to work round it, but I don't think they'll see it as a pressing need if we can convict McAndrew of murder.'

Daisy's desire to push it further was derailed by the sign for the Letterkenny supermarket. Half an hour later, they were back on the road. Daisy had had two bacon rolls and a hot chocolate with whipped cream; Karen had settled for a toasted cheese sandwich and a large coffee. And they'd changed from their walking clothes into their normal work clothes. 'More intimidating,' Daisy said approvingly.

Karen let Daisy take over the wheel for the next stretch of the journey. She learned more than she wanted to know about the choir that Daisy sang in and her future plans for exploring the Greek archipelago. They crossed seamlessly into Northern Ireland at Strabane and left it again at Aughnacloy. 'I wonder how easy that'll be after Brexit?' Karen mused.

They talked about the implications for the island of Ireland of a post-Brexit world. 'We'll see a unified Ireland inside five years,' Karen said. 'And that'll be the start of the break-up of the UK.'

'Only if Scotland doesn't get there first.'

Karen sighed. 'Let's hope so, eh.'

'So what's the plan in Dublin?'

'We'll be having a wee conversation with Francis Flaxner Geary. What happens next depends on how cooperative he is.' Karen's smile would have made hard men run for cover.

It was late afternoon by the time they strolled past Gallery Geary. It was a double-fronted shop, each window displaying a single canvas. One was a large modern abstract featuring drips of paint in dozens of shades that ran from the top of the canvas to the bottom. The other was an older piece, a Victorian evening street scene with horse-drawn trams and people shrouded under umbrellas. Beyond them, the gallery stretched back, broken up by staggered walls that provided more hanging space. A young woman with long blonde hair and tight black clothes perched on a high stool behind a laptop on a cocktail table. 'Do you think she's an installation or staff?' Karen wondered.

'Only one way to find out,' Daisy said.

They had to ring a bell for admission. The young woman looked up and tapped her trackpad. The door buzzed and Karen led the way inside. 'Can I help you or are you just browsing?' the woman asked. Her accent sounded East European, matching the slant of her cheekbones.

'We're here to see Mr Geary,' Karen said.

The gallery assistant raised one eyebrow, as if dubious about their provenance. 'I'm not seeing anything in the diary. Do you have an appointment?'

'Tell him it's about six paintings by Scottish artists that he sold in the early 2000s.' Karen's level stare was implacable. 'He'll want to see me.'

She frowned. 'Can you be more precise?'

'Not to you. Away and tell him we're going nowhere till we see him.' Karen's voice had deepened, rough round the edges, a threat in itself.

The assistant slid off her stool and stalked down the gallery towards a door at the back. Karen followed, with Daisy on her tail. She held out an arm to halt Daisy in her tracks a few feet from the door that had closed behind the blonde. She counted to thirty in her head, then opened the door and walked in, shoulders back and head up, making the most of her presence.

The assistant whirled round. 'You can't just walk in here.'

Karen looked around in mock-surprise. 'Oh, did I just walk in here?'

The man behind the desk stood up, urbane and polite. Not a trace of panic. 'It's fine, Elvira. I'll deal with these ... women.' He nodded at her. 'Away back to your post.' He waited for her to leave, then gestured towards the client chairs. 'Please, sit down.'

Karen took a moment to absorb the room as she moved to sit. Dove grey walls, each with a vivid modern abstract. Knowing next to nothing of art and artists, all she could say was that they all looked different in their composition and choice of palette. 'Thanks for seeing us, Mr Geary,' she said, taking in at a glance his neatly trimmed iron-grey hair and skin that had spent a lot more time in facial spas than hers had. Large-framed tortoiseshell glasses gave his face a serious, cultured impression. He wore a silk shirt, open at the neck to reveal a tuft of chest hair and a heavy silver chain. In one ear, a substantial diamond stud.

'You have the advantage of me. I don't have the faintest idea who you are.'

'I'm Detective Chief Inspector Karen Pirie and this is Detective Sergeant Daisy Mortimer of the Historic Cases Unit of Police Scotland.'

'Then you have no jurisdiction here. This is the Poblacht na hÉireann. That's the Republic of Ireland, to you.'

'You should be grateful for that. I'd have thought the last thing you'd want would be a senior detective from the Garda Siochana sitting here.'

He scoffed. 'I have nothing to hide from the guards,' he said. 'My business is entirely above board.'

Karen gave a harsh bark of laughter. 'Sure it is. But before we get on to the interesting question of the six Scottish paintings you brokered sales for fifteen or so years ago, I want to talk about David Greig.' She let that hang in the air. His head moved a fraction, tilting slightly to one side.

'What about David?'

'You've been his dealer for a very long time.'

'I was his dealer. He's been dead for ten years, in case you hadn't noticed. With you being concerned with history, and all.' His relaxed smile was almost a smirk.

'Yet you're still selling his paintings.' She took out her phone, tapped the screen and read, '*Jarvis Cocker in the Year 2000, Rihanna Disturbia, Barack/House Black/White, Madonna of the Celebration, Dame Judi, Time Out for Stephen Hawking*, and *Passing Divine*, to be precise. All sold since his death and all previously uncatalogued.'

His smile widened. 'And all authenticated. You do know how he authenticated his paintings?' An edge of sarcasm now.

'Yes, I know all about the fingernail clippings. I presume you have a legally certified copy of Greig's DNA?'

Now it was a shit-eating grin. 'That's right. Every one of those paintings has been matched to the verified DNA. Not even a shadow of a glimmer of doubt.'

'I didn't think for a moment there would be,' Karen said coolly. 'So you'll have no problem with providing me with a copy of that certificate?'

'No trouble at all, officer. I presume this is a question of authentication?'

'Something like that. The certificate, if you don't mind?'

Geary sighed. He stood up and crossed the room, lifting one of the paintings from the wall to reveal a small safe. Careful to hide the combination from them, he opened it, rummaged among the contents and returned with an A4 envelope. He emptied the contents on the desk. Karen recognised the familiar pattern of a DNA profile on the sheet of paper. Geary turned it over. On the reverse was a stamped and notarised confirmation, signed and witnessed by a Dublin lawyer with an impressive letterhead. 'Satisfied?'

'Very. The copy?'

Another sigh. He turned to the printer table behind him and rapidly copied both sides of the paper. As he did it, Karen said, 'I don't suppose you could scan it too? And send it to me? Just to speed the plough.'

This time he tutted, but he did as she asked, sending the

scan to a computer. 'What's your email address?' he asked. Karen passed him a business card. He went to the door and called for Elvira. They heard him instruct her to forward the scans on to Karen.

'Thank you,' she said.

'Now, if that's all? I'm a very busy man.'

Aye, right. 'Not quite. These recent David Greig paintings? What can you tell us about their provenance? Do they come from collectors who want to capitalise on their good taste? Because dead artists do see a spike in prices if they're any good. Especially if some of their works have been burned to a crisp in an arson attack.'

His perfectly shaped eyebrows drew down slightly. 'I deal with David's estate. The paintings come to me via them. They may be from other collectors or they may be held by the estate. It's none of my business as long as the paintings are authenticated by the estate. And they are.'

'The estate? That would be Daniel Connolly?'

'If you know, why are you asking me?' Now he'd moved on to the front foot. His voice was sharper, his back straighter.

'I'm trying to get a clear picture here. Was it Daniel Connolly who brought you those six Scottish paintings you sold in the early 2000s?' She consulted her phone again. 'Raeburn, MacTaggart, Redpath, Eardley, Crawhall, Doig. Or was it David Greig himself? He was the one who stole them, after all.'

'I don't know what you're talking about.' The denial was flat, no sign of fear.

Yet. 'I appreciate they won't show up on your books,' she said. 'What with them being stolen. But if you genuinely have no idea what I'm talking about, why was the very mention of them enough to get us into the private office of a very busy man? And there will be traces, Mr Geary. The kind of traces the Garda's Financial Intelligence Unit are well accustomed to digging out, once they know what they're looking for. Is your house a bit bigger than your legitimate figures would account for? Have you got art hanging on your walls that's beyond your official means? Is your car a bit too close to the top of the range? Once they get started, there's no hiding place.'

Geary steepled his fingers together. They were surprisingly short and stubby, out of keeping with the elegance he aspired to. 'What *I* don't appreciate is being accused in my own office of crimes of which I have no knowledge.'

'You don't seem to understand the difference between a threat and a promise, Mr Geary.' Karen busied herself with her phone again then held it out to show him that morning's shot of Iain Auld. 'Is that Daniel Connolly?'

Now there was a flicker of something in his eyes. A moment of decision. 'It certainly looks like him,' he said.

Karen flicked back through her images till she found the blow-up of the Brighton fire scene. 'And this?'

'Yes, that looks like him.' A trace of impatience.

'That photograph was taken outside the Goldman Gallery in Brighton the night it burned.'

'And what has that to do with me? I'm getting quite tired of this conversation,' he said, breathing heavily through his nose.

'I find it an interesting coincidence that on the night when David Greig's market values were pumped up, Daniel Connolly was on the spot.'

A one-shoulder shrug. 'As I said. Nothing. To do. With me.'

'Maybe not, but your association with a man who

benefited directly from the Brighton arson isn't going to be a good look for the Gardai. Especially since you also ended up making money as a result.'

'I have no knowledge of anybody's involvement in a fire in Brighton. My dealings with Daniel Connolly are purely to do with David Greig's estate, of which he is the legal executor and beneficiary. There's nothing illegal in that.'

'Except that Daniel Connolly doesn't exist.'

A long silence. At last, Geary shifted his shoulders inside his shirt and said, 'What are you talking about? Of course he exists. You've just shown me a photo of him, for God's sake.'

Karen leaned forward. 'The man I have a photo of is called Iain Auld. He disappeared from his life ten years ago and he was declared dead two years ago. Can you tell me how it is you've been doing business with a dead man all these years?'

'I've never heard the name Iain Auld before now.' He clamped his lips tight together as if to stop anything untoward spilling out.

'You must have done due diligence before you started dealing with him?'

'I'm a businessman, not a fool.' He turned away and opened the bottom drawer of his desk. It was a double-depth file drawer. His fingers walked across the file tabs and he drew out a thin red folder. 'My dealings with Daniel Connolly.' He selected two sheets from the bottom of the pile and handed them to Karen. 'His passport. His bank account details complete with his address.'

It was an Irish passport, due to expire later in the year. And the address on the bank statement was Hill House, Ramelton.

'Why would I doubt that?' His voice was mild now.

He thought he was past the worst. He spread his hands wide. 'Ladies, I'm an art dealer. I sell work on commission. Nothing more exotic than that. If you tell me Daniel Connolly is not who he says he is, that's a matter for you and the Gardai, not me.'

This wasn't going quite the way Karen had hoped. Time for the last ace up her sleeve. She returned to her phone and brought up one of the photographs of the two men she'd taken that morning. She pinched the screen and enlarged David Greig's face. She showed it to Geary. She was taken aback by the look of genuine shock on his face.

'What the fuck?' He recoiled in his chair. 'How the fuck? Where's that from?'

'You know who that is, don't you?'

Geary swallowed hard. 'If I didn't know any better, I'd say that's David.' His tongue flicked along his lips. 'But it can't be. David's dead.'

49

Either Francis Flaxner Geary was one of Ireland's finest thespians or he genuinely knew nothing of David Greig's resurrection. He stared down at the phone, the colour gone from his face. 'I don't get it,' he murmured. 'Why would he hide from me? I loved the man like a brother.'

Now she was flying by the seat of her pants. The plan she'd worked out and gone over a dozen times in her head was predicated on Geary being in on the whole devious plot. Time to improvise. 'Every time you share a secret, you multiply the chances of exposure.' Karen gave a snort of laughter. 'If he'd told you, he'd have had to kill you. That's what he did to the last person who found out. I can show you a picture of the dead man, if you like?' She reached for her phone again.

Geary had the look of a man who's been caught on a sandbank by the tide. 'You're making this up. I don't know why, I don't know what you're trying to ... This is a fucking fantasy. David was never a killer. He ... we ... Look, we were lovers. Way back when he first came to me and asked me to represent him. He never so much as lifted a hand to me. David couldn't ... kill someone. You've got it wrong.'

'Those paintings you've been selling, the ones that were

supposedly in a private collection – they've been painted since David supposedly died. That's why the fingernails are authentic.'

'No, this is crazy. You're making this up.'

Karen shook her head. 'Francis, listen to me. We can prove what I'm saying. All we need to do is send a fingernail from one of the recently sold paintings to a forensics expert. They can do what's called a stable isotope analysis and that will tell you that David Greig has been living in the north-west of Ireland for some considerable time. Which, as far as I'm aware, he never did before his presumed suicide.' She took in the stricken look on his face. 'I'm not making this up. He's living in Ramelton with the man calling himself Daniel Connolly.'

'I don't believe you.'

'There's one way to find out,' Karen said, thinking furiously on her feet. 'Get Daniel Connolly over here and confront him with the evidence. See what he has to say for himself.'

Geary jumped to his feet and opened a tall cupboard. He poured himself two inches of Black Bush and returned to his chair. 'You're lying to me. David would never deceive me like that. He'd have no need.'

'You've seen the pictures.'

Geary gave a hoarse shout of laughter. 'I spend half my life looking at video installations, collages and deepfakes. The camera does nothing *but* lie these days.'

'You want to know the truth, don't you? So let's get Connolly in this room and see whether he can explain himself.'

'And how are you going to do that? Kidnap him?'

'Will he come here if you ask him?'

'What? "Come to tea so I can interrogate you"?' Geary's lip curled to match his sarcasm.

'I was thinking more along the lines of, "Something's come in that I need you to take a look at. The seller claims it's by David but I'm not sure." You could text him. Suggest he comes over to have a look tomorrow.'

Geary took a pull on his whisky. 'Why should I do this? What's in it for me? You said yourself, the last person who found out about him was killed.'

'You've already found out, though. You know now. I was only going to throw you to the Gardai, but if you'd rather I throw you to David?' She turned to Daisy. 'That would work, wouldn't it? Then we could stake out Francis here and wait for David to show up. Of course, we might not be quick enough off the mark.'

Daisy nodded. 'David's a smart operator. I bet he could get to Francis, no bother.'

He dropped his head into his hands. 'Youse are bastards,' he wailed, all his debonair polish tarnished.

Karen exchanged glances with Daisy, who gave her an almost imperceptible thumbs-up. 'A text, Francis. That's all you'd have to do. And we'll be here waiting tomorrow morning when Daniel arrives. Then we can straighten all of this out.'

He raised his head slowly, as if it had become very heavy. His eyes glistened with self-pity.

'Otherwise . . . ' Karen left the word hanging.

'Bitch,' he said.

'Get your phone out.' Her tone saturated with contempt.

He took his phone from his pocket and laid it on the desk. He unlocked it and stared at it as if he'd never seen it before. 'What do you want me to say?'

'Put it in your own words. Something he needs to come and look at.'

He sighed and began slowly tapping out a message. When he'd done, he pushed the phone towards Karen. She read:

Daniel, I had a walk-in this afternoon with a small canvas she says is David's work. I've never seen it before but she's got some paperwork. I need your authentication. She wants a quick deal. Can you come over tomorrow? Cheers, FFG.

She could see no grounds for suspicion, so she pressed send.

'Now we wait,' she said. 'I don't suppose Elvira could manage some coffee?'

The coffee came from a nearby café, but it didn't make the time pass any more quickly. Thirty-three minutes ticked by before Geary's phone vibrated.

Can't you scan it and sent it over?

'What do you want me to say?'

'Unlock it,' Karen said. Then she typed, She wouldn't leave it with me. She's coming back tomorrow at noon.

This time, there was no wait. Pain in the arse, but I suppose I have to check it out. See you between 11 and 11.30.

'Thank you, Mr Geary,' Karen said. She stood up. 'We'll be back tomorrow morning. You'll understand why we need to borrow your phone. In case you're tempted to try a wee double-cross. It's tempting to cuff you to a radiator overnight, but I'm going to trust you to understand that, if you fuck with me, I will make sure David Greig knows you

389

know. And before we go—' She reached across his desk and filched the original verification of Greig's DNA. 'You can keep the copy,' she said across his howl of rage.

'Wow,' Daisy said as soon as the door of Gallery Geary snecked shut behind them. 'That was some performance. I had no idea where you were going with that.'

'Neither did I. I was sure he was in cahoots with Greig. But you saw the way he reacted. He was gobsmacked when I talked about Greig being still alive.'

'I know. His face! No way was he putting that on. He's obviously been totally taken in by Iain Auld's Daniel Connolly routine. How did they get away with that?'

'I suppose because they'd been so secretive about their affair. Even someone as close as Geary had never encountered Auld. I assumed he was in on it, that because he'd brokered the stolen painting sales, he'd have the dodgy contacts to sort out Irish passports. They must have come at it another way.'

They wove through the crowded rush-hour streets towards the car. 'So are we going to book into a hotel for the night?' Daisy asked.

'We are, but not here.'

'I don't understand,' Daisy said, dodging a burly man who was not willing to cede the centre of the pavement.

'Think about it, Daisy. There's no point in us confronting Iain Auld in Geary's office. We've got no jurisdiction here. I've already jumped through the hoops of a European Arrest Warrant once this week and I've no intention of doing it again. I have very different plans for tomorrow morning.'

'Are you not going to tell me?' Daisy pleaded as they turned into the car park.

'I want to see whether you can work it out for yourself. Now, give me a minute, I need to send that DNA scan to Charlie, so he can get the wheels turning on comparing it with the DNA on the crowbar as a matter of urgency. It shouldn't take long, it's nothing more technical than setting the two profiles side by side. I want an answer by the morning.' Karen worked her phone, then started the engine. 'Right, now we're going to head for Omagh.'

'That's in Northern Ireland, right? Didn't they have some horrible bombing there?'

'Right on both counts. It was an atrocity. No other word for it. An IRA splinter group who didn't like the Good Friday agreement set off a car bomb. I can't remember the exact number of casualties but it was somewhere in the region of thirty. I do remember that one of the dead was a woman pregnant with twins. That stayed with me, because my cousin Kim was pregnant then. Not with twins, but still. It freaked me out.'

'Did they get the people who did it?'

Karen unlocked the car and got in. 'Historically, justice in Northern Ireland was a complicated beast. You should read Irish crime fiction if you want to get a handle on what was going on during the Troubles and afterwards. Nobody was found guilty of the Omagh bombing in the criminal courts but there was a civil verdict that named the guilty men and made a massive damages award against them.'

'That's terrible. Those poor families. I mean, I know it doesn't make the pain of losing someone go away, but there has to be some sort of consolation in seeing the killer lose their liberty.'

Karen thought of Phil's death and the price the law had demanded from Merrick Shand. She'd spent years thinking it didn't even touch the sides. But their encounter on the News Steps had shifted something inside her. His losses were different from hers. Some might say they were trivial compared with what had been wrenched from her. But he'd live with damage and it would change him, just as it had changed her. 'It does make a difference,' she said slowly. 'I wouldn't call it consolation, though. Nothing consoles you for the loss of someone you love. You absorb it into you. You move forward but you move in a different way.' She caught herself. What was she doing, saying these things to Daisy? She hardly knew the woman.

'Sorry,' Daisy said, colour rising in her cheeks. 'I wasn't thinking. God, I'm so crass, I didn't mean to—'

'It's OK. Anyway,' Karen added brightly, 'that's got nothing to do with why we're going to Omagh. Get your phone out and start looking for a hotel. Ideally, close to the main police station.'

50

Friday, 28 February 2020

Chief Inspector Callum Nugent frowned at his computer screen, considering the two images Charlie Todd had sent Karen late the evening before. 'I can see right enough that these two DNA profiles match each other. But you're telling me that this David Greig, or whatever he's calling himself now, lives in Ramelton. Now, that's in the Republic, so we've got a big problem there from the off.'

'I understand that,' Karen said. 'But I do have a plan to lure him over the border.'

Nugent raised one bushy black eyebrow. 'I hope you're not talking entrapment? We've a strong tradition of not liking that around here.'

Karen gave him her best smile. 'More like persuasion,' she said. 'I happen to know his partner, Daniel Connolly, will be driving from Ramelton to Dublin to keep an appointment this morning. By my reckoning, that means he'll be coming through this way. We have the details of his car – make, model, registration. All I'm asking is that you pull Connolly over and let me interview him with a view to arresting him for conspiracy to commit a whole range of offences ranging from theft, fraud and arson to murder. And I'm hopeful that in the course of that interview, we can see our way to making a wee deal with Mr Connolly. Who is better known to us as Iain Auld, as I explained.'

'And how did you come by this information, DCI Pirie?'

'We had a meeting yesterday with the gallery that represents David Greig's estate—'

'How can you have an estate if you're not dead?'

Karen held fast to the knowledge that honey catches more wasps than vinegar. 'He faked his death, remember? So his will went through probate and as far as the art dealer is concerned, the person he has been dealing with for the last ten years is the executor, Daniel Connolly. Except that, as we know now, Daniel Connolly is in fact Iain Auld and Greig's lover of many years.'

Nugent shook his head as if the wasps were bothering him. 'This isn't straightforward at all.'

'Trust me, we've been struggling to get our heads round it for the past wee while. It's a very clever scam the pair of them have pulled and it only started to unravel because an actress in London thought she'd seen a ghost.'

'Stop it,' Nugent exclaimed. 'You're making my brain bleed. Let's go back to the simple stuff. So this dealer told you Connolly is coming for a visit.'

Karen nodded. 'He's due in Dublin between eleven and half past. Which suggests to me he'll be here around nine.'

Nugent looked startled. 'That barely gives us an hour to get set up.'

'You look like a man who relishes a challenge,' Karen said.

'You're sure about this?' Nugent pushed back in his chair. 'I'm all for inter-jurisdiction cooperation, but this feels like it's hanging by a very slender thread.'

'As soon as we get both of them into custody, that thread will turn into a rope that'll hang the pair of them,' Karen said, letting the grim creep into her voice.

'I hope I'm not going to live to regret this, DCI Pirie.'

'Trust me, if the wheels come off, it won't be your arse in the fire,' she said, spirits sinking at the thought of the joy on the Dog Biscuit's face if it all went wrong.

'Well, let's give ourselves a wee bit more leeway,' he said. 'We'll pick him up on the ANPR cameras and put someone on his tail. But we'll set up a roadblock a few miles down the road at Garvaghy and pull him in then.'

'I might be able to give you a better idea of where he is right now,' Karen said.

'How's that?'

Karen spread her hands in a gesture of innocence. 'Modern technology, Chief Inspector. We all leave an electronic trace wherever we go. Me, I'm a bit of a digital bloodhound.'

Nugent guffawed. 'When you came in here, I thought you were going to be one of those big-city coppers who thinks we're all bumpkins out here. But you're a woman after my own heart. Let's be having it, then. Where the actual fuck is he?'

Karen took out her phone and checked the app. The BMW had moved some distance while she'd been charming Nugent. 'He's on the A5 between Sion Mills and Victoria Bridge.'

He stood up. 'We'd better get our skates on, then. Wait here, would you? I need to set some wheels in motion at the double. I'll send your bagman in to keep you company.' He strode across the room, a man with a purpose. 'Tiernan,' she heard him shout as the door closed behind him. 'Get me Traffic Control, right now.'

A few minutes later, Daisy stuck her head round the door. 'Wow, your pal is stirring up a whirlwind out there. Can I come in?'

'Sure. I think he's thrilled to have something a bit different to get his teeth into.'

'So what do we do now?'

'We wait. Like the surfer in the Guinness advert.'

There wasn't much to divert her in the chief inspector's office. He manifestly didn't like clutter. On his desk, he had a set of stacking trays, none of which held more than a few sheets of paper. The box files stacked on top of his filing cabinet were all neatly, if obscurely, labelled. There were three framed photographs on the wall. Nugent in an eye-wateringly bright outfit standing by the flag on a golfing green shaking hands with a young man who looked unmistakably Irish. Karen vaguely recognised him but couldn't put a name to him. One of Nugent in dress uniform being handed some kind of award by Arlene Foster, Martin McGuinness behind her. The third, Nugent bursting out of black tie with his arm round a woman in an evening dress who looked like she brooked no nonsense. Presumably Mrs Nugent, Karen thought.

And that was the extent of it. The office looked on to the car park at the side of the building. There had been a swift flurry of activity, three liveried vehicles having left in short order, followed by two unmarked cars. But now it was quiet.

Karen checked her emails while Daisy talked to her world on Snapchat. A message popped up from Ruth Wardlaw and Karen opened it immediately.

Dutch unimpressed by McAndrew's complaints about
due process. She'll be back in Scotland by the end of
the week. We owe ourselves a large drink.

'No argument from me on that,' Karen said under
her breath.

She messaged back: Nice one. Stand by your bed, I may
have need of you later today. Speak to Charlie Todd about the
James Auld case, tell him you need to get the DNA ducks in
a row.

Ruth came straight back to her. Any more cryptic and
you could get a job on The Times crossword. Good luck with
whatever you're up to.

Buried further down among the routine Trash fodder was
an email from Jason:

Hi boss. I'm back at my mum's. I have a massive
stookie that Ronan's already drawn a willy on. My leg's
still pretty sore but I've got painkillers so its not to bad.
Did you get her?

Karen was annoyed with herself for not letting Jason
know what had happened. She'd meant to email him so it
would be waiting for him when he was well enough, but
in the general whirl of events, it had slipped past her. At
least now she had time to put that right. She started writing a message, but soon realised it was too complicated, so
she called him instead. He sounded not only pleased but
also relieved to hear from her. She guessed his mother was
doing his head in. It had been a while now since he'd lived
at home; he'd lost his acquired immunity to her fussing over
him. 'I'm sorry you got hurt,' she said.

'It wasn't your fault, I got railroaded by a pensioner,' he said.

'What do you mean?' A pensioner? Surely even the Mint could outwit a pensioner? Karen listened to the whole sorry story. It had clearly cascaded like a row of stacked dominoes when he'd asked for directions looking more like a polis than an art lover. She couldn't entirely blame him for that. She'd probably sent him into battle unprepared in the wardrobe department.

'Anyway,' he wound up. 'Thanks for coming to get me. So where are you now? In the office?'

'I'm in an office. But not mine. I'm in Northern Ireland with Daisy, hot on the trail of Auld and Greig.'

'Daisy? You're with Daisy?'

'Aye, she's been seconded to the unit while you're on the sick.'

A pause. She hadn't expected him to see Daisy as any kind of threat. 'I could come into the office and do all the stuff I do on the computer,' he said. 'Next week. Eilidh wants me to come back to Edinburgh anyway. It would be no bother.'

Her heart went out to him. He tried so hard, even though he kept butting up against his limitations. 'Only when you're ready, Jason. It's not the same without you. Now away you go and annoy your mother, I've got to show Daisy how we catch killers in this team.'

'OK, boss. Thanks.'

Before she could replay the conversation, Nugent was back, rubbing his hands with satisfaction. 'We spotted him on the ANPR and there's an unmarked car picked him up at Newtownstewart. The lads are setting up the roadblock at Garvaghy and they'll bring him straight back here so you can interview him. You'll have him in your hands within the hour, I promise.'

Karen hated tempting fate. To her ears, Nugent's speech had the ring of famous last words. She really hoped she was wrong.

51

For once, Karen was delighted to be wrong. Nugent had been as good as his word. In under an hour, he barged back into his office and announced, 'Your man is waiting for you in Interview Room Two. Now, I don't know how youse do things in the Historic Cases Unit, but I'm going to want to sit in on this, DCI Pirie. So's I know exactly how it played out if there are questions down the line.'

Karen was reluctant but she knew there was a price to pay for Nugent's cooperation. 'I can live with that. DS Mortimer and I will conduct the interview because we know the ins and outs of the case, but I'm happy for you to be in the room. And of course you can chip in if there's anything you're not clear about.'

Nugent's face radiated self-satisfaction. 'Grand.'

'But before we go in, I'd appreciate a word with the officers who brought him in.' Firm but frank, that was the way to play Nugent.

'If you think that's necessary, I'll get the sergeant in question.' He opened the office door and roared, 'Tiernan? Get yourself in here.'

The sound of hurrying feet then a man who could have been Jason's older brother barged in, pink-cheeked and ginger hair in disarray, his cap rammed under one arm. He was long-limbed and his uniform seemed to have been made for someone wider in the shoulders and the chest. 'Sir,' he barked, far louder than the small room demanded. He caught sight of Karen and straightened to attention. 'Ma'am.'

Nugent introduced everyone then said genially, 'DCI Pirie would like a report on your roadblock stop.'

'Sir. As per instructions, myself and four constables proceeded—'

'Hold on, Sergeant,' Karen interrupted. 'Relax. You're not in court, nobody's taking notes—' A stern look at Daisy, whose hand froze over her notebook. 'Give us the pub version.'

Tiernan smiled shyly and blushed, turning the pink cheeks puce. 'We knew your man was on his way from the unmarked car on his tail so we were ready to pull him over. I asked him for his documents and he produced his ROI driving licence and passport. He seemed quite relaxed.' He shrugged. 'People round here, they're used to routine checks from time to time. I asked him to step out the car and he was, "For why?" and I was, "Because I say, so, sir." So he grumbles a bit but he gets out and then I ask him to accompany me back here to assist with an inquiry. He wasn't keen, he was all, "What's this to do with? I'm off to an important meeting in Dublin," and I just acted the eejit, said it was my boss's orders. He says, is he under arrest, I says no, he says, "So I'm free to go?" And I go, "Well, no, because if you don't come willingly I will arrest you."' He took a deep breath. 'So he decided he'd maybe make the best of it by coming along peacefully. All the way back, he was going on about being an Irish citizen and this being totally out of order. Me, I ignored him and delivered him to the interview room.' His face twitched in the kind of involuntary frown that Karen recognised from years of working with Jason. 'Did I do right, ma'am? Not arresting him?'

'You did, Sergeant Tiernan. Thank you.'

Nugent patted him on his shoulder. 'Off you go, Sergeant. Good lad.' He gestured towards the open door in Tiernan's wake. 'Shall we, DCI Pirie?'

Interview Room 2 resembled its equivalents in every other modern police station Karen had been in. It was anonymous, bland and smelled of bodies and anxiety. Iain Auld sat on one side of the table, dressed in a tobacco-brown needlecord suit, a mushroom-coloured flannel shirt and a knitted heather-mixture tie. With the curling hair, the facial hair and the glasses, he could have escaped from a conference of curators. He looked relaxed. Palms resting on his thighs, feet flat on the floor. He barely turned his head when they walked in. 'Finally,' he said. 'Is someone going to tell me what's going on here?'

Karen sat down opposite him, Daisy next to her. Nugent moved the third chair behind her other shoulder then moved round the table to press record. He recited the formal opening of the interview and the officers present. 'Also present is—' He frowned and looked at Karen. 'What do we call him?'

'My name is Daniel Connolly.' The voice strong and steady.

'Also present is Iain Auld, alias Daniel Connolly,' Karen said. There was a momentary flash of something behind his eyes as he clocked her accent. 'Iain Auld, you are attending a police station voluntarily and this an interview under caution.' She recited the familiar mantra about the right to remain silent and the possible damage to a future defence by doing so.

He looked her straight in the eye and said, 'My name is Daniel Connolly and I am a citizen of the Republic of Ireland and you have no right to hold me here.' He pulled a passport from his inside jacket pocket and slapped it down on the table, the unmistakable clarsach symbol of the Irish Republic on the front cover.

'Three lies already. That's pretty good going for an opener,' Karen replied, picking up the passport and thumbing through it as she spoke. 'Let me correct you. Your name is Iain Auld, you are a UK citizen and I have every right to hold you here to answer questions about crimes you have committed or been an accessory to in various UK jurisdictions.'

'You're mad,' he insisted, leaning forward slightly. 'I have no idea what you're talking about. I am an Irish citizen, I have lived in the same house in Ramelton for ten years and I have no criminal record.'

'Another lie. According to the stamps in your passport, you seem to have spent . . . ' she made a show of scrutinising it more closely, 'between three and four months a year in St Kitts and Nevis. A handy wee tax haven, I believe?'

'We have a cottage on Nevis. That's not a crime.'

'As long as it's tax avoidance and not tax evasion. A bit more expensive than a fortnight in the Canaries, though.' She switched tack. 'Your passport says you were born in Dublin. Your accent says the east of Scotland.'

'I lived in Scotland as a boy. It was the accent I heard around me when I learned to talk.'

'Good try.' Karen leaned back in her seat and gave him an indulgent smile. 'It's over, Iain. Better get used to the idea. You've had ten good years of living off the fat of other people's land, but that's history now. I can prove you're Iain Auld in a matter of minutes. Your fingerprints will match the ones we have on file, the ones lifted from your home when your wife reported you missing ten years ago. You remember Mary? She certainly remembers you and it will break her heart when she finds out what you've done to her.'

A muscle in the corner of his mouth twitched but that was the only tell that her words had hit home.

'You might get a good lawyer who would question the validity of the fingerprints, I'll grant you,' Karen continued. 'The same argument with the DNA samples the Met Police took at the time of your disappearance. You might argue against their accuracy, or you might even claim you'd been in Iain Auld's flat and used his toothbrush. Disgusting, but better to be thought disgusting than a thief, a fraudster and an accessory to murder.'

The last line jolted him. His lips tightened and she could see his hands ball into fists. But still he said nothing.

'So you maybe think you can still wriggle out from under Iain Auld? Well, I suppose there is a universe where that might enter the realm of the possible. But that's not this universe. You see, since you did your disappearing act, the science of DNA has come a long way. I don't know if you're familiar with the concept of familial DNA?'

She waited. He said nothing but he blinked more rapidly for a few seconds. 'I'll explain it to you, shall I? Close family members share some of their DNA. The closer the relationship, the more extensive the sharing. So you can look at two DNA profiles side by side and say, "These two are siblings. But these two are no more than cousins." I take it, by the way, that you know your brother Jamie's dead?'

He breathed in deeply through his nose and dashed the back of his hand across his mouth. 'My name is Daniel Connolly. I have no brother.'

'Stop it,' Karen said gently. 'We are entitled to take a DNA sample from you right here, right now. Because we are holding you on suspicion of involvement in a homicide. And, Iain? You know as well as I do that your sample will prove that you're the brother of a murder victim. You've got a few hours of hiding behind, "I am Daniel Connolly", and then it's truly over. You'll be facing quite an array of charges. Wasting police time. Theft of art worth millions of pounds from the Scottish national collections. Conspiracy to defraud by replacing the originals with forgeries. Conspiracy to obstruct the police by colluding in David Greig's fake suicide. Travelling on a false passport. Arson. Money-laundering . . . Stop me when you've had enough. No? Then the big one. Conspiracy to commit murder.'

Auld maintained his pose but a tiny trickle of sweat crept down one temple.

'You're taking this very calmly,' Karen said. 'But then, I suppose if you've aided and abetted the cold-blooded murder of your own brother, this is a walk in the park to you. Your brother Jamie, who was always a friend to you. Always had you in his heart. First you stood by when the finger pointed at him over your disappearance back in 2010. You skulked in your hideout in Ramelton while he faced police interrogation and fingers pointing. Was it you or David who put the bloodstained T-shirt in the bin to incriminate him? Did you secretly hate the brother who loved you?'

Auld shifted in his chair and folded his arms across his chest. But still he met her gaze. Karen was beginning to wonder if he was ever going to crack. What would it take, she wondered. There had to be the perfect pressure point. But she hadn't found it yet. 'Jamie learned one thing from you, though. How to go on the run and become somebody else. You forced him to do what you chose to do. Seven long hard years in the French Foreign Legion fighting other people's wars while you swanned around being Daniel Connolly in your lovely big house in the country. I bet you didn't even know where he was or what had happened to him. But then you didn't care, did you?

'The only person who knew, the only person who actually cared about your loyal brother Jamie was the other person who was loyal to you. Mary. The woman you married. It broke her heart when you vanished into thin air. You didn't even have the guts to tell her you were leaving her for someone else, you left her high and dry in a wilderness of pain and ignorance. All those nights she lay awake in the bed she'd shared with you, working her way through all the terrible fates that could have happened to you. Because how could she believe you'd condemned her to a fate like that for your own selfish pleasure?' Karen let the disgust show. 'What a contemptible piece of shit you are.'

Now he looked away. He stared up at a corner of the ceiling. 'My name is Daniel Connolly. I don't know these people you are talking about and I demand that you release me at once. If you had a shred of evidence of these insane claims, you'd be arresting me.'

Karen refused him a direct response. 'And then Jamie discovered you were still alive. What happened, Iain? Did he contact Daniel Connolly, the executor of David Greig's estate, looking for you? That must have freaked out the pair of you. After ten years, you must have been feeling absolutely secure in your gilded lives. Then out of the blue, your brother finds you. He must have been raging after what you'd done to him and Mary. But still, he agreed to meet you, didn't he? Because deep in his heart, Jamie still loved you.'

'Can I get a drink of water?'

Clever move, Karen thought. Break up the rhythm of her relentless attack. 'Sergeant, get Mr Auld some water, would you?'

Daisy stood up as Nugent leaned in and said, 'DS Mortimer is leaving the room.'

'Jamie loved you. So it never crossed his mind that agreeing to meet you was a dangerous thing. He came over from France – did he tell you anything about his life in Paris, by the way? He played saxophone in a well-respected jazz quintet. If you're ever in a position to listen to Spotify again, you can check them out. Comme des Etrangers, they were called. They're gutted at losing him. Oh, and he had a girlfriend too. We met her. Pascale. Lovely woman. She owns a jazz club in Caen. She's devastated. She really loved him. She doesn't understand why he was murdered. To be honest, I don't understand either. The very fact that he'd agreed to meet you says to me he was a long way down the road of forgiveness. So what happened, Iain? How did it all go wrong? How did it end up with David whacking him round the head with a crowbar?'

Shock flashed across Auld's face. He tried to cover it with a cough, but Karen was no stranger to the bombshell moment. He'd had no idea. He hadn't been there and, whatever story David Greig had concocted, it hadn't involved a crowbar.

Daisy couldn't have picked a worse moment to return with a paper cup of water. 'DS Mortimer has entered the room,' Nugent sighed. She put the water on the table in front of Auld and sat down, her expression puzzled.

Auld seized the water and drained the cup. By the time he put it down, he had almost recovered his composure.

'I know what you're thinking, Iain. You're thinking I'm making it up. You're sitting there clinging to the hope that I'm making it up. You don't want to believe that the man you love, the man you tore up your life for, the man you committed all these crimes for – you can't bring yourself to believe he caved Jamie's head in. That David could ever do that to your lovely brother. But it's true. I'm not making it up. Sergeant, show Iain the DNA analyses.'

Daisy opened the folder she'd brought to the table and took out three sheets of paper. Karen took the first and showed it to Auld. 'Look at this. It's a lab report from the Police Scotland lab at Gartcosh. See what it says? "DNA profiles extracted from Exhibit 73, Case 5/13022020." See the labels? The top one, that's your brother's DNA, the victim. That's the DNA we'll be comparing to yours. But see the other one? "Unknown" it says.'

She placed the page that showed David Greig's certified DNA next to the Police Scotland report. 'They match, don't they?' Her voice sharpened. 'Don't they, Iain?'

'If you say so.' His voice was so soft she could hardly hear him.

'Could you say that more loudly, for the tape?'

'If you say so.' This time it was almost a shout.

'You know what this piece of paper is, don't you, Iain? It's the piece of paper that confirms the identity of the unknown assailant who brutally beat your brother to death.' She dropped in front of him the final piece of the jigsaw. The legal confirmation of David Greig's DNA.

Auld stared bleakly at the papers in front of him. He rubbed his forehead with the tips of his fingers. He looked up at Karen, a plea in his eyes. 'How do I know that piece of paper' – he flicked the legal document with a finger-nail – 'refers to this? It could be anybody's DNA. This is entrapment.'

'Why are you even trying this? I took the original from Francis Flaxner Geary yesterday. Right before he texted you to come to Dublin for an important meeting. I didn't bring the original into this interview in case you decided to rip it up. Geary's not on your side any longer, Iain. He's all about saving his own skin now. I bet he's closeted with his lawyer right now, concocting a version of events that covers his back. That'll be why he wasn't answering his phone when you tried to call him from the police car on the way here.' She took Geary's phone from her pocket and tossed it on the table. 'Three missed calls from Daniel Connolly.'

There was a long silence. Karen could hear Nugent breathing. She leaned forward, forearms on the table, hands clasped. 'All you've done over the years, you've done for David. All the hazards you've faced, all the laws you've broken, you did that for David. You were never the one in love with risk. That was David. Iain, the man you live with killed your brother. In cold blood. There's nowhere for you to hide from that. How safe do you feel now?'

52

When Iain Auld broke, he shattered into pieces. It was as if Karen had taken a crowbar to the shell he'd been hiding inside since the interview had begun. He threw off his glasses and buried his face in his hands, weeping like an inconsolable child. The dam had burst, yet Karen felt no satisfaction. It was grief and not guilt that possessed him; to her that was obvious. Grief for his brother, but also grief for the lives he would never recover.

Karen cast a quick look over her shoulder at Nugent. He gave her an approving nod. Auld continued to weep, great shuddering sobs that shook his whole body. It felt like an unconscionable time before the tears subsided but it was probably only a couple of minutes. He sat with his head bowed, panting as if he'd run a hard race. Daisy took some tissues from her bag and passed them across to him. He looked up then, his eyes swollen and red, his face strangely mottled.

'This wasn't where you expected it to end up when you fell in love with David,' Karen said gently, transforming herself into the caring face of interrogation.

He shook his head and blew his nose. 'Nobody was supposed to get hurt.' His mouth twisted up at one corner